SEASON OF DEATH

Also by Will Thomas

Some Danger Involved

To Kingdom Come

The Limehouse Text

The Hellfire Conspiracy

The Black Hand

Fatal Enquiry

Anatomy of Evil

Hell Bay

Old Scores

Blood Is Blood

Lethal Pursuit

Dance with Death

Fierce Poison

Heart of the Nile

Death and Glory

SEASON OF DEATH

·———·———·

WILL THOMAS

MINOTAUR BOOKS
NEW YORK

First published in the United States by Minotaur Books,
an imprint of St. Martin's Publishing Group

SEASON OF DEATH. Copyright © 2025 by Will Thomas. All rights reserved.
Printed in the United States of America. For information, address
St. Martin's Publishing Group, 120 Broadway, New York, NY 10271.

www.minotaurbooks.com

The Library of Congress Cataloging-in-Publication Data is available
upon request.

ISBN 978-1-250-34360-4 (hardcover)
ISBN 978-1-250-34361-1 (ebook)

Our books may be purchased in bulk for promotional, educational,
or business use. Please contact your local bookseller or the Macmillan
Corporate and Premium Sales Department at 1-800-221-7945, extension
5442, or by email at MacmillanSpecialMarkets@macmillan.com.

First Edition: 2025

10 9 8 7 6 5 4 3 2 1

SEASON OF DEATH

CHAPTER 1

L ondon is a labyrinth, even for those like me, who have taken the cabman's examination, which was a condition of my employment as an enquiry agent to Mr. Cyrus Barker. The East End is a particular nightmare. I suspect that the city planners threw everything east of London Bridge together higgledy-piggledy, then went out for a pint and patted each other on the back for a job well done. There are districts, there are subdistricts, there are neighborhoods and wards and hamlets. Then there are arteries that snake through all of them, haphazardly named after districts without actually being in those districts at all, though they might be. It's anyone's guess.

Take my own little slice of heaven, for example, Camomile Street, where my wife Rebecca, our daughter Rachel, and I reside near the Bevis Marks Synagogue. It is in the City of London, hard by the ancient wall that separates the City from the East End. It is in the Lime Street Ward, but I've also heard it called Bishopsgate. One will also find it referred to as Old Jewry, although the street with that name is farther west. There is no rhyme or reason to any of it.

It was November of 1895, and Barker and I were in Shoreditch at four o'clock in the morning, in search of a gang of criminals the newspapers had dubbed the Dawn Gang. They struck in the early hours of the morning, when most constables had sore feet and just wanted to go home for a sausage and bun, and a well-deserved kip, and the merchants were tucked snugly in their beds, counting profits in their dreams. The gang was in, out, and gone as quick as you could say knife. In fact, they were so careful that often shop owners wouldn't know they'd been robbed for hours after they opened. I heard a rumor that the gang even swept after themselves. They had been so successful that a merchants' committee had been formed and visited us at Craig's Court the day before, demanding action.

"We'll look into the matter," the Guv promised after listening to an extended tale of woe. Our reputation at that point was such that the men breathed the proverbial sigh of relief and went on their way. What cheek we had to assume we could solve any problem with the snap of a finger. But such is the folly of man, I suppose, or so Barker would have said. He is the philosopher, not I.

It was just after All Saints' Day and autumn had set to in earnest. Leaves were blown off trees and gathering in the gutters. We had been on the enquiry for four days, but our promise to the deputation had proven to be easier said than done. The gang seemed impossible to find. We trudged up one street and down the next. We tried gridding the area and circling it. Our visits had become a patrol, which we both despise, seeing it as a sign of defeat. A patrol is an optimistic term for wandering aimlessly.

"Their luck can't hold out forever," I said, before biting my tongue. Luck is not a term one uses in front of a Baptist deacon. A Scottish one, at that.

"Now, Thomas," Barker admonished as we walked, happy to have a subject to correct me over. "You know luck is an illusion. We shall find them or not find them without any help from foolish human notions, like fate or luck."

"Yes, sir," I said, deciding to change the subject. "Were you aware that the district was named after Edward IV's mistress, who died in a ditch here in 1527?"

"Nonsense," he replied. "It was named after a watercourse of the Thames called Walbrook. You mustn't listen to tales."

He was in an irritable mood after not having found the gang for three days, and my feet were tired. We'd surveyed the entire district of Shoreditch, which might have been Hackney, and was definitely one of the Tower Hamlets. We were passing the Shoreditch workhouse for a fifth or sixth time when Barker stopped and raised his head.

"What is it?" I asked.

"Wheesht!" he said. "Listen!"

I did for a minute but heard nothing but the sounds of the town beginning to stir: dray carts loaded with produce from out of town, hansom cabs freshly polished, and the rattle of the night soil man's wagon in the alleys.

"The birdy, lad. Can you not hear it?"

A bird twittered somewhere nearby, but there were no trees in the area. I reasoned it must be perched on a building.

"I hear it," I said. "What about it?"

"It's a robin, Thomas," he replied. "Robins fly south in September, sometimes even late August."

I looked him in the eye. To be more precise, I stared into

the darkness of the black-lensed spectacles that he is never without.

"A birdcall from a lookout, then," I said. "He must be somewhere nearby."

We paced along the entire building, circled around it, and passed by again. As if on cue, the bird twittered again, but I couldn't tell from which direction it came. The sun began to break, as if it were hanging on to the horizon by its claws.

"He's got to be here somewhere," I muttered.

"What's by the door there?" my partner asked.

There was a pile of rags on the step of the workhouse. Last week's laundry, I supposed, save that the pile appeared too grim and gray even for that hard worn institution. Then we heard the robin call from some distance away.

"No," I said. "We were mistaken."

"It's an old music hall trick, Mr. Llewelyn. It's called 'throwing the voice.'"

Barker stopped in front of the workhouse door and lowered himself onto his haunches, a trick he'd learned in far-off Canton, where business is conducted in so lowly a position. His balance was perfect. I wouldn't dare try such a thing myself. I'd fall on my beam-end.

Barker reached toward the heap of rags and removed one from the top. The odor coming from the mass gave me no desire to move closer. I did lean forward, however, close enough to see an eye regarding us from within.

"Good morning," my partner said, as if addressing a gentleman in Hyde Park. "A brisk one, is it not?"

There was a rough squeak in answer, like a rusted hinge.

"My name is Cyrus Barker," the Guv continued, as if he'd come just to speak to him. "What's yours?"

"Dutch," came the answer after a hesitation. "They call me Dutch."

"You've got a fine talent, Dutch," my partner stated. "Mr. Llewelyn and I are most impressed. We'd like you to tell us which shop the Dawn Gang is burgling this morning," he said. "No, there's no use denying it. If you tell me, I promise no harm will come to you, but if Scotland Yard hears of you, you'll be tossed in stir with the rest of them as an accomplice."

"Doesn't frighten me, sir," the voice rasped. "I'll be dead by year's end. The season of death is upon us."

"Very well," Barker answered. "If I cannot frighten you, let me tempt you. If you help us, we will take you to the Mile End shelter for the night. You'll have a warm bath and a meal. You'll get fresh clothes and your own bed and blanket. When was the last time you had your own blanket, Dutch?"

"I don't remember," the beggar confessed.

"And what would you like to eat? I'm certain you must be hungry."

The form on the steps moved. Again, I smelled the acrid odor of unwashed flesh. The man wore an old waterproof in a grimy, grayish brown, the same shade as the rest of his clothing. One of his broken shoes was oddly positioned. Something was wrong with the limb.

"Best not to talk to me, sir," he croaked. "Best for you, best for me."

"Which would you prefer, Dutch, beef or haddock?" Barker continued, ignoring the warning.

"B-beef?" the man asked in wonder, as if it were a magical substance from a fairy book.

"A proper choice," my partner continued. "You'll be wanting potatoes and gravy with that, of course."

"Gravy," the bent figure murmured.

"I prefer mine with sprouts," the Guv continued. "There's nothing like sprouts when they are soaking in butter and properly salted."

It was cruel, I supposed, tempting a starving man with food you don't have to give him, but it was necessary that we learn the location of the Dawn Gang.

"Mr. Llewelyn, can you suggest a proper dessert?" my partner rumbled, looking over his shoulder. He wasn't much for sweets.

"Gooseberry fool, I'd say," I replied. "Although a humble custard tart has its merits."

The poor beggar squirmed in a kind of restless agony.

"We need to know which shop they've gone to, Dutch," Barker rumbled in his deep basso voice. "You're going to have to tell us."

"No, Push," Dutch said. "No, you mustn't ask. Let me alone for all our sakes!"

The Guv and I glanced at each other again. "Push" was the moniker much of the East End used for Barker. Dutch knew who we were, yet he was still too frightened to tell us where the Dawn Gang was working. I was certain my partner would find it unflattering that anyone or anything here should be thought more dangerous than he.

"We can protect you," Barker promised.

"No, sir, you can't," Dutch moaned, huddling on the hard step in his ill-fitting coat. "You don't know what you're asking. You can walk away, go anywhere, but not me. I'm here, and I'm going to die here."

My partner shook his head. "Not if I have a say in the matter. Tell us about the gang."

"I don't know any gangs, Guv. I swear!"

"Very well."

Barker rose smoothly from his squatting position. He stepped over the deformed limb in front of him and settled on the step beside the beggar. Even sitting, Barker towered over the unfortunate.

"What are you doing?" Dutch demanded.

"Me?" he asked, all innocence. "Why, I'm merely passing the time with a new friend. I could sit here for hours. Couldn't I sit for hours, Mr. Llewelyn?"

"For hours, sir," I agreed.

"Of course, you wouldn't be able to alert your friends and everyone in Shoreditch will see us conferring together," he said. "I cannot be responsible for any conclusions they make about our relationship."

"Then we'd go back to our offices, and where would you be?" I remarked.

Barker shook his head. "No, lad. We should get some breakfast first. I'm a bit peckish. We've been walking for hours."

I noticed something in the corner behind the beggar. It was a dented metal teapot, much the worse for wear. It appeared to be his sole possession. How much twice-brewed tea had been poured from that cheap tin pot? What did he eat with it? Stale bread, I presumed. There was a time in my past when I would have been glad of a crust of bread myself, but not as a steady diet.

"You're right, sir," I agreed. "A plate of eggs, some rashers of bacon and sausages, and those black and white puddings you fancy. There's nothing like a good sausage sizzling in its own juices."

"Stop! I can't stand it!" the beggar burst out. He clutched Barker's sleeve with a dirty claw, his arm no thicker than a broom handle. "They're in Hassard Street at Hesse's, the jeweler!"

"Excellent," Barker said. "And how many of them are there?"

"Four, sir. Just four," the beggar answered, beginning to weep.

Barker was on his feet again. Without a word, he turned

and ran in the direction of the jewelry store. I reached into my pocket and retrieved a shilling. I tried to push it into the dirty hand, but Dutch shoved me away.

"A penny, sir," he whimpered. "Just a penny, no more."

I looked about. The workhouse was to open soon, and there were already people milling about, all of them in poor straits. I saw what he meant. As soon as I stepped away, they'd be on him, and he'd have nothing. He could not protect himself. Perhaps a penny he could keep, although there was no certainty. They were like those fish in the Amazon that can strip flesh from an animal in seconds.

"Take it," I said, pushing two pennies into his skeletal hand, hoping he could retain one. Then I went in pursuit of my partner.

Hassard Street was more prosperous than its neighbors. Jewels, rings, and brooches could be ordered from Hesse, who was probably a German Jew who had emigrated to England for a safe life with his family. It was not a shop as such. He also made necklaces for wealthier merchants in the West End. A certain percentage of the area was Jewish, and for a number of reasons, they thrived here just as they thrived everywhere. I was married to a Jewess and I admired their industry. To carve out a living in the mean streets of Whitechapel was a hard thing, even a foolhardy one. Mr. Hesse was going to find that out this very morning.

I knew Hassard Street was northeast of the workhouse. I ran, threading my way between hansom cabs and costers' barrows, following the Guv. The sun was rising, traffic was increasing, and if I wasn't fleet of foot the gang would be up and gone with their swag. Wouldn't that be a treat to explain to the merchants' committee? I soon caught up with the Guv. He was taller than me by more than half a foot, his heavy boots pounding on the cobblestones as he ran.

"Did you pay Dutch?" he asked over his shoulder.

"Yes, sir!" I replied. "I offered the man a shilling, but he only accepted a penny or two."

"What man?" he asked.

"The beggar."

"Thomas, that beggar was a woman."

"No!" I cried. "Surely not!"

"Did you not notice her kettle? The woman's a crawler."

He pulled ahead of me again, a hound upon the scent. As for me, my mind was racing as fast as my feet. Barker had spoken to me about crawlers before, but I'd rarely seen one. They kept out of sight. I wondered if he were pulling my leg, but he doesn't have a sense of humor.

London crawlers are the British equivalent of India's Untouchable class. They are beggars who beg from other beggars, unfortunates with one foot in the grave. They are more than half starved, living on scraps of stale bread like pigeons. Often, they can't digest solid food any longer. Many can no longer walk, or stand upright, they are so weak. When they become too weak even to beg anymore, they sit and wait patiently for death. As he, or rather she, had said, it was the start of the season of death, which a beggar must survive in order to see spring. Most crawlers don't. They are like midges and mayflies, who last only a day or two and are gone.

"No dawdling, Thomas!" Barker called.

The crawlers have an odd relationship with the community in the Tower Hamlets. They both feed them and feed on them. Someone will steal a penny from them to feed their family, then bring them a cup of soup or gruel afterward. Local merchants and publicans who are generally hard-hearted will provide water to them for their ever-present teapots, the crawler's sole possession, and residents offered used tea leaves to put into them. It is a beggar's sole opportunity to give alms, and they do it willingly, more willing than their betters. Barker has claimed some crawlers have been well known, their names remembered, and their funerals well attended. Crawlers are almost always women. Men in such conditions often kill themselves out of shame, but then I've always considered the female of the species to be braver than the male.

Cyrus Barker noticed a beat constable and flagged him, as he slowed to a halt. He gave the policeman our card and told him that a robbery was taking place at Hesse's.

"Where did you acquire this information, sir?" the constable asked, suspicious of a pair of men running through the early morning streets. We might have been the burglars ourselves.

"From a beggar nearby," Barker said.

"Very well, sirs," the man answered. "I shall pass the word along to 'H' Division. It might come to something, might not. Thank you for your help. We'll handle the situation ourselves. The two of you may go."

Of course we wouldn't interfere, or try to stop the Dawn Gang ourselves, and bust a few skulls in the process. Not us. We were just going to observe the area and wait for Scotland Yard to arrive, after they'd had their tea, reflected on the meager information we'd provided, looked up who we were, and debated how reliable our word might be. Then, the night inspectors would gather a dozen constables from neighboring districts and argue over who was in charge or had jurisdiction, and they'd trot in squad formation to the shop. Which was exactly what they did. I'm not complaining about the Metropolitan Police. They are for the most part fine chaps. It's a bureaucracy problem, mixed with a little professional jealousy all 'round.

When the constable left, Barker and I ran to Hassard

Street, where I spied Hesse's sign at the far end. I slowed, but my partner quickened his pace.

Fifty yards. Thirty. Fifteen.

He struck the door with his boot, and it sounded like an explosion echoing through the streets. It hadn't occurred to the Guv that the door might be too thick or strong for him, or even that it might be unlocked. The obstacle in his way shattered into boards. There was a bellow, and a hue and cry. I shot through the doorframe behind him and was just taking my bearings when I was punched in the side of the head. My ears began ringing, and I was unsteady on my feet for a moment. It was not what one would call a propitious start.

CHAPTER 2

The Dawn Gang was hot as hornets, and we found ourselves in a fight for our lives. The shop was too small to support six men battling at close quarters. Glass broke all around us and jewels danced across counters or were trod underfoot. One of the men pulled me off my feet, then objected when I jammed a thumb in his eye. A second tried to get his arm around my neck, but I slid under it and booted him in the stomach. The first returned and clouted me on the ear. The Marquess of Queensberry Rules had no part in this fight.

When I glanced over, I saw Cyrus Barker banging two men together as if they were cymbals. He smacked one facedown on the counter and watched him slide off onto the floor. The other, who outweighed the Guv by two stone at least, charged him. I sensed something odd here. We'd been in dozens of skirmishes over the last ten years together, but this one was different. The men seemed frantic over and above the general possibility of being caught. The one I'd kicked came off the floor with a knife and lunged at me, but I was prepared. My partner and I ran an antagonistics school in Glasshouse Street twice a week. I slapped the blade hand away and jabbed the man in the throat with a knuckle. He dropped the knife and went down with a hoarse rasp.

"Thomas!" Barker bellowed, pointing toward the door, where one thief was escaping. I ducked as a half dozen sharpened pence flew over my head with a ringing sound, some embedding themselves in the poor blighter's back and arms, others clanging against the doorframe. They are my partner's weapon of choice, an odd affectation he'd acquired in China. The man staggered but I pulled my Webley from my waistband and followed him out the door. He fell in the street, and I clapped the pistol to his head.

Having made short work of the Dawn Gang, Barker stepped out into the night and raised an Acme bobby's whistle to his lips. I'll wager he awakened a hundred sleepers at least. He blew loud enough to wake the dead.

"What in hell?" the man at my feet asked, lifting one of the bloody pennies he'd plucked from his shoulder. I pushed the short barrel of my pistol against his neck.

"Shut it, you," I said. "You're the reason I'm not tucked in bed right now."

Within a few minutes a dozen constables arrived. Scotland Yard had been after the Dawn Gang as we had, and extra patrols had been engaged to apprehend them. I pocketed my bulldog pistol and tried to look innocent, something I'm good at.

An inspector from "H" Division arrived a few minutes later, and what was now a fully assembled squad stepped through the broken door and took the other three men into custody. Even with their wrists locked in darbies, the thieves were not inclined to give up the fight. The one I'd stopped was being carried away by three constables and still struggling to escape, despite his wounds. The fellow was nearly frothing at the mouth in panic. The patrolmen didn't have sharpened coins, but they did have truncheons. One tap and it was all over. As violent as the altercation had been in those crowded moments, I cringed a little at the brutality of it. I'd been clouted once or twice myself. I wouldn't recommend it.

The night inspector in charge was a man named Dew. Though only a detective constable, he was the most senior officer at "H" Division at that moment. He looked too young for the duty. The rest of his men were hunting for the gang now in his custody, a fortunate set of events for him. He would eventually get the credit for the arrests. Save for advertisements in *The Times,* the Guv prefers to keep our names out of the newspapers.

"You must be Barker," Dew said, glancing at the sea of shattered glass strewn along the aisles of the narrow shop. "I recognize you from the descriptions I've heard at the station. I wasn't aware you were involved."

"We were hired a few days ago," the Guv explained. "We have been patrolling the area since three o'clock this morning."

"How did you manage to track them down when half of the Met has been out looking for them for over a week?" the detective constable demanded.

"We found an informant at the Shoreditch workhouse, a beggar named Dutch."

"We'll have to speak to him after you've answered some questions at 'H' Division," Dew replied. "I presume you don't mind."

"Inspector!" a voice shouted from the next room.

The Guv and I looked at each other. What had we missed?

"No inspectors here, Constable Beeching," Dew barked. "I'm a workingman. What have you found?"

"Body, sir!"

We stepped over the shattered glass and through a beaded curtain into the back room, which was a workshop. There were scarred tables with vises, hammers, and tools in neat rows against a wall, beside a smelter. Ahead of us was a door which opened into a vault. From where I stood near the entrance to the storeroom, I could see a pair of boots motionless on the floor. When we filed into the small room, a man lay prone, a sturdy safe open beside him. Dew rolled him onto his back and went through his pockets for a card or some kind of identification. From where I stood, I could see his bloodstained shirt.

"Mr. Ibraham Hesse, the man who owns this establishment," the detective constable said. "He must have been protecting his interests. The Dawn Gang will swing for this. It's been all larks and skittles until now. Sergeant, collect a barrow and bring the victim to the station."

Barker and I looked in every direction, making observations. It is a habit people in our occupation develop. Nothing seemed out of place, but then we had not seen the body closely enough to determine how the man had died. We later learned he had been stabbed under the rib cage. We stepped back through the curtain into the front room again.

"Crikey," Dew remarked, looking about at the devastation. "You ain't half left a mess!"

"They were . . . what would you call them, lad?" Barker asked, turning to me.

"Spirited, sir," I said, ever helpful.

"Aye," Barker replied. "They were spirited. We'll meet you at the station, Detective Constable."

"No, sir," Dew stated. "I can't take that chance. I'm afraid you must come with us now."

Dew was very earnest. He was trying to ape his superiors, not only in manner, but in appearance. He had a short mustache, which would need a few more years' growth to be as thick as those of the Criminal Investigation Department, or of Barker's own, for that matter. Dew seemed to know what he was about, however, and I thought it likely he would do well. For one thing, he'd challenged my partner without his voice quavering.

Dew left two constables in charge of the premises, so that his superiors would see the scene in situ in a few hours' time, after they'd had their tea and boiled egg. This might even bring the commissioner from his office. On the way to "H" Division by the Embankment, I found a diamond in the cuff of my trousers. I thought how my wife would look with a new ring or necklace but knew she would be prouder of an honest husband, so I gave it to one of the constables. Goodness knows what happened to it afterward.

Cyrus Barker and I were well acquainted with "H" Division from our investigation during the Whitechapel Murders a half dozen years earlier. That's what we called them, both Scotland Yard and the Barker and Llewelyn Enquiry Agency. It was the press who tagged them the "Jack the Ripper" murders. We had tracked the killer to his lair and seen him carted off to Colney Hatch, but the powers-that-be had swept the matter under the mat and sworn us all to silence. I've heard the decision went as high as Queen Victoria herself, but you can't believe what you hear nowadays, or don't hear, as the case may be.

The constabulary hadn't changed since we had seen it last. Battered and scarred wooden benches in dire need of paint flanked the entrance under the eye of a sleepy-looking sergeant who was not a patch on the one we knew in Great Scotland Yard Street. "H" Division is not a plum assignment, but Dew looked keen. *Keen and ambitious,* I thought to myself.

The interrogation room wasn't much larger than a closet, and Barker's presence seemed to fill it. Dew sat and began to write on a form. They had typewriting machines in Scotland Yard now, but few inspectors felt comfortable enough to use one. I reckoned this constabulary wouldn't see a typewriter until the dawn of a new century.

I hoped we wouldn't be arrested, but that decision was up to the night inspector. As far as I knew, our agency was considered competent and honest. However, we were also known to be stubborn and crafty. Barker works to his own timetable and his own code of ethics and devil take the hindmost. We'd warmed many a cell cot in the districts and divisions of London Town, but I had no wish to do so that morning. We were at the mercy of this green detective constable. *We'd done nothing wrong,* I told myself, *but when has Scotland Yard ever taken my word for anything?* I was a former convict myself. I'd gone straight from Oxford University to Oxford Prison for theft. I was innocent, of course, but I suppose everyone says that.

Dew was completing an incident report in our presence. This was done in a leisurely fashion, as if we weren't even in the room. He sighed. He coughed. He crossed out a word or two and wrote others in the margins. It was just the sort of thing that gets right up my nose. He was trying to stall, to break us down, hoping we'd confess, when we hadn't done anything of which to confess. It was mere routine for Dew. Nothing personal, you understand, just duty. *Yes,* I told myself, *this tyke would make a fine inspector someday.* That was not a compliment.

"Tell me, gentlemen, are you armed at the moment?" Detective Constable Dew asked.

My partner and I looked at each other. Of course, we were. We were private enquiry agents, not tobacconists or bakers. We nodded.

"Would you be so good as to place your weapons on this table?"

Barker shrugged his wide shoulders. He pulled a Colt Single Action pistol from inside his coat and set it in front of Dew. He reached into his sleeve and retrieved a knife he carried in a sheath strapped to his wrist. Meanwhile, I pulled my Webley bulldog pistol from the waistband of my trousers. Dew examined the knife, knowing Hesse had been stabbed.

"That was fine work, tracking down the Dawn Gang," he said at last. "How did you happen to become involved?"

Cyrus Barker coughed. "We were hired by an organization of merchants to find the gang and stop them."

Dew raised an eyebrow. "Was Mr. Hesse a member of this organization?"

"He was not among the men who hired us," the Guv admitted. "He must have preferred to guard his premises himself."

"Have you ever seen this before?" Dew continued, holding up a penny.

"If it is sharpened, it is mine," Barker replied.

"Have you any others?"

"Detective, you know I haven't. You told me to put my weapons on this table."

Dew frowned. "Do you always carry sharpened pennies about with you?"

"Not to church, of course, but generally speaking, yes."

"What is their purpose?"

"To slow or stop a suspect from escaping without the need

to shoot him. It is a scatter weapon, like a rifle filled with buckshot."

We were staring at the top of Dew's head. He'd removed his helmet and was writing laboriously, like a child forming his letters. His hair was parted perfectly, each to its own side. A precise man was our detective constable. Precise and careful. Barker would approve.

"I see," he answered. "How came you to know where the thieves would be?"

"As I said, we came upon a beggar in front of the Shoreditch workhouse," the Guv replied.

"How did this beggar know where the gang would be?"

Barker shrugged his burly shoulders. "I did not ask, but I assume it was a matter of self-preservation. Do you mind if I smoke?"

The detective constable shook his head. The Guv retrieved a sealskin pouch from his pocket and began to stuff his personal blend into a meerschaum pipe carved like the head of a Zulu warrior. It must have been white as ivory when he'd purchased it, but time and smoke had turned the figure into a realistic shade of yellowish brown. Lighting it, he blew a large plume across the table. Dew's incident form rustled, and the detective constable coughed. As I said, it was a close room. I was accustomed to the smell, but our captor would be choking soon. It was Barker's way of encouraging the fellow along. The Guv never does anything randomly.

"Did this beggar approach you or did you approach him?" Dew asked.

"As a matter of fact, I saw someone perching on the steps of the workhouse and asked a question. Money changed hands, just a penny or two. We received the information and went on our way."

"He knew where to go, then?"

"Aye, he did."

"Do you suppose he's still there?" he asked.

Barker shrugged again. "I don't know. There was food and drink nearby, and Dutch looked starved."

"As well as parched," I added.

"You were there, Mr. Llewelyn?" Dew said, looking at me. "Can you elaborate on what Mr. Barker has said?"

"Just that Dutch was in rags and needed a bath as much as a cup of tea. The beggar also had a bum leg." I turned to Barker. Had it been right to mention the limb? He gave the smallest of nods behind the smoke.

"Did you proceed directly to the jewelers?" Dew asked.

"We did," Barker replied.

Dew consulted his paper. "When you arrived, you broke right through the door?"

"We feared they would escape otherwise," I answered.

"Just the two of you, against four men?"

"Mr. Barker prefers those odds."

The detective looked me in the eye as if I were joking, but of course I wasn't. One of Barker's dictums is that the truth makes the best lie.

"Did you have to bust the place to pieces?" Dew asked.

"That wasn't our plan," Barker stated. "They were very intent, weren't they, lad?"

"Yes, sir," I said. "Very intent. But we've already explained that."

"In-tent," Dew muttered as he wrote.

"Everything they did was unorthodox," I added. "That's u-n-o-r-t–"

"I've heard of you as well, Mr. Llewelyn," Dew added, pointing at me with the blunt end of his pencil. "Someday someone's gonna smack that mouth clean off your face."

I smiled. Discretion is the better part of valor.

"Have you any further questions, Detective Constable?" my partner asked. "We'll need to open the doors of our agency soon."

"No, sir, but I'm certain my superiors will have a few."

He glanced at me to make certain I had no remark about the word "superiors" on my tongue. I had five, in fact, but I chose not to use any of them. He was the wrong audience. Metropolitan constables are not issued a sense of humor.

When he was done questioning us together, he separated us and questioned us individually.

"Tell me more about Mr. Barker," he said. He had left the door open, but our eyes were still stinging from the smoke.

"He is a private enquiry agent," I replied. "He has chambers by Scotland Yard."

Dew frowned.

"I know that!" he said. "What are his antecedents?"

I smiled. "You've been wanting to use that word for a while, haven't you? I suspect you're using it wrong. However, an—"

"Shut your gob, Llewelyn, or I'll shut it for you."

I put up both hands. If he wanted silence, silence was what he would get. I refused to answer another question after that.

Barker went into the interrogation room. A smoke-filled room is his natural habitat. I took a seat by the constabulary door and traded banter with the desk sergeant while Dew tried to crack the hard nut that is my partner. If he thought the man would open himself to a jumped-up detective constable, he was sorely mistaken. The Guv didn't even grin as he came out. Defeating low-level officials was a matter of course.

"May we go, Detective Constable Dew?" he asked.

"First you'll follow me to the workhouse and point out this beggar to me."

Dew opened the front door of the constabulary. We were marched to the Shoreditch workhouse. From time to time, he shot me a cautious eye. I seem to have a knack for vexing authority figures. And vice versa.

However, Dutch was no longer there on the steps. Dew looked disappointed. I presumed he wanted to present the wretch to his inspector as a fait accompli. However, we'd given him enough to get a pat on the back, and possibly a promotion. He looked satisfied enough when he left us.

"We'll have to find Dutch before the authorities do," my partner said after we left. "She can't have gone far. Some questions are in order."

"A bath wouldn't go amiss, either," I suggested.

CHAPTER 3

S he could be anywhere by now," I complained as we left the steps of the wretched workhouse. A long line of vagrants stood where Dutch had been. The day had dawned in one of the largest and busiest capital cities on earth. The street in front of us was choked with vehicles. Men were pushing street carts along, women opened stalls to sell their meager wares, and children larked about in the cold morning air with few garments and even less supervision. The East End hadn't changed since Dickens wrote of it in his first book, *Sketches by Boz*. Unlike Whitechapel, however, Shoreditch had a certain Old World charm. One could picture Boz himself wending his way along these stalls and purchasing a bag of hot chestnuts.

"She can't have gone far," the Guv reasoned. "She doesn't have the energy."

"Do you suppose she can walk at all?" I asked. "What I saw of her boot was oddly twisted."

"I cannot begin to imagine what horrors that woman has faced, Thomas. You noticed the grime on her face?"

"Of course, I did," I said. "One could hardly miss it."

"It has a purpose, and she won't say thank you if we remove it. Crawlers are helpless against lecherous men, so she does her best to look undesirable."

"What a way to live," I remarked. "It's worse than dying."

"Aye," he admitted. "But it's remarkable what one will do to survive. You lived nearby after your release from prison, didn't you, Thomas?"

"I was in Islington, sir, but it was poor enough. We slept on the floor, eight to a room. I skipped out on the rent, but I still had enough for breakfast, meager as it was. I came to your door without a sou in my pocket. Why do you suppose she crawled away? You mentioned the warm bed and beef. I'm certain the poor woman has not eaten a proper meal in months if not years."

"I suppose she feared that we'd tell the police about her, which is just what we did," he answered. "She feared she'd be placed in the workhouse where she would be forced to do menial work twelve hours a day for poor food, and a rude bed. Once you get in it's difficult to get free again. Some inmates don't escape their clutches for years. In fact, there are whole generations of families living there. You were fortunate to miss it."

"But Dutch was sitting on the very step in front of it," I pointed out.

"She was," he agreed, "but merely to inspire pity. She had no intention of going inside. Crawlers frequently sit in front of workhouses, hoping to gain sympathy."

"How would she feel about the Mile End Mission?" I asked.

"That would depend on what she knows about the Salvation Army. General Booth has taken the mission in hand."

I cocked my head. "Has he? I hadn't heard. Is it going to become a Salvation Army mission, then?"

"Not if I have my way," the Guv replied. "I'm on the board of governors for Mile End. If they take control of it, I fear any sign of Brother Andrew's works will be expunged. I don't want that to happen."

"Nor I," I replied. "I have nothing against Booth, but I'd like Handy Andy to be remembered. He was my friend as well as yours."

"He liked you," Barker replied. "He said I'd made a wise choice for an assistant."

I remembered the first time I saw Andrew McLean, sitting in his office with a chop held to his eye to stop the swelling. He'd broken up another tavern. The man was adamant about temperance, saying that alcohol was the chief cause of misery in the East End. I don't know if he was right, but he certainly wasn't wrong. His life's work, the Mile End Mission, had been responsible for much good in the East End, especially in converting streetwalkers and ferrying them out of London's tentacled grip for a new beginning in the countryside. Andrew had been heavyweight bare-knuckle champion of London for many years, and a man with a reputation for drunkenness and violence when he had a road to Damascus experience and turned his life around. It wasn't just that I admired him. I'd loved the man like a favorite uncle. He'd died during one of our enquiries and we both still mourned him. He was in Heaven now, going three rounds with Saint Peter.

"Do you intend to take Dutch to the mission against her

wishes?" I asked my partner. "She seems determined to be let alone."

"I do," Barker stated. "As she said, the chances are high that she'll be in a pauper's grave by year's end. Consumption, diphtheria, typhoid. Cold and want. I feel duty bound to help her. I promised, and my word is my bond."

He believed it. He'd protect unto the point of death someone whom he had not known a moment before. I had to remind him at times that we are an enquiry agency, which requires payment for services rendered, but the heart of this large, rough-hewn Scotsman is the only soft part of him.

We found the woman just three streets away, crawling determinedly through an alleyway like a tortoise, dragging her crooked limb behind her. The moment I saw her again, I realized Barker was right. We couldn't leave such a wretch without doing something for her, even if she objected to our aid.

Sometimes the poor are too proud to ask for help. No one wants to confess to being in need. It is an admission of failure. However, Barker and I had each tasted poverty in our time and would do what we could to ease our neighbor's burden. Otherwise, what else is a man good for?

"It's you," she said when we came upon her.

"It is," Barker said. "Where did you go?"

"I had a ha'penny for a cup of tea and a doorstep, so I came out ahead."

The latter was a slice of stale bread slathered in butter.

"Ma'am, you undervalue yourself," Cyrus Barker said.

"How do you know?" she retorted. "Perhaps people have overvalued me my entire life."

My partner let out a bray, which made both the woman and me jump.

"Dutch, you are a natural philosopher," he said. "However,

your protests mean nothing to me. You are coming with us to Mile End Mission. Have you got your kettle?"

"Always," she said, clutching it to her breast. "But you have no idea what trouble you will cause."

Barker put his hands on his hips and looked at the pitiful morsel of humanity at his feet.

"Now, woman," he said. "That is the second time you have intimated that. What aren't you telling me?"

She gave a cold smile. "You'll learn soon enough, sir."

The Guv stepped out of the alley and whistled for a cab. The driver stopped but balked when he saw the passenger he was to convey. I had to promise him twice the fare. Dutch preferred to sit on the floor of the cab with her misshapen limb dangling over the side. We took our seats, the odor already permeating the small enclosure. As we bowled east, she looked out onto the street with her teeth set as I wondered how much pain she had endured.

We reached Mile End Road in ten minutes. The Guv and I could have walked there. I paid the fare, while my partner lifted the woman out of the cab, odiferous rags and all, and carried her to the gate of Mile End Mission as she moaned in pain. That limb needed looking after.

The mission began life as a knacker's yard; now it was more like a fortress. The walls were ten feet tall, and the iron gate was like a prison entrance. Many people didn't like the mission. Women of easy virtue found refuge there, as well as beggars, thieves, and worse. As we stepped forward, two matrons came toward the gate in white mobcaps and starched pinafores over dresses made in the same drab brown as the building. They were big, strapping women, but their faces weren't warm and inviting. Quite the reverse, in fact.

"How can we help you, sirs?" one demanded of us. She

was the size of a barrel, and her forearms were brawnier than mine would ever be.

"We have brought this woman for aid," Barker stated. "I'm on the board of directors here."

They removed the bar from the iron gate, gathered the woman from Barker's arms, then closed and barred it again. Wordlessly, they melted away, and we were left alone.

"There's that sorted," I said. "Shall we go to the office now?"

"Perhaps," he answered. "But I want to see her tomorrow after she is settled. The woman intrigues me."

We broke our fast at an A.B.C., where I had three cups of abysmal coffee to stay awake.

Afterward, we arrived at our offices in Whitehall no more than half an hour after our usual opening. Our clerk, Jeremy Jenkins, was in residence although he did not ask why we were late. Our official day began. I typed all I could recall of the morning's events, while Barker spread out all five of the newspapers Jeremy had brought with him from a newsstand in Northumberland Street. Our clerk reads them through, soaking in the information, retaining most of it.

A shop owner from the merchants' committee arrived at our door, declared that our clients were highly satisfied, and paid the bill. I didn't know how they received word so quickly. However, I took the check to the Cox and Co. Bank on the corner of Craig's Court and Whitehall Street and deposited the sum. Then I looked about, wondering if anyone was watching me. After several years of training, one develops a second sense about these things. The subtle warnings Dutch had given were concerning, but no one seemed to notice me. I returned to our chambers and read the newspapers through myself, although I read only the parts that interested me. Jeremy had bought a copy of *The Idler,* a personal favorite, and

I read that last. Meanwhile, the Guv reflected on whatever it is he reflects upon.

No one called for our services for the rest of that morning. Eventually we went to lunch, where I had more undrinkable coffee. Afterward, I purchased an afternoon edition of *The Times* and read the scant but lurid account of what had occurred that morning, before handing it to the Guv. He nodded in acceptance, if not appreciation. The Yard took the credit, but then we expected it to, and Barker had given them leave. Dew was mentioned, which must have brightened his day.

No clients came that afternoon, either. The Guv would have called it the nature of the beast. Enquiry agents, even those with a royal warrant above their door as we had, must learn to expect periods of inactivity. However, the man I work with does not like inaction. It irks him. He starts to fidget. He glances through the books on his shelves as if the authors vexed him. He paces the building and even the courtyard behind, scouting for something to complain about. As five o'clock approached he felt he must have accomplished something for the day. One would have thought the morning's events were enough.

Alas, the day bested him. I saw him off to Newington, No. 3 Lion Street, to be precise. I'd let his butler, Mac, deal with his moodiness. I hadn't slept the previous night and dozed in the cab on the way to the City, awaking just as it reached Camomile Street. All was pleasant there. The street lay under a layer of multicolored leaves like a down quilt. Neighbors were having either a late tea or an early dinner. I shook my head to scatter the cobwebs and paid the cabman. The small hedges that lined our walkway had been neatly trimmed by a man whom we had in once a week. I wondered what would be served for our dinner. More than that, I wondered who would be cooking it.

We had not yet hired someone for the kitchen. Our maid Lily had prepared meals for us when we moved here, but since the baby had been born, she wilted under the strain. One cannot expect a maid to both cook and clean indefinitely. Likewise, our nanny, Mrs. Skaleski, had her arms full, quite literally, with our infant daughter, helping only occasionally in the kitchen. This left my darling wife. Once she attempted an omelet and we nearly had to send for the fire brigade. Anyway, I didn't particularly care what was to be served that evening. Sleep was what I needed. Blessed slumber. *Ten uninterrupted hours seems perfect,* I thought as I stepped inside.

There was some kind of noise blaring through the house. Mrs. Skaleski ran across the upper landing, then Lily ran in the opposite direction. A minute later Rebecca rushed out of the kitchen, holding our daughter, Rachel, who had been teething for two days.

"Oh, thank heavens, Thomas, you're home!" my wife cried. "What kept you? She's been crying for hours. I'm exhausted! I can't do this anymore! Take her before I send your daughter to a foundling home!"

She put the baby in my arms and fled as well. Meanwhile, Rachel continued to screech, her small body hot and damp in my arms, showing no sign of abating anytime in the foreseeable future. She made sounds of which any bagpiper would be proud. The women in my house have assured me that I have an ability to soothe the baby, as if it were a special gift like second sight. It was rank collusion on their part, but I was too tired to argue. I leaned against the doorframe and let her cry herself to sleep. I could not think of anything else to do. Dinner was forgotten, sleep a far-off hope.

If it is possible to catch forty winks while leaning against a door and holding a child, I came as close as any man can.

Later, I shuffled to the kitchen and ate a wedge of cheese and some digestive biscuits, the kind that look and taste like pasteboard. They could have been pasteboard for all I cared. I ate mechanically, and drank tea, which I don't like any better than digestive biscuits.

I'm not certain what happened afterward. Rachel finally fell asleep, and the nanny took her. I staggered to my study chair and lay shattered for an hour or two. Then I took down a copy of *Sketches by Boz,* having thought of it that morning, but never successfully opened it. I don't recall going to bed.

Sometime near midnight I staggered downstairs to the kitchen from our bedroom and sat in a chair, vaguely aware of the quiet. I poured a glass of milk and cut a piece of Dorset apple cake. The Lord only knew who brought it. Perhaps Rebecca's sister had shown mercy on us. A few minutes later my wife, another refugee, wandered into the kitchen and sat. I took down a second glass and plate for her. We didn't speak. We sat and ate and stared at the walls opposite.

"How do people do this?" she asked. "Are we just poor parents?"

I had no answer for her. To reply seemed more fraught with danger than anything I'd ever attempted since raising a child. I once compared babies to squid, all bulbous heads and slack, slippery limbs. Rebecca did not find this amusing. How someone keeps from dropping a baby on its head is beyond me. I'd almost done it a dozen times, though I'll never admit it. I suspect everyone in the house had, as well, but we all kept our secrets. Poor Rachel, dangling high in the air, unable to bear her own weight, at the mercy of cruel fate or gravity, and incompetent parents. I'd cry as well.

There is an old Persian adage that says, "This too shall pass." I say let that old Persian watch my bawling daughter for an hour and then ask him what he thinks.

CHAPTER 4

The next morning, I shaved and dressed, kissed Rebecca on the cheek, and stepped into the nursery to see our daughter, who was sleeping soundly for once. It was half past five o'clock. I found a cab in Commercial Road and took it to Newington. Five days a week I met the Guv in his oriental garden at six o'clock in the morning to train. Barker's half acre is the envy of the staff at Kew Gardens. It is particularly beautiful in autumn, when the winged seedpods of the Japanese maples sedately whirligig to the ground. The walls were high enough that the wind blew over our heads. Water gurgles under the wooden bridge, and everything seems a fairy-tale paradise.

The ogre that protects the garden is named Harm, Barker's prized Pekingese, who was born in the Forbidden City and has been exiled on our barbaric shores since his youth. He followed me and sniffed the toe of my boot with suspicion, obviously because I am a barbarian. Finding me singularly devoid of interest, he found a rock warmed by the early sun and returned to the sedate guardianship of his private kingdom, occasionally giving me a look of disapproval. I had been on sufferance for a full decade. Meanwhile, Barker came down from his growlery at the top of the house and crossed to where I stood in a grassy patch near the center of the garden. The day had begun.

I had subsisted for two days on very little sleep, but as far as the Guv is concerned, any complaint I had was due to poor planning on my part. I had no idea what we would be studying that morning, so I leaned my neck to the side until it popped and swung my arms about to look as if I were eager. I should have known he'd see through that immediately.

"Horse stance," he barked. He turned and crossed the bridge again. He went inside for a cup of tea in the warmth of the kitchen, leaving me at the mercy of the most mundane yet difficult exercise in Barker's bag of tricks.

The position is simple enough: one spreads one's feet wide apart then settles into a low crouch as if riding a horse. It's easy enough for the first half minute, then the pain begins to settle into one's joints and increases exponentially every few seconds. My best achievement so far was to stand unmoving for just over three minutes. The Guv did not consider this to be satisfactory for an assistant instructor in his Barjitsu class. My limbs would barely keep me upright the rest of the day, but I've seen my partner stand like a statue for nearly ten minutes. I suspect he only does it to crush my wayward spirit.

Cyrus Barker enjoys seeing me in pain; I believe it gives him genuine pleasure. He was tortured by his own martial teacher, Dr. Wong Fei Hung of Canton, who was tortured by his father in turn, Dr. Wong Kei Ying, et cetera. It is an inheritance of sorts, passed from one generation to the next. I could not wait to have students of my own to torment. I'd give those lazy layabouts what for.

Three minutes later my knees gave way and I fell to the ground. I pulled myself up and tried to get circulation going again, before dragging myself over the bridge. My limbs had frozen in that position, causing me to walk like an American cowboy in a dime novel. I stepped inside the warm kitchen, where Barker looked at me witheringly over his teacup. His turnip watch was open on the table.

"I'm sorry, sir . . ."

I stopped myself. Never give an excuse when you fail. I heard him say so in my head. Don't blame the weather, infirmity, or anyone else. Confess your own weakness. It's the only way.

"I failed, sir."

Barker nodded, looking thwarted. I believe he was hoping I'd make an excuse.

"Surely you can do better than that," he said. "Let us go out again."

I nodded, though I doubted the man would get another full minute out of me that morning. I hobbled behind him to the same spot and crouched again. Then came my deliverance.

"Sir!" I heard Mac's voice calling from the direction of the house. He was trying to forestall a man attempting to cross the ornamental bridge and having a time of it. The man was in full stride and would brook no interference from a mere domestic. He wore a long mackintosh and a gray fedora, and it wasn't until he removed the hat that I recognized him. It was Chief Detective Inspector Terence Poole of the Criminal Investigation Department at Scotland Yard. He was an old friend of sorts, the kind who had locked us in a cell on many occasions.

"Let him in, Mac!" Barker called, as if a dandified butler could stop him. Jacob Maccabee dropped back and disappeared into the house with a look of disapproval while Poole strode forward until he reached us on the lawn. The Guv waved at an octagonal pavilion near the moon gate at the back of the property. Once there, the inspector fell onto a bench.

"You could have called us on the telephone set, Terry," my partner chided. "You need not have come all this way."

Poole stopped to appreciate a cool breeze that wafted through his thinning hair. Even someone as hard-pressed as a policeman could appreciate the garden.

"I wanted to see your face when I told you the news," Poole replied. "There's been a hanging in the cells at 'A' Division overnight."

"Within Scotland Yard?" I asked, stunned. "Are you serious?"

"As Death itself."

Barker's mustache curled into a frown. "Who was hanged?"

"You remember the Dawn Gang?"

"Of course, I remember the Dawn Gang!" the Guv growled. "I gave them to you for safekeeping just yesterday morning. One of them has died?"

"All of them," Poole said grimly. "Every last one. They must have hung each other one by one in the middle of the night. They took off their trousers and tied them together to make a noose. There's nowhere to jump, so they tied a knot on the top bar of the cell, and the others dragged each one down until his neck broke. Nasty business."

"My word," I said. There seemed no other response. I tried to imagine myself in that situation but couldn't.

"We found them this morning when the other inmates started crying out," he continued. "Three bodies lined up in a row on the floor, and the fourth hanging from the bars with his tongue out. It didn't half give us a turn. The last one would have had it the hardest. Death by asphyxiation."

"I don't understand," I confessed. "The cells are facing each other, and clearly visible. How did they manage it?"

"Bloody quietly is how," Poole muttered. "The other prisoners slept through it."

"Have you identified them yet?" Barker asked.

Poole shook his head. "We're checking the cards. We should have at least one match within a few hours. There is a finite number of safecrackers in London."

The cards he mentioned were the Bertillon forms, containing a full description of each criminal, including height, weight, and meticulous measurements, as well as a photograph. It was the best way of recognizing a suspect so far and allowed the various stations and staff of the Metropolitan Police to pool their knowledge.

"The commissioner is livid, the turnkey has been reprimanded, and the reporters smell blood in the water," Poole continued. "We look like fools, although that's nothing new. I need you to come to the Yard and verify that these men are the ones you captured."

"That's absurd," the Guv countered. "I saw them arrested myself."

"Very well," Poole said, shrugging. "I've also come to escape Whitehall. I swear the commissioner was about to burst like a balloon. I wanted out of there before the explosion came. I also thought you should know, since the collar was yours, no matter what the newspapers claim."

"Very thoughtful of you, Terry," the Guv said, nodding. "Where are they now?"

"In Vandeleur's Body Room," he said, referring to the coroner, whom we all knew as a hawkish fellow. "You should nip over quick before he starts carving on them."

Barker stood, preparing to leave. "Did they confess under interrogation?"

"Not a bleedin' word all yesterday, Cyrus. Shut up like clams. Then, there they were this morning lying on the cell floor, sans trousers. What a terrible way to die! You'd have to help your mates hang themselves in front of you. And they were so young! I don't believe any of them were over thirty yet. Now I'll have to see if they have families. You think you've seen everything, and then this!"

"They were very game yesterday," Barker admitted.

"They would be," Terry said, as we crossed the little bridge. "They'd have swung for it. That would have made anyone game enough. But then they hanged themselves! I've come to ask you about the witness in the report. Some sort of beggar, was it?"

"She called herself Dutch," my partner replied. "We suspected she may have been warning the gang with birdcalls. She was gone by the time we returned with the men from 'H' Division."

"I've heard of her," the inspector responded. "The Canary, they call her. A novelty beggar. I'll go look for her. She's bound to know their names."

"We took her to the Mile End Mission," Barker stated.

"That may be the best place for her," Terry Poole said. "The commissioner wants a word with you. Shall we get a cab, gentlemen, and make our way to Scotland Yard."

It wasn't a question. In Newington Causeway, Barker hailed a hansom cab, and the three of us climbed aboard. We headed west to St. Georges Road and Westminster Bridge, still considering Poole's tale.

We left the cab in Whitehall and were soon near the Embankment. Parting ways with Poole, we entered through the familiar doors, climbed to the second floor, and were shown into the commissioner's office.

James Munro is a short man with no neck to speak of. His head is shaped like a bucket and his hair shaven close to his skull. We first met him as the head of the Special Irish Branch, a division most of the personnel at Scotland Yard did not trust. The man was a law unto himself, and when Commissioner Henderson retired, he gobbled up the position like a mastiff might Sunday dinner. My partner and I had little use for him until Barker was offered the position of head of a secret society known as the Knights Templar. Unwilling to discharge all the duties himself or risk shutting down the agency, he split them with Munro, who was also a member. It seemed an odd decision at the time, since the two disliked each other intensely, but the Guv said his antipathy was not because of any flaw in the commissioner's character, merely his personality. Privately I suspected the men were too much alike and neither enjoyed taking orders. The pair made a truce and had been working together for a few years now. Barker kept Munro's secrets, and he kept Barker's, and by association mine. Munro had to swallow the fact that I was a former felon and I the fact that he was a dyspeptic toad. There was swallowing to be done on all our parts, but it is sometimes necessary to get things moving along. We're not all friends here, but we don't need to be chums to do business together.

"Congratulations on finding the Dawn Gang," Munro said as we entered his office. "I regret we couldn't keep hold of them for you. I've just sacked our turnkey; he was lax in his duties. I shall be raked over the coals myself by the British press tomorrow morning, but it won't be the first time. Sit."

We removed our coats and hats and sat with them in our laps. The man is known for his directness, so there was no need to look for a hat rack. He cleared his throat and continued.

"It will make an interesting story for a day or two, but you caught them, and we saved Her Majesty's government the cost of a trial. Again, I thank you."

Barker nodded in acknowledgment. He's no more effusive than Munro.

"I understand there was a witness," the commissioner continued. "A beggar. Have you found him yet?"

"It was a woman," my partner replied. "She was somewhere in the East End when we last saw her."

It was true, but it wasn't precisely what the commissioner had asked.

"We're patrolling the streets for her, but I suspect she's gone to ground," Munro said.

"Did she appear to be working with the gang?"

"Aye, she did," the Guv confirmed. "She was keeping an eye out for constables and sending messages to the gang using birdcalls. She is very proficient."

"What did she look like?"

"A heap of rags," I spoke up. "She had a voluminous mackintosh, and a filthy cloth tied around her head like a scarf. Her face was caked with mud, and she was lame."

Munro made no comment but scribbled the description on a sheet of paper.

"Was she Dutch?" he asked.

"No," Barker answered. "She uses the moniker 'Dutch,'

but we don't know her real name. She didn't have a trace of a foreign accent."

"Did she give up the gang?"

"She did, readily," the Guv replied. "She told us the exact shop where we could find them. Of course, she had disappeared from the steps of the workhouse by the time we returned."

"She couldn't have been too badly crippled if she disappeared so quickly," Munro said.

"I thought so at the time," I stated. "But her leg looked as if it had gone through a wringer. It's possible she was helped away by someone before Detective Constable Dew and his men arrived."

Munro sat back in his chair and put down his pen. "What was your impression of Dew?"

"Satisfactory," the Guv pronounced. "By the book. He had an air of authority for so young a fellow and kept the constables from various districts in line."

"Cyrus, I appreciate your willingness to share this arrest with him."

Barker waved his hand. "The merchants I worked for understand who caught the safebreakers. It's immaterial to me whether the public knows."

"I agree with your assessment. We'll give Dew credit for the official collar, then."

"Are we done?" Barker asked, ready to stand. Munro put up a hand.

"A final question," he asked. "Did the beggarwoman indicate that the Dawn Gang was working for someone else? Did she say who hired her, for instance?"

"She didn't," I replied. "But then she didn't say much. Her voice was very rough, as if it hurt her voice to speak. Goodness knows how old she must be."

One of Barker's beetling brows peeked over the tops of his black lenses.

"Is something going on, James?" he asked, lowering his voice.

Munro sat back in his chair, glancing at the ceiling. His fingers drummed on the armrest of his chair. Then he stood and closed the door.

"Something is, I fear. Some crimes are up, others down. The Dawn Gang is an example. They were too professional: ruthless, violent, proficient. Not the usual incompetent rabble. I haven't seen such good planning since my days with Irish Branch."

"Aye, when Seamus O'Muircheartaigh was running the East End," my partner added. "The Irishman had attempted to unify the local criminals."

"But he's dead," the commissioner said. "He died on the Continent. We sent a Bertillon card and photograph. The body was shipped here and buried. The man is definitely dead. Something's changed, however. I can feel it in my bones. Might you look into it? Dew's just out of nappies. I need an experienced man, and currently the Criminal Investigations Department is spread very thin. The Dawn Gang is only the most public matter."

I stifled a smile. Scotland Yard needed our help. Was the Yard to be our next client?

Barker nodded. "Of course, James. I'll investigate the matter."

"Discreetly," Munro suggested.

"I am the soul of discretion."

Munro and I glanced at each other, as if trying to ascertain whether that was true or not. Neither of us answered. The two men nodded, and we left his office.

"Scotland Yard is asking for our help," I said, as we descended the stairs to the lobby. "I can't believe it."

Cyrus Barker stopped at the bottom of the stair with his hands in the pockets of his ulster, contemplating the ground as if he would find the answer there.

"It can only mean one thing, Thomas," he said. "I suspect Munro no longer trusts his own men."

CHAPTER 5

When we reached the front desk, Sergeant Kirkwood sang out.

"Gents!" he called. "Your presence is requested downstairs!"

"Thank you, Sergeant," my partner said, in his rich basso voice, which sets wooden floors to reverberating. "Shall we go, Thomas?"

"Not if there's a choice," I muttered.

We went down a flight of stairs to what "A" Division colorfully calls the Body Room. It is the domain of a minotaur named Edward Vandeleur, coroner, surgeon, barrister, and author of various articles in medical publications. He's also a bit of a tyrant.

"Out!" he barked as a matter of course, then seeing who we were, invited us into his sanctum sanctorum, which was the morgue for the whole of the Metropolitan police force. Corpses found all over London made their way there. We were responsible for several bodies whose stories appeared in his articles, and I had no doubt he would soon write one about the Dawn Gang. He wore a snowy white coat over a gutta-percha apron stained with blood, bile, and every other fluid a corpse can leak. Vandeleur always reminded me of the composer Franz Liszt, with a waterfall of pale hair that flowed over his collar, though he was only fifty years of age.

"Ah," he grunted. "I wondered when you two would be along."

He lit a cigarette with a vesta, transferring bloody finger-marks to both.

"Quite a haul you've brought me," he continued. "I'd have been satisfied with one. You have gilded the lily."

"It was not my intent, Doctor," Barker said, his voice echoing in the tiled room. "We merely captured them. The rest was their own doing."

I'd been in this room dozens of times, and very little startled me. However, we had fought these fellows only the morning before, and now they were lying naked on metal tables, shriven of all dignity. I wondered whether they imagined such an abrupt ending to their choice of careers.

One of the bodies especially bothered me, the one I'd held a pistol to and taunted about getting me out of bed. Now he lay with his throat angry and red, his protruding tongue the color of liver. His body was a waxy gray. Rigor mortis had come and gone, and he lay as slack limbed as a marionette. I wanted to say something to assuage my feelings of guilt at the gibe I'd made at him, but I couldn't take the words back now.

"Have they discovered their names yet?" my partner asked.

"Not to my knowledge," Vandeleur replied. "Constables have been running in and out, comparing the faces to Bertillon cards, trying to identify them. So far, they have been unsuccessful."

He dropped the fag end of the bloody cigarette on the postmortem room floor and crushed it under his boot. If he did such a thing at home, I felt sorry for his wife.

"You're just in time," he said, handing me a yardstick. Barker took a second.

"What are these for?" I asked.

"Measuring, obviously," he answered.

The Bertillon method was conceived by the Sûreté in Paris to identify criminals. A photograph is taken, or a drawing made, then various parts of the body are carefully examined and measured, such as the length of the arm from wrist to elbow. Bertillon was mad for ears, and they were carefully and painstakingly drawn or photographed. Personally, I thought the man a nutter, and the methods haphazard at best, but it was a crude answer to a pressing problem, criminals who moved about Europe and Britain.

Obviously, the inspectors could not run down here for every measurement, so we were the equivalent of the mountain coming to Mohammed. It was a very tactile experience. I would have made a poor embalmer. However, Cyrus Barker was humming to himself as he measured, the way I'd seen him hum while he built a model of his ship, the *Osprey*. He showed no more awareness of the macabre nature of the duty we were performing than Dr. Vandeleur. Meanwhile, the doctor was weighing a kidney in a glass bowl. I wanted out of the room and into the fresh air as soon as possible. I would even accept a sooty London particular over this atmosphere.

A half hour later we were able to return to our offices. I wanted to bathe but had to settle for a wash in the room behind our offices. Afterward, I stepped out the back door and let the frigid air comb through my wet hair for as long as I could bear it. Then I came in and shook myself like a dog. Barker was grinning when I returned. His face was never intended for smiling. He looked like a mastiff baring his teeth.

"Presentable again, lad?" he asked.

"You tell me."

"One of the men had a tattoo which can only have been scriven in Manila," he said. "I'll wager he was once a sailor. Another was missing the tips of two fingers, long healed. He must have once worked in a meat or fish market."

"Could we change the subject please?" I asked.

"Certainly, they were trained thieves and safebreakers," he continued, oblivious to my discomfort. "I wonder what Mr. Hesse did to provoke his own death. As a rule, safe artists do not resort to murder. He must have put up quite a fight to be silenced that way."

Chief Detective Inspector Terence Poole entered within the hour, a triumphant look on his face. He held four buff Bertillon cards in his hand.

"Once we had the measurements, it was just a matter of comparing the numbers," he stated. "Here are our suicides, gentlemen, every one of them on record."

He fanned them across the table like a hand of whist and we studied them. The man I had menaced bore the name James or Jamie Dunn. He did five years for safecracking in Holywell Prison. Apparently, he didn't learn his lesson. The others were named Alfred Keller, Nigel Smith, and Graham Lester.

"We have their last known addresses, gentlemen," Poole

stated. "I suppose it is too much to hope the swag they got from their other robberies hasn't been fenced and spent already."

"If you are going to interview their families, may we accompany you, Terry?" Barker asked. "The commissioner has asked for our help."

"As did you," I put in, looking at the inspector.

"I suppose I did," Poole replied. "If you gentleman wish to be present when wives are told that their husbands have killed themselves in the most violent way possible, and they have been cut off without a penny, I won't stop you."

"Good, then," Barker said, nodding.

Poole and I glanced at each other. As I've noted before, Barker doesn't understand sarcasm. His yes means yes and his no means no. The three of us went to the Public Carriage Building and hired a brougham. We weren't going to be squashed into a small cab with the Guv again.

Against his better judgment, Terry gave us a glance at the files that "A" Division had collected. Each of the gang members had minor records and had spent a brief time in prison. All had resided in the East End.

"Perhaps one of them recruited the others for the job," Poole speculated. "This fellow, Dunn, was a known safecracker. He'd be the one to form a gang."

Barker settled back in his seat. "Unless another criminal recruited them, and all of them worked for him."

Poole looked at him, mildly annoyed. "You seem determined to find a conspiracy here."

"Four men caught in a robbery and murder do not kill themselves en masse," Barker argued. "Each of them had learned to cope with prison life."

Poole shrugged, conceding the point.

"It's a theory," Terence Poole admitted. "I doubt it, but

then I have no argument to counter it. Perhaps we'll never know. That's the problem with solving cases; we can generally work out how someone committed a crime, but not necessarily why. Sometimes, it's as plain as the nose on your face, but at others it's a complete mystery. Let's hope their families are willing to shed light on their reasons."

The first address was in Watling Street in Cheapside, the address of the late Mr. Nigel Smith, a former locksmith. It was a typical low-rent row house. Poole knocked politely on the door, then more forcefully the second time. There was a face in every neighbor's window watching us. Poole was not dressed like a Yard man, being head of the Plain Clothes Police. Perhaps they thought him that other symbol of grim authority, the rent man. The inspector stepped back to deliver a kick to the lock, but my partner stopped him.

"Let me, Terry," he insisted, reaching into his waistcoat pocket to extract a "betty" or skeleton key. I kept a penknife in mine. He inserted it in the lock and waggled it around for a minute or so until it finally acceded to his demands.

"I won't ask how you learned that trick, Cyrus," Poole stated flatly.

"It's probably best," came the reply. "I'll teach you how to use it sometime. There is no damage to the door, and no sign you were there."

Poole rolled his eyes upward and shook his head as if dealing with an incorrigible brother, who could not help but get himself into trouble.

We stepped inside and found the front room full of old but respectable furniture. A stuffed monkey lay on the floor near the door, along with a small pair of knit stockings, which I imagined had been improvised as a pair of mittens. Poole went into one of the adjoining rooms.

"They've scarpered," he said when he returned. "Drawers opened, and some of the clothing taken."

Barker went into the kitchen, and we followed after him. There was an icebox, something one rarely finds in this part of London. It was a step toward gentility, even legitimacy. The couple who lived here passed as respectable. They might even have been married. Stranger things have happened in the East End.

Poole opened the icebox and then jumped back. The meat had spoiled, the ice long since melted and evaporated.

"They haven't been here in days, perhaps longer," I remarked.

"Agreed," the inspector replied. "They must have cleared out of this flat in a hurry before the last break-in. Let's try another on the list."

Barker stopped him and relocked the door with his betty as Poole gave him a scornful look.

"Why so careful?" he asked. "You kicked the jeweler's door into firewood."

"That was a business," the Guv said. "This is someone's private home, and if they did return, they'd discover that their neighbors had stolen them blind. Where is the next address?"

"Worship Street," Poole said, reading the Bertillon card he carried. "Graham Lester, former rampsman."

The address was not far away. We climbed into the four-wheeler and traveled through the downtrodden streets. When we reached the door, we knocked. Again, there was no answer, and when we unlocked it, again we found an abandoned flat. Well, not fully abandoned. There was a half-starved dog there. It looked frantic. I left my companions to look over the deserted flat and carried the small creature into a butcher shop in the next street where I bought a few scraps of beef. She devoured them, poor thing, and swallowed a bowlful of water. She was small and spindly, and of uncertain parentage. A terrier of sorts perhaps, with short hair, and ginger spots. When she was done eating, I carried her back to the flat. With her short hair and the fear of being around strangers, she shivered in the cold. I could not deduce her age with any certainty.

"They left a week ago, by the number of messes left behind," Barker stated.

"I'm inclined to agree with him, not that I intended to count them," Poole informed me, looking at the dog. "What are you going to do with that beast?"

"It's a frail little thing." I replied. "A pet for children, rather than a guard dog. They wouldn't leave it behind if they could help it."

"They cleared out quickly," the C.I.D. man admitted. "Drawers open, clothes strewn on the floor. Valuables left behind, like lamps, books, even silverware."

"Thomas is right," Barker pronounced. "They didn't leave voluntarily. They were taken."

"Perhaps they didn't pay their rent and were tossed into the street," Poole said.

"All four of them?" I asked, scratching the dog behind the ears.

"Even the most negligent of landlords wouldn't have left a dog to soil his floors," Barker agreed, as if it settled the matter.

He chucked the dog under the chin. She wagged her wiry tail. He had a way with small creatures. It was only people who found him intimidating.

"Be careful!" Poole warned. "Don't name her. If you name a dog you have to keep it."

"Is that true?" I asked my partner.

Barker shrugged. "I don't know, but in either case, until we find the family, you're taking care of it. You know how jealous Harm gets."

I thought of Rebecca, and her expression when I came in the door with a dog, then what would happen if the family was found, and we had to give her back again. It was one of those domestic heartaches that happen every day in London. But what was the alternative? I glanced at Poole, who put up both hands.

"Don't look at me," he said. "I own a boarhound. That thing would be a snack for him."

"Blast," I said.

"See, it was meant to be," the inspector pronounced. "But don't get too accustomed to it. We might find its owners safe and sound."

We stepped out into the street and locked the door behind us. The cabman gave me a look but allowed the dog in his carriage and took us to the third flat on our list.

"James Dunn," Poole read from the next card. "Safe-cracker."

The Dunn house was little more than a hovel, but there were several small cots in one room, so we knew more than one child lived here. Clothes were strewn about, little more than rags. Rancid food sat on the table, and bottle flies danced against the windows trying to escape, though it was nearly winter.

"I'm sensing a pattern here," Poole remarked.

"Perhaps the gang hid their families away ahead of their big heist," I said.

The thought occurred to me that we didn't think of a man's family when we arrested him. That was supposed to sort itself out, which meant it was the wife, common law or otherwise, who must handle the consequences. It was always thus. Women bear the burden for us all.

"Let's go," Poole said. "I need fresh air."

"Do you suppose these families knew each other?" I asked after we stepped outside.

"Why would you think that, lad?" Cyrus Barker demanded.

"Their husbands worked together," I reasoned. "It's possible the wives knew one another as well. Then their husbands are arrested and kill themselves—"

"Each other," Poole corrected.

"The women took everything they could carry and left the area together."

"Cyrus," Poole asked. "Do you believe this theory?"

"There's no way to know yet, Terry," my partner admitted. "But I'm certain all will be revealed in the fullness of time."

"Look at him," Poole complained to me. "You ask the man a straight question and he spouts Bible verses at you!"

The final house was in Bethnal Green. The Bertillon card listed him as Alfred John Keller, but his aliases included Johnny Keller and Alf Johnson. The fellow was not very imaginative. The room we entered was stale, and a mouse jumped off the dining table as we entered the kitchen.

"Eggs," Poole said, pointing at the table. "It happened at breakfast, then. First thing in the morning."

Barker pointed to the door. "It appears to have been broken into with some kind of tool. There may have even been a struggle. Let's ask the neighbors."

We knocked on doors. No one had seen anything. No one wanted a dog, either. After half an hour of trying to find answers, we met back at the brougham where the cabman sat on his perch reading an afternoon edition, his collar up around his ears.

"It was a waste of time, but we had to look," Terry Poole said. "If the Old Man asks, at least we were thorough. I'm peckish. Let's visit the Prospect."

"Will they allow dogs?" I asked, looking at the pup in my arms.

Poole shrugged. "That sounds more your problem than mine."

CHAPTER 6

The Prospect of Whitby is an institution. The old riverside tavern opened its doors in 1520 and had once been called the Devil's Tavern. Despite an evil reputation in its early days, it was now beloved by Londoners, and few locals sailed through the year without docking at the tavern at least once.

The Prospect was at the loop in the Thames where the river turns and flows south. The river police dock was nearby, and under one particular twist in the river was a tearoom owned by Barker's friend, Ho, a Chinaman. Not far away was another well-known pub we favored called the Grapes.

The publican at the Prospect frowned at the dog under my arm as we entered, but I took it that Poole was a regular, so he wouldn't toss me out the door. I was glad, because I liked the place, with its old ship models and quaint view of Lime-house Reach. It's one of those places where, if you squint, you can feel as if you're in the eighteenth century, having a pint with Isaac Newton.

We found a table by the back window and ordered ale along with a large steak and kidney pie. Barker dug out his travel-ing pipe and soon had it going. While waiting to have the pie delivered, we began to discuss the day's strange events.

"Have you any theories, gentlemen?" Poole asked after that all-important first gulp of ale, which must never be rushed. He sat back in his chair and set the pint glass on the table, amidst a myriad of circular rings from thousands upon thou-sands of previous pints.

"They've gone," I said, referring to the Dawn Gang's families. "And have been for a while. They could be in John O'Groats by now."

"Agreed," Poole said. "But for the sake of argument, let's say they are still in town. Where could they be hiding?"

"I can't picture a group of women and children moving about together, especially if they are being threatened," I an-swered. "It would be too difficult. They would separate and return to their families."

"Cyrus?" Poole asked, scratching his sandy side-whiskers.

Barker was sitting in his chair, his pint of stout still un-touched. He was making random circles on the arm of his captain's chair with the broad tip of his finger.

"Hmmm?" he asked. "I beg your pardon. I was thinking."

"About what?"

"About a child's stuffed monkey and a family dog."

Here, the aforementioned creature raised its head and looked at him.

"What do you mean?" Poole asked.

"If a mother were attempting to flee the family home for whatever reason, with a frightened and confused child, I would imagine the first step would be to pacify the child with a favorite toy."

"Or the family pet," I remarked.

The dog turned to me then, cautiously wagging its tail. She seemed subdued in a strange place, surrounded by strangers. However, she was no longer shivering, so she must have felt at least marginally safe in my lap.

"That's true," the inspector agreed. "But generally speaking, children drop their toys a dozen times a day, especially when going out with their parents. They can't keep hold of things. That has been my experience, anyway."

Belatedly, Barker took a pull of his stout, then strained a thin layer of froth from his mustache with a finger.

"Do you suppose they all evacuated their flats at once, or did they go from one to the other, accumulating children and items as they went along?" the Guv asked. "Thomas, how many beds did you count?"

"Let's see," I said. "There were two children's beds in the first flat, four in the second, and another two in the third. The fourth only had just the one, but I saw a child's chalk and slate, so I assume it slept with its parents. That's at least ten children, sir, give or take."

"That's quite a gaggle," Terence Poole stated. "They would be noticed. I'll send constables to question neighbors. We'll get names and whatever information we can gather about the families."

Our pie arrived then, brown and fragrant and fresh from the oven. We tucked in. The dog was curious, and I would give her a little after it cooled, but not too much. It would only make her ill. She wasn't a young dog. There was gray in her muzzle, and the fact that she knew the word "dog," and presumably her own name, meant that she was intelligent. It made me think of Dutch: half starved, living by her wits, and cautious.

"What an odd thing," I said, "for four men with families to form a gang and stage a series of daring robberies."

"Well," Poole said, waving for a second pint. "Perhaps it's not so unusual. Safecracking was their only bankable skill, after all, and the only work that would bring them together."

"It was well planned," the Guv said, nodding. "One would need a locksmith to open the door, a safecracker to get to the jewels, a housebreaker to know what was worth stealing, and a rampsman to keep an eye out for constables and help them escape. It was organized."

"I see what you're saying," I said, scratching the dog between the ears. "Normally a gang is a group of random fellows with one skilled man. This group seemed . . . what's the word?"

"Handpicked," my partner said. "Well organized, and successful. They must have made hundreds of pounds in the past month of robberies. Yet look at their criminal record. They were captured easily in their earlier careers and spent time in various prisons. The Met jugged them with no problem."

"Here now," Poole said. "We're not incompetents."

"No insult intended, Terry."

"We're only the most celebrated criminal investigation organization in the world, that's all!"

"A reputation that is well deserved."

The inspector set his glass on the table, sloshing the ale. "We solve thousands of cases every year!"

"Of course, Terence," Barker agreed. "No one is arguing that."

Poole turned to me, perhaps to start an argument. I have

occasionally been vocal in my criticism of the Yard. Fortunately, I was face deep in my pint, and the dog was blinking
up at him. For a criminal's dog, she did not seem inclined to
bite a C.I.D. man. In fact, she looked a little frightened of
him. He was being contentious.

"I brought the two of you along," he said. "I didn't have
to do that!"

"That's true," I replied. "You didn't."

Sometimes Scotland Yard inspectors can seem petty. The
system tends to set them in competition with one another,
and the more public successes are trumpeted in the newspapers. Also, the public is never slow to show its displeasure,
either in print or in letters to the government. Sometimes
private agencies like ours step in at the last minute and steal
the glory. It's a thankless job. I wouldn't be an inspector if
they were paid weekly in gold sovereigns.

I concentrated on the food. The Prospect makes what many
consider the best steak and kidney pie in London. The bar-
maid even gave me a small plate for the Dog-I-Would-Not-
Name. I refused to give her more than a few bites. Despite
the fact that I'd already given her a scrap at the butcher's, she
bolted the food. The rest of the pie was divided among the
three of us.

"Thomas is right," Poole continued, pointing at me with
his fork. "The women could be anywhere. If they have the
money their husbands stole, they could be on the Continent
by now and long out of our hands."

A picture formed in my mind of four women on a spree in
Paris, shopping for Worth dresses and toys for their children. I
shook it away. These women had probably lived grim lives and
never knew luxuries. Their flats attested to that.

"The matter that concerns me about the Dawn Gang is
why they were so quick to commit suicide," Barker said,

frowning. "If found guilty they might have received a sentence of five to seven years. Had they hidden away the money, they would have been free and clear by the time their children were youths. Why kill themselves? There appears to be no obvious reason for it."

"Granted," Poole said. "What do you suggest as an alternative?"

"Let us turn this entire matter on its ear," the Guv said. "Let us imagine a criminal leader in the East End. He creates for his own needs a group of criminals with unique skills to perform a certain task, such as breaking into jewelers' shops. But to be certain his name remains anonymous, he kidnaps their families. If the gang attempts to notify the authorities, or if they are captured, they understand that their families will die. Therefore, when they are taken to jail, they reason that the only way to safeguard their wives and children is to kill themselves."

Poole and I looked at each other.

"That can't be it, surely," I said.

Barker let out a gust of air. "Look back on the rooms we've visited this morning. Toys forgotten. Pets left behind. Belongings pulled from drawers piecemeal. These women didn't pack in a hurry to escape. Someone pushed their way in, made them stuff their clothing into sacks there and then, and herded them somewhere for safekeeping. The men were helpless. They had no idea where their families were. They had never asked to be a part of this man's plans."

"It's rather far-fetched, Cyrus," Terence Poole said.

"You didn't fight the Dawn Gang that morning," Barker replied. "They were frantic. They tried everything they could to stop us, but only one knew how to defend himself, and even he was not well prepared."

"I'll concede the possibility that there was someone

planning but not executing the robberies," the inspector said. "I don't know about the rest."

"It seems an odd arrangement, sir," I remarked to my partner. "It's overly ruthless. Why force men to perform thefts they'd have been willing to perform themselves if given the proper opportunity? Why not offer them more money?"

"Look, lad, there's no way to foresee every aspect of this matter, but I sincerely believe one thing: despite any promises made to the members of the Dawn Gang, now that the men are dead, the women and children have become a liability. They can offer nothing."

"Well—" Poole began.

"Man, can you not tell the difference between a woman packing her possessions neatly, and someone else throwing things into a sack in a disorderly fashion?"

"I'm sorry, Cyrus," Poole said, shaking his head. "I just can't believe it."

"But you'll alert the stations in the East End to look out for a group of women and children who may be held hostage in the area."

"Yes," Poole conceded. "Yes, I will."

There was silence around the table. Barker pointed at Poole's empty glass, but the detective chief inspector put his hand over the top.

"What happened with Commissioner Munro?" he asked.

Barker looked innocent, which is hard to do when one has a face like thunder even on his best days.

"Come along, Cyrus," Poole continued. "Spill it."

"I'm sorry, Terry," the Guv replied. "What he told me is private."

"Private, my blessed mother," Poole snapped. "I know Munro has a bee in his bonnet about something. You can see the stress in his face."

"Very well," Barker conceded. "He called me in as a consultant. He wants me to go about and observe things in the East End in a general way and report back to him. That is all."

"He's been secretive lately, and ill-tempered to boot," Poole said. Then he shook his head.

"Well, he's always ill-tempered. I think he's got himself an ulcer. What else?"

"You can bounce a pebble off the commissioner's windows," the Guv answered. "Ask him."

"It's that secret society business, isn't it? The rich and powerful men running everything."

The Guv set down his glass. "You know I am a common man."

"Common, my eye," Poole parried. "You could buy my house ten times over. Heaven help all of London if you were common, as well. One Barker's hard enough."

"I wasn't born with a title or a plot of land to my name. I was a missionary's son."

"Well, what's Munro looking for?" Poole asked.

"That is what is called open-ended."

"He doesn't know," Poole said, looking at me. "Why doesn't he ask the C.I.D., then?"

Barker shrugged. "It is his choice, not mine."

"Very well. Be all silent and mysterious. Just remember, I've saved your life more than once."

"And I yours."

Poole hooked a thumb in my direction. "Does this one know?"

"This one?" I demanded, putting down my now empty glass. "I've known you for over a decade. I've been to your house and met the missus!"

"Of course, he knows," my partner replied, ignoring the

banter. "He was there. But we didn't discuss societal matters."

"Then it does concern the Templars!" Poole said, pointing at Barker's broad chest.

"Join and you may find out."

"Not me," Poole replied. "I couldn't afford the dues. And for the record, I don't like human sacrifice."

"I knew it!" I cried, smiling.

Even Barker smiled at the corners of his mustache.

"It is only ceremonial, of course," he remarked. "You can gibe at me all day long, Terry, but I'm not going to tell you."

Our friend sighed. It was no use. He took a pull at his pint but found it empty. It made him irritable.

"Very well," he replied. "But don't expect any help from the C.I.D."

"We never do," I put in.

Barker leaned forward. "Terry, have you noticed anything unusual in the East End, over and above the Dawn Gang?"

"Oh, so you're allowed to ask questions."

"Of course. You're a public servant. We're private."

"As in, 'no rules,'" Poole muttered, shrugging. "Offhand, there's nothing of any import. The Dawn Gang was one for the books, but everything else has been dull by comparison. Even the *Illustrated Police News* is reprinting old articles."

There was silence again. I glanced about the room, which looked like the forecastle of a ship.

"Four families gone at once," Poole repeated. "It can't be a coincidence. They must be together, the lot of them."

"None of the gang were bachelors," Barker pointed out.

"There is no handle here to turn the pot," I remarked.

Both men nodded. It was an enigma. I hate all enigmas and mysteries. The dog looked up questioningly. I think she was trying to keep up with the conversation, but not succeeding.

"What say you, Cyrus?" the inspector asked. "Are they in town or in the country?"

"That's not the question, Terence. It's 'Are they alive or dead?'"

Poole shook his head. "That's too fanciful. It would never happen."

"You would have said that yesterday if I'd told you four men would hang themselves in the cells at Scotland Yard."

CHAPTER 7

That was that, at least as far as the Dawn Gang enquiry was concerned. We had found them, fought them, and captured them, and they had been suitably punished, although we had no part in the latter. In fact, they had been punished beyond what we and the merchants' committee had hoped, and by their own hands, a bizarre end to the case. The victim, Hesse, had been murdered, but he had not joined the organization who hired us, and had paid the price for attempting to take the matter into his own hands. We tendered our bill, and they paid it with neither a hem nor haw. This is a satisfactory outcome in my opinion, I who handle the accounts. Barker takes no part in this end of the business. If he did, he'd dispense with a fee entirely, and then where would we be? Very close to charity work. Too close, in fact.

Poole had promised to hunt diligently for the missing

women and children. As the Guv has said to me at various times, we are like a scalpel. Our incision is quick and narrow, but deep. We are but two men. The Metropolitan Police has a vast pool of dedicated constables to draw from. This sort of work, tracking a group of missing women across the entire city, and possibly beyond, is ideal for their skills. Neither entity is better, and sometimes both are necessary.

The matter was over and done with, although Barker had promised Poole that we would keep our ears to the ground. We were free to take a new case, which was fortunate, because one arrived at our door that very afternoon. Our visitors were a man and his wife in their early forties, perhaps late thirties in the wife's case. She was a handsome woman with pale skin, blond hair, and the kind of delicate chiseled nose one finds on Greek statues. However, the woman looked fragile and sickly, as if standing was a trial. She gazed about the room with some trepidation. Obviously, she had never been in an enquiry agent's den and was uncomfortable doing so now. However, Mac had alighted on our chambers a few days before like one of the cobbler's elves in storybooks, and the floor had been shined with beeswax to a high gloss, the furniture polished, and every speck of dust in the entire chamber removed. A few bouquets from the Guv's glasshouse had appeared in small vases, and there was a scent of lemon in the air for which I could not account. In short, there was nothing of which our visitor could complain, save perhaps the bloodthirsty pair of ancient cutlasses on the wall at the back of the room which flanked the Barker coat of arms.

The gentleman was a well-set-up fellow in a morning coat with a white rose boutonniere and a Turnbull & Asser tie. His sleek hair was black, with a few wisps of gray at the temples, and an eye color to match. He was well-built and well-dressed, and a fine example of the aristocratic class, unlike many these days. He was also recognizable from the images and engravings in the press. He introduced himself as Sir Hugh Danvers, the current opposition leader in the House of Lords. He, too, was taking in our chambers with interest. The woman was his wife, Lady Jane Danvers. Barker and I had stood at her entrance into the room. His Lordship helped her to one of the visitors' chairs with a look in Barker's direction, and receiving a gesture, seated himself as well. They were an elegant couple, who set off the yellow leather chairs. Barker introduced us and we settled into our own. I couldn't help but notice mine was not polished and a bit dreary. The rivalry between Jacob Maccabee and myself had been a long-standing one.

"How may we be of service to you?" Barker asked, leaning back in his tall green wingback chair.

"My wife's sister has disappeared," Lord Danvers explained. "It was remiss of me not to have come earlier, but we were concerned about this court you work in and some of its inhabitants, no insult intended. There is a royal warrant on your door, however, and I reasoned that if you were recommended by the royal family, we can feel safe in your hands. My sister-in-law has been gone since June."

Cyrus Barker took no offense. It was my partner's mission to make our profession reputable and downplay its sometimes seedy aspect. His Lordship wasn't the only visitor to voice such concerns.

"June?" my partner remarked. "It is November! It's been five months. She could be anywhere."

"May suggested to Hugh that she intended to go to Rome," Lady Danvers explained. "She was too ashamed to talk to me. The following morning, she was gone without a word."

"Ashamed?" the Guv asked. "How so?"

"We suspect an affair of the heart," Danvers said, looking

abashed. He did not enjoy airing family secrets. "She was either running to or running from a suitor."

The Guv tented his fingers on his desk. "You know this, or are you speculating?"

"The latter," Lady Jane admitted. She could have left the matter to her husband but seemed determined to play her part in the discussion. "Hugh volunteered to go to Rome himself, but I convinced him to hire a professional to do it. There are always matters in Parliament that require his attention."

"You wish us to go to Rome?" Barker asked.

I'd been taking notes, but my pen stopped of its own accord.

"Oh dear," Danvers said. "Is there some difficulty, sir?"

"Not in the least," Barker said easily as if he went to Italy twice a week. "We have no objections, do we, Mr. Llewelyn?"

"None whatsoever," I lied, wondering who was going to soothe poor Rachel for however long it took us to find this woman. Not to mention Rome held no charm for me. Rebecca and I had honeymooned there and had found it far from quaint.

"What is your sister's name, Lady Danvers?" the Guv asked.

"Miss May Evans," she replied. "Our father is Harold Evans of the Evans Shipbuilding Company of Newport, Rhode Island."

That was it, I realized. I noticed there was something unusual about the way she spoke. Her tones were flat, but her words strung together like cursive, unlike the British, who clip their sentences the way a man does a cigar. She was an example of the American heiress who marries into an old British family that has more pedigree than pounds sterling. As a group these young pioneers were not welcome, but some persevering Americans with enough charm, wit, and flawless manners had wormed their way into British society. I assumed Her Ladyship was one of them.

"Are you aware of any reason she would go to Rome?" Barker asked. "Has she shown any interest in the city before?"

"My family is Roman Catholic, Mr. Barker," Lady Danvers replied. "But I don't recall her ever mentioning a wish to travel to the Holy City before."

"We're certain she's never spoken of taking holy orders or that sort of thing," Lord Danvers said. "Though I understand some jilted women have."

Lady Danvers turned to face her husband. "First, you've accused her of running off with a lover. Now you suspect some swain has jilted her. It can only be one of them."

"Have you a name?" the Guv asked.

"We do not," Lord Danvers stated. "It is pure speculation on our part. She had been maudlin since Easter. Secretive as well."

"May is a romantic, Mr. Barker," Lady Danvers said. "She's unworldly and innocent. I believe she's been adrift since coming to London. Too many young men want to marry an heiress, and too many society mothers are willing to help them. I suspect this mystery suitor, and I am convinced there is one, has turned her head. He is unsuitable."

"Ma'am, do you believe she went to heal a broken heart, or to meet a lover?"

Lady Danvers leaned forward, color coming to her face. "I hope it was the former. I don't want my darling sister ruined. She would be unhappy for the rest of her life! I've even suspected she might do away with herself, and that is the reason she left Camberley."

"The poor wee girl," Barker said. "You live in Camberley?"

"Yes, Mr. Barker," Danvers replied. "If some bounder has taken her, I want you to find him, sir. And when you do, I'll go to Rome and settle the matter myself."

"Do you intend to pay the man to let her alone?" the Guv asked, looking at him curiously.

"Ball and pistol, more like," Danvers stated.

"Now, Hugh, you promised!" Her Ladyship chided, touching his arm. The opportunity to vent his bottled-up feelings in front of other men had been too much for him.

"We had been hoping for a proper suitor for her, gentlemen," Lady Danvers continued. "In fact, we had introduced her to Phillip Chalmers, of the Hampshire Chalmers. Such a dear boy! But by then May had become moody and distracted. I don't think she was impressed with him at all."

"Dear boy," I noted in shorthand.

"Had she any friends in whom she might confide?" my partner asked.

Lady Jane nodded. "There was one girl, the daughter of a tenant on our estate who owns a dress shop. Her name is Henrietta Styles. I often saw them meeting together in town, though we didn't care for her coming to the house."

"We shall need to speak to her," Barker said. "Tell me, Lady Danvers, have you an idea of your sister's dowry, or how much money might be settled upon her were she to marry?"

She looked unsettled at the question, but then so did the one who asked it. Barker dislikes talking about money. I suspect it has something to do with the Asian culture he grew up in as the son of missionaries from the London Missionary Society assigned to Foochow.

"I haven't spoken with Papa about the matter," she said. "I assume it would be similar to my own, which is approximately five million dollars."

My pencil ran off the edge of the notebook. I quickly recovered my composure, wondering to myself what made an American girl worth so much more than an English one. Nothing, of course, save that her father or grandfather, through a combination of luck and hard work, had made a fortune in gold or silver, and could then use her to form alliances to gain power and influence across the globe. It had been so for centuries, even millennia, yet it still seemed mercenary to me. But then, I'd been raised in a Welsh coal-mining town, where heiresses are few and far between.

"I see," Barker said, not reacting to the sum of money she had discussed. "Did you at any time suspect that she was taken instead of leaving of her own accord?"

"I assumed if that were the case, we would have received a note for her ransom, but there have been no threats so far," Lord Danvers said. "None in nearly half a year."

"It's as if the world has swallowed her up, Mr. Barker," Lady Danvers said. "I'm certain she would have communicated with me were she able, even if she were ashamed of her actions. She knows I would forgive her anything."

Barker turned to Lord Danvers. "She spoke to you about leaving?"

"Yes, sir," the man replied. "I had come from my pied-à-terre in London on the first train and saw her waiting on the platform. She looked maudlin and said that she wanted to leave England, and that she thought Rome must be beautiful that time of year. But there was something odd about the way she said it, as if she were trying to convince herself. I tried to talk her out of it, and I thought I'd succeeded, but she never returned."

"Did you notify the local constabulary?" Cyrus Barker asked, leaning forward.

"We dared not," Her Ladyship answered. "News would be all over the village by noonday. There would be a scandal."

"We needed to safeguard her reputation," her husband added. "I'm sure you understand."

"Of course. Did you attempt a little investigating of your own?"

Lord Danvers smiled. "Merely to ascertain if her luggage had been sent along. It had, to London. From there it could have gone anywhere."

"You didn't question her friend, Miss Styles?"

The couple looked at each other.

"It hadn't occurred to me," Danvers confessed. "Obviously we are unaccustomed to this sort of thing. Stupid of me not to think of it!"

"My husband is often preoccupied with matters of state, gentlemen," Lady Jane said. "He didn't have much time to devote to my troubled sister."

Aristocrats, I thought to myself. If my sister-in-law were to disappear, Rebecca would track her to Australia like a panther and make short work of the man who took her.

"Very well," Cyrus Barker said, rising to his feet. "I believe we have enough information to work with. If I have questions, I will visit the House of Lords. Discreetly, of course, and only if necessary."

"Shall you go to Rome, then?" Lord Danvers asked.

"I'll exhaust what information I can find here first, but I'll send a telegram to Rome this morning. I have a friend or two among the Carabinieri there. If there are leads, I will go there, locate her, and bring her back to London if she is willing."

"You will be discreet?" our client asked.

Barker turned to me. "Mr. Llewelyn, do I strike you as a discreet man?"

I nodded. "Mr. Barker, you are the most private person I have ever met."

The couple rose from their seats. His Lordship reached into his breast pocket.

"I assume you'll require a retainer," he said.

"It isn't necessary just yet," the Guv answered. "However, I do not have a description of your sister-in-law."

"Stupid of me!" the man said, rummaging about in his pocket.

"I gave it to you this morning, Hugh," his wife said.

"So you did," he replied. "Here it is."

He handed a small carte de visite to Barker, and then ushered his wife through the door. I glanced at the picture in my partner's hand.

"Pretty," I said.

She was blond like her sister, and I suspected her eyes were just as blue. Her smile was a bit coquettish, as if she were keeping a secret from the casual viewer. Most of all, she looked refined and beautiful. Nearly five million dollars' worth of beauty, I supposed. I could not help comparing the situation to horse breeding.

"I assumed you'd refuse the enquiry," I said to the Guv once they were gone. "Generally, you don't accept cases about silly young girls and their self-inflicted problems."

"That's rather harsh, Mr. Llewelyn," my partner said, though we both knew it was true.

"She's probably slipped off to Rome without considering the matter fully, and now goodness knows what's become of her," I continued. "She's gotten herself into one scrape or another, and now she's too ashamed to tell them where she is."

"You're speculating," Cyrus Barker said.

"I am, but that doesn't preclude the possibility that I am right."

"For now, let me compose a telegram."

I keep a sheaf of blank telegraph forms in my desk. I was just handing him one when the door opened again. Lord Danvers had returned.

"May I have another minute of your time, gentlemen?" he asked. "There are a few matters I wanted to discuss when my wife wasn't present."

"Of course," my partner said, waving him to the chair again.

"There are reasons why I haven't come here earlier," Lord Danvers confessed. "At one point I considered the possibility that she was with child and had gone to Rome to have it in seclusion. If she sent the infant to a foundling home, I wish the silly girl good fortune, but if she returns with it unwed there would be a scandal that would affect my political reputation. I'll admit that is one of my considerations. I've been on pins and needles waiting for some word. May is something of a flibbertigibbet, I'm afraid. She's flighty and headstrong and doesn't have her sister's good sense."

"Have there been suitors for her hand?" the Guv asked.

"There have. That's why Jane and I wanted to find a proper candidate for her quickly, a young and bland fellow who can keep her out of trouble. American women will be the death of me yet. Thank goodness my wife has good sense, but why did she have to have all of it?"

"I take it then that at least one gentleman was unsuitable," Barker stated.

"Very unsuitable, indeed! In fact, I had a few village toughs knock him about a little, to send the message that he should move along. Do you see? That isn't my normal behavior. I'm a sensible fellow, not the kind for that sort of thing, but I'm at my wits' end! The tension is starting to affect my work. I care for my sister-in-law, but this is maddening!"

"Can you tell me his name, sir?" the Guv asked.

"His name is Alan Dunbarton, the youngest scion from an ancient and noble family. I suppose there is a rotten apple in every barrel, as they say. He's a throwback to the Georgian days: a drinker, gambler, and roué. He keeps a flat in the East End, close to Whitechapel and its excesses. You might inquire after him before heading to Rome. She may have been foolish enough to fall for his charms and not told us. It's my fault, I suppose. I should have watched the man more closely. I don't know which would be worse, leaving an unwanted child on the Continent in an anonymous orphanage or returning with an infant ready to destroy our family and my career. The man's a swine, but as is often the case, he's got a silver tongue. It's got to be Dunbarton unless she's fallen in love with an Italian lothario and run off with the blighter. My nerves are ruined. Is that brandy there?"

He crossed by Barker's desk to a table behind him and splashed some into a tumbler. The Guv sent me a look of disapproval while our client poured the contents down his throat. To my partner's puritan mind, brandy is medicinal, but Danvers's nerves were shot. I shrugged. Nerves are a part of the body as well, and some circumstances require a dose of courage. The man wasn't intending to get sozzled.

"The last I heard Dunbarton had accumulated debts," the man continued. "You could imagine how he would feel about the mere thought of five million dollars in his grasp, and nothing between him and it but a strip of a girl without any sense."

"You're very severe about your sister-in-law, Your Lordship, without knowing her situation yet," my partner reminded him.

Hugh Danvers hung his head. "You are correct, Mr. Barker. I have no excuse. I shouldn't think poorly of May. She's not wise to the ways of the world, while I face them every day. Politics would jade a saint."

"You haven't spoken to Dunbarton since June, I trust?"

"No, but if I had, I'd at least know what I'm facing. This not knowing . . . I can't sleep at night. I'm distracted."

"I'll handle the matter, Your Lordship," Barker assured him. "Rest easy and concentrate on your duties. We'll look into the situation."

"Very well."

Despite Barker's refusing payment earlier, our client reached into his pocket and tossed a lump of banknotes onto the glass top of Barker's desk.

"I just stopped into Cox and Company," he said. "Use this when you go to Rome. Find her, gentlemen, and bring her safely back to her sister. We're counting on you. Please don't let us down!"

He fled as quickly as he had arrived. Barker watched him leave and made no comment for a few minutes.

"Excitable fellow," he finally pronounced.

CHAPTER 8

B y then I knew my partner well, better than anyone save for his lady friend, Lady Philippa Ashleigh, who lived in the South Downs. He and I had worked together for ten years, lived together, shared innumerable injuries, baffling enquiries, and to a small extent confidences. Though I could not think the way he did, I tried to understand how his mind worked, in order to predict his next move. Sometimes I was able to. Other times, I admit I hadn't a clue.

"Where do we begin?" I asked. "We should have asked what date May Evans disappeared. I could go to Victoria station and track her luggage from there."

"Later," he replied. "Let us go to the mission first."

"The mission?" I asked. "I thought the Dawn Gang case was finished."

"Is it?" he countered. "No one has questioned Dutch. She was in effect, a member of the Dawn Gang. Certainly, an accomplice at the very least. Do you not wish to hear her story, Thomas?"

"Not particularly," I said, setting my notes aside. "And if our past conversation is any indication, you won't get a full sentence out of her mouth. It would be a waste of effort."

He stood and reached for his coat and stick. "Still, I am willing to try."

Mile End is not bedraggled like Whitechapel, nor fascinating like the Docks. It is cold and impersonal; anonymous even. There are industrial businesses there with no signs to tell their address or purpose. No children play in the gutter after a rain. No wives await their husbands' return. There may not have been husbands to return.

We reached the gate and alighted from our cab. It was ten o'clock or thereabout. Barker raised his stick and hammered on the iron railing with it, causing it to echo. The sturdy woman in brown we had encountered before stepped out of the building and came to the gate.

"Back again, are you?" she asked.

"Like a bad penny," I replied.

"We need to speak to whomever is in charge," Barker stated.

"Sorry, sir," she said. "He ain't here."

"Miss, I support this charity, sometimes single-handedly, and I was a close friend of your founder, Andrew McLean. I wish to enter."

"I'll take care of this matter, Bertha," a voice said.

We turned to find a man standing behind us. He was about

forty, I thought, a thin fellow in a black military uniform with frogged buttons and a peaked cap. Despite his relative youth, he wore a long beard, dark as pitch.

"You are Cyrus Barker, are you not?" he asked, looking at the Guv.

"Ah, Brigadier Booth!" Barker said as we all shook hands. "We are delighted to see you. This is my partner, Thomas Llewelyn. How is your father?"

"The general is slowing a bit these days," Booth answered. "He takes on too much, no matter what we tell him."

"And his life's work?" Barker asked.

"I would like to say the Salvation Army is thriving," the man continued. "At least we are surviving. Times are hard and there have been many setbacks. Last night someone poured a bucket of slops over a poor major's bonnet. It made the poor girl cry, I'm afraid. Your Brother Andrew would not have put up with such a thing. Nor would you, I suspect, sir. No insult intended, of course."

"None taken," Barker said. "Andrew would turn a cheek the first time, but heaven help you the second. Is the boxing ring in the mission still standing?"

"It is, in Brother Andy's memory," he said, gesturing for us to follow him through the gate. "It is cleaned regularly, but rarely used, and the room itself is available to our residents for physical culture. I would show you about, but of course the ladies are wearing their exercise costumes. Come into the office instead."

We passed along an alleyway between two rows of barracks like structures, painted in the uniform drab-colored paint. At the end there was an office sign. We went inside. A woman sat at a typewriter, while a second lounged against a desk, looking at the ceiling while tapping a pencil between her teeth. I suspected she had been dictating a letter.

"Gentlemen, may I present Miss Eliza Orme and Miss Re-ina Lawrence," Booth said. "Ladies, this is Mr. Cyrus Barker, our benefactor of whom you've heard so much. Mr. Barker, you are fortunate to find me. I only come in once or twice a week to oversee things, but the truth is, there is little for me to oversee. These two ladies handle everything perfectly, which is as it should be. As you know, this is not strictly a Salvation Army facility."

"We are pleased to meet you, Mr. Barker," Miss Orme said. "You're something of an enigma here. One doesn't know what rumors are true."

"Most probably are," I remarked.

"This is my partner, Mr. Llewelyn," the Guv said. "He is the one who sends our monthly donations."

I bowed to each of them. The pair was much of a type: in their forties, with dark hair pulled back, and plain blue dresses of a similar hue. They appeared efficient and busi-nesslike, very suitable for their positions.

"Miss Orme and Miss Lawrence command everything," Booth said. "They are solicitors as well."

"You practice law?" Barker asked, looking at them with interest.

"Not yet," Miss Orme conceded. "But we have received degrees in law from the University of London over the last few years. In our opinion, it is only a matter of time until women are given the legal right to practice in court. We are pushing to have the restrictions removed so that we can do the work we were meant to do."

"It seems to be taking forever," Miss Lawrence added, looking up from her typewriter. "For the most part we are devils."

"Devils?" my partner asked, one side of his mustache curling upward a little.

"It's a legal term," she replied briskly. "We work in law offices typing, proofreading, and preparing briefs for the barristers who defend or prosecute."

"These two ladies work tirelessly for the good of their sisters in the East End," Booth added. "And in the West, as well, I should say. No woman is completely safe from mistreatment."

I decided I liked Booth. He saw the drollness of being placed in charge of these women who were older and probably far more qualified than he to run the mission. He understood he was there because of his connection to his famous father, General Booth. I wondered if the mission was a source of contention the charity could do without. It seemed to have become a shelter for women only. I think Brother Andrew would have approved, but then he had never cared for any opinions but his own, save perhaps his Maker. He held strange values for the East End, such as the belief that fallen women should be returned to society, and that being beaten like a rug by an abusive husband was justification for leaving him. Some people didn't agree with either of those values, and so far British law, always late to change a political stance, had defended them.

"How many women are sheltered here?" Barker asked.

"Twenty-seven?" Miss Orme asked, looking over her shoulder at her colleague for confirmation. "Yes. Twenty-seven. We often have thirty or more."

"How did they first come here?"

"In our chambers in the City, we've encountered several poor women who have left their husbands due to excessive abuse," Miss Lawrence answered, warming to her subject. "The problem is that the husbands feel justified in taking them back by force, and the current law gives them that right. However, within a single day we had two women murdered by their husbands. At that point we started looking about for a place to protect anyone who is in peril."

"And you discovered Brother Andrew's mission," my partner stated.

"Precisely," Bramwell Booth answered, nodding. "Meanwhile, my father was trying to decide what to do with Brother Andrew's bequest to us. We have missions in the East End already, and they are expensive to staff and maintain. I believe we would have sold it to fund our other programs were it not for you, Mr. Barker. If I may say it, sir, you have been the proverbial fly in the ointment."

"You are not the first to call me that, Brigadier," the Guv said, shrugging.

"These ladies came to us and asked if they might house a few women in the vacant buildings," Booth continued. "Then more women were encouraged to seek refuge when they saw what was happening."

"These fortresslike walls are ideal," Miss Lawrence said. "Many angry husbands have come looking for their truant wives, demanding that we release them. They have become violent to the women and to us."

"I got a black eye once," Miss Orme said, as if proud of it. "But there are many mouseholes in these old buildings. It's so easy for a woman to get lost here. It seems that whenever the police arrive with an angry husband, his wife is nowhere to be found."

"I'm sure it's difficult to keep hold of everyone's name and location," I stated. "So many comings and goings. So many anonymous women. I suppose they give aliases rather than using their real names."

"You are correct, Mr. Llewelyn," Miss Orme said. "However, there is more. Some women arrived, having escaped their minders, recalling that Andrew McLean's mission was a haven for fallen women extricating themselves from their terrible lives. They were in as much danger as the women who were here already. We felt ourselves unwilling to judge, if for no other reason than that some of the women within our sanctuary had been out on the street themselves from time to time, even on the orders of their husbands."

"Our work is difficult here," Miss Lawrence added, coming from behind her desk. "Some women come to our gates for food because their families are hungry. It would break your heart. However, we must divert them to other missions. Half of Mile End is starving, and unfortunately, we can't feed everyone."

I had a sense that despite the struggles, Miss Orme and Miss Lawrence enjoyed their work and found it rewarding. The moment I glimpsed the first, leaning against a desk dictating, while staring at the ceiling, there had been a smile on her face, one she shared with her colleague. I didn't think it right that they could receive a degree after several years' work, yet not be able to use it. I also noticed that both women became more sober when we entered the room. Were they attempting to appear more businesslike or was it because of our sex? The entire place seemed a kind of sanctuary, and though Barker was financially supporting the mission I felt as if we were intruders. They did not need us here. The women sheltered in this place had seen the worst of men, and no longer would trust the best of them. Barker's sword of justice was sharper than mine, being ground on the whetstone of his conscience, and I'm sure he felt it keener than I. Like Brother Andrew, he drew upon his own instincts of right and wrong and society with its muddleheaded and arbitrary laws be damned.

My partner crossed to a window and looked out at the gate at the women passing by.

"Ladies, you have been using my funds for various purposes without my knowledge," Barker rumbled.

"If so," Bramwell Booth stated, "the fault is mine. I gave them permission. The money was to hand. The mission was boarded and gathering dust."

"Mr. Barker, do you feel your funding has been utilized for something with which you don't agree?" Miss Orme asked.

I already heard the barrister in her voice, questioning a witness.

"I would have preferred to be informed of the radical change in boarders here, but I don't see that my pounds sterling have been misused," he replied. "I fund the mission for good, and you appear to be using it for that purpose, though I haven't toured the facilities yet."

"We'd like to accommodate you," Booth replied. "But it would take some time for the women here to prepare for some kind of inspection."

"I understand the difficulty, Brigadier," the Guv conceded, nodding. "However, without seeing the mission I have a limited knowledge of how I can best provide what you need."

All eyes were raised. I don't know how much Cyrus Barker is worth, but he supported a good half dozen charities, and at least one church. He'd been a sea captain in China when he found a treasure ship at the bottom of Bias Bay. Its sale brought him to London to open an enquiry agency, which must have been some kind of dream for him. That is all I know, and I was glad to have discovered that much. He is the most stoic and reticent of men. After ten years I still knew so little about him.

"That's kind of you, sir," Miss Orme replied. "But of course, we would need at least a day to prepare for it."

"Very well," he countered. "Let us say a week. That should be sufficient time."

The two women looked at each other, and then at Brigadier Booth. The young man merely shrugged his shoulders.

Miss Orme nodded. "Very well, Mr. Barker. We will see you then."

"Satisfactory," he replied. "However, I insist upon seeing the woman we brought here yesterday, the one calling herself 'Dutch.'"

"She's in the infirmary," Booth replied. "I'll take you there myself."

Before either woman could object, he opened the door, and Barker and I tipped our hats as we left. We stepped out into bright but heatless sunshine. Descending a set of wooden steps, we followed him along a gravel path. There was something ravenlike about the fellow, head down, hands clasped behind his back, dressed all in black. I had noted the same aspect in his father.

"Your volunteers are intelligent," Barker noted.

"More intelligent than I," he admitted. "And quite possibly the barristers they work for."

"Do they chafe under your leadership?" I asked. "I sense an air of distrust regarding men in general."

"One can hardly blame them," Booth replied. "The only men they see are either drunken or belligerent. Or both together."

"Save for you," Barker answered.

"True. This facility is a duty my father passed to me, but both of us are overworked. Often, I'll come along, see that everything is shipshape and Bristol fashion, which it always is, and be on my way within half an hour. I wish that my other duties were as easy."

"Is there ever trouble with Scotland Yard?" the Guv asked.

Booth wrinkled his nose. "There is, but it never comes to

anything. Whichever truant wife they come looking for suddenly goes missing again. It's unaccountable."

"No doubt there have been altercations," Barker growled.

"Oh, yes," he conceded. "But the husbands or fancy men only use the constables as a last resort. First, they beat on the gates and yell. Light torches, throw bottles, that sort of thing. So far, they have not organized, which is a blessing."

We reached a doorway and the brigadier stopped.

"Ah, here we are," he said, pointing at a stone building that had been abandoned and looked older than the rest. "Watch your head, Mr. Barker. Welcome to the infirmary."

Booth opened an ancient and scarred door for us. We removed our hats and stepped inside.

CHAPTER 9

There were a handful of patients in the infirmary, all with their blankets lifted to their throats out of modesty, their eyes locked on the spectacle of our advent. Wards are lonely, dull places, and any bit of excitement is divided among all. There can be no privacy when the next bed is two feet from one's own.

A glance around the room did not reveal a phoenix newly risen from its ashes. One woman held an infant in her arms, an inauspicious start to its new life. The next patient was elderly and toothless, wizened with age. Another was stout, which left only three candidates for our canary. Then it occurred to me to look for the mangled limb and I found her immediately among the women. Fully scrubbed, she looked to be about thirty years of age. Her features were regular enough, but her skin had been roughened by exposure to the elements and mottled from the miserable conditions under which she had lived. Her hair had been combed severely behind her ears while wet, and now lay flat and lank about her shoulders. Her eyes were as blue as the sky at twilight. She sat upright in her berth under a blanket, her hands clasped around her good knee, the other limb stretched out upon the thin mattress. She wore only a sleeveless white shift, and that was well worn.

Surely this couldn't be the crone we had spoken to, I told myself, the one with the rasping voice and crow's-feet about her eyes. If what Barker said was true, she must have drawn lines on her face with dirt, as subterfuge against unwanted male attention. At present, she looked very gaunt, but then I knew she was more than half starved.

On the bed stand beside her lay a half-empty bowl of gruel, and a copy of the Bible. Both were wholesome and necessary for nourishment, I supposed, but rather grim. It might be fanciful, and I've been called that more than once by my partner, but she had a nunlike appearance, a combination of austerity, patience, and world-weariness. There was a listlessness about her, as well as an acceptance of her fate, however soon it came. The season of death, she'd called it. The poor creature's fate was sealed.

"Oh, it's you," she said, with little inflection.

Cyrus Barker removed his bowler hat and bowed, and I followed suit. A smile played at the corners of her parched lips. She saw the irony as keenly as I, a rich man bowing to a beggar. Lower than a beggar, in fact.

"It's good to see you again, miss," he said.

"I wish I could say the same, sir," she replied. "I thought I'd seen the back of you."

"Not quite," he answered. "How are they treating you here?"

"No better or worse than on the street," she admitted. "I am rushed about, while people do things to me for which I didn't ask."

The diction shook me. It was almost cultured, far different from the rusted hinge of yesterday.

I couldn't imagine how such a woman could find herself destitute and broken on the streets of Shoreditch. Then I realized I could, having once found myself in Oxford Prison for eight months among some of the most depraved men I've met before or since.

"You have misrepresented yourself, I'm afraid," the Guv purred. He was playing with her, a cat with a captive mouse. I knew he had a half dozen methods for interviewing a witness, for breaking her down and revealing all.

"I did not ask to be spoken to, sir," she replied. "In fact, I went out of my way to avoid speaking to you. Now you are here, and I still prefer that we not converse."

A thought rushed in upon me then. It was her! Dutch was the woman we were looking for, Miss May Evans. I reached into my pocket for her photograph, having been the last to have it. I often find myself in possession of the evidence in a case. My desk is littered with them.

I compared the woman before me with the photograph Lord and Lady Danvers had given me and then realized I was wrong. There was no resemblance between the two women, not by any stretch of the imagination. An enquiry agent learns to note differences between features, the placement of eyes, and the shape of the ears. It was similar to the Bertillon method Scotland Yard and the Sûreté used. Even starvation and hard living could not turn one woman into another. A shame, really. I would have dearly loved to be the one to solve a case first.

"We can speak freely here, miss . . ."

"Dutch," she insisted. "Just Dutch. And no, we can't, not really. It's no safer here than on the streets. They named you right. Push, push, push. It's all you ever do."

She was correct. Push. Poke. Prod. The ever-curious tom with his captive victim.

"You are a pessimist, if I may say it."

"Why don't you let a woman alone?" she asked, pulling the sheet up in a protective manner. "I have not requested your attentions."

"Aye, but you were aiding some criminals I was determined to stop," he rumbled.

"Yes, and look what became of them, Mr. Detective!"

Cyrus Barker cleared his throat. "Private enquiry agent, if you don't mind."

The woman sat up in her bed, color coming to her raw cheeks.

"It's not as if I had any say in the matter!" she insisted, her hands balling into fists. "They met me in the street and told me what to do, and what would happen to me if I didn't. I had no choice but to obey. No one expected you'd get involved."

"What have you heard of me?" my partner asked, but it was a rhetorical question.

"Just what everyone east of the City of London knows," she replied. "You're Whitehall's hound, eager to jump after every bone they throw. You thump people hard, then run off to church and put a little extra in the collection plate to ease your conscience. You leave bodies in your wake without comment, without remorse. You walk about like you own the city, rich as Midas, lording it over everyone. You claim to be a benefactor, as long as we pray to your God, and do as

He orders. Oh, and we must be thankful for your largess, or you'll take it elsewhere. Thank you, Mr. Barker, sir! Bless you for your kindness!"

I held my breath. We all did. One of the matrons heard her and came running over to silence her. For the first time I was aware of a clock on the wall, ticking off the seconds of our lives. I wondered how the Guv would react, but he was as stony-faced as ever.

"That was harsh," I murmured, to no one in particular. She rounded on me.

"And you, you're just as bad. Barker's little terrier, how many men have you shot since you started working for the man? Did you wonder if any of them had families? Mothers? Sisters and brothers?"

"They were criminals," I corrected. Barker reached out and seized my arm to restrain me. I was agitated if he wasn't.

"Oh, and do criminals not have families?" she persisted. "Do they not need food and drink or beds to sleep in?"

Barker and I looked at each other, but before we could react the matron slapped her face. The sound reverberated in the room, making everyone but my partner jump. Dutch ducked her head while the ward nurse lay into her, saying she should be respectful and mind her tongue, that she'd be dead in the street by now if it weren't for us. It was a little too close to what Dutch had just described.

My partner stared at the woman through his dark spectacles without a display of emotion. He seemed capable of divining people's thoughts and motives during a thousand or more enquiries. Surely that proved some kind of empathy, and if he chose to show it by giving to charities, let the man be, I say. Our work was to help people, to accomplish something they couldn't do on their own. It involved starting early, working late hours, putting our very lives in danger, while we had people of our own to care for and support.

Barker and Dutch stared at each other in silence. The latter was fish-belly white, save for the ruddy mark on her face, each finger delineated on her damaged cheek. Finally, he turned to the wardress.

"What has become of her clothes?" he asked.

"Those verminous rags?" she asked. "Burnt 'em."

"But you kept her kettle?"

"Yes, Mr. Barker, sir."

Dutch smiled. Yes, everyone did his bidding, and called him sir, me included, but now we were conscious of it. I noticed she had good teeth. Remarkable, even. Some poor women sold theirs to make dentures for others, I've heard, if they were in extreme want. It was reminiscent of Victor Hugo, but how had she managed to keep hers?

"Well, Push, what have you got to say for yourself?" she asked. "Can I recover without being pestered any longer?"

"I'm going to send for a doctor to look at that leg," he replied. "That's our priority at the moment."

For the first time, Dutch looked at us with something other than contempt. Now it was alarm.

"No, you're not going to take my leg!" she cried.

"My good woman, I don't want to take your limb," he stated. "I want to help you!"

"You're going to put me and mine into an early grave!"

Barker crossed his arms. I could hear the fabric of his coat stretching. One side of his mustache curled up. He had caught her out.

"'Me and mine'?" he repeated. "You are not alone, then."

"Mr. Barker, have a heart, if you've ever possessed one," she argued, with a look of defeat on her face. "I am the most alone woman you've ever met, but it's better this way. I'm a danger to all I meet."

My partner turned to the matron again. "I'll send that doctor along, but he is merely to examine her. Do you keep clothing for those in need?"

"Yes, sir."

"Excellent," he replied. "Provide some for her, please."

He bowed again. We donned our hats and left the wretched woman to her misery. Barker had his head down on his breast, his hands folded behind him as we left the room.

"What's that phrase you are fond of quoting, lad?" he asked as soon as we were outside the building, away from listening ears. "The one you claim was written by an Oxford don, as difficult as that is to believe?"

"Lewis Carroll?" I ventured. "He said, 'Curiouser and curiouser.'"

He nodded. "That's the one. It describes Dutch very well."

We stepped into the front office, but the brigadier appeared to have left for the day.

"Did you find what you were looking for?" Miss Orme asked.

"That is what I am asking myself," Barker stated. "That woman is a loose thread on an old jumper. One wants to pull at her and see what will fall apart. Tell me, what sort of medical equipment have you here? And do you have a doctor in residence?"

"Not in residence, no, but we have a student who comes in once a week," she answered. "We purchase such medicine as we need and keep it in a locked cabinet."

"That's wise," the Guv replied, nodding. "Would I be able to bring my own surgeon here? I want him to look at Miss Dutch's limb, if you do not object."

"I don't object, sir, but she might," the woman said.

"You've spoken to her, then," he rumbled.

Miss Orme raised a brow. "Oh, yes, the two of us had an animated conversation before she was forcibly bathed. She had an objection to lye soap and screamed like a banshee."

"Was there anything about her you thought odd?" the Guv asked.

"There was," Miss Orme admitted. "When she was admitted, I thought her toothless. She had covered her teeth in cobbler's wax."

"Clever woman," the Guv replied. "Did you notice her diction?"

Miss Orme smiled. "She has a vocabulary one would learn on the docks, which she conjugated for my benefit. When she found me unimpressed, she reverted to proper English, the last thing I expected. I'm not saying we made friends, but I would assume she prefers me to you, Mr. Barker."

"Aye, ma'am," he said, nodding. "I got that impression myself. Have you any theories as to her origins?"

"An unimaginative one, I'm afraid," she replied. "It's a situation I see here too often: a governess or ladies' maid, who was taught proper grammar, and then seduced by the son of the house. She is inevitably blamed for his transgressions and sacked, while he is sent off to university or the Continent to forget the matter. No one will hire her without a reference, and so she finds herself on the streets without a proper vocation or means of getting one."

"And the limb?" the Guv asked.

"She wouldn't say, but I thought perhaps she'd tried factory work and was injured. I'm only conjecturing, of course."

Barker nodded. "You do it well. Have you heard her birdcalls? She's quite talented."

"She does birdcalls?" Miss Orme asked, looking at him skeptically.

"She does," he replied. "An inspector I know calls her the Canary."

"Imagine that!"

"You couldn't get her to reveal her real name?" I asked.

"No, but then I'm not surprised," replied Miss Orme. "Most women here use monikers: Tall Sally, Meg o' Putney, Coffin Street Rose."

"Thank you for your assistance, ma'am," Barker replied.

We all nodded as the Guv and I left the office.

"She was insufferable," I said. "Rude beyond imagining."

"Miss Orme? I thought her pleasant enough."

"You know what I mean," I said. "I was talking about Dutch."

"Aye, it was quite a performance."

I looked at my partner. "You think that's all it was?"

"The only real concern she showed was about her damaged limb," he said. "The rest was trying to insult me enough to let her alone."

"So why don't we?" I asked. "I'm highly in favor of it."

"I might have considered it if it weren't for the phrase 'me and mine,'" he replied. "Who is she protecting? Is there a child?"

"That seems unlikely," I said. "Although not impossible, of course."

He grunted in agreement as we passed through the iron gates into Mile End Road again.

"I've never heard anyone speak to you that way before," I confessed. "And you said nothing. It made my blood boil."

"'Sticks and stones will break one's bones,'" he quoted.

"They certainly will, in my experience. However, she's diverting us from the new enquiry. Are we going to Rome soon, or aren't we? I'll need to inform Rebecca."

"We shall see," was all he would vouchsafe.

"You promised Lord Danvers you would go!" I remarked.

"You must pay closer attention, Mr. Llewelyn," Cyrus Barker replied. "I did no such thing. I said we would look into the matter. When beginning an enquiry, one must be certain to give oneself proper leeway."

CHAPTER 10

I'm a poor sleeper. Insomnia, physicians call it. It isn't that I don't sleep at all, I just don't fall into a deep slumber until the early morning hours. Or conversely, I'll sleep well but wake at four o'clock and cannot return to sleep afterward. It's a curse of sorts, but it allows me to consider matters overnight while my body lies dormant. At least that's what I tell myself. It's also why I was one of the few in London awake during one of the most bizarre catastrophes ever to occur in Her Majesty's reign. In fact, our home was less than a mile away from the scene of the accident. I'm speaking of course about what has been called the Fall of Calcutta.

It isn't the destruction of the colonial city, but rather a sinkhole in the East End caused when an abandoned railway tunnel collapsed in the wee hours, killing dozens. There was never an accurate account of the number dead, but Barker privately estimated it at close to seventy-five souls, including those who fell from the houses above, and those below who were crushed under stone and rubble.

London is rife with tunnels of all sorts going back two millennia. It forms a labyrinth of subterranean passages: abandoned sewers and railway properties, hidden tunnels from centuries past, secret royalist lairs created during Cromwell's reign, and clandestine Puritan burrows from the rule of Charles II. Then there were tunnels created for criminal intent. This was one of the latter.

Barker and I had been in that tunnel several years before. There had been an conclave of the underworld there, consisting of various guilds: thieves, gangs, rag-and-bone men, mendicants and beggars, bawdy house madams, and many other such occupations. We had been invited on that occasion because enquiry work was considered part of the underworld at that time, in that it was not considered strictly lawful or respectable, a situation Cyrus Barker had made it his life's work to rectify.

This particular tunnel had been built by one of the early railway companies trying to lay tracks under London, but as they were consolidated many went bankrupt or were bought out. This left some lines abandoned, filled with rubble, or taken over for other purposes. This one was blocked at both ends and lay forgotten for decades. Then an unusual investor calling himself "Mr. Soft" bought the land above it and while examining his new purchase discovered a subterranean kingdom below. Soft had a mysterious past and the work he did was in the shadows as well. The tunnel became a secure meeting place for criminal organizations. Many plans and crimes were hatched in the depths of Calcutta, no doubt including those of the Dawn Gang. But now Humpty Dumpty had fallen, and everything was yolk and eggshells.

I didn't know what was happening, but shortly after midnight heard what I took to be a bomb exploding. Then all went silent save for a whooshing noise, as if the earth itself were inhaling. No one else in my household heard it. Even Rachel slept through the commotion. I threw on my clothes quickly and went downstairs, intent upon stepping outside to see what had happened, for it sounded extremely close. I was nearly at my door when the telephone set in the front room jangled. I seized it immediately, assuming it was Barker. It wasn't.

"Thomas! It's Victor," the unfamiliar voice said.

"Who?" I asked.

"Victor Soho!"

"Vic?" I exclaimed. "Why are you calling at one in the morning?"

"Calcutta has fallen!"

When I first met Stasu Sohovic he was a twelve-year-old dirty-faced Artful Dodger of sorts, calling himself Soho Vic. He ran a gang of messenger boys who just happened to also be pickpockets. He doubled as Fagan to them as well, squatting in an abandoned hovel and providing for his smaller brethren. Barker saw his potential talents and provided him with an education. A decade later, he had entered the University of London at the Guv's expense and was now working in a law office. He and I had a complicated relationship. I hated him and he hated me. Well, I suppose it wasn't that complicated, really. We took every opportunity to insult each other, but only in the spirit of good fun. He'd never called me on the telephone before, and certainly not in the middle of the night.

"Why are you calling?" I asked.

"The Guv isn't answering his telephone line," he replied. "Also, I wondered if you'd fallen in, which is no less than you deserve. Are you up and about?"

"Just about to step out the door. Are you nearby?"

"I'm standing within fifty feet of the crater. It's in Wentworth Street. Do you know where the Guv is?"

"Haven't a clue."

"Gormless, as expected," he said. "I thought you might come. It's pandemonium here, and they need all hands on deck, as the Guv would say."

"On my way," I replied.

Hanging up the receiver, I threw on a coat and hat, patted our visiting dog on the head, and ran out the door. It's an odd thing, but some wives like to be notified when their husbands leave in the middle of the night. Not that it occurred to me at the time. Most everything I learn is hard-won.

The night seemed quiet enough in the City, but when I reached Commercial Road a fire brigade bowled by as quickly as the horses could pull it. I saw two constables running past, and half-dressed pedestrians hurrying by, either to help or to gawk. Probably a little of each. I trotted faster, wondering what I would find when I arrived. Vic had been economical with the details.

As I reached Wentworth Street, I was met by people coming from the disaster. They were covered in dust and plaster, and ghostly in the light of improvised torches created on the spur of the moment from wooden fence pieces. The air was full of chalky dust that settled in one's mouth and throat. I wrapped my face with my scarf. Until then I hadn't realized how cold it was. Cold and still. It was quiet as well, the kind of hush that occurs after a snow.

A Black Maria brushed past brimming with more constables, and a second fire brigade bobbed along in its wake. Up ahead, a large knot of people had gathered. It seemed a simple local matter. I didn't realize then that the event would be discussed for generations.

Finally, I arrived and gawked with the rest of the crowd.

The crater seemed enormous and at that moment, I couldn't imagine how it would ever be filled. All the buildings nearby were coated in dust, making the area look like midwinter. Entire residences, two or three stories tall, had been rent apart, revealing the interiors and the people inside, blinking at the devastation. Drainage and gas pipes twisted out into nothingness like tree branches. Children ran about underfoot, chattering and yelling to one another, as if it were a holiday, while their parents were in tears, tracks running down their powdery faces.

I wondered how many had died. Then I wondered who would get the blame. Surely the government should have known about this potential disaster, although I wondered. Decades before, railway companies were floating bonds and trying to outbid competitors. Building was done secretly, and the companies spied on one another, trying to arrest each other's progress. I thought it likely Her Majesty's government had no idea about Mr. Soft's little bolt-hole. This was the East End, after all. Who really cared?

"Thomas!" I heard a voice call.

I turned and saw Vic coming toward me. His eyes were hollows in his chalky face. His dark hair was dusted gray.

"Can you believe it?" he asked, trying to brush the dust from his sleeves.

"No," I replied. "It's unimaginable. Are we safe here, do you think? Are these cobblestones underfoot about to crumble?"

"I don't know," he replied, looking about. "I suspect no one does. Do you think the Guv is coming?"

I blinked and rubbed my face with a handkerchief, realizing I was already as covered in plaster as everyone else.

"Of course, he's coming!" I said. "I mean, I'm certain he is. He wouldn't miss this, but his house is on the Surrey side, and I reckon that the bridges are already jammed with traffic."

"Gor," he said, forgetting all his elocution lessons. If there was a time for it to happen, however, this was it.

Things began to happen quickly then. Several other fire brigade wagons arrived from outlying districts. Cabs disgorged what I took to be government officials, all of them dressed carelessly, fresh from their beds. A group of men arrived in boilersuits. They walked to the very edge of the disaster, which was in extreme danger of having the ground crumble underneath their feet. Some carried thick dockland ropes.

"Royal Corp of Engineers," Soho Vic said in my ear. "How do we help?"

"By giving them time to decide what to do," I answered. "I'm sure we'll be allowed to help soon enough."

Ill-advised as it was, everyone began cramming forward, now that the engineers had shown it could be done. Victor and I took a few tentative steps, then found our shoulders gripped from behind. There was a chorus of screams ahead of us, and the sound of rock crumbling into the chasm below. I don't believe anyone fell in, but I wasn't certain. Someone took me by the shoulder, holding me fast.

"Sir!" I said, realizing who had seized me. "I'm glad to see you."

"Rather a change from our last visit here, is it not, Thomas?" Cyrus Barker asked. Unlike the rest of us he was neat as a pin, having just jumped from a cab. "Good morning, Victor."

"'Morning, sir. I rousted this one out of bed."

"You didn't!" I insisted. "I was walking out the door."

The Guv cleared his throat, and we both went silent.

"What has happened so far?"

I let Vic explain what had occurred since he had arrived first. My partner nodded and walked the hundred feet or so to the edge, as if he weighed nothing, as if he could just fly away if the ground fell from under him. His hands were in his pockets as he surveyed the scene below. Everyone watched, as one watches a circus performer on the high wire, and some beseeched him to step back from the abyss.

"Whatever God pays that man's angels, it ain't near enough," Vic quipped.

Barker turned and walked back to us, the front of his suit dusty now. It would gather a great deal more dust that night before we were through.

"What could you see?" I asked.

"A mountain of rubble, topped by a corpse in a white suit."

"Mr. Soft wears white suits," I reminded him.

"Aye, and his office was on the top floor of this building."

I remembered the man, with his dandified ways and his linen suits. With his white suit and doughy body he had reminded me of a white rat. I recognized him as the sort of fellow whose father had put him through Eton and Cambridge, then spent the next ten years bailing him out from one scrape or another. I had inferred a rupture between the two of them. One doesn't associate with criminals unless one is extremely hard up.

Belatedly, an anonymous brougham arrived, and a man sprang down to the pavement. I recognized him at once. It was our client, Lord Danvers. He slapped the side of the cab and walked to the edge of the hole, looking down. The crowd encouraged him to step back, but he didn't seem to hear them. Finally, he turned and noticed us.

"Ah, Barker," he said. "Some business, eh? I wonder how many are lost. Where did this bloody hole come from?"

"I do not believe anyone examines this part of town intimately, save for casual observers," the Guv replied. "What say you, Your Lordship?"

Danvers pinched his lower lip in thought. "Money is tight this session, but something will need to be done here. Are there any officials about?"

"Scotland Yard has arrived," I replied. "Along with the volunteer fire brigade, and the Royal Corps of Engineers."

"What about the press?" he asked. "Government officials?"

"None that we've seen, Your Lordship," said Barker.

"Thank you, sir," Danvers answered. "Let's see what we can do, shall we?"

At His Lordship's request, ropes were brought from the docks, and soon I was stripping my coat and preparing to descend into the breach. I've never had a problem with heights, and I was eager to do what I could for the poor wretches below, so I was one of the first civilians to climb down. The devastation was appalling. The first thing I noticed was the twisted wreckage of a hydraulic lift. It must have replaced the long ladder that had been affixed to the roof by Soft, allowing him control over who entered. It was now crumpled and lay across the rubble. Looking down below I saw incongruous objects such as window frames, some still with the glass in them, and a wardrobe that must have stood in the corner of a bedroom for years.

There were broken chairs and dining tables half submerged in rocks and boulders. The closer I came to the bottom I saw bodies and shattered limbs of people who had gone to bed the night before expecting to wake the next morning. Safety is an illusion. We know not what lies beneath our feet.

I unwound my limbs from the rope, which smelled of salt water and tar, and landed atop the rubble, instantly losing my balance. Before attempting to stand I looked up over my head and was amazed at how high the street soared above me. I tried to gauge the distance from the surface to where

I sat, but it was impossible. I recalled the one time I stood in the tunnel that I had the same trouble. Was it twenty feet? Forty? Then I heard a moan from somewhere nearby and pushed myself to my feet.

I lost sight of Barker and Vic for an hour or more. There was grim work to be done. It would take weeks to locate all the bodies. Having worked around crime for over ten years, I knew that there would need to be guards posted here at night, or thieves would be down here searching for watches, coin purses, and wallets left by their late owners.

What I didn't know was how Humpty Dumpty could be put together again. It seemed an impossible feat. Would sand or gravel need to be brought by rail? Would stone and cement be better? How does one even build ground stable enough to be walked upon?

"Oy, over here!" I cried, uncovering a groaning man, a scrawny old fellow with side-whiskers.

We began uncovering bodies and dragging or carrying them to one side. There were men, women, and children there, bearing testimony to the fact that they had lived hard lives, and this was the sad end.

Each body I found was clad in night attire: women in gowns, men in pajama sleeping suits or nightshirts, barefoot. The scene was ghastly, and I did my best not to look into their blasted faces. I tried but failed.

There was an eerie silence over everything, punctuated by calls from the rescuers for help moving rubble. Looking up from my work, I saw bodies stacked along one side like cord-wood. How would they be lifted to the surface? I supposed that was for the Royal Corps of Engineers to decide.

I was trying to excavate a corpse stuck between two blocks of broken cement when I realized that the man who was helping me was Lord Danvers. I hardly recognized him. His hair was so full of ash, his face so covered in dust and soot, that he looked an old man. His clothes were white with plaster. He nodded at me.

"Mr. Llewelyn," he said. "This whole thing is . . ."

"Hellish," I supplied.

"Good of you to help."

"We're needed here, sir," I said.

"Additional help should be coming soon," he replied, nodding. "I've sent for everyone I can think of."

We returned to our work, and eventually separated. I noticed Barker on the other side of the hole, excavating souls. Would I have climbed down into this crater if Barker weren't about, I wondered? Would I have come on my own to help my fellow man if he hadn't set the example all these years?

There was a sudden hue and cry, and I leapt to the side just as another section of street crumbled over our heads and landed no more than fifteen feet away. It was the size of a hansom cab. If I hadn't moved, I'd have been crushed instantly.

I crawled away from the wreckage, and sat for a moment, shaking. I tried to settle myself and not breathe too heavily or quickly. It hadn't occurred to me until then that I wasn't alone in this, that I was no longer a carefree bachelor. I had a wife not far away that I had neglected to inform that I was leaving. Just stepping out for a moment, dear. Back soon.

I had a daughter, who would not remember me if I put one foot wrong in this infernal pit.

I'd never see her grow up. I'd never get to walk her down the aisle. My grandchildren would hear tales of their granddad, who had died during the Great Disaster of 1895. I'd become an anecdote. That and a faded photograph in out-of-date clothing.

"Lad, are you well?" the Guv called.

"Fine, sir," I replied.

I looked up to see him standing over me. His clothes were chalky with dust and soot. He'd lost his jacket and tie, and his sleeves were rolled to the elbows, exposing his thick forearms like loaves of bread. What is it about this man that makes one go out and risk life and limb for the good of the agency? We would do practically anything to not disappoint him. That included Jeremy Jenkins and Jacob Maccabee. We believed whatever he was doing must be the right thing.

The three of us worked alongside the other volunteers for another few hours. As soon as we were released by the Corps of Engineers, we climbed the ropes to the blessed surface again. Immediately, I scribbled a note in my notebook, ripped it out, and passed it to an urchin with a penny, to take to Rebecca in Camomile Street.

On the street level, I saw a sooty politician speaking to a group of reporters. It was Danvers, of course. He had impressed me, I must say, going down into the hole to rescue what some might consider beneath his attention. Someone took his photograph, with another puff of smoke from the camera. His Lordship tried to wave them away.

Barker, Vic, and I were utterly filthy. If one but lifted one's heels and stomped them, a cloud would fill the street around us. We leaned against a brick ledge, and watched the progress, not speaking. We did our best to not think about what we had just witnessed and what we had done in that infernal hole. Finally, Barker turned to us, running the back of his hand across his forehead, smearing the dust.

"What do you say to some tea, gentlemen?" he asked.

CHAPTER 11

It had been a long morning, though it was barely six o'clock, and the sun had finally shown itself like a truant child. It was cold, and our noses and ears were red. Our suits were caked in dirt and might never be clean again, dross for the rubbish bin. We could do with a proper cup of tea, but none of the nearby cafés and public houses had opened yet and wouldn't be for hours. It was possible that they wouldn't open at all. The water had been shut off in some streets, as one fireman at the scene had complained.

Fortunately, the Guv spotted a pushcart selling tea coming around the corner. An enterprising vendor had come to help the workers and spectators, himself included. He must have kept the water from the night before, but we weren't particular. We joined the queue and within a quarter hour stood in the shelter of a recessed shopfront holding tins of tea so hot we were switching them from one hand to another. The November wind was biting, blasting the powder from our soiled suits until it looked as if we were smoldering. We were tired and dull. At least, two of us were.

"Tell me, lad, do you suppose the fall of the old tunnel was an accident?" the Guv asked, studying me through his dark lenses, which he'd had to polish with a pocket handkerchief.

"Of course," I replied confidently. "The old pile should have fallen a decade ago or more. You've been down there before and seen it. Safety was never the main concern when it was built."

"Agreed," the Guv replied. "And yet . . ."

Soho Vic huddled over his cup, his shoulders hunched. I sipped my tea and immediately regretted it. But it was hot and wet, and we were parched. We sipped and were glad we had it, even if it had been obtained at twice the usual price, which it had. As I said, the owner of the cart was an enterprising fellow.

"And yet what?" I asked, wishing he'd stop being coy and say what he was going to say.

"And yet it occurred after midnight."

I frowned. "Why is that significant?"

"Thomas, you've been trained in the making of satchel bombs. Is it not your habit to set the timer to a specific time, the hour, perhaps, or half hour?"

"Yes, that's correct," I agreed.

"You know the old tunnel has been used for underworld meetings before. Let us say one was set to go off at midnight. What would happen? Think, man, think! You're the Oxford scholar. Reason what comes next!"

"Well," I said, trying to think. "Most, although not all the gang leaders would show up on time. There'd be a struggle for precedence as to who would descend the lift first to get the best seat for the meeting. Tables and chairs would have already been set out, possibly with food and drink."

"Granted," he said before turning to his second pupil, Victor Soho. "What would happen at midnight?"

"Nothing much, sir," he answered. "The meeting would begin."

At that point the horrid tea in my veins began to work its magic.

"The most important criminal leaders will have assembled there," I stated.

"Aye, to meet their doom, Thomas," Barker rumbled. "I'm speaking hypothetically, of course."

"You're saying someone might have bombed the tunnel on purpose?" I asked. "Calcutta didn't merely collapse on its own?"

"I'm entertaining the possibility," he admitted. "Should such an event occur, what would be the logical conclusion?"

I swallowed the bitter brew, huddling in my coat. It already felt like January.

"The logical conclusion was that the bomb was set deliberately."

"Aye, Thomas," the Guv said, nodding. "And who would die?"

"Everyone present, sir," I replied. "The leaders of the costermongers, the rampsmen, the mudlarks, the dolly-mops. Everyone!"

"Everyone!" Vic repeated, picking up the thread. "In one fell swoop, every underworld leader would be dead! Then the seconds-in-command would have to defend their right to leadership, which could be a long and bloody campaign. Crikey!"

"There would be chaos in the streets," I added. "Not to mention more deaths. Gangs hoping for new territory would naturally have a go at one another."

"Really, Thomas," my partner chided. "'Have a go'?" Is that what your professors taught you to say?"

"I'm sorry, sir. I forgot myself."

At least once a day the Guv insisted that our occupation was poisoning my well of English vocabulary. Unfortunately, he wasn't wrong. Every time I crossed into the East End, I picked up something new.

Victor took the opportunity to stick out his tongue at the admonishment.

"Lickspittle," I murmured.

"Milksop."

"Blatherskite!"

"Gentlemen!" the Guv rumbled. "This is not a nursery. Thomas, if you were to set a bomb to bring down that railway tunnel, how would you go about it?"

"It would be nothing at all," I said. "Even a single Gladstone device could bring down the entire house of cards if it were placed in the right spot. It's the sheer weight of the buildings above, you see. What do you know about Mr. Soft, the man who supposedly owned the property?"

"His name is, or was, Colin Forsby," Barker replied. "He was invited to leave the University of London due to gambling debts and raucous living. His father paid him ticket-of-leave money to stay out of good society. However, instead of leaving England, he bought a tenement to fund his gambling addiction, and by chance found the tunnel underneath. The Metropolitan Railway had no record of it, so he took advantage of the situation. He dropped out of sight and changed his name to Soft. As I recall it was a remark he made about a 'soft' living. He has rented the tunnel for various purposes, over twenty years or more, from gang negotiations to informal gatherings. I didn't know he had installed a lift."

"Where did you acquire this information?" I asked.

"The Templars, of course."

Vic and I glanced at each other. The secret society had its tentacles in everything. No one knew how long they had been in London, or where they got their money, or even how much the society had in its kitty. Well, one man probably did. Barker was now, along with Commissioner Munro, co-leader of the organization.

"Very well," I said. "So, who could have planned his death?"

"O'Muircheartaigh?" Vic asked.

"The man's dead," Barker stated.

Seamus O'Muircheartaigh had been a criminal and Irish patriot, who attempted to take over the entire underworld in London almost ten years before to fund Irish Home Rule. We had clashed with him once, but he was poisoned by an assailant, who had left him debilitated. We did not know his full story, but eventually his body had been found at the bottom of a gorge on the Continent a few years ago.

"You're certain?" Soho Vic asked.

Barker set down his cup on the ground in front of him. His fingers are so thick they could not fit into the handle.

"Certain enough," the Guv replied. "I have met the Swiss inspector who found the body, and I believe him to be an honest man."

"Who else could it have been, then?" Vic asked. Patience isn't one of his virtues. That is, if he had any.

Barker shrugged. "That is unknown to me so far. If this sinkhole is any indication, however, we shall hear of him soon."

"Jolly," I said.

"Would you prefer we sit on our hands in the office with nothing to do?" my partner asked.

I would at the moment, but I knew better than to admit it.

"Victor," my partner said. "My face is too well known in the East End. Would you be willing to use your resources to look for someone brazen enough to stage this?"

"Of course."

"Be very careful."

"I shall," he said, nodding at my partner before turning to me. "I'll see you later, baboon-face."

I was about to reply in kind, but Barker frowned.

"Have a good morning, Victor," I called, with a dollop of venom.

He took himself off. It was Sunday morning. We had worked all night, and even the Guv seemed to be flagging a bit.

"I must change before service," he said. "Are you attending this morning?"

"Yes, sir."

Cyrus Barker attended the Baptist Tabernacle in Newington. He had quit for a while after his pastor and friend, Charles Haddon Spurgeon, had a schism with the church over matters too ecclesiastical for me to understand, and left London for the Continent. Since then, Barker had floated from congregation to congregation, looking for a slot he might fit into spiritually, but eventually returned to the Tabernacle. I privately thought he did so chiefly because it was on his own doorstep.

As for me, I attended the synagogue close to our home in Camomile Street where Rebecca's father was one of several rabbis, but we also attended a messianic church on Sunday mornings.

Our spiritual beliefs were complicated; we were neither fish nor fowl.

"Will we be going to work today, sir?" I asked. We'd already labored for several hours that morning.

From time to time, I worked on Sundays, because as Barker says, "Calamity has no respect for the Sabbath." However, I was exhausted after crawling up and down the rope in that blasted hole for hours and wanted a hot bath, a stout loofah sponge, and a generous supply of Pear's soap. Filthy did not begin to describe my appearance.

"Not today, lad," he said. "Go home and attend your service."

"Thank you, sir," I replied. "Are we going to Rome this week in search of May Evans?"

"We cannot go this week, Thomas," he rumbled. "Half of London has fallen apart. We must be on hand to see what happens."

That woke me from a daze far more than the abysmal tea.

"Not for a week?" I exclaimed. "But Lord Danvers is expecting us to go!"

"His Lordship seems as busy as we are," came the reply. "Besides, he has waited six months. What is a week more?"

"Perhaps you're accustomed to tweaking the nose of members of the House of Lords," I rebutted. "But I'm not."

"We'll not make a habit of it, then," the Guv said, shrugging his burly shoulders. "And we are not doing nothing. I have wired the polizia in Rome. I have an acquaintance or two among them who will pursue the enquiry. We live in modern times and must use modern methods, lad. If they find her, I'll collect her and bring her back to her family immediately."

"Provided you can convince her to come back," I grumbled. "What shall we do while the Roman police are doing our work for us?"

"If what I suspect is true, the East End will descend into chaos for at least a week, if not a month," he answered. "We shall tour the Tower Hamlets once or twice a day to keep abreast of matters. Of course, we will have to separate. It's too large an area for one man. You patrol north of Commercial Road, and I'll take the South and Dockland."

"Yes, sir," I said.

There was that word again: patrol. I pulled my notebook from my pocket, shook the dust from it, and began to scrawl in my Pitman's shorthand.

"We'll be communicating with the Royal Corps of Engineers and Scotland Yard for the latest details," he continued. "So, you see, I cannot leave London yet. I promised Munro I'd look into the matter, and by the heavens he's been right so far. My thumbs are pricking, and if I know that old devil, his are as well."

He studied me with a frown on his craggy visage. Meanwhile, my mind was racing. He'd just sent Vic into the East End to gather information. Both of us would be doing the same work. That's not generally how the Guv operates, unless there are special circumstances. Therefore, these must be special circumstances. And, if they were, why waste time chasing after a silly girl in Italy?

"Have you any other questions?" he asked pointedly, knowing I had hesitated.

"Always, sir, but I'm a mere junior partner."

"Aye," he growled. "And don't forget it. Off with you, then."

"Where to, sir?"

"Home, of course!" he said. "Your home that is. Get ready for church, Thomas. You look a mess."

Rebecca was waiting for me when I stepped in the door.

Both hands were on her hips, and she was tapping the toe of her shoe on the polished floor. Then she saw my face and condition and helped me off with my jacket. She asked if we were attending services, and when I said we were, she called for Lily to draw me a bath. Rebecca had questions and I needed to talk, so she sat in her vanity chair and combed her hair while I told her all I had seen and done. I'd been fine an hour before but talking about the devastation was like seeing it all over again.

"Are you certain you're up to the service?" she asked, concern in her voice. "You've just been through a trying ordeal."

"I'll be fine, I think," I replied. "If I start to become upset, I'll warn you."

After my bath, I looked at myself in the mirror. I didn't fully get the dust out of my hair and looked as if I had aged a decade overnight. However, when we reached the church, I saw that I wasn't the only man who had suddenly gone gray. It was something of a badge of honor for those who had gone down to rescue those poor souls. Unfortunately, there were few alive to save. As I recall, one tyke lived, and he retained a certain celebrity for doing so, as if survival was its own feat. Illustrations in the popular press had him bouncing about the crumbling structures like a rubber ball.

It was chaos in the East End, and in our part of the City, as well. Half the pews in the church were empty. Brother Malachi was teaching, but everyone was distracted and murmuring to one another. Who had lived? Who had died? There was so much to say, so many questions to answer. I reckoned that if someone brought a newspaper fresh from the press into the church the entire congregation would leap at it. The pastor persevered, but he must have promised himself a glass of sherry afterward. No one was more curious than the woman on my arm.

"He expects you to patrol the East End for an entire week?" my wife whispered in my ear. "What does he want you to do, Thomas? You're a father now! And why are the two of you working separately when everything is falling about our ears?"

"Excellent questions," I answered. "I believe he wants me to record what I see, and help when I can, but mostly the former. I suspect the Guv wants me to prepare a report for Commissioner Munro."

"Note-taking is good," Rebecca reasoned. "Climbing into dangerous pits is not. You could be killed."

"I agree," I said, nodding. "However, if Barker is correct, anything could happen this week."

"That makes me feel so relieved."

I was a bad influence on my wife. She did not acquire the habit of using sarcasm until after we were married. In her defense, she had gotten even less sleep than I.

After lunch, we spent a half hour playing in the parlor with Rachel. She was just considering the possibility of standing while supporting herself on the leg of a chair, and if she mastered it, she would be even more of a hazard for her beleaguered parents. Meanwhile, the dog watched her from under a table. Infants can be unpredictable, especially for creatures with long, skinny tails. I began to consider that trembling was the poor thing's natural state.

The dog was there on sufferance. Rebecca had not been raised around one and was not certain what to think of her. The creature, who was still unnamed, slinked about the house, concerned about being in Rebecca's territory without permission. It was my wife's domain, in her eyes. I was of little importance.

After we returned home, I went upstairs and took a short nap. That is, if one considers five hours short. I awoke just long enough to eat and attempt a conversation with my wife. Then I returned to bed. If Rachel woke that night, I didn't hear her. I was busy battling nightmares of blasted bodies and crumbling chasms.

CHAPTER 12

The following morning, I returned to Craig's Court and we started the workday as we usually did, by reading the morning newspapers. There was a lot to learn concerning the railway collapse. Thirty-one bodies had been found so far and they had still not reached the floor of the old tunnel. Many railway lines had been temporarily closed as a precaution, with no certainty when they would open again. A rumor circulated that there were many more abandoned tunnels under the city that would inevitably collapse due to weight and pressure. The whole of London would be subterranean by the end of the week and the Thames would flood its banks. It was nonsense, of course, but so far, Her Majesty's Government had done nothing to dispel the rumors. Sewers had been blocked as a precaution, and gas mains shut off, despite the low temperatures expected that day. Telephone service east of Liverpool Street station had stopped, including lines to constabularies. As traumatic as the events we had witnessed had been, they were too insignificant to cripple the whole of London, although they had come close. Now I became concerned that matters would deteriorate until they affected the entire city.

I continued to read. Electricity had been shut off in various areas as a safeguard, as well. Our chamber was heated by coal, but our modern electric lights were not functioning, and we were forced to light the room with candles. It was all very Dickensian. It did not help matters that the day was overcast, so that one could not tell morning from noon. We had lost half a century's progress overnight.

The inconvenience was novel for the first hour, tiring for the second, and irritating by lunchtime. It might have been the perfect opportunity to type some notes on the events in case they became relevant later, but it was impossible to type by a flickering flame. Even Whitehall was inconvenienced. The difference was that the West End could complain about it, whereas Whitechapel had succumbed to resignation.

"No one can type by this light," I complained.

The top half of our clerk's face appeared over a copy of *The Times*.

"This article says all Underground services in the East End have been stopped," Jeremy Jenkins said. "Even the omnibuses aren't running."

"Omnibuses?" I asked. "But they are pulled by horses!"

"Something to do with the rails, it says," Jenkins replied. "Some went out of gauge. Could go off track and fall over."

The Guv said nothing. He stared out the window at the wall across Craig's Court as if it were a crystal ball foretelling the future.

I looked up from my shadowy Hammond typewriting

machine, my eyes beginning to strain. I longed to be out in the sunshine, not that there was any. Perhaps I would find some if I went looking for it.

"Are your thumbs pricking again, sir?" I asked.

"Decidedly," Barker replied. "I'm wondering what is happening in Great Scotland Yard Street. Munro is as cut off from the East End as we are, but surely he'll be getting information more quickly than we can. Perhaps I should go there and see what they've learned."

"Do you think whoever did this knew it would cause such a disruption?" I asked. "If both the Metropolitan Police and the London Fire Brigade are occupied, any number of crimes could be happening this very moment."

"Wyn'cha head east and look about, Mr. L.?" Jenkins suggested. "Mr. B. will find out the latest from Scotland Yard, and I'll mind the office. No one's likely to look for an enquiry agent today. You do love a good stroll, and there will be some novel sights today. I need to catch up my scrapbooks."

Jenkins collected articles from several periodicals, from *The Times* to *The Illustrated Police News*, and pasted them into large books. There were dozens of them on a shelf behind his desk. This news was just the sort of work he liked. He could measure and cut and paste to his heart's content. I knew, however, that he wanted to get rid of me so he could have my candle.

"Gentlemen, events will occur all day and I need to be kept abreast of the situation," the Guv said. "When you are out, Thomas, look for anything out of the ordinary. If you are able to meet me at Ho's around noonday, we can discuss what to do this afternoon. It's too early to predict our schedule at this point. If I don't appear, have a quick meal, and make your way back here. It's likely that London is coming to a standstill."

Jenkins and I exchanged glances. I donned my coat and gloves and then stepped out into Whitehall Street. Traffic, both foot and hansom, was slow. I knew cabs would be at a premium that day. Therefore, I stepped out onto the curb and lifted a pound note. A hansom bowled to the curb two minutes later. The cabman set his brake eagerly.

"Where to, sir?" he asked.

"Go east until something stops us," I said as I climbed aboard.

"Righto."

We headed northeast through the Strand. Save for the traffic there was nothing to suggest that it was any other day. However, a few streets later the shops were dark, and people stood about looking befuddled with nothing to do. Commerce was impeded. Traveling by vehicle began to be nearly impossible.

"I say, driver!" I called, rapping on the roof of the cab. "I'll give you another ten shillings if you can get me to the Minories!"

"Worth the attempt, I reckon," he called down from his perch. At least there was money to be made for them.

The Minories had once been a Franciscan abbey, I've been told, but it was now a part of Whitechapel known for its Jewish population. It also contained the closest stable to my home. I had complicated memories of that stable, having nearly been killed there during my first case working for Cyrus Barker. I wasn't superstitious enough to avoid it, however. It was close, and the stabling fee was reasonable, and there you are.

A quarter hour later I gave the cabman his fare and stepped down in front of the old structure that stabled my mare, Juno. The cab behind me was instantly besieged by desperate customers. There was still an air of chaos in the East

End, but it was quiet when I stepped into the cool stillness of the livery stable.

The calm made me realize how little peace I'd had recently. Between the baby, the disaster of the tunnel collapse, and work, I was exhausted. There was something so peaceful here I wanted to sit down for an hour and rest. I didn't, but I would take my time tacking Juno. I was only pushing myself. There wasn't anywhere important I had to be at that moment, I merely needed to move forward with the enquiry. The East End and its myriad of problems had no interest in my doings or was even aware of my existence.

I greeted the stable boy, who was sixty if he were a day. In her stall Juno nickered, having recognized my voice. I heard her moving about in her stall, disturbing the straw. I hadn't visited her in almost a week because of the weather.

"Hello, girl," I said, rubbing her velvety muzzle. Horses aren't especially affectionate as a species, but the minute I touched her head she rubbed it upon my breast. I scratched her between the ears, and we communed silently for a few minutes. The stable boy must have thought me barmy.

I preferred to saddle her myself, so I threw the saddle pad over her tawny back and settled it squarely, then wiped dust from the seat. She began stamping her hooves expectantly, anticipating an outing. I swung the saddle onto her back, before cinching and buckling the girth and then decided to change her bridle, so I unbuckled and removed it, and settled the bit and chin strap on her securely. I adjusted it about her ears, examined her hooves for any debris, then backed her out of the stall. Juno looked ready for a gallop, but one can hardly do so in the streets of Aldgate. I put my boot in the stirrup and settled onto her broad back. Then we trotted out slowly into the Minories.

A sharp wind curled around us, trying to squeeze under

my coat. Children played in the gutter, chasing one another and ignoring the chill. A coffee stall was set up on the corner of Leman Street, and I stopped for a drink in my saddle. It was scalding hot, but I swallowed it down and headed toward Commercial Road. Everything flowed through that old artery as it had for centuries. I reckon old Julius Caesar may have ridden the exact bit of road below me and complained about the broken cobblestones.

I remembered what I had come for, following Barker's vague instructions to look for things out of the ordinary. There were indeed things to notice. A young man ran by while being pursued by two others, and unlike the children in the street, they weren't playing. I hoped he wouldn't be floating in the Thames the following morning.

Foot traffic had been orderly in Whitehall as people walked down one side of the street or up the other. Here people wandered in every direction. They darted into the middle of the street, skirting vehicles. They lounged in the gutters or lurked in alleyways for no apparent reason. Many were poorly clothed for the November weather. Everyone seemed dumbstruck by the catastrophe.

I came to what was now being called the Wentworth Street Hole by the press. It looked far different from what I had encountered the morning before. Barricades had been put in place two dozen feet from the devastation, and constables guarded the perimeter. Signs were posted, some warning about public safety and others about the consequences of looting. Dozens of houses were torn apart. It wasn't Holland Park, but people were removing their furniture and household items from nearby flats in case there was another collapse to come.

I rode close to one of the constables, standing high in the stirrups, although I couldn't see better on horseback than anyone else. There was a large canvas tent off to the right. Without asking I knew what it was for.

"Are they still excavating bodies, Officer?" I asked the young constable.

"A few this morning, sir," he replied. "We're on the floor now, shoveling debris from one side to another, looking for the last of them."

"How many so far?" I asked.

In response, the peeler cleared his throat. I rummaged in my pocket, then dropped a shilling at his feet, which he immediately stepped on. He'd pick it up at his leisure.

"Sixty, sir. Maybe sixty-one. Found one an hour ago, flat as a plate."

I nodded and returned to Commercial Road. The East End constables have a reputation for corruption, though I believe most are on the level. Many of them were raised here, and they know whom to touch and whom to let alone. None of them, for example, would be stupid enough to ask Barker for a half sovereign. I looked more like a workingman, however, and I'm more philosophical than he. I look behind the uniform and see a poor blighter whose children needed shoes. It is the price one pays for doing business here.

I trotted along, noting a recent attempt at beautification in the area. A fire pumper sprayed water on shopfronts, to get dust off the windows. Money was changing hands. The area may look down at heel, but money was to be made. If I didn't know that then, I would a quarter mile farther.

I heard the sounds first, sounds of construction: hammering, heavy things falling, men yelling to one another, but it did not appear to be connected to the catastrophe nearby. I reached the cross street and gawked. The entire street was beautiful. It looked as it must have looked when it was first built a century ago or more. The cobblestones were clean and flat, and none were missing, and there was even an attempt at uniformity in their color. They had been taken up, arranged, and set down again with care. There wasn't even any dust on them.

The buildings themselves were of the original brick, but much work had been done to them.

Glass had recently been replaced, and worn steps turned and polished. There were even hanging baskets of flowers, though the cold would soon make short work of whatever was growing in them. I saw a small sign that interested me enough to cross over to it. It read:

FINE BACHELOR FLATS

FOR SALE

H & D ASSOCIATES LTD

A strip of paper had been pasted diagonally across the middle line that read SOLD.

There had been talk about developing this area for five years or more. The City of London was so crowded that even a mouse could not find a berth there. Goodness knows they had tried. Bank workers, court clerks, legal assistants, and the like were forced to commute from out of town. A few, the most wealthy and fortunate, found pieds-à-terre in which to stay through the week and returned home to their families on Friday by train. The problem was lack of space and high prices for flats. The buildings I was staring at solved both difficulties.

Despite its dangerous reputation, parts of the East End are habitable, particularly for young bachelors who work in the City. Streets connected to Commercial Road are an example, as long as one avoids the dodgy ends. Some can be mistaken for Oxford Street or Pall Mall and if one consults one of Mr. Mayhew's maps of the poor, one can find slums in the West End as well, Seven Dials being a prime example.

Many of these structures in Poplar or Bethnal Green were beauties when they were built, when this part of London was countryside, but they'd seen a century or more of wear and neglect. If a builder with enough of the ready could buy out tenants' leases, and set to work, the area could be restored to properties worth buying at a premium. There would be no more roach-infested tenements, but clean, quaint streets a city worker could live in, whether or not he owned property north of town. There's always money to be made in London. That's why people came from all over England to live there.

Juno told me then that she could just as well be in her stall if we were going to stand about all day. She had come for some exercise, so we headed farther east, toward the din. There I found a second street also under reconstruction. I heard hammering and wood being sawn. New, unpainted wooden lintels were being affixed to the fronts above freshly hung doors bearing gleaming new brass hardware.

As a property owner myself, I appreciated the effort. It pushed the undesirable element farther east, with its crime and poverty. Now that I was a father, I wanted Rachel to be safe when I wasn't watching her, particularly when she was old enough to go about the neighborhoods on her own.

I wondered how much of the area would be rebuilt. It would require a lot of money, but then it would reap still more. Land here was cheaper than other districts, however, and the quality of these buildings was superior to more modern flats in the west, besides being so close to the City. Messrs. H and D, whoever they were, could make themselves a fortune.

I continued deeper into what General Booth called "Darkest England." There was still a good deal of work to be done. Whitechapel would not become Paris overnight, although I've visited parts of that city that would give Whitechapel a run for its money in terms of squalor.

The deeper I moved into East London, the more normal it looked, though no gas was lit. I decided to stop in and see how Dutch was faring. I wondered if that game leg of hers would need to be amputated. Barker would want to know as well. I had just turned in to Mile End Road when I saw trouble ahead. The gates were open and one of the female guards was arguing with a man in the road. It was just the sort of disturbance Barker would want to know about.

CHAPTER 13

The Mile End Mission looked deserted, after the argument broke up and both parties went their separate ways. There was an old post and ring near the gate, and I tied Juno to it. Then I looked about. I went to the first door I came to, the gymnasium, and found it locked. On the other side of the compound, I saw a man running, but by the time I reached the gate again, he was gone. I assume he was an angry husband searching for his wife and finding the place shut up and vacant. But, if so, who opened the gates? Where were the women?

I stopped at the office, which was also locked, and then proceeded to the infirmary where we had found Dutch. Again, there was a locked door and no signs of life. What had happened, I wondered? Had Brigadier Booth moved the women to another location for some reason? Surely, he would have told us when we visited before. The area seemed neat; the gravel walkways not especially scattered as if people had been fleeing the premises. It was a mystery.

I returned the way I'd come, and as I passed the office, I saw movement inside. Finding the door still locked, I tapped upon it.

"This is Thomas Llewelyn!" I called. "What has happened here?"

After a moment, the door was thrown open.

"Mr. Llewelyn, is it really you?" Eliza Orme asked.

"Yes, Miss Orme," I replied. "What's going on?"

"They broke in a little while ago!" she said. "Some men entered the building next door, then climbed out the second-floor window with a rope and unlocked the gates from the inside. I gather there were angry men waiting in the street, looking for their women. I don't think there were many, but they were too much for us to handle safely. We were overrun. Everyone knows if they hear the gong, they are to lock the doors and hide."

"That's a wise system," I said. "So, everyone is still here, then?"

"Yes, sir."

"Give me a moment," I said.

I stepped outside the building, reached inside my waistcoat pocket and found my bobby's whistle. Then I trotted down the alleyway in the direction of the front gates and blew it as hard as I could. I wasn't convinced any constables would come, but it might clear out any men who were left. Miss Orme and Miss Lawrence came up behind me, too curious to stay barricaded in the office.

"Did you frighten anyone, Mr. Llewelyn?" Miss Lawrence asked.

"Sorry, miss, there was no one there," I answered. "So, there was just a small crowd?"

Miss Orme nodded. "That's right."

The two women looked at each other. I noticed they looked frightened and haggard. I also noticed they were a little afraid of me, as well.

"We weren't here when it happened," Miss Lawrence said. "We were called from our flat by the matron, Bridget. We only arrived a half hour ago."

"Either they only came for a few women, or they did not organize with any competence," I surmised aloud. "A count of heads will be necessary as soon as possible. I have called for a constable."

Both women gave me a skeptical look.

"It won't do any good," Miss Orme said. "Nothing gets done here. If they answered every time a man argued at the gates or made an affray, the Metropolitan Police would be here every other day. We'd need our own constabulary. They don't approve of our work here and claim most of the wives are glad to return to their husbands. One woman swore to it, but I'm sure she was threatened by her husband into making the complaint, or else she was paid to. You can call them to come if you wish, but I'm certain it will be a waste of time."

I should have stopped the man who ran by for questioning, knowing Barker would have done so. I sighed.

"Everyone has scarpered," I said. "What building is next door?"

"It's a warehouse," Miss Lawrence replied, glancing in that direction. "Pipes and things. We never see anyone inside it."

Looking up, I noticed a window on the second floor was open and a long rope hung from inside.

"I'll have a look," I told her. "You should close and lock

the gates until I return. And as I said, check to see if anyone is missing."

I walked through the gates to the building next door. Old Town Pipe Fittings, it was called. The door was ajar, and the lock had been battered open, though not as roughly as Barker had done to Hesse's Jewelers. I stepped inside and immediately saw numerous footprints on the dusty floor. When I leaned over and inspected them, I counted at least three separate sets of prints. I followed them up a flight of steps to the first floor, then continued up the stairs. Nothing appeared to be missing. No one comes to steal pipes in broad daylight, I knew. They had come with the sole purpose of breaking into the mission.

The window on the second floor overlooking the compound was small, but a man had crawled through it, perhaps even a youth. I looked through the window to the mission below. It would have been easy work. The rope was tied to a water pipe that ran up the inside of the wall. I untied it and let it fall to the ground below, then I shut the window and locked it, as if that would stop anyone from breaking in again. I went downstairs and met with trouble at the gate. Bertha, or was it Bridget, refused to let me in.

"I just left," I explained. "I was checking the building next door. I'm helping Miss Orme and Miss Lawrence sort this out."

"No visitors," the woman said. I noticed she had a bruise under her eye that was swelling quickly. *She was ashamed*, I thought. She had let the enemy through and considered it a dereliction of duty. Unfortunately, I was bearing the brunt of her shame.

I thought for a moment and then pulled my Acme bobby's whistle from my pocket again, taking in a bushelful of air. Scotland Yard would eventually come, force their way in, and the disturbance would be in the newspapers in the morning. The citizens of this fair city would learn that the Salvation Army, a charity that so far had not exactly covered itself in glory, was running some kind of secret mission in the East End, and goodness knows what they were doing there. People were probably already suspicious of their military titles and strange uniforms. Why did they hold military ranks if they were a Christian charity? Why did they let some into their missions and not others? Where were they getting their money? The whole thing sounded like a secret society. No one even knew where the money went. It was all very suspicious.

"No!" the woman screeched. "No police! Stay here!"

She hurried away. I waited five minutes with my collar pulled up about my ears. I should have brought my gloves, I told myself as I looked around the area. The Mile End Road seemed to have returned to normal.

"All right," the woman said in my ear a minute later, making me jump. She pulled on the gate in front of me and it opened.

"It isn't locked," she said, giving me a gap-toothed grin.

I could have been in the office by then, in front of a roaring fire if they had one. When I entered, the two women were as serious as anyone I had ever seen.

"Ah, Mr. Llewelyn," Miss Orme said when I entered, as if I hadn't seen them a quarter hour before. "Won't you have a seat?"

I didn't take one. A feeling came over me then, a certainty, without being told.

"Is someone missing?" I asked.

"Yes," Miss Orme replied.

I frowned. "Just one person."

"Yes, sir."

"The one called Dutch," I continued, with a sinking feeling.

"I'm afraid so, Mr. Llewelyn."

I gave a long sigh. If the women weren't present, I would have expressed myself forcefully.

"We're sorry," Miss Lawrence replied. She was the quieter and more sympathetic of the two.

"There was nothing you could have done," I said. "Is there a chance I might see her bed?"

"Of course. I'll take you there at once."

She donned a long coat and a pair of thick gloves, then we stepped into the cold air.

"I apologize for the trouble," I said, raising my voice. "I could have gone on my own."

The wind wasn't strong, but it whistled in the alleyway.

Miss Lawrence shook her head. "No. The infirmary has been locked from the inside as a precaution. We are responsible for this. You brought a woman here for her safety and she was taken. It's never happened before. If word gets out that we cannot defend our own residents, no one will come here for shelter. Eliza is beside herself! Here we are."

She unlocked the door, and we stepped inside. A fire burned in the grate and the long room was as warm as a fresh blanket. I surveyed the room, which now housed a single patient, the woman who had watch us interview Dutch the last time we were here.

"May I have a moment?" I asked.

"Certainly."

I turned and studied the prints on the floor from the dung-filled streets. Men's boots, not shoes from the marks there, hobnailed boots which were common to most gangs. Two men had been in this room. It must have required them both to carry her, not because she was heavy, but because it was awkward to carry her with the damaged limb. She had been in pain when Barker had lifted her, and he had taken care not to hurt her further.

I didn't find what I was looking for underneath her bed: her teapot. At least she could get her tea now, her chief source of sustenance. How would she live? A woman like Dutch would fade quickly. A touch of catarrh could kill her in a fortnight, poor woman. She had gone from a life as a teacher or governess to the lowest form of existence imaginable and without a doctor and the women at the mission, along with her precious kettle, she would die and be forgotten, just as she said she would.

A book lay on the table beside her bed, on top of the Bible. She'd been reading *Return of the Native* by Thomas Hardy, one of my favorites. I wondered what insights she might have had unless her precarious grasp on life had prevented a serious study. Anything to occupy the slow unspooling of time in that dull room.

I lifted one side of the mattress, then I examined her pillow. A note of some sort was in there, folded several times. I opened it and read.

> *I don't know why you haven't written. Or perhaps I do. If you don't wish to see me, I understand. I've been a rotter as a suitor. Let me know, however, or I will pine away and die.*

That was all. There was no signature or address. A letter from an old beau. The scrap of paper must be part of a longer note, I thought. A man so ardent couldn't resist a final endearment and signature. I wondered how old the note was. The paper was stained brown, but then so was most of Shoreditch where we found her. The writing was turgid, but the hand-writing showed typical grammar school training by a masculine hand. The paper was so fragile and alternately bleached and stained there was no way to determine if the paper or ink had been of good quality. I carefully folded the note and put it in my wallet, or rather, Barker's. I carried it for him, an idiosyncrasy of his.

"I believe I'm finished," I told Miss Lawrence. "Mr. Barker will be determined to find her."

"On the chance she returns, I will send word."

"Thank you."

"Mr. Llewelyn, I'm truly sorry. We did all we could."

"Of course, you did, Miss Lawrence. I do not blame any of your staff."

I pulled up my collar and held my bowler hat. It would fly off if I tried to jam it on my nest of gypsy curls. I stepped out into the alleyway between the buildings. It hadn't snowed yet that autumn, but it looked as if it might.

As I passed, I saw there was a constable in the office arguing with Miss Orme. I stepped inside. My blood was up.

"Is there anything I can do for you, miss?" I asked, frowning at the man in the room who suddenly went silent.

"No, Mr. Llewelyn," she answered. "I believe everything here is fine."

"You will call our chambers if you need our assistance, won't you?" I continued. "The Guv will be here in a tick. You know he considers this mission his personal responsibility. I don't want to think about what he will say when he hears about the assault. You know his temper."

The constable looked at me, trying to decide whether to question me. It seemed like a lot of work over a simple break-in.

I stepped outside again and caught my hat before it blew down the alleyway. Really, a bowler is next to useless in a stiff wind. I sprinted to the gate to take hold of Juno's reins, but there were no reins to take. They, like Juno, were gone.

CHAPTER 14

I have somehow developed a reputation for being maudlin. However, I see the future as a glorious time of in-
novation. Telephone sets will be everywhere, and people
can communicate from long distances, so if, for example,
I wanted to talk to Cyrus Barker, for advice or orders, all I
would need to do is lift the closest receiver and the operator
could put me through, day or night, as simple as that. Even
someplace as humble as a stable would own such an instrument, and if I wanted to find if a missing horse had returned
on its own, I wouldn't have to walk from Mile End to find
out. That would make the world a utopia all in itself, in my
opinion.

I was distraught over Juno being missing. I loved that horse.
We had been through a great deal together. I had been aboard
her hansom cab on our first case, when her then owner, John

Racket, had tried to strangle me. Barker had purchased her after the fellow was killed, and later I'd bought her from him, as she spent nearly all her time in the stable, well cared for, of course, but locked up like a prisoner. I'd been a prisoner before myself; I know what that feels like.

As the new owner, I began riding her on my own. I found a trainer to teach me how to ride and look after her. We rode in Battersea Park, and sometimes farther afield. Once or twice, before I was married, Juno and I got ourselves polished up and took a ride along Rotten Row in Hyde Park, where the fashionable set goes to find a mate. I'd like to think I turned a few heads. After all, I had purchased a new top hat, and a boutonnière, for the occasion. One cannot ignore the power of a perfectly placed boutonnière. I am sure that Juno and I broke a few hearts that day.

The truth is, I am closer to that horse than I've ever been to my brothers and sisters. At times, especially during a good run, I feel as if she and I were one. I can sense every twitch of her muscles and she can read my every thought. I drove her on, and she drove me. I wouldn't let a stable boy brush her; the currying comb was mine. She and I communed in that little stall of hers. I know that buying and selling breeds is a business, and that only a dolt falls in love with one particular horse, but this son of a coal miner never expected to own one for something as posh as riding. She was a symbol of my success in life, and a celebration of it, as well as a true friend.

Now she was gone, and I was panicking over the situation. Obviously, she had been stolen, but who had taken her, and why? What an idiot I was to bring a creature so valuable into a slum district! Perhaps I'd wrapped her reins about the post negligently. The latter had been put in a century earlier, when this was considered the new, smart end of London. It wasn't intended to be used now when the area was rampant with crime. In fact, the post probably hadn't been used for half a century. They really shouldn't leave them just lying about.

I had to decide what to do next. Certainly, I couldn't return to the mission office and ask Miss Orme or Miss Lawrence if anyone had found a horse in the vicinity. I'd be a laughingstock. Taking her out in the streets for such an occasion had been foolish.

I left in search of an omnibus. I knew they had been halted due to the tunnel collapse, but perhaps it was temporary while they examined the rails. If the line got me as close as Liverpool Street station, I could walk to the stable in the Minories from there. I headed west, and for once in my life I was fortunate enough to have a wish granted. I sprinted to the omnibus and leapt aboard just as it left.

It was moist and warm inside the vehicle, and the windows were fogged. I dropped a coin into the box and fell into a seat. I remember being impressed by omnibuses when I first came to London, though I couldn't afford to use one. They looked so smart. This one, unfortunately, was shabby.

My stomach tightened when it occurred to me that people ate horse meat in the East End. Not many people, of course, only the desperately poor. Mostly, they sold it to feed dogs and cats. But surely that couldn't happen in this case. Juno was far from a knacker's yard. In frustration, I tried to blot the entire thing from my mind.

Wiping the window condensation with my sleeve, I peered out onto the street. I was struggling to recall something but couldn't remember what it was. Perhaps it would come to me when I saw it, I reasoned. As it turned out, it did. What I remembered were the flats that had been renovated in George Yard. I thought they qualified as "out of the ordinary." When the vehicle slowed near there, I jumped out again.

It certainly was pretty, this quaint little street. It looked exactly as it had when it was built in 1790. The exteriors were of red brick with wood window frames painted white. The only obvious modernism was the window glass, so smooth and glossy. As I stood there, I noticed a sign at my elbow. It read NO HORSES OR VEHICLES ALLOWED.

There was also a delicate wrought-iron railing that came up to my knees. The space was such that only a bicycle could go through it. I squeezed through the rails and poked about. There was no sign that any of the bachelor flats were occupied, but then a young man in an expensive Prince Albert suit sailed down the stairs on his way to the office or the Exchange, looking satisfied with the world.

Very nearly perfect, I thought to myself, and it was a good thing they came along now when I was safely married. I would have spent an inordinate amount of money to live here, and I didn't even work in the City.

I studied the area for five minutes or more. The walls were not plastered with brown dust from horse refuse, I noticed, and I'm certain the constable on patrol slowed when he came by the street and hurried along afterward to keep to his scheduled beat.

I walked down Commercial Road to George Yard, the first street I had found of the bachelor flats. Renovation of the oldest homes was still going on. The flats had been gutted and were now mere brick shells, from which both light and loud construction sounds were emitted. The road had not yet been repaved with cobblestones, and the colors of the old stones were muted. I assumed they would be cleaned and tumbled to a high gloss.

I went up to an open doorframe and looked inside. Men were hard at work sawing and hammering. They appeared to be putting the breast of a fireplace over the original structure.

Glancing up, one of them happened to notice me. He leapt to his feet and charged at me. His mates did the same.

He seized the lapels of my coat and began to yell at me in a foreign language, spraying spittle in my face. I broke and ran while they followed at my heels. I headed as quickly as I could down Commercial Road, through its ruts full of stinking puddles.

My pursuers began to slow, having successfully driven me off. Perhaps they realized I wasn't worth the effort, but more likely they saw that they had abandoned their precious buildings.

I hopped the next omnibus and managed to reach Liverpool Street station, which I assumed would eventually take me to the safety of Whitehall. I nearly succeeded, when someone tugged at the hem of my coat.

"Please to come with me," a Chinese boy in blue pants and a tunic said. A hat like an overturned bowl covered his head, and he wore rope-soled slippers. He bowed so deeply his pigtail flopped over his shoulder.

"Who's your master?" I asked. "Mr. K'ing?"

"Master Ho," he said. "He wish to see you."

"Don't give me the celestial music hall act," I said. "What does he want?"

"Don't ask me," the boy said, slipping into East End patois. "'E don't consult me."

"But I just came from there," I argued.

"'E says you come, you come," he said, grinning. There was a space between his teeth you could hang a pencil in.

"No, I don't come," I replied. "Not if he's going to order me about."

The cheeky boy nodded. "He said you might cut up rough. He's got some information. 'Zat good enough for you?"

"Fine," I conceded. "Tell him I'll be along directly."

"Will if you give me sixpence. Otherwise, I'll stick to you like a tick."

I laughed. "Fair enough. Here you go. I'm heading to the tearoom now."

I gave him the coin and sent him along before consulting my watch. It was a little past two o'clock. I could have used some coffee, but tea would do, if it were strong enough and didn't taste like peat water.

Ho's tearoom is in a narrow street hugging Limehouse Basin. It is entered through a long, dark tunnel under the river. Ho is Barker's oldest friend. He's not exactly a criminal, but not a choirboy either. He is a senior member of an Asian secret society you wouldn't want to tangle with.

When I reached the tearoom, about a dozen people pointed toward the kitchen. Apparently, everyone knew my business. I passed through a doorway, and continued until I found his office.

"What took you so long?" Ho demanded. He sat at a desk with the legs sawn off and was smoking a metal water pipe that looked like a watering can. Cyrus Barker sat cross-legged on the other side.

"I came as fast as I could."

Ho is tall for a Chinaman, and his head is shaved except for a thick queue, which hangs over his shoulder like a pet python. Rings dangled from his earlobes, and his shirt was stained in various colors from the food he cooked. I realized I was starving.

"Something smells good," I noted.

"Feed me! Feed me!" he mimicked. "You have no discipline!"

Ho's accent was on a sliding scale between Chinese and Etonian English, depending how he felt on any particular day. I've even heard him imitate the Guv's broad Scots accent. The Chinaman began complaining to Barker about me as my partner listened patiently. He'd heard it all before.

It wasn't my fault that I was raised in a wealthy country where there was food to eat and no societal upheaval, where all the young men were fat and lazy. He claimed I had not endured enough hardship and privation. I assumed he considered my time in prison to be like a rest cure at a sanitarium. I had no backbone, no discipline. I must be retaught. If Barker would only give me to him to work in his kitchen all day and train with him all night for a particular span of time, he could correct some of my deficiencies. Not all, but some. After all, I was nearly ruined. Ho even suggested that a *guailo* like me—a foreign devil—would never fully master what he could teach, a martial style called the Lion's Roar. He also complained I was too old now, in my decrepitude at thirty-one, and that if he'd only got hold of me when I was nine, he might have made something of me. Might, mind you.

"Fine, then," I said. "Don't feed me. I'll pick up a boiled potato at a street stand."

"Don't say things like that!" Ho roared, clapping his hands to his ears. "Very well, I'll feed you. Wait here!"

He crawled from behind the desk and exited the room. I had no idea what he would serve, but there was bound to be something unpleasant in it.

"You really shouldn't tease him like that, Thomas," Barker said, having watched the exchange.

"Are you really going to lend me to him like a mule or a dog to be trained?" I asked.

"I am considering it, but then I've been considering it for ten years. So far you have slipped the noose, but don't tempt me, you rascal. It would be the making of you."

"Sir, I have some news," I said. "The mission has been broken into and Dutch has been taken."

"Aye, I've just received word," he said, pointing to a small, crumpled paper on the desk. "Is there any indication as to where she has gone, or who has taken her?"

"No, but then we haven't started looking," I replied. "There is something else. Juno is missing, too. I rode her to Mile End, but in the search, someone stole her."

"You let them steal my horse?" he asked. However, instead of anger I saw bemusement on his face.

"It's my horse, sir," I said indignantly. "I bought her from you, as I recall."

"So, you did," the Guv answered. "It appears you have gotten yourself in a spot of bother, Thomas. However, there are more important matters afoot. Ho was waiting for you to arrive to tell us."

When he returned, Ho shoved a bowl in my hand. It contained some kind of noodle soup, with a reddish oil on top. There was an unidentifiable meat swimming in it, which it would be best to remain so.

He held out a pair of chopsticks. "You do know how to use these, don't you? This end goes in your mouth."

"I know how to use them," I replied. "I've been coming here every week for ten years or more."

I ate. There were so many ingredients I wondered which flavor would dominate the bowl. I was enjoying what I hoped was pork when the hot spice came to the fore. My throat ignited, but if I showed any sign of it, I would disgrace myself.

"Delicious," I squeaked.

"Szechuan," he replied.

Both men watched me closely, as if I were a bottle fly and they were trying to decide which wing to pluck. They are a bloodthirsty pair. The two had met during the Taiping Rebellion and had been friends ever since. Ho was the first mate aboard the Guv's boat, the *Osprey*.

My throat was seared, and I was being boiled alive from the inside, but I dared not admit it without losing face. I looked about for a drink, but there was nothing. Of course, there was nothing. This was Ho, destroyer of taste buds. He had been waging war against me for years. I had to keep eating to save face. I swallowed a piece of pork that had been brined and braised in the pit of Hell itself.

"What did you need to tell us?" I asked.

"They have finished the excavation of the tunnel they call Calcutta," Ho said. "There were many bodies at the bottom of the tunnel. The Corps of Royal Engineers believes they were having a meeting when the roof fell in."

"Fell in, or was dynamited?" I asked.

Ho shrugged his bared shoulders. They looked fat and flaccid, but I knew better.

"Who can say?"

"There was a secret meeting in the tunnel around midnight," the Guv said. "I assume it wasn't about a church raffle sale."

"No," said Ho, thumbing tobacco into the water pipe, which gurgled when he applied a match. "It was a meeting of all the leaders of the guilds in the East End. The gang leaders, the costermongers, the pickpockets, betel-nut sellers, gamblers, streetwalkers. I could go on."

"All gone?" I asked, Barker's speculation verified. "You're saying there is a sudden vacuum of leadership in the criminal underworld."

"There is."

"And everyone wants to be the new leader of their clan. Which means they'll be fighting for it, probably in the streets."

Ho nodded, crossing his arms over his broad chest.

"Which means what's happening now is nothing compared to what's coming," Barker stated.

"Correct!" the Chinaman said.

"Where was K'ing during all this chaos?" I asked. "Was he down there as well?"

Mr. K'ing was a secret society leader from Macao who ran the Heaven and Earth Society, whose purpose was to bring down the corrupt Chinese government, no easy task. Barker had a long and complicated history with the criminal leader. In a way, K'ing was his son-in-law, the husband of his former ward, Bok Fu Ying.

"He is in Guangzhou, at a meeting," Ho continued, cocking his head. "I hope the two events are not connected."

I reached for a cup of cold tea on the far end of Ho's desk and downed it in one. Ho raised his fists in the air and crowed. Yes, I was a sniveling little foreign devil, who couldn't do anything right, but that had already been established. I saw no reason to have to prove it over and over.

"What happens now?" I rasped.

"The battles and the chaos will continue until each group chooses a new leader," Ho said. "All territories will be reclaimed, boundaries established, and new alliances made. It could take years."

"Wonderful," I said, setting down the bowl. "What about the Blue Dragon Triad? You have territory of your own."

The Triad was the local version of the Heaven and Earth Society.

"We are not interested in acquiring any more land," the Chinaman said, shrugging. "Mr. K'ing is content to milk London like a goat to fill our war coffers in China."

"That's a fine way to treat your adopted city," I said.

I noticed Barker glowering at me from behind his black-lensed spectacles. Somehow, I had put a foot wrong.

"I had a brother who died of opium; opium which was brought to China from India at the request of the British government, in order to trade with us for tea." Ho paused, and then in one move sent the offending teacup sailing across the room until it shattered against the wall. "We did not want it, but we were forced to buy it. Now my people are enslaved by the poppy. I live here, but that doesn't mean I wish to. I burned a shipment on the docks in Shanghai and now there is a bounty on my head from the Manchu government. I can never go back."

I nodded in defeat and bowed to Ho.

"Forgive me," I said. "I have offended you. I did not know about your brother."

The tearoom owner shrugged. If he forgave me, he displayed no obvious sign. I glanced at the Guv, who gave me the very subtlest of nods.

"Very inconvenient, this upheaval," Ho said, changing the subject.

"It was fortunate that Mr. K'ing was in China when a gang war began here," the Guv said in Cantonese. At least that's what I believe he said. My knowledge of the language is spotty at best. What little I learned was to better understand conversations like this one, from which I was being deliberately excluded.

"You think K'ing may have planned this?" Ho spat in English.

"Yes, and so do you," Barker replied. He had no concern about insulting his friend, nor was he worried when the tearoom owner grew angry.

Instead, Ho gave a slight smile. "One never knows with K'ing."

"How do you think he will react to a new leader in London, if he wasn't the one behind this?"

"Who can say?" Ho answered. "When he returns, he will need to take counsel and consider the matter. But remember, he shall be like the willow and bend whichever way the wind blows."

"Thank you for the meal," I said.

"I'll make more for you the next time you visit," he said, giving me an evil smile. His face was no more made for grinning than the Guv's.

"Tell us everything that happened at the mission, Thomas," Barker remarked as Ho filled his bowl with tea. It was half the size of a teacup.

I told him all I could remember, including climbing the stairs in the building next door, and discovering Miss Orme and Miss Lawrence hiding in the office. As an afterthought, I mentioned the construction in the nearby streets.

"Who?" Barker inquired, concentrating on the latter.

"A group of Russians or Poles," the Chinaman said. "Stout men. Strong. Good workers. Above the average."

"Were all of them foreign?" Barker asked me, swallowing the contents of his teacup.

"All that I saw," I replied. "No one seemed to understand what I said."

Barker glanced at Ho. "Mercenaries?"

Ho nodded.

"Interesting," the Guv pronounced.

"To say the least," I added. "You think they are here for more than carpentry?"

"If you want to take on territory in the East End, military training is helpful."

"Strong men, well trained, battle hardened against half-starved rabble, most of whom are youths," Ho stated.

"But they are actual carpenters," I said. "I saw the work."

"One can be two things at once, if properly trained," my partner remarked.

Ho looked at me. "Not you, maybe."

CHAPTER 15

The following day, Cyrus Barker and I took a morning train southwest to Camberley, a small town near Basingstoke, where Lord Danvers's estate lay. A frost covered the fields and towns but would be gone long before noon. It would have been a quaint and bucolic journey if the Guv wasn't watching everyone who passed our compartment, considering them a potential adversary.

"Are we going to see Lady Danvers?" I asked, as the countryside slipped by our window.

"Perhaps," Barker replied. "However, my intention is to interview Miss Henrietta Styles."

"May Evans's friend," I recalled. "I'm sure she'll have some insight. Perhaps Miss Evans would reveal to a confidante what she would keep from a sister."

"Let us hope, Thomas," he said, looking over my shoulder.

"It may seem we are turning over every rock, but we cannot know what's under each one."

"Why the wariness?" I asked. "Surely no one is following us into the countryside."

"Thomas, yesterday you would have said that surely no one would steal a horse in the middle of London."

"You have me there," I admitted. "I hope Jeremy might help me look for Juno when we return. Also, I am curious to see if Miss Styles has some information for us."

"We need to find whoever took Dutch and why, as well," he said. "It would have been easier to kill her. The attack on her was well orchestrated. There was no obvious reason for taking her."

"There must be an explanation, sir," I replied. "She is a crawler, of no use to anyone, and a danger to none. Even she believes so."

"And yet they came for her alone," the Guv replied. His coat collar was up, and his bowler hat brim rested on his spectacles. He leaned against the window frame, a disguise in itself. Normally his posture is impeccable. "No errant wives were taken, and there was no attempt to break into the office, where funds might be kept."

"Perhaps," I conceded. "I can only conclude that she witnessed something."

"True," he said. "I admit I'm being overly careful. I'm going to the smoking car."

I was glad to avoid the latter. I rarely smoke, and prefer not to spend an hour or two, and sometimes five or more, sucking in the fumes from someone else's pipe, cigar, or cigarette. My partner sits in the private car until his suit smells like a tobacco shop.

When we exited the train in Camberley, Barker once again scanned the crowd for someone following us but found no one. We stepped out from under the station canopy. The area around it had been improved with new shops and a memorial park, but in the distance, I saw signs of the quaint village Camberley must have been a half century before.

"Are we pouncing on Miss Styles unannounced?" I asked.

"I sent a telegram yesterday," the Guv answered. "However, I did not receive a response in reply, either because it has not yet arrived, or it was refused. Our journey may be a complete waste of time, but I felt the need to get out in the country, away from unwanted scrutiny."

We weaved our way through the crowd as people found vehicles or met loved ones. Barker remained vigilant. Had a man been trailing our steps I was certain the Guv would have spotted him.

As it happened, during her friend's absence Miss Henrietta Styles had married and become Mrs. Briggs. Her husband was a wheelwright and she a dressmaker and milliner whose shop was in the High Street. We found it with little difficulty and went inside, where Barker asked to speak to the proprietress. A woman of around five and thirty came out of the back room and greeted us with a smile.

"So, you're Mr. Barker!" she said. "I apologize, sir. I didn't expect your arrival today. I've barely had time enough to read your note, let alone answer it."

"No apology is necessary, ma'am," he replied. "We decided to come, anyway, which was quite presumptuous of us. Our apologies. It is a pleasure to make your acquaintance."

"Charmed," I said, which was true. She was the kind of woman who laughed easily, and made others laugh in turn. Though of a different class, one could see what drew the attention of Miss Evans to her, and at least one man as well.

"Are you really detectives?" she asked. "That must be so exciting!"

"It has its moments, Mrs. Briggs," my companion rumbled. "We prefer the term 'private enquiry agents.'"

"My mistake, sir," she said. "Allow me to speak to a customer in the back, and then I'll be able to give you my full attention. I see you're married, Mr. Llewelyn. We just had some lovely handkerchiefs arrive. They're in the wicker box on that table if you'd like to see them. I won't be more than a moment."

Mrs. Briggs was not especially pretty, but she was so personable she could win one over in a minute's chat. She was over the common height, which made her taller than I, and she volleyed conversation so unerringly one eventually succumbed to it. Even my taciturn partner gave a slight smile under his mustache. However, she was more serious when she returned.

"Have you found May?" she asked. "I've been beside myself with worry."

"It has only been a few days since we were hired, Mrs. Briggs, but we won't stop until she's found. Do you subscribe to the theory that she ran off with a lover?"

"I made a trousseau for her," Henrietta Briggs replied. "I know she intended to be married."

Barker and I turned to each other. At last, we had a break.

"Whom was she marrying?" Barker asked.

"Half the boys in town had set their cap at her, not to mention the lads of her acquaintance who would cross half the country to court her. Who could resist a beautiful girl who is worth millions of pounds?"

"But was there someone in particular whom she favored? Did she not take you into her confidence?"

"That's her way, Mr. Barker. She could talk for half an hour together, but if she held a secret one couldn't pry it out of her. No amount of sweet talk or browbeating would pry it from her lips."

"How did you meet?" my partner asked.

"She came into the shop one morning, needing a hem re-sewn," Mrs. Briggs explained. "She stepped on it, you see. Next time she ordered a dress for a ball, and we got to talking about this and that. I hear rumors from the local women, both high and low. What boys to encourage and which to keep at a distance. She didn't know anyone in town of her set. I suppose she didn't have a set at all, being American, but I know her sister and brother-in-law were trying to force one on her."

"What do you know of her background?"

"She said her father made his fortune in a place called Virginia City digging ore by hand and now he wears the most expensive suits to be had in all Europe. With his money he bought a house and a shipbuilding factory in a place called Newport and sent the girls to a finishing school. Now her family has been dangling her like a worm on a hook over the heads of dukes and earls. I think she'd have preferred a nice boy of the common sort. In fact, I've wondered whether she'd found one and run off with him. I'd have preferred that for her."

"Did she ever say anything you thought was unusual?" I asked.

"Only once," Mrs. Briggs admitted, furrowing her brow. One could tell she was concerned for her friend.

"And what did she say, precisely?" Cyrus Barker prompted.

"I made the comparison one day to the worm on a hook, or perhaps she did," she said, turning to Barker. "I don't remember. Anyway, she said the problem with being one was that one became a meal for any fish ruthless enough to swallow her up. She was not usually so arch. It worried me, but I couldn't get another word out of her. It gave me a turn. I thought . . . well, never mind what I thought."

"No, please, Mrs. Briggs," the Guv said. He could be persuasive when he needed to be. It is part of an enquiry agent's arsenal. "We value your opinion. What did you think?"

The woman ducked her head and looked away. As vivacious as she was, she was not comfortable talking about her friend to complete strangers.

"The thought occurred to me once that she might be absolutely wretched and hiding it from us all. From her sister, from her brother-in-law, even from me. I wondered if she'd do something foolish like harming herself."

"Thank you, Mrs. Briggs," Cyrus Barker replied. "I have wondered much the same. Tell me, did she ever mention a suitor named Dunbarton?"

"Of course," she answered. "He was one of her more ardent admirers. A duke of some sort, I think. Apparently, he was a bit of a rake. I believe her family talked her out of seeing him again. She cut him off without a word. He followed her about for a week or more, like a puppy. It was the talk of the village, and he didn't leave until His Lordship warned him away."

From what Danvers had told us, he did more than merely warn him, but then he was defending his sister-in-law. Some men will not accept no for an answer.

"Did Lady May's father become involved?"

"No, Mr. Barker," she replied. "I understand he is much occupied, both in Newport society and in politics. May said he is acquainted with the president and contributes to his campaign. I believe he hopes to become a senator, whatever that is. Excuse me a moment!"

She went to help a customer. I took the opportunity to lean toward my partner.

"I wish all our witnesses were this loquacious," I murmured.

"Aye," he replied. "I just wonder which is wheat and which chaff. At least we are getting a better view of the lass's state of mind, if we believe her."

"I think it likely that if anyone knew May Evans best it would be Mrs. Briggs," I said. "Her sister seems rather formal, while her friend is excellent at winkling secrets. I wish she had been able to break through the girl's reserve regarding suitors."

The Guv nodded. "I suspect it would be a waste of effort to track every gentleman who sat beside Miss Evans at a dinner party, or whose mother plotted to find an heiress for her son."

Before I could reply, the former Miss Henrietta Styles returned from the back room.

"Is there anything more I can tell you, sirs?" Mrs. Briggs asked. "The shop is busy this time of day."

"We are sorry to have taken up so much of your time," Barker answered. "Allow me to turn that question back upon you. Is there anything you haven't told us, anything else that struck you as unusual?"

She thought for a moment and then nodded. "Just one, I think. It was the talk of the village for weeks. After May left, and it became obvious that something had happened and she might not be back soon, Mr. Dunbarton went on a drinking spree for a month."

"Did he attempt to speak to Lord and Lady Danvers?" I asked.

"Both, sir," she replied. "But then he got himself in more trouble and spent two days in the constabulary jail. It was a pitiful sight. But mostly, he just cried into his drink all the time. It was romantic in a way."

The Guv bowed. "It was a pleasure meeting you, Mrs. Briggs. If all witnesses were as straightforward and insightful as you, our work would be too easy. Mr. Llewelyn will take those handkerchiefs."

"How many?" she asked.

"All of them."

She wrapped the kerchiefs and I paid for them. I didn't see how many there were, or what pattern they had. They could have been hideous for all Barker cared. I would look through them when we were in London again and take the best home to Rebecca. As the man who keeps track of the agency's financial books, I considered it a business expense.

We dined at the Carpenters Arms on Park Street. I had Welsh rarebit, and he a cutlet with mushrooms. Then we settled back in front of the fire.

"Did we learn anything?" I asked.

"I believe so," Barker said, having just consumed a pickled onion. "If Mrs. Briggs is any indication, May Evans was much loved in the village. She did not give herself airs, whereas her sister was very much the lady of the manor. She was sensible and not given to revealing secrets. Not a . . . what was the word her brother-in-law used, Thomas?"

"Flibbertigibbet, sir."

"Exactly," he said, nodding. "I believe our clients have a lower opinion of the young lady than the people of the village. Also, regarding Mrs. Briggs, if one were a stranger to a town where one expects to stay for some time, wouldn't your first task be to find a talkative member of the community to explain the history, individuals, and customs?"

"Yes, and Mrs. Briggs would be able to give to the village a positive report of the new lady staying at the manor house."

I watched him upend the half-pint glass and swallow the last of his ale in one gulp. The food, I noted, was excellent.

Good rarebit requires a knack, a skill. This was perfect, and I hadn't had such a meal outside of Wales. London's is consistently rubbery.

"Shall we take the next commuter back to London?" I asked.

"I don't mind dawdling an hour if you don't, Thomas. I haven't been to this part of Surrey before. Have you?"

"I have fished here once or twice, sir," I said. "Fine trout."

"Mmmph," he nodded in agreement. More probably he'd discarded the answer, my response being not pertinent to the enquiry.

"I suppose visiting the manor house is not out of the question," my partner said. "We are so close to it, after all. Her Ladyship might think us rude if she learned we were here but did not bother to visit."

"It makes us look as if we are working," I remarked.

"Thomas," he said in a reprimanding tone, "we are working."

"Yes, I know we are, but now they can see us doing it. We're certainly not in Rome."

"Cheek," he stated. "Let's go."

We toured the town. There was an old center to the village, and a more modern street or two full of shops and hotels. We were walking along one and passed between two buildings. On the other side, we found a better view of Camberley.

"There, sir!" I said, pointing. "There's the manor house."

It was on the other side of town, a large lawn sloping down from a venerable old pile to a copse bisected by a stream. It was something of a walk, but we had come some distance, and this was definitely a stone worth turning over.

A warm sun was at our back as we walked, and there was nothing of the chill from the morning's frost. Crossing the stream over a quaint stone bridge, we began the long walk up the hill to the manor. I could feel the rise in my heel cords. The lawn had lost much of its green, but was immaculately cut, and there were architectural structures, fountains, and a terrace.

"Should we use the servants' entrance, do you think?" I asked my partner.

"Do we look like servants?" he demanded.

"No, sir," I said, shaking my head. "With certainty I can say you do not look like a servant."

After the long, sloping walk, my limbs were sore as we approached the entrance. We came to a tall front door made of ancient oak. Barker reached for the iron knocker, but I forestalled him, and rang the doorbell. Half a minute later the massive door opened, and a burly-looking butler inspected us unfavorably.

"May I help you?" he asked.

"We've come to see Lady Danvers," Barker said.

"I'm afraid Her Ladyship is not receiving visitors at present," he stated with finality.

"We are working on her behalf," Barker explained. "She hired us to find her sister, Miss May Evans. We've come from London and have a question or two before we proceed. Our names are Cyrus Barker and Thomas Llewelyn. We are . . ."

The door closed in our faces. Barker and I looked at each other, and then at the door, which looked even larger and more forbidding when one's nose is pressed against it. Barker sighed and turned about. Not every request a private enquiry agent makes is accepted.

"Perhaps we should have used the servants' entrance after all," I remarked.

CHAPTER 16

Back in Whitehall again, Barker and I returned to our chambers. Jenkins said no one had called, so I sat back in my caster chair and thought. I had various, unconnected pieces of information and was trying to fit them together in my head if in fact they were just one puzzle. Possibly we were working with several unrelated mysteries: The Dawn Gang, Dutch and the mission, missing wives and children, a vanished heiress, and a tunnel accident, if in fact it was an accident. Then the telephone set jangled, interrupting my train of thought.

"Barker and Llewelyn Agency," I said, trying to sound professional and succeeding a bit too much.

"What's wrong with you?" a voice asked.

"Nothing," I said. "Who is this?"

"It's Poole. Put Barker on."

"Terry Poole," I said to Barker, brandishing the telephone set. When I sat back, I could hear them both talking from my chair across the room.

"You'll want to come over here," Poole said. "We've found the missing wives of the Dawn Gang."

"Excellent," Barker told him. "We'll be right along."

He hung the receiver on the hook and stood.

"You heard?" he asked.

"I did," I replied. "He could have simply told me."

"Jeremy!" the Guv barked. "We're going to the Yard. I don't know when we'll be back."

Our clerk nodded. "Right, Mr. B.!"

Cyrus Barker and I went around the corner to Great Scotland Yard Street, and down to the Embankment where the Yard overlooked the Thames like a giant wedding cake. We stepped through the heavy doors and waved at the desk sergeant.

"His nibs!" Sergeant Kirkwood called in greeting.

"We've been called to the interrogation room!" I told him, removing my hat. "Not to be interrogated this time."

He waved us on. Poole was in the room when we arrived but was just finishing an interview. He left the witness, a bedraggled woman of about thirty years. He stepped out and waved us inside.

"Some doings!" he muttered.

We were brought into the small room and stood behind the inspector. The next witness matched virtually the same description as the first. This one was crying into a handkerchief. Detective Chief Inspector Terence Poole began the interview.

"State your name, please," he said.

The woman composed herself and took a deep breath. "Margaret Dunn."

"You are the wife of the man whom you have just identified, is that correct?" Terry Poole asked.

"Yes," she murmured. "I am."

Poole wrote something on the paper in front of him. "You are aware, are you not, that your husband was a safecracker, and a member of the Dawn Gang?"

Jamie Dunn's wife looked up at the Guv and me before nodding. "Yes, sir. I thought he'd given it up."

"Would you please tell me where you have been for the last week or so?"

She had a miserable look on her face. "We were in an abandoned cellar in Poplar. Locked up tight, with very little sunlight. It were like a ruddy tomb! We were sure we were going to starve to death in there."

"Who put you there, and why?" Poole asked.

"Don't know no names," she said, wringing her handkerchief. "Didn't ask. Some men. Ruffians, you'd call them. We were being held as assurance, one of them said. If Jamie didn't do what they asked, they'd do for us."

"Please be more precise," Terry Poole instructed. "Do you mean they threatened to kill you?"

"That's right, sir."

There was a moment's pause before he continued. "Are you saying that if the Dawn Gang was unable to fulfill their mission, you'd be punished for it?"

"Murdered, sir," she said, nodding vigorously. "Me and Sarah and Jess, the youngest. All the other women and their families. And if we didn't do what we were told, my man'd be the one who'd pay the price."

"You say you were locked in, unable to leave?"

"Said so, didn't I?"

"Were you being watched?" the inspector asked.

She nodded. "All day, every day. There was even a man

who slept in the hall outside at night. Silent as a clam he was, except when he was snoring."

"How many men were there?" he continued. "Could you tell?"

"'Course I could tell," she replied. "There were six of them. Only one talked to us. The rest, all mutes. Didn't say a word. It made your flesh crawl."

"Describe the one who talked, please."

"He was a toff," she answered. "Nice clothes. Good teeth. Dark skin, clean shaven. A pretty boy, if you know what I mean."

"How dark?" the Guv asked. "Was he African?"

"No," she said, shaking her head. "Indian maybe, or Italian. I couldn't say."

Poole looked at the paper in front of him before he continued. "Did he threaten you?"

"Well, he didn't come to hold my hand, did he?" she snapped. "No, but he was clever. Didn't say what would happen to us or Jamie if things went south. Left me to think the worst."

The inspector frowned. "Were you locked in the cell day and night?"

"No, most of the day we were taken to a room and forced to make paper flowers. We made thousands! So help me, I never want to see another bleedin' paper flower as long as I live! It's bad enough we had to be locked up there, they wanted us to earn our keep and pay for the privilege!"

"What did the other men look like?" Poole said, refusing to react to her emotional statement. "Were they dressed as well as the one in charge?"

She shook her head. "No. They looked like laborers. All dusty and banged about."

"Do you believe they were foreign?"

"How would I know with them all dummied up? They weren't Zulus or Chinamen."

Poole turned the paper over and looked at Mrs. Dunn, who seemed to be holding her own. "How long were you kept there? Could you count the days?"

"The last girl did, Frannie Smith. Eleven days, she reckons, locked up in a room with table and chairs and full of dirty cots. No blankets and a bucket. "Coming in all day and glaring at us. Threatening the children! They was terrified. It was . . . oh, gor, it was bloody awful!"

Poole turned and looked at us. "Cyrus, have you any questions?"

"Who the bleedin' 'ell is he?" the woman demanded.

"These are the gentlemen who captured your husband's gang."

Officially, the interview ended there. Unofficially, she tried to scratch us to ribbons. Poole could barely restrain her and had to call in the constable from the hall. She spat at me on the way out the door.

"Thanks for that," I said, wiping the spittle from my eye with a handkerchief.

"You were the one responsible," Poole said, shrugging. "The others said pretty much the same thing. Their husbands' bodies are awaiting a pauper's grave. Doesn't it just make you ill?"

"How did these families get loose, Terry?" the Guv asked.

"They didn't," Poole replied. "Apparently, once the leader found out the gang had hung themselves, their captors just walked away. The women and children were left there with the door still locked, and no food or water on the premises. Fortunately, someone in an alley nearby heard them screaming after several days and called for the police, or they'd be dead, every last one of them."

"Criminals preying on other criminals," I muttered.

"'No honor among thieves,'" the inspector quoted.

"Cicero," I responded automatically.

"Well, la-di-dah," Poole replied.

Barker still had one or two questions for Poole to ask the witnesses, so I returned to the office. I put my boots up on my open rolltop desk and frowned. That's the problem with our work, or the Metropolitan Police's, for that matter: you see the most horrendous things. People killing people for little or no reason. Others unwilling to help one another with a sixpence for a family's meal. It's a wonder that a neighbor was willing to hunt for the source of those screams, else there would be a hideous sight within the week.

"You're looking down in the mouth," Jenkins noted as he came into our chamber to water Barker's penjing tree by the window.

"A hazard of the trade," I said. "One sees the darker side of humanity. Convince me there is another side."

"I can," he said readily. "There is beer."

I looked at him. The man was serious.

"Well, I can't argue with that," I said. "Did I tell you my horse has gone missing? I left her tied to a post at the mission."

"I'm sorry to hear that, Mr. L.," he said. "Is there anything I can do? Shall we go and look?"

There it was, a person actually willing to help. It restored my faith in humanity. To a point, that is.

"No, but I was wondering if you'd be willing to print some signs for me," I suggested. "I wouldn't know where to begin."

"You'll have to offer a reward, I'm afraid, if you want to see Juno again," Jenkins answered. "A good amount, but not too dear. Whoever has her is probably not a horseman and knows nothing beyond that it's worth money."

"Will twenty-five pounds do?" I asked.

"Twenty-five pounds it is," he said, nodding. "How many broadsheets do you need made up?"

I shrugged my shoulders. "I have no idea. I hadn't thought about it."

Jenkins inhaled and shook his head. "You don't want to post signs in Holland Park or Leatherhead. Let's choose the area between the stable and the mission, say, one street up and one down, in every direction in case she strayed."

"Jeremy, she's been stolen," I told him.

There, I said it. She'd been stolen. The reins hadn't come loose. She hadn't wandered away.

"Either way, it's worth a chance, sir," he insisted. "You can't give her up without a fight."

"No," I agreed, nodding. "She's important to me, that horse, and I want to see her safe and sound."

"That's the spirit, Mr. L.," Jenkins said. "We'll find her. I'll help you look, however long it takes. I'll trot along then to a printer I know in the Strand. You decide what to do next."

"You'll need money," I said, reaching for my wallet.

"Don't worry yourself. He owes me a favor. If she was taken when you were working, it is an expense, isn't it?"

"I suppose it is," I replied. "Thank you, Jeremy. You don't know what this means to me."

"Fine," he said, standing. He reached for his coat from the rack. "You just sit there and worry."

"Worry?" I asked.

"I know you, sir. It's what you'll do, no matter what I say."

Jenkins went out the door. I heard his footsteps in Craig's Court.

An hour later, he returned and lay a broadsheet on Cyrus Barker's desk. The Guv had arrived by then, and we looked it over together. It was larger than I expected, about half the size of *The Times*. It had a stock illustration of a horse on it, with large and easily visible lettering.

LOST

BAY MARE, LAST SEEN IN

MILE END ROAD.

A REWARD IS OFFERED OF

TWENTY-FIVE POUNDS

ENQUIRE AT 7 CRAIG'S COURT

The reward had the largest lettering.

"This is good work, Jeremy," Barker stated.

I always liked their relationship. It was formal, but the Guv complimented or thanked him often.

"I like it," I said. "How do we send it out?"

"We shall give them to a lad with a shilling," my partner replied. "He'll get a bucket, some paste, and a brush, and mount it on every wall and post in the East End. Give the lad three shillings for his work and you'll be a humanitarian."

"Thank you, sir," I said. Then I turned to Jenkins. "And thank you, Jeremy. I knew I could count on you."

He left the offices and looked for a worthy boy in Whitehall Street, while I went back to doing what I did best, which apparently was worrying.

CHAPTER 17

That evening Barker met me at the Barjitsu school in Glasshouse Street. As he unlocked the door, a cab pulled to the curb and Sarah Fletcher hopped down. She was probably the only female detective in London, and certainly the only one to start her own agency, which specialized in ladies' enquiries. Her office was situated approximately fifteen feet overhead in the office above ours, and Barker was her landlord.

She was a no-nonsense sort of person, and favored the Guv with a greeting, before giving me a stare that would curdle milk. We did not care for each other, but she and my wife had formed an unaccountable friendship.

She had barged into our class one evening requesting to join the club, and my partner admitted he had not specifically excluded women and she was welcomed. In the class we have partners, and of course she found herself mine, our being of a similar height, and I a secondary instructor. At the end of most sessions we both hobbled out the door, she with a triumphant look. There's nothing like thumping a fellow you dislike and tossing him to the ground repeatedly to cheer a girl.

We changed into our uniforms. Miss Fletcher wore a canvas jacket tied at the waist with a belt, over a Japanese pleated skirt known as a hakama. The men wore canvas breeches reinforced at the knee, and we all wore leather shoes appropriate for boxing.

Being the junior instructor, I was often the one Cyrus Barker demonstrated upon, and the student who had the most control, by which I mean I could throw a punch and stop it before I hit someone, as close as an inch away from the face. The others had varying abilities, so I often woke with bruises the next morning, many administered by Sarah Fletcher.

"Class!" Barker bellowed, and we scurried into position, two lines facing him. We bowed to him and he to us. Class began.

"Horse stance!" the Guv growled, and we all groaned, internally at least. Barjitsu, literally "Barker's style," is a combination of Chinese boxing and Japanese wrestling. From time to time, a little stick fighting or French savate is thrown in to keep the classes from growing stale. Sometimes an instructor of another art is brought in for a class or two. We all crouched into position, hoping for a way to end the torture.

It happened, but not as we hoped. The large front window facing Glasshouse Street shattered suddenly in front of us. Everyone in the room leapt back or fell to the ground. Which meant, of course, that Barker leapt forward. He jumped through the empty space formerly occupied by glass and wooden framing and was gone before most of us understood what happened.

"I thought I heard a carriage," I said.

"Look!" Miss Fletcher called, pointing.

On the floor in front of us lay a brickbat. I stepped carefully through the glass and retrieved it.

"There's no message," I stated, turning it over in my hand. It was almost a full brick, heavy enough to shatter the window.

"Should we follow after Mr. Barker?" someone asked.

"No," I said, eyeing the damage. "Let the Guv handle the matter. He'll want everyone to be safe. Class can't go on with all this glass on the mats, however. I'm afraid you've come out for nothing this evening."

Everyone accepted my decision. They went back to the locker room to change into their street clothes. A few left, but most others stepped out to the street and looked about. Meanwhile, I called the Soho Constabulary to report the incident.

Barker appeared a few minutes later, blood seeping from a cut on his forehead and spattering his spotless white jacket, a gruesome sight.

"I almost reached the vehicle on Adams Street, when I was hit with a brick," he explained. "It was a pony cart, one man driving, the other throwing bricks at our windows. Thomas, have you notified the police?"

"I have, sir."

"Gentlemen, Miss Fletcher, my apologies," Barker said to the group, most of whom were still milling about. The urge to stay and see what catastrophe happens next lurks very strongly in our breasts. My partner stared at the glittering glass, his brows digging into the tops of his spectacles.

"It's my own fault for having this plate glass window installed," he admitted. "It was expensive, but I was hoping to attract more members."

It is his way to take responsibility for any act taken against him. Everything in life is a lesson, he believes, and like all of us, he was still learning. His sieve is particularly fine.

Miss Fletcher came out of the changing room in her street clothes. She stepped lightly through the standing glass and glared at the offending brick for daring to have been thrown at her teacher.

"I wish to hire your services," my partner growled at her. This was the primordial Barker, primitive and grim. One could picture him throwing handmade spears at antediluvian mammoths.

"Of course, sir," she said, awaiting her orders.

She looked ready to chase after the cart on her own. With her straight hair and freckled face, she seemed unremark- able, but inside her rib cage beat the heart of a Valkyrie.

"I want you to volunteer at a mission on Mile End Road," he continued. "You can't miss it. It has been used for dis- placed women who have left cruel husbands. They have been badgered for the past few weeks by a group of local men. If the mission is breached again, I want you to identify the leader and follow the suspect."

"Should I defend it as well, Mr. Barker?" she asked.

"Miss Fletcher, do as you think necessary to protect the women in the mission," he said. "We cannot have a repeti- tion of the event that just occurred. I should have expected an attack upon us."

The woman smiled, something I had rarely seen. She been raised in what I've heard described as a Dickensian orphanage and was a product of what the late Mr. Darwin called "survival of the fittest." My wife and I still found it extraordinary that she steps out with Barker's effete butler, Jacob Maccabee, but she does. I couldn't imagine what they had to talk about. Miss Fletcher walked to the door and disappeared into the night.

"What now?" I asked after she had left.

"Find a broom and get rid of this glass," he instructed. "I'll see if I can find a carpenter willing to come out in the middle of the night."

Glancing over my shoulder I saw that the students had disappeared. That sort of thing wouldn't have happened in China or Japan, I'd heard. They would have pitched in until the entire school was as clean as when the Guv engaged it. I began to appreciate Ho's remarks about lazy Europeans. We had no proper concern or discipline. We would not practice when we should, as long as we should, or as vigorously as we should. But then, we were merely British, a country which had subdued much of the known world.

I was left with a broom and dustpan. Who knew how long it would take Barker to find a carpenter willing to come at night. I was certain the fee would be twice the usual price, at least. I thought it would be nice to retire to my own bed sometime before midnight, seeing how we so often found ourselves working into the early hours of the morning. Sleep is an unimportant matter until you don't have it.

I set to work, knowing the Guv would skin me alive if I left so much as a sliver of glass on the mat. I found an ash can and began filling it. There was an infinite amount of glass before me: sizable pieces, shards, smaller fragments, pebble-sized bits, and the kind of powder that gets on your hands and stings. Meanwhile, people passed by in cabs or on foot, watching a man in what looked like night attire sweeping the floor of a windowless room by gaslight.

The following morning when we arrived in our offices, Jenkins was already putting articles into his scrapbooks, a pot of paste at his elbow. He looked up as we entered, a guilty look on his face.

"I bought extra copies of the newspapers, gentlemen," he explained. "I knew you wouldn't want me desecrating your morning editions. Crime is obviously increasing in the East End. There have been stabbings and beatings all over. The hospitals are full to bursting."

Within five minutes we were nose deep in the printed word. Jenkins was correct, of course. There had been a riot on the docks, with two dead. At least three men were found stabbed in blind alleys from which there was no escape. One man was shot, a rarity in Bethnal Green. Judges in London have trouble believing a man with a pistol is defending himself. The sentences are severe as a warning to others.

"Here a man was thrown from a roof," I said, shaking my head. "He broke seven bones but is expected to live."

"Two found floating in the Thames, one on each end of the river," Jenkins read aloud.

"Most of them leaving behind common-law wives and children with no means of support," Barker remarked. "And yet the government does nothing that will find its way into their pockets."

"It's enough to make a man a Socialist," I said.

The Guv grunted, which I realized was an attempt at a laugh.

"Let us not go that far, Thomas."

I folded my copy of *The Sun* and set it on top of the others on Barker's desk.

"You think it all connected?" I asked.

"Inasmuch as the events stemmed from the bombing of Calcutta, yes," he replied. "It destabilized everything. One event, from which we may infer that a single man saw the chance to take over the East End, due to the meeting in the abandoned tunnel. This begs the question of whether he staged the meeting himself. If so, he is intelligent, resourceful, and ruthless."

"And wealthy, sir," I added. "One can't gather a group of criminals based on bonhomie."

"It ain't just the East End, sirs," Jenkins called from the outer chamber. "There was a stabbing in the Seven Dials pub, and a man was hung from a streetlamp not a quarter mile from Buckingham Palace."

"It seems—" Barker began, but just then the outer door opened, and a man stepped inside our chambers. I heard and felt his arrival rather than saw it. He went up to the desk and Jenkins looked up. The man's lower face was wrapped in a sturdy wool scarf that encircled his chin several times. He wore a tan-colored wool top hat that impressed me, as well as a burgundy-colored overcoat I wouldn't have the panache to wear. He removed his kid gloves in no particular hurry, and finally addressed our clerk.

"May I speak to Mr. Llewelyn?" he asked.

Barker and I turned to each other. Never in my eleven years as associate to Cyrus Barker had anyone come to our offices expressly to see me. We watched as our visitor began to unwind the scarf. It went on and on, as if a weaver in the Shetland Islands had forgotten her pattern and made two in one.

"I am Thomas Llewelyn," I said. "Won't you step inside?"

By the time he reached my desk he had divested himself of both scarf and top hat. He was olive-skinned, with black brows and an aquiline face. I was reminded of a young Disraeli, and wondered if he were a Jew. Or was he Arab or Spaniard or Egyptian? I couldn't guess.

"Mr. Llewelyn?" he asked, putting out a hand. Cautiously, I shook it.

"I am he," I replied. "This is my partner, Cyrus Barker. Won't you have a seat?"

"Thank you," he replied. "What exquisite chairs! One rarely finds yellow leather."

He settled into it as I noticed his stick. It had two strips of metal on the ferrule near the handle. It was a sword cane. I could see that Barker noticed it as well.

"How may I help you, sir?" I asked.

"I have your horse," he said.

I sat up in my chair. "You have her?"

"I do indeed."

"An odd choice of words," I noted. "How did you find her?"

"Oh, you know," he said, shrugging. "She was wandering down Commercial Road and strayed into the court where I live. She's very affectionate. Look, I've found a horse, I thought, but then I saw your placards pasted on every sign-post, so I decided to return it, though of course, I desperately hoped it wasn't the one you were seeking."

"Is she outside?" I asked, looking toward the bow window behind me.

"No, I've put her in your stable in the Minories."

There were a few ticks of the clock over our grate.

"There was no address on the poster," my partner stated, immersed in his sixth newspaper, and not looking at our visitor. "How did you know where to deliver it?"

"I suppose I'm a bit of a detective myself, Mr. Barker," he answered. "You'd be surprised how many people can recognize the two of you in the East End. I triangulated the address of your stable using several accounts I've heard about you. Both of you, really."

His words were polite enough, but why did I feel a trace of menace in them? The Guv leaned back in his wingback chair, where the pistol under his desk was in easy reach. Mine was in the cubby of my rolltop desk, a foot away. We tensed. Our visitor did not, however. He draped himself languidly in our chair.

"I'm glad to hear it," I said. "She is safe and sound?"

"So far."

There it was: the menace come to the fore.

"I owe you a reward, Mr. . . . ?"

"Havelock," he replied. "G. C. Havelock. And no reward is necessary. I am glad to be of service."

Cyrus Barker tented his fingers in front of him.

"Is there anything I can offer you?" I asked.

"I would prefer if you would cease menacing my workers," he replied. "They're rather touchy fellows."

Barker and I looked at each other again. The dull winter sun made Barker's spectacles look gray and smoky.

"I beg your pardon?" I asked, and wondered for a second whether the man was crazed.

"My workers in Osborn Street. You interrupted them the other day and caused them no end of bother."

"You're the 'H' in 'H and D Associates'!" I said, recalling the incident with the foreign workers. "Tell me, why were they so nervous?"

"I have a confession to make, gentlemen," he pronounced. "They are in the country illegally. It's how we keep our expenditures low. They hope doing satisfactory work will allow them to stay here permanently. Very little money changes hands. We give them room and board and a few bob for drinks. I am ashamed of it myself, but Mr. D. insists."

"Mr. D.?" my partner asked.

"Yes, a silent partner, so to speak."

Cyrus Barker stared at his blotter and drummed on it with his index finger. "I see. He prefers to remain anonymous?"

The man nodded. "A very discreet man, my partner. But in fact, I came to speak to Mr. Llewelyn."

"So you did," Barker said. "My apologies."

Havelock's head swiveled in my direction.

"Have we a deal, then?" he asked. "I have done my good deed for the day. You have your horse back, safe and sound. We only want our privacy. From you, from both of you, actually. Shall I relieve my partner of his worry? He prefers that our workers not be harassed."

I looked at him soberly. "I fear I cannot give you what you ask. I have to please my own partner, you see."

Havelock turned his head swiftly, but Barker didn't look up from his newspaper. Our visitor sighed and began to wrap the wool about his throat again.

"I tried," he said. "You can see I've tried. Mr. Llewelyn, your horse is safe and sound now, but don't expect her to be alive by the time you get there."

The Guv and I let him leave without incident. I couldn't think of any reason to detain him save for the foreign workers, and London businesses used them all the time.

"Go after Juno," my partner stated.

I grabbed my hat and shot out the door. A hansom cab was coming up the road.

"The Minories, please, and hurry," I called, clambering aboard.

Traffic had improved since the tunnel collapse, and we moved steadily through the City as my heart was in my throat. I'd never understood the phrase before. I was terrified about what I might find when I reached the old stable.

Finally, I saw it up ahead, and the minute the cab skidded to a halt I threw coins at the driver and vaulted out of the hansom. I ran into the stable, rushing to Juno's stall. Then I stopped, unwilling to take the final step, lest I find gouts of blood in the straw and my beloved horse dead.

"'Ello, sir," the stable boy said, bringing a bucket of feed to fill Juno's trough. "A gentleman found your horse for you this morning."

I opened my eyes. Juno nickered at me from inside. I hurried in and touched her face, her neck, her ears. She was fine. There wasn't a scratch or mark on her body. I put my arms around her, and she leaned into me as if she'd missed me.

"Do you have any carrots?" I asked the hired man.

"Carrots?" he asked, cocking his head. "No, sir."

I pulled some shillings from my pocket. "Buy some for me. Give her two but no more. I don't want her to get sick. She loves them."

The man scratched his head, as if to say, "These rich young men with their pampered horses." Juno was in the barn half the time. The man put on a coat and cap and stepped out of the dimness into the sunlight as I sat on an overturned bucket and tried to compose myself.

"Thank God," I muttered.

Juno nickered and nudged my ear. We sat like that for a quarter hour until he returned.

"Don't leave the livery stable unattended for a couple of hours," I requested. "I fear someone means her mischief."

CHAPTER 18

Cyrus Barker looked up when I returned. There were reference books on his desk that hadn't been there before. One was *Debrett's Peerage,* listing all the aristocrats and royals to be found in Britain. Another was the Kelly's Directory, containing the telephone numbers of every household and business in Greater London that owned such an instrument.

"How is Juno?" Barker asked as I came into our chambers and dropped into my chair. "I assume you found her safe and sound, by your expression."

"No worse the wear for her adventure," I admitted.

"Tell me every detail you can recall about H and D Associates."

I told him again about finding the new-looking streets in the heart of the East End and the rough-looking workers who tried to attack me. I gave him a full account of the business.

"Is it folly to build fine gentlemen's flats in Whitechapel?" the Guv asked, brushing a finger over his mustache.

"I couldn't say," I answered. "It depends on what the market will allow. The exteriors are quaint, and the street itself is impressive. If someone needs a bolt-hole close to his offices in the City and H and D offers one at a price he can just afford, then they will take it. Still, it's a financial risk. It could flourish or fail."

Barker settled back in his chair with his hands crossed over his stomach. It was approaching ten o'clock.

"I'll assume the 'H' in the company name is Havelock. I wonder who the 'D' belongs to. I've been looking into it while you were gone."

I came 'round and looked over his shoulder at the *Debrett's*.

"Do you think it's Dunbarton?" I asked. "May Evans's unsuitable suitor, the one Sir Hugh warned away. So, he lives in London!"

"He works here and his office is in Bethnal Green."

"Right in the thick of it, then," I remarked. "That's an odd location for an aristocrat, even a disgraced one."

"Odd enough to visit, lad?" he asked, though he knew the answer without asking.

"Certainly," I agreed. "He's another stone we should kick over as soon as possible."

Barker signaled to Jenkins that we were going out and we found a cab quickly. There was no sign that a catastrophe had occurred in London as far as Whitehall was concerned. Everything here was as it had been and would be for some time to come. When we crossed into the East End, however, there was still dust caked on many of the buildings, as if it had snowed. Construction to repair the damage had begun in earnest. As we passed the crater, we could see wooden scaffolding had been set up around the entire area, so that one could no longer look into the pit below.

"Do you believe the Fall of Calcutta and the odd events in the East End are coincidental?" I asked my partner.

The Guv crossed his arms. "I concede the existence of coincidence, but by its very definition it is rare. Therefore, one must investigate each instance, but in this case, we must await developments and move on to something else in the meantime."

"By that you mean Dunbarton."

"I do," he replied.

Just then, a man jumped into our hansom cab and exited through the other side. As we watched, a second man approached, chasing after the first.

"Things are still volatile in the East End," Barker said. "I suspect they will continue to be so for a while. One of those young men will not be alive by nightfall."

I wouldn't vouchsafe an answer, but I thought it highly likely that events here would not improve any time soon.

"This isn't a safe time to purchase property in the East End," I remarked. "If there ever was such a time."

Alan Donald Pettyjohn Dunbarton was the duke of Mansford, according to *Debrett's*. I wondered what he was doing with an office in Bethnal Green. Lord Hugh Danvers had claimed he was a ne'er-do-well and a gambler. It was a mystery. Surely, the suitor of a wealthy young woman like May Evans would have gone for all the shiny trappings and baubles of the West End, and a proper address to go with them.

"Stop here, jarvey!" the Guv called as we came to a halt. Barker sprang to the ground and looked about as I paid the fare.

The building had been a shop at one time, but the windows were now painted over in green.

One could still see a chink of yellow light here and there through the paint. SECOND START, the hoarding over the entrance said, but I couldn't make head nor tail of what that meant. I was still puzzling over it, when Barker opened the door and marched in as he always does. He doesn't wait for invitations.

It was not a business at all. Second Start was a charity. I saw at a glance it was a small operation. The room was full of crates of varying sizes with their tops pried off, mostly containing clothing, toiletries, and other necessities. A few men were stuffing items into pasteboard suitcases.

"May I help you, gentlemen?" a man asked at my elbow, startling me. He was neither fish nor fowl. He did not wear piety as if it were a badge, nor did he look ground down with poverty. He wore the plainest of suits, but I could see it had been properly tailored in Savile Row. The man had an intelligent face, green eyes, and dark hair that had begun to recede at the temples.

"We are looking for Alan Dunbarton," Barker told him.

"Look no further, then, for I am he," the man said. "And you gentlemen are . . . ?"

I gave him my card and he glanced at it.

"You are detectives," he said.

"Private enquiry agents, yes," the Guv replied.

"The two of you are the first I have met," he admitted. "What brings you here?"

"Mr. Llewelyn and I have been hired to look into the disappearance of a Miss May Evans."

The man suddenly seized my partner by the sleeve. It is not something one does lightly, and can get one killed, but it became obvious that he was agitated at the very name of the woman we were hunting.

"Please, gentlemen, come into my office!"

He herded us through two rooms before we finally reached a private chamber as unadorned as Mr. Dunbarton's suit. There, he practically threw us into seats and rounded the desk like a wrestler about to close on an opponent.

"Have you found her, gentlemen?" he demanded. "Tell me you've found May after these many months."

He gripped the desk and leaned forward as if nothing in his life had ever been so important.

"I'm sorry, sir," my partner said, crossing an ankle over his knee. "We have just been hired to look into her disappearance."

The man looked crestfallen. He heaved a sigh before he continued.

"You haven't been to Rome, then?" he asked.

"No, sir, not yet," Barker admitted.

"Yes, well, don't bother," the duke answered. "I spent months there hunting for her and hundreds of pounds searching. She's not there."

Barker turned to me with a knowing look.

"Was there a sign that Miss Evans had ever been there?" the Guv asked.

"Her trunk arrived at a small hotel, L'Albergo Pantheon, and was taken to her room," Dunbarton said. "The register was signed, but no one recalls seeing May there. No one matching her description was seen by the staff. I didn't arrive until a day later."

"Was her luggage sent back home?" Barker asked, leaning on the ball of his cane.

"Her trunk is right there, gentlemen," he said, pointing to a corner. "I found it in storage at the hotel as assurance for the bill, which I paid."

"You kept it?" Barker asked, looking delighted.

"Yes, sir. This trunk and its contents are the only material property I have of hers. I should have returned them to her sister, I know, but she has many mementos and what little I have of her is in this one trunk."

"May I?" Barker asked.

Dunbarton seemed reluctant. He was afraid if it were taken away he'd lose all of her.

"It is private," he stated. "It contains her personal things."

"Very well, Mr. Dunbarton," the Guv said. "I won't touch it. You open the case. If I wish to see something I will ask for it. Is that satisfactory?"

It almost wasn't. Reluctantly, he reached into his waistcoat pocket, inserted a key into the lock, and opened it. I peered inside.

"It's a wedding dress," I stated. "She was getting married. To you, Mr. Dunbarton?"

"It's Lord Dunbarton now," he said. "My father died three months ago."

"She agreed to run away with you to Rome to get married?" Barker pressed him.

"She did, but we never told anyone."

The Guv shook his head. "When did you see her last?"

"We met at the lych-gate of St. Michaels in Camberley the night before she left. We often met there. She was still afraid. Her sister's approval is important to her. I freely offered her the chance to back out of the wedding, but she didn't desire that either. I could have forced her. On my weaker days I wished I had. But it was her choice, however long it would take her to make it."

"Why didn't you marry in England?" the Guv asked.

"Because we knew May's sister and brother-in-law would oppose our union, and we would begin married life with a scandal."

"And why Rome?"

"May thought it romantic, and we are both Catholic," he said. "We hadn't decided which city to marry in."

"You did not travel together, I see," I pointed out.

"I was being followed by Lord Danvers's man to stop such an event from happening. Even Dover wasn't safe. We thought it best to arrive in Rome separately. I arrived the day after and went to her hotel immediately, but she was nowhere to be found."

"What do you suppose became of her?" Cyrus Barker asked. "In your heart of hearts, I mean."

Dunbarton peered into the open trunk as if it were a tomb.

"I suspect she drowned herself, Mr. Barker," he said. "I think she jumped into the Tiber. She fancied herself Ophelia. She was a romantic; that's what I loved about her. That's one of the many, many things I loved about her."

"Are you convinced, sir?"

Dunbarton slumped in his chair. He wiped one of his eyes with the palm of his hand.

"Mr. Barker, I no longer believe in love, in joy, in happiness on this earth," he replied. "There is only duty, at least for me. You know, I have wasted much of my short life. There is a wild streak in my family history, going back several generations. A dissipated youth followed by what is hoped a chastened adulthood. You may have heard, or will hear, that I am a wastrel, a drunkard, and a gambler. All of those were true, but I am not that man now. I work so that former libertines like me can have a second chance to mend their lives and to help restore confidence to the people they have hurt. I do my best to counsel them, to offer them a way to regain their dignity and dare to be worth something to someone again. I failed May. Perhaps I can help a few men to not ruin their lives as I did."

I studied Alan Dunbarton for a moment. It seemed a consummate waste. He was a good-looking fellow of about forty, a peer of the realm, and if he wasn't wealthy before, he was certainly well off enough to marry an heiress now. He cut a romantic figure, yet here he was in Bethnal Green, performing a self-imposed penance in a dull suit.

"May I take it you have been hired by Sir Hugh Danvers?" Dunbarton asked.

"At the insistence of his wife," I answered.

The man nodded. "She's a good woman. At least that's what her sister has told me. I've only met her twice, the second time after the incident."

Barker raised his brows. "Incident?"

"Yes, when her husband had me beaten by a pair of toughs."

"Tell me about that," the Guv said, leaning back in his seat.

"There isn't much to tell. I had a room in Basingstoke, not far from Camberley. I'd had a good night at cards and was celebrating with a few cronies. They were chaffing me about meeting an heiress. We were traveling from pub to pub, sampling the town, because I'd never been there before. I was in my cups and suddenly realized I'd left my favorite stick at our last public house, so I told my friends I would return and then hied it back. The next I knew I was on my back looking up at an exceedingly ugly pair."

"Were they local lads?" my partner asked.

"Surely you know Danvers would only hire the best. The two were Cockneys born and bred. They warned me that certain people were concerned about my bothering Miss May, and it would be best if I put London between us, if not the whole of England. The dutiful brother-in-law driving away the stage villain. It's classic melodrama."

"What did they do?"

"They nearly broke my jaw, knocked out two of my back

teeth, and kicked in two ribs. Almost punctured my liver. Then they left me there to consider my choices. My friends happened onto me a half hour later, unconscious in the road, and called for a doctor. It was touch and go for a while. I stayed at an inn near where I was beaten because the doctor said I was too badly injured to be moved."

"When and where did you meet Miss Evans?"

"We met at a soirée in Mayfair at the home of Lady Taylor-Archer. My mother sent me there on my best behavior. I was to find a suitable girl, get married like a sensible chap, and produce an heir, or I could go on gambling with my own money, not the family's. My first thought about May was to wonder what was wrong with her if she wasn't married already. Then I was introduced to her, and she smiled at me. I was flummoxed, sir. It was like being a schoolboy again. I kept tripping over my own tongue. Later Lady T. told me I was red as a beet during the exchange. She was just the sort of girl a successful rake avoids: the reforming kind. No drinking or gambling. No snatching kisses from barmaids. No hijinks of any kind. So far, I had avoided her type, but when she found me, I was doomed. I'd go through any radical change to be with her, including the yoke of marriage. I wasn't the only moth hovering around that flame however, her with her millions of dollars, so I retreated to the punch bowl to ruminate. I was about to chuck it in and get a proper drink, but suddenly she was there at my elbow. She'd come to me despite my reputation, which I'm sure everyone in the room had shared with her. I'd never been so happy in my life."

Cyrus Barker gave me a scalding look. I don't think he had expected a tale of budding romance. He'd come for fodder, for cold hard facts, but that's the way it is with being an enquiry agent.

"Did you contrive to meet her again afterward?" I asked, hoping to steer the conversation away from romance.

He nodded. "Oh yes, I made my way down to Camberley to find a way to see her again. It was rather difficult. Danvers guarded his sister-in-law like a hawk. I managed to see her twice at service, and she seemed pleased to see me. Then one night I went to retrieve a stick after winning at cards, and we're right where we started, gentlemen."

Barker nodded again. His arms were crossed, then he reached up and raked the underside of his jaw with his thumbnail. He was thinking. It's always a good sign.

"This is a kind of 'reformed rakes' club, then, this establishment?"

It made the duke smile. "If you like. There are enough reprobates in a city of this size to occupy me. Of course, I don't need money anymore, but this is something I can do for a segment of the population that no one else cares about. I'm temperance blue, now. I've sworn off cards and horses. My old friends despair of me, but I've managed to save a few men, and even paid off their debts."

Here Dunbarton took a deep breath, as if looking back at the last few months. He had learned a bitter lesson.

"So, gentlemen, I've kept you talking overlong," he remarked. "Are you here as a second warning from Danvers? If you are, I'm more than ready for you. I box at the Athenaeum Club now."

"It won't help you, I'm afraid," I said. "Mr. Barker is a teacher of antagonistics."

"Oh, well," he said. "One can but try."

The duke removed his jacket, held up his fists, and came around the desk. He threw a right cross at Barker, who caught it easily in his hand. The Guv lowered it, and I expected the coup de grâce, but it didn't come.

"I'm sorry," he said. "I only give lessons for a fee."

Dunbarton looked relieved. "Thank the heavens. I box, but I admit I'm not very good at it. Are you that Mr. Barker they all talk about with reverence at the Mile End Mission?"

"He is," I said. "You're familiar with the place?"

"Oh, yes," Dunbarton replied. "The charities in the East End are all familiar with each other. Are you really just here to talk?"

"We are," my partner said.

"Imagine that."

The Guv cleared his throat. "We just want to learn what has become of Miss May Evans."

"Why didn't you hire an enquiry agent?" I asked.

"My father was still alive and I didn't have the money."

The Guv turned to me. "Can one reach Newhaven or Dover from Camberley?"

He considers me something of an expert on trains and timetables because railways are an interest of mine.

"Not easily, no," I responded. "Through London is the easiest way, though it is to the north."

"Into the valley of sin," he said, Baptist that he was. "She wouldn't be the first woman to be swallowed up in our fair city."

CHAPTER 19

After we left Dunbarton's office, Barker turned to me. "Thomas, would you let me think for fifteen minutes together?"

At first, I thought it an insult, but Cyrus Barker isn't the sort to get irritable over my volubility. On the odd occasion when he does, he'll growl something like "belay that!" from his days as a ship's captain, so that I know if I said one more word I'd be keelhauled, whatever that is. So, I gave him his silence, difficult as it was. Silence was never one of my gifts. We were by a bank in Bethnal Green with a short set of steps flanked by two low brick walls. Barker sat on one, facing the street, and did little for a quarter hour.

Sometimes when London seems too much for me, or I've just finished a particularly taxing enquiry, I gather my rod and creel and take a train to the closest trout stream. There

I throw a line thinner than a horsehair tethered to a Royal Coachman fly into a stream for a full hour without saying a word. It looks dull to the casual observer, but I'm calming myself and concentrating. I'm looking above the surface for mayflies, to see if they will attract a brown trout that morning. Temperature is important, both above and below the surface of the river. Knowing what brush is submerged nearby is equally necessary, as the prey may be hiding therein. They aren't stupid; the fish know I'm there.

Barker was doing so now. He watched traffic go by, pedestrians walking to their destinations, customers entering and leaving the bank, hawkers doing business nearby. His head turned left and right, noticing everything. He looked down in the gutter and overhead in the windows. Sometimes his gaze followed a vehicle from the minute it came into view until it turned a corner and was gone. He watched the dogs and cats on the street, and the smoke spiraling from chimneys. He was taking impressions, as if he were a ball of wax. I spent the time sitting on the other brick wall, willing myself to be silent. The Guv did not need my thoughts; they would merely throw off his conclusions, so I sat.

Finally, I heard him sigh.

"They haven't taken Dutch, lad," he stated. "She is nearby."

"What do you mean, sir?" I asked. "Of course, she was taken."

"Aye, but only to be set free again," he said. "You've been a student. Have you ever seen a rat in a maze?"

"Of course," I answered. "In natural science tutorials at Oxford."

"What happens when the rat reaches its destination?" he asked, sounding professorial himself.

"I don't know what you mean, sir. It's put in a cage."

"Or . . . ?"

"Or returned to the beginning of the maze, I suppose."

"Ha!" he cried, pointing at me as if I'd just made a brilliant observation. "If you were consolidating all the crime and criminals in the East End, and there is one person who could reveal your plan and endanger your operation, what would you do with her?"

"Silence her," I said.

"Let us not be coy, Thomas," he stated. "You'd kill her."

"But she wasn't killed!" I exclaimed.

"Correct. I believe she was moved elsewhere. Dutch could not have crawled to where we found her that first day in the brief span of time between our leaving her to find the Dawn Gang, and our return. Therefore, she was taken there deliberately by whoever controls her."

"For what purpose?" I asked.

He didn't answer for a moment. "We found her again and brought her to the mission. A few nights later there is a raid in Mile End, but she was the only one taken. What became of her? Was she murdered as an example to others? No, I believe she was whisked away, as she had been the first time."

"Perhaps they killed her later," I reasoned.

"No, Thomas. Leaving her dead at the mission would have sent a clear message to the East End. Alive, she has no one's attention but ours."

"I don't know," I answered skeptically. "She was a proper lookout for them. Who would suspect a crawler, of little use to anyone? However, I see what you're saying. He took the rat out of the maze, so his next step is . . ."

"To put her at the beginning again," Barker replied.

"You're saying he staged an assault on the mission and took her, merely to let her go again? Why?"

"I don't know yet," the Guv admitted. "But I need to find

out. I suspect their relationship is personal. He's enjoying himself."

"But if I may ask again, sir, why waste our time here?" I inquired. "She is not part of an active enquiry, and our plate is completely full. Why are you bothering about it when we're supposed to be looking for May Evans?"

"Why?" he repeated. "Because no one else will. Dutch needs our help. She is a rat in a maze and goodness knows how many times she's been prodded through it. We don't know why, and we don't know how she came from being an educated woman to what she is now, but I do know this. The poor woman is being tortured."

Surely, Barker was wrong, I told myself. He was looking for a damsel to rescue and found her in this dried husk of a woman with one limb mangled and the other in the grave. The Guv was off the mark, but was I the one who had to tell him?

"So where is she, then?" I demanded. "She could be anywhere! Scotland, the Continent."

"No, lad," he purred, pointing at the paving stones under our feet. "She's here."

"In Bethnal Green?"

"Aye, or Poplar, or Shoreditch, or Canning Town. She's nearby."

"How are we going to find her, then?" I asked. "Cab fare is still at a premium. Remember, we have no client. Oh, wait, we do! He wants us in Rome."

"No, Thomas," he chided. "We won't find the woman by cab. We must walk."

"Walk?" I asked, aghast. "We've already patrolled the area for days."

"Shoe leather is still the best option, I think. A cab can only give you impressions."

Once again, I had no say in the matter. We combed the area for more than three hours before we found her again sitting in one of the narrowest alleys in the East End. Barker had to squeeze himself into it sideways and I noticed his shoulders brushed both sides. She was an obstruction in the middle of the alleyway, which I noticed only because I saw a flame in the shaded alley. She was making her ever-present pot of tea.

"Oh, no," she said scornfully when she saw us. "Go away! Quit pestering me. I haven't asked for your help. You're only mucking everything about."

"Who are you protecting?" Barker demanded. "You're alone in the world with a damaged limb, yet when I offer you aid, you figuratively spit in my face. Who are you protecting, and whom are you protecting them from?"

"Mr. Barker," she replied. "I don't believe the two of you could find a mouse in a barrel."

The Guv winced, and I thought he would explode. I'd never heard anyone insult him so in all the years I've worked with him. Then his features relaxed again.

"Thomas, we've just walked into a trap," he said casually, as if discussing the weather.

I turned. There were two men at one end of the alley, blocking the street. I looked in the other direction. Another blocked the entrance to Commercial Road. *This woman will be the death of us yet*, I told myself. Barker began to trot down the narrow alley in one direction, his movements impeded by his brawny shoulders. I headed toward the other two, who in turn, were running at me with blades drawn. I reached into my waistcoat pocket and retrieved the knife I kept there. How did this happen so often, my being outnumbered in a fight?

What to do? I asked myself. Then something came to me. An

idea, or part of one. A perfectly hideous idea, but I had nothing else at the moment. I began to climb, my limbs splayed across the alley. The two men looked at me as if I'd gone barmy, which in hindsight may have been accurate. However, I managed to make my way eight feet above one of their heads, and no amount of jumping and waving his knife at me could hurt me. His blade wasn't weighted, so he couldn't throw it with any degree of accuracy. He looked perplexed as I passed over his head.

The second fellow wasn't. He began to climb toward me. We were twenty feet apart and moving toward each other step by clumsy step. It would be useless to try to reach the roof. Even if I tried, I wouldn't be able to get over the ledge. However, if I could climb over the fellow's head, I might be able to come down again on the other side and go for help, not that Cyrus Barker required any. He carried his pistols, while mine were back in the cubby of my desk, safe and sound.

Of course, it began to rain. Moving about on the vertical walls became more difficult. For a moment I saw the futility of it all, and as I considered it, I heard a shot from my partner's pistol. I turned my head to look but saw that the first man I had passed had decided to start climbing after me, as his mate had. They were a couple of brutes, but for once being smaller was an advantage for me.

I looked about. Both walls were sheer brick. There had been no need to put in windows that would only face others three feet away. There were no stairwells, no projections of any sort to grip onto. It was raining, and my hat had become sodden, which somehow angered me. The rain was cold, and my collar was like a pitcher being filled. The frigid water slipped between my shoulder blades. Suddenly, the man in front of me nearly fell. I waited a moment, expectantly, but he managed to right himself again.

My only hope was to climb over him, or at least it was the only idea that came to me, poor as it was. I set to in earnest, climbing as fast as I could between the walls. However, he worked out what I was doing, and began to hurry as well. We were ten feet above the alley floor, and I nearly escaped. Then he seized me by the ankle at the last moment, and I fell.

Perhaps "fell" is not the correct word. I let go. Realizing he was directly below me, I relaxed every muscle in my body and dropped on top of him. He gave way, of course. He couldn't hold my weight when his feet had such a feeble connection to the brickwork. I fell, we both fell, landing in a pile.

I struggled to my feet just as his comrade dropped and landed in the alley. He cried out, clutching his ankle, which looked broken. I looked from one of them to the other, both of them grimacing in pain. I stepped over him and headed toward Barker. I heard a laugh, and looking over my shoulder, saw Dutch cackling nearby.

"That's one way!" she cried.

"Just need one," I replied.

One of the men helped the other and they hobbled away.

When Barker returned, he asked, "What happened to the two men who were after you?" the Guv asked.

I explained the situation and then asked a question of my own. "Were these men following us?"

"No, Thomas. They were here to keep an eye on Dutch."

"Four men to guard the one woman?" I asked. She was within our hearing, so I didn't state the obvious, that she couldn't walk.

"Now will you not understand what I have been telling you?" my partner demanded.

"Who are you?" I asked the shapeless bundle. She was wrapped in one of the mission's blankets by the look of it, which was as soaked from the rain as my bowler hat.

"Nobody," she replied. "I am nobody."

Barker squatted until they were nearly eye to eye. He filled the alley like a stopper. "Who are you protecting?"

"Again, nobody!"

"A nobody with four guardsmen watching her every move!"

She waved an angry fist at us. "I didn't ask them to follow me! I can't order them to do anything!"

Cyrus Barker stood again, his arms akimbo, staring down at her.

"That's it," he said, as if he'd reached his limit. "I'm going to do what I should have done on the first day."

He reached into his pocket and retrieved his bobby's whistle. He breathed in as Dutch gave a long wail. Then he blew loud enough to reach the constabulary in Brighton.

"No!" she howled. "Let me alone! You don't know what you're doing!"

"I'm not arguing with you anymore. You've brought this on yourself!"

My partner turned and marched toward the street.

"He'll ruin everything!" Dutch cried, seizing the hem of my jacket.

"No," I said. "But he'll finish everything."

An hour later we were at "A" Division, shivering from the cold, with towels on our heads. The two men we had encountered had been arrested at "H" Division and taken to London Hospital with broken bones. The third had been shot, although it was not fatal. Terence Poole was in Sussex and might not be back until the following morning. Commissioner Munro was at home, but the inspector handling our arrest did not know why. Inspector Lang, the highest official in charge, was bullheaded, and I suspected he didn't like private enquiry agents any better than the rest of the Metropolitan Detective Police Force.

We were stuffed in the interrogation room with Lang, the four of us together, Barker taking up most of the room. Dutch was laughing at our discomfort. Lang was tall and thin, with blond hair and ruddy side-whiskers. He sniffed as if he had a cold. He didn't know Barker or I from Adam, and somehow felt that shooting a possible criminal was not the best way for us to handle a dispute. Barker and I were locked in darbies, the metal cold against our skin. To think we had called for the police ourselves.

"You claim you were defending this woman," Lang said, pacing in front of us.

"That's correct," Barker answered for the record.

"And yet she claims to have never seen you before."

"Of course," I replied. "She's lying."

Lang pointed a severe finger at me. "I didn't ask you. I'm interviewing Mr. Baker here."

"Barker, sir," the Guv corrected.

"Whatever. She claims you came into the alley where she was talking to her friends, and immediately started an affray. They assume the two of you were drunk. You challenged them to a fight, in the course of which you wounded all of them. This gentleman here, Mr. Clew . . . Mr. Lew . . ."

"Llewelyn," I supplied. "Three l's."

"They say he was climbing the walls. How much did you have to drink, sir?"

"Not enough, apparently."

"Shut it!" Inspector Lang reprimanded. "You are in trouble here, and you are handling the matter as if you find it a joke."

The Guv shook his head at me, but it was too late.

"Oh, believe me, Inspector, this is a joke."

"Guard!" Lang bellowed.

"Now you've done it," Dutch muttered in my ear.

Five minutes later my partner and I were locked in a cell.

"That did not go well," I noted.

"Whose fault was that?" asked the Guv.

"Not the fellow who shot someone in daylight on Commercial Road."

We sat on the cot until we heard Big Ben down the street sounding four o'clock.

"I don't have time to lay about here," Barker complained. "I need to know how the East End is reacting to Dutch being taken to Scotland Yard."

"Do they all know about it?" I asked.

"Aye," he replied.

"Have you got your betty?"

"No, it was taken, along with everything else I own," he answered. "You as well?"

"Yes, sir."

"Did they take your penknife?" he asked. "The wee one with the mother-of-pearl handle?"

I reached into my waistcoat pocket. It was still there. Lang had missed it; it was only three inches long. I handed it to the Guv, and he looked at it with satisfaction.

"Surely you're not going to—" I began, but he ignored me, jabbing the tiny knife blade into the lock.

"It's not going to work, sir," I assured him. "It's too small."

"Aye, but how else are we going to spend our time?"

Two minutes later, he successfully opened the cell door. Of course, the other prisoners had witnessed what had just happened, so Barker passed my pocketknife to the closest one.

"Gentlemen, if one of you would please call the guard?"

They did, and within fifteen seconds the turnkey came in

with threats. One of us who is not named Thomas Llewelyn took him by the arm and swung him into the hands of the prisoners reaching through the bars, who clapped a hand to his mouth. Meanwhile, Barker and I passed through, locked the door from the outside, hung the keys on a hook near the door, and left. We waved casually to Sergeant Kirkwood at the front desk and stepped out the large front door.

"What next?" I asked. "We are in serious trouble. We can't return to the office and Scotland Yard will go immediately to both of our homes looking for us. They'll have patrols looking all over London for us."

"My blood was up," he said in his defense. "Inspector Lang had no excuse for detaining us."

"You're not used to inspectors who don't bow and scrape to you," I observed.

"He did have a nerve," the Guv admitted.

"Granted. But where do we go? They'll be looking for us everywhere."

"I'm a bit thirsty," Barker said, looking across the street. The Rising Sun was there in all its beery glory, facing the entrance to Scotland Yard. Before I knew it, we had crossed the street and stepped inside.

"Mr. Barker, sir," the publican said when he saw our faces. We were well known there. It was Jeremy Jenkins's choice of public houses.

"Rupert," said the Guv. "We'll have a booth in the far back. You know, I'm feeling generous today. Would your customers object if I offered a round of drinks?"

"Why, I don't believe so, Mr. Barker," the man replied. "They'll bear up under the circumstances."

We passed through the room to a dark booth in the corner. To do so we passed a dozen off-duty constables. The Sun is a favorite of Scotland Yard staff, as well.

A minute later our pints arrived. Barker took a pull of his stout as if it were his last, which it might have been, before wiping the foam from his thick mustache.

"What next?" he asked, as if we'd just had a romp, and the future was full of possibilities.

"I shudder to think," I replied.

CHAPTER 20

Did you ever break a vase when you were a child, and experienced that feeling of dread until it was discovered? We all have. Now imagine it a thousand times over. We had just broken out of jail; specifically, the jail of Scotland Yard itself. Technically, Cyrus Barker had broken out and I had followed him, but I don't believe justice would parse the matter so fine. I imagined calling Rebecca on the telephone set and saying: Darling, I won't be coming home to dinner tonight. I'm in jail. Again.

I could have simply stayed put while Barker fled, and hoped for the best, but it had been my pocketknife he had used, or what our counsel Bram Cusp would call "Exhibit One." We were in deep trouble. One couldn't explain this away or merely make a generous donation to the London Police Widows' and Orphans' Fund.

"What are you thinking?" the Guv asked, breaking into my thoughts. "You've been staring into your ale for ten minutes."

"Sir, why did we just break out of Scotland Yard?'

"Oh, that?" he said. "Because I didn't like the cut of Inspector Lang's jib. The man had no right to arrest us. We saved the life of an unfortunate woman and what did he do to thank us? He tossed us in a cell whilst the men using Dutch as bait are in the hospital, probably unguarded. It's prejudice, lad. We are all of us likened to the worst of us."

"Perhaps we are the worst of us," I said. "We've just committed the most recent crime in London."

"Why?" he challenged. "Have we stolen property? Beaten someone who didn't attack us first? Committed fraud or murder?"

"No, sir, but Commissioner Munro will consider that mere semantics."

"Munro will smooth over the matter," my partner said. He set down his glass. "I used to be more like this when I was younger. Impulsive. Be there first and then gone. Out the door before anyone knows what happened. I'm sorry. Thomas. I had forgotten you have a wife and child awaiting you at home now. I shall do my best to show you had been coming with me under protest. Remember, they cannot hold your previous incarceration against you. It was expunged from the record."

Leaning out of the booth I saw that nearly the whole of the room was looking at us. I leaned back again. The room bristled with constables' helmets.

"Scrutiny?" the Guv asked.

"Decidedly," I answered.

He nodded as the publican shuffled up to our table with a solemn face.

"Mr. Barker, sir?" he asked.

"Yes, Mr. Lynch?"

"We was wondering, sir, if, that is, if you might . . ."

"Yes?"

"Like another?"

A Cheshire cat smile spread across my partner's face.

"Thank you, Rupert, but you know one's my limit."

"Sir, we're going to close now," the man continued. "I'm hoping you won't cause too much damage to the place. We just got the chairs replaced last year and we're still a-paying on them. And the glass, Mr. Barker. Glaziers is ever so expensive."

"You've heard, then."

The man turned, holding the platter against his chest.

"Yes, sir. We're certain you had your reasons."

"Are there officers awaiting us in the street?" he continued.

"There are, sir. Dozens."

"I see," Barker purred. "Not just any officers? The strongest and brawniest? I'm not going to waste my time on a group of ticket writers."

The man shuffled away, and the Guv and I looked at each other patiently. The publican finally returned.

"A regular football scrum, sir," he said.

"That's champion," my partner replied. "What Scots whiskey have you got? Give us a glass of your best!"

"The Cameron, sir, from Dufftown."

"Bring it, laddie."

"Right away, Mr. Barker."

He brought us our drinks. One could hear the proverbial pin drop. I had the sinking feeling that we'd be dropping in a minute.

I gulped, but my throat refused to swallow. Our backs were against the wall.

Cyrus Barker lifted a silent toast to me and poured it down his gullet. Afterward, he savored the feeling it engendered for a few seconds. *And he a good Baptist,* I thought. Then without ceremony, he turned and charged out of the room. Charged as if it were the bloody Battle of Culloden. I followed after more sedately.

They were awaiting us in front of Old Scotland Yard, which now housed the Criminal Investigation Department. Twelve men they were, an even dozen. Barker paused a moment, preparing to charge into them. Then they raised their rifles. They were a bit dusty from lack of use, but I was certain they could still fire.

I wouldn't be going home that day, or ever again. Rebecca would be a widow again as her mother had always predicted. Rachel would not remember my face. My parents would outlive me, and I'd never see home in Gwent again. I'd never meet my sister Bronwyn's new husband, or trade jokes and tales with my cousin, Arthur. I wouldn't see my mother a final time. Worst of all, I'd disgrace every last one of them.

I stared at the barrels facing me, one of the constables in particular catching my attention. He had short whiskers and acne and looked little more than a youth. We eyed each other. I held my breath and prepared myself.

"Rifles down, boys," a loud, rough voice ordered. Commissioner James Munro stepped out from behind them. "Who gave the order for rifles? Are you mad? In Great Scotland Yard Street in front of all Whitehall?"

The constables lowered their weapons and stood at attention while my knees nearly gave out.

I would swear that Cyrus Barker looked disappointed.

The commissioner stepped up to us and put his hands on

his hips. "Cyrus, go back inside. I've got something to tell you."

We stepped into the Rising Sun and returned to our dark little booth with its church pew seats. If the inhabitants had been interested before, they were doubly so now. I squeezed against the wall, as Munro took up most of the seat.

"Are you trying to get the both of you killed?" he demanded. "Of all the stunts to pull. Our turnkey resigned on the spot in disgrace. He claimed it was too much excitement for a man over sixty. Oh, and passing the knife to an inmate? You're just looking for trouble. You even upset Sergeant Kirkwood, and that's a deucedly difficult thing to do. The man is the very definition of phlegmatic."

"What's to become of us?" I asked.

"Keep your shirt on, Llewelyn," he barked. "I'm only getting started. Barker, where were you last night?"

The Guv looked at me, then back again at the commissioner of Scotland Yard. I was sweating like a farmer on a hot day in August.

"Last night?" Barker repeated. "At home. Why?"

"I told you there was a meeting of the Templars," Munro said. "Cyrus, you were voted out of office last night. Some of the members claimed you missed meetings. We had an agreement to run the society together. There are powerful men there doing important things, while you're out beating thugs in the East End!"

"I'm sorry, James," the Guv replied. "You are perfectly right. I have an agency to run, but I apologize for leaving the work on your shoulders."

I'll say this for Barker. He apologizes well. I truly believe he was repentant.

"That's fine, but it's done," Munro stated. "They voted you out. You're technically still a member, but you've no more power than an initiate."

"No less than I deserve," the Guv said, nodding. "And you?"

"I resigned on principle."

I watched my partner's face change. This genuinely concerned him.

"But you love this work," he said. "You resigned in protest because of me? You should have censured me like the rest."

Munro shook his head. "Actually, it was convenient. I'm resigning from Scotland Yard at the end of the week."

We stared at him openmouthed. He'd been in office long enough that I had trouble picturing anyone else holding the position of commissioner. Originally, we had trouble with him when he was the head of the Special Irish Branch. They were known for rough dealings and bribes. Neither of us trusted him, but when Barker found the work of running the Templars too much for one man, he had asked Munro to run it with him. The commissioner was ill-tempered, and they butted heads like rams in spring, but he proved himself to be honorable.

"I wish you good fortune, James," Barker said. "Will you retire to the country?"

The man smiled. He had a mouthful of square little teeth, like cubes of sugar.

"In a way," the commissioner replied. "I'm moving to India to become a missionary. I'm forming a Christian medical mission in India."

Barker reached across the table and shook Munro's hand fervently.

"Congratulations, sir! A fine calling late in life. You've made an excellent choice for your latter years."

"I want to tuck in there and do some good while I still can."

"And who is left in charge, may I ask?" Barker said. "Who is your replacement?"

"Where? Among the Templars or at Scotland Yard?"

"Both! Either."

"I have no idea as far as the Templars is concerned. They will take a private vote."

"So, what's to become of the lad and me?"

"I have a little leverage that I've never used. I'll cover up your madcap adventure of this afternoon, though heaven knows why. You both deserve a long, restful prison sentence."

"And what of Inspector Lang?"

"I've given him a proper dressing-down. I've sent him to 'H' Division, Whitechapel. I'll leave his future career in the hands of my successor."

"When do you leave for India?"

Munro took a sip of his drink, a cup of black tea, no cream, no sugar. "In a few days. I've got a great deal to do, as you can imagine."

"I'll speak to you before you go."

Both men stood and shook hands again. Then James Munro, newly minted missionary, left the booth. Barker seemed nonplussed when he was gone.

"Did you know this was coming?" I asked.

"I did not."

"You're out of the Templars," I remarked. "How do you feel about that?"

"Relieved, I think," he replied, stretching his arms out like a man who has had a burden lifted. "It had become like a straitjacket. You know I am a private man. Leave it for the fellows who enjoy that kind of thing."

"Things were dark for a few minutes there," I admitted.

The Guv chuckled. "No more than this morning when a man was menacing you with a knife halfway up a wall."

"I can't argue with that."

We stood. Immediately there was a round of applause from the bar. Money was exchanged. The rest of London would never hear about Barker's escapade, but the gambling fancy made some proper money that day due to him, and not for the first time.

"What's our next step?" I asked when we were in Whitehall Street again.

"Home!" he said, raising his hand for a cab. One arrived immediately. The cabmen of London know the heavy tippers at a glance. We climbed aboard and bowled off.

I hadn't known we were both going to the Guv's house, but light eventually dawned in the old Llewelyn noggin. We arrived a few minutes later. When I entered the front door Barker's dog, Harm, capered about as if his best friend had returned. He hadn't given me the time of day during all the years I lived there, and now he was in a paroxysm of joy. I reached down to stroke his ear and he nipped my finger to the bone. Then he tried to shred my ankle with his innumerable teeth. It was good to be back.

"Mac!" I called.

Jacob Maccabee came out of his pantry, much in the way a cuckoo comes out of a clock. He was in his shirtsleeves, which were rolled to his elbow. Of course, he wore one of his several Liberty waistcoats, a leafy pattern in silvery green. He is a dandy of the first water.

"Good afternoon, Thomas."

"We were just almost shot by a squad of armed constables," I said conversationally.

"Just almost?" he asked. "I wish you better luck next time. It's good to see you. How are your ladies?"

"Thriving," I replied. "You need to visit Rebecca. She thinks you're avoiding her. The woman did make you a godfather to her child."

"I'll call her on the telephone," he said. "We'll set a date."

"Has Sarah told you about her assignment?"

"She has," he replied. "It's dangerous; she's having a marvelous time."

Barker mounted the stair as soon as we arrived, but he did not invite me to join him. One does not stroll into his lair uninvited, even after so much time together. With no set plan, I let Harm out into the back garden and then followed him.

It was not as cold in the garden, thanks to the surrounding brick walls. I followed the dog over the little bridge and across the stepping stones. We circled around the rock and pebble garden and arrived at the small pavilion. There we sat together.

Harm barked at me, goggling his bulging eyes at me like a Chinese demon. He chewed my finger as if he considered it a fine delicacy. Then he hopped down and began making loops around the lawn at a furious pace.

"I missed you too, you little monster!" I said.

In my opinion, there is no spot in London more peaceful than Barker's garden. The November sun beat down in spite of the cold, and if I dared sit out in the sun too long, I'd grow drowsy. When my daughter was older, I would bring her here for a visit now and then. Barker would forget his prejudices against children. She would be a perfectly behaved child, after all, in spite of her father.

Eventually Harm tired himself out, and he went inside for

a plate of chicken livers, his favorite. He'd been temporarily deranged, but now he was quite himself again. After he ate, he would retire for a rest. It is difficult, the life of a rich man's dog. Most of Houndsditch don't eat as well.

Barker was in the hall when I returned to the house, speaking into the telephone transmitter. He lowered his voice when I entered, so I followed the dog into the library and examined the shelves for new treasures. It occurred to me that I could start a library in the mission, possibly have a woman in to give reading lessons.

There was an interesting book by a Chinaman named Sun Tzu, Henry Mayhew's *London Labour and the London Poor,* and a volume of Christopher Marlowe's plays. Barker doesn't generally go in for novels of the nineteenth century, considering them too modern and dangerous. The standards are slipping and all that. A few minutes later, the Guv came in and sat. He had a scowl on his face.

"Bad news?" I asked.

"Perhaps," he admitted. "I consulted a ledger upstairs of members of the Templars, then called an acquaintance who is also a member. There is a secret group within the society that speculates on events. Who do you think is the most likely new leader of the Templars?"

We looked at each other for a moment.

"I have no idea," I said.

"Hugh Danvers," he replied. "But he won't if I have anything to do about it."

"You're only a member now, sir."

He struck a match and applied it to his pipe.

"I have concerns about our client," he remarked. "He seems to be everywhere these days. Let us see what kind of trouble we can stir up tomorrow."

"I'm for home, sir," I replied. "I've had enough trouble for today. Good night."

"Good night, lad. My best to Mrs. Llewelyn."

Harm took a final nip at my ankle, and I stepped out the door.

CHAPTER 21

I suppose many husbands find listening to their wives talk about decorating to be a chore, even a trial. A single false step and one finds he has agreed to an expenditure of more than a hundred pounds for a dresser that looks just like the one it replaces. However, I'm glad when Rebecca prattles on about Chesterfield sofas and Axminster carpets, because I'm learning what she likes and why she likes them. Also, she can bathe in the warm glow of envy from her friends when she tells them I said one cannot have a Chesterfield sofa without a proper Axminster carpet. It simply isn't done.

I was sitting on said Axminster carpet watching Rachel kicking her little legs in the air while the dog lay beside her. It was an antidote to a hard and stressful day. I'm sure some husbands flee to their club in Pall Mall at the earliest moment. Some even stay for the weekend. However, when one has been stabbed at and arrested, one wants to come home to one's chair with a book and Grieg playing *Peer Gynt* on the gramophone. The nerves need soothing and looking about at hearth and home, with a contented wife discussing decorating and a child kicking on the carpet and nobody trying to stab me or shoot me is just the cure.

Dinner was served. If I have given anyone the idea that my wife has no other interests beyond the home, it isn't so. Rebecca is an intelligent woman, who can discuss politics, religion, and literature, sometimes all three at once. However, no number of classes in elocution or piano at the Jews' Free School had prepared her for life as we knew it.

"You climbed a wall to avoid being stabbed?" she asked, lowering her knife and fork. "Honestly, Thomas, I despair of you. I suppose that was your idea. If you recall, you tried climbing down a wall last year with poor results. What made you think changing direction would be any better?"

"I wasn't climbing up," I explained. "I was climbing over, you see."

"And where was Mr. Barker while this was going on?"

"He was on the other side of the alley. There were four men altogether."

She frowned. "Why should it require four men to guard one woman? And why was she being guarded in the first place if she's a simple beggar?"

"There you are, dear," I said. "You've got it in one."

She paused, ate a bite of her dinner, and pondered as she chewed.

"Tell me more about the mission," she said.

As best I could I repeated what Brigadier Booth had explained to me.

"That's a positive movement, isn't it?" she replied. "I'm sure there are dozens of women in the East End who have left their husbands, or desperately need to, due to ill temper. Not just there! The wives in the synagogue know which sisters are in danger, as well. I'm so glad you're not the kind of man who slaps his wife like a donkey."

"I wouldn't even slap the donkey," I responded. "I consider myself a man of peace."

"Really?" she asked, looking at me out of the corner of her eye. "I saw you shoot two men dead in the hall a few years ago."

"No, one of them lived," I argued. "Anyway, I was protecting you. That's different."

"What else is the mission doing?" Rebecca asked.

"I believe they call it a shelter now. There is a gymnasium, a clinic, several wards, and a chapel. Most were left over from Brother Andrew's day, but there have been a few improvements. I like Booth, but even he admits he's just a figurehead. The work is done by two barristers named Eliza Orme and Reina Lawrence. They appear to run a tight ship."

Her fork was arrested halfway to her lips. "Did you say the women were barristers? Surely, they can't practice law."

"No," I admitted. "But as I understood it, they can prepare briefs until such time as they are allowed. They seem to think the time is coming. The work they do at the mission is pro bono. That means—"

She slapped my hand. "I know what pro bono means, darling. I've had Latin classes as well as you."

"Sorry. Of course, you have. The women seem quite competent. The area is dangerous, however, and several men have tried to break in. They did, in fact, this very week, and the woman I spoke of was taken. They have two impressive women guarding the gates, but they were outnumbered. Now Barker has hired Miss Fletcher to volunteer there and keep an eye on matters for him."

"Sarah!" Rebecca said, surprised.

"She seemed suitable to the task," I replied. "I pity the poor oaf who strays in her path."

"Sarah is a dear."

"Sarah is practically feral," I argued. "As Shakespeare said, 'Though she be but little, she is fierce.'"

"We are working on that," she remarked. "Not all of us were fortunate enough to have someone sponsor us to Oxford. I've been giving her a few lessons in deportment, here, with the ladies' auxiliary."

"Here? You mean here in our house?"

"I thought she could do with a little polish."

I shook my head. "I'd call her a hopeless case. She comes from a very rough orphanage, you know."

Rebecca sighed. "Yes, she told me. What a tragic story! It makes me think of the mission. That could be me in there, battered and bruised."

I frowned. "It most certainly could not!"

"I don't mean you, darling, but you know what I mean," she said. "No woman is proof against it."

"I know. I can't understand it," I murmured. "I mean, you chose a woman to spend your life with. Blood of my blood and all that. Why would you strike her? What kind of person would do that?"

"Never you, dear. Although you will shoot people on the new linoleum."

I wagged a finger at her. "You're never going to let me forget that, are you?"

"No, Thomas. Never."

Later I was sitting in the study, reading *Crime and Punishment* by the Russian, Dostoyevsky, and having a hard go of it, when there was a knock at the door. I looked at the timepiece on the fireplace. It was nine o'clock, not the time for someone to come calling. Why didn't we live in a nice, normal street, the kind with picnics and garden parties and ice-cream socials? We seriously needed that sort of thing if we were going to become acceptable to the neighbors, although I wondered if I truly wished to ingratiate myself to them.

It was late, but being an enquiry agent, I don't allow the maid to throw open the door carelessly at that time of the evening. Therefore, I intercepted her, and made my way to the door, thinking to myself that I needed the pistol in a drawer nearby just in case. Lily was behind me with a stout broom I had never seen before. I gave her points for trying.

I flung open the door and immediately she screamed. She had reason to. A man was crumpled on our doorstep. His back was to us, and as I gazed at him my eyes took in the trail of blood that had dribbled along the walk. Goodness knows how far it went. He had to have walked here, or staggered, or crawled to reach our door. I stepped over him and gazed into his pale, perspiring face. It was Victor Soho.

"Vic," I cried, slapping his cheek lightly, trying to get him to wake. His eyes rolled in their sockets. His shirt and waistcoat were soaked in blood. Only heaven knew how much he had lost, and whether he would ever recover. I turned to the maid, who was in hysterics, and saw the dog was barking behind her at the commotion.

"Lily," I said, trying to calm her. "I want you to call St. John Priory on the telephone and give them my name. The number is in the address book. Have them send an ambulance. After that, I want you to get the mop bucket, fill it with water and pour it over the walk. Don't use a mop, just pour the water over it. Do you understand?"

"St. John Priory," she replied in a strangled voice. "Pour the bucket."

She ran off, the event having given her hiccups. I threw

off my dressing gown and seized a cushion from an obliging chair. Gently, I lifted Vic's head and settled it on the pillow, knowing the latter would have to be sacrificed.

"Vic," I said, watching as his eyes tried to focus. "Victor, we have called for an ambulance. Hold on. Don't die, do you understand? The Guv would never forgive you if you died."

He murmured something. An insult perhaps? An insult would be a good sign; he was still with us. I leaned forward, my ear close to his mouth, trying to make out what he was saying.

"It was him," he murmured, no louder than a whisper. It was as if he had no breath. Perhaps a lung had collapsed. There was so much blood I couldn't find the wound.

He's going to die, I told myself, *right here on my doorstep.* I remembered him as a dirty-faced twelve-year-old, climbing over the office wall and stealing Barker's cigars. He called me egregious names, yet Barker had always treated him like an adult colleague. Now he was an adult, who was lying on our doorstep, and unaccountably I considered him a colleague as well.

Rebecca arrived belatedly. She gave a short scream, then clamped a hand over her own mouth.

"Who is it?" she asked. "Is it Mac?"

I looked down at him. He did look vaguely like Barker's butler: long, lean, and dark-haired.

"No, he's an informer named Victor Soho," I answered. "Barker has employed him since he was a tyke."

"Is he dead?"

"Not yet," I replied. "But I don't know his chances."

We live and die, I thought, *some into a comfortable old age, while others are picked early, like spring flowers.* There seemed no rhyme or reason to it.

"Should we carry him inside?" my wife asked.

I became unaccountably irritable with her, pestering me with questions. Then I realized it was merely nerves. The maid came out of the house again, carrying the galvanized bucket full of water. She dribbled it over the puddles of blood.

"Thank you, Lily," I said. "Bring another. Perhaps the stains will be gone by morning."

"Sir, they go all the way along the street as far as I can see," she replied. "Do I wash those as well?"

It was futile, but we had to try. "Whatever you can. I appreciate it. Thank you."

She dipped a curtsey and left for another bucket. I realized then that my wife was holding the pillow that cradled Vic's head, droplets of blood staining her nightgown and robe. It was her way to care more for a perfect stranger than what she was wearing.

"It's cold," I said. "We should put a blanket on him, and I must call Barker."

As I went into the house, I saw that my sleeves were bloody up to my elbows. I retrieved a blanket to put over Vic and then went to the telephone in my study and dialed Barker's house. It was a quarter past ten, but he retires late.

"You have reached the Barker residence," Jacob Maccabee's lugubrious voice crackled over the line.

"Mac, it's Thomas. I need to speak to Barker immediately."

"Hold," he said.

He lay down the receiver. Off in the distance I heard a sedate pair of shoes climbing the stairs. After a moment I heard a second pair clattering down.

"What has happened?" he demanded.

"Vic has been stabbed," I replied. "He's bleeding profusely all over the front walk. He may have walked for miles, I'm not quite sure. There's no idea what happened unless he comes 'round."

"Have you called St. John's Priory?" the Guv asked.

"Yes, sir," I answered. "The ambulance is coming. I only hope Vic will be alive when it arrives."

"Are you going to the priory as well? You don't have to come."

"Of course, I have to come. What a question! I'll see you there."

I hung the receiver on the hook. Turning, I went back to the front step and looked at my wife.

"How is the patient?" I asked. "Better or worse?"

"I have no idea," she admitted. "He is moaning, which I suppose is a good sign."

"I'm going to meet Barker at the priory after the ambulance arrives."

"Go and change. Mr. Barker will need you."

The priory is a religious center founded in the twelfth century. I understood the Crusades were planned there. A few years ago, it was decided that there needed to be some aid at railway stations when someone was hurt. From that idea, the St. John's Ambulance was founded, providing vehicle services and instruction in first aid. A small hospital is attached to the priory, but most of their ambulances drop patients at major hospitals. For some reason, Cyrus Barker always goes there to recover after his worst injuries. Perhaps he likes the monks praying over him. The Guv was waiting there for us when the ambulance arrived. I paid my cabman and alighted, meeting him at the door.

"He's naught but a bloody mess," he noted, shaking his head. "I hope Mrs. Llewelyn was not inconvenienced."

"She held his head in her lap," I said.

"You've got a good woman there, lad. Mind you treat her well. Let's go inside."

We walked along the corridor, our footsteps echoing on the ancient stones. Reaching some scarred wooden seats that only a monk would be penitent enough to sit in, we sat and waited, knowing we would be there for some time.

"Tell me everything," he ordered.

I related what happened, but there wasn't much to tell. Our conversations in Camomile Street had not been important, nor was watching Lily washing the steps.

"He said, 'It was him'?" he asked.

"Yes, sir. He said it distinctly."

"What information was Victor imparting?" Cyrus Barker asked. "Who was he speaking about, do you think? And are you sure that's all he said?"

I nodded. "He was barely conscious, sir, and probably delirious. Perhaps he didn't know what he was saying. Or perhaps he had a message but could no longer remember it because he was in so much pain."

Barker thought for a second or two. "We'll know soon enough."

"Or we won't," I replied.

"That's the spirit, lad. Always optimistic."

A doctor came into the lobby a half hour later.

"Soho?" the man asked us. "An odd name for a person, if I may remark upon it."

"It's short for Sohovic," my partner explained. "How is the patient, Doctor?"

"He'll recover, but it will be painful. Stomach acid gets in the wound. He was stabbed on the right side, under the lowest rib. We're taking him into surgery to see what organs have been damaged. His arrival at your door in such a condition is a minor miracle. Have you any idea where he was or what he was doing?"

"He worked for me, sir," Barker said. "We are private enquiry agents."

"I see," the doctor replied. "So, it was in the line of duty, then."

"Aye, it was."

"He'll need a good month of bed rest," the doctor stated.

"As soon as he can be moved, we'll take him to London Hospital," the Guv answered.

"Good idea," the man replied. "They'll need to keep him for at least a week. Afterward, he'll need a proper physician to check on him weekly. He must use laudanum for the pain. I've given him a dose now."

Barker frowned. "May we question him?"

"He's unconscious, I'm afraid."

"Blast," the Guv growled. "I need some answers."

The surgeon wasn't impressed. "Not half as much as he needs the bleeding to stop."

Barker let him have the final word.

CHAPTER 22

We waited for a couple of hours in the dim hall of the priory, comforted by the knowledge that the physicians there were used to emergency cases. We were fortunate as well that their best surgeon, Dr. Treves, performed the operation. He is considered an expert in anatomy, and in particular abdominal surgery. We were told he had been about to leave the building, and briefly considered leaving the work for a younger colleague but changed his mind when he saw Victor's condition.

All the same, I was concerned for Vic. I am no great champion of hospitals. I have had friends go in and not come out again, and feared he might be one of them. It wasn't until that moment that I realized I had just considered him a friend. Fiend more like, I'd have said a week ago, but despite our constant gibes, I didn't despise him as I had years before, when he insulted me continually while stealing items from my desk to hawk later that day. He had a talent for it. I used to make an inventory of my possessions whenever he left our chambers.

Now he was an adult, of sorts. Twenty or so, I imagined, if he ever knew his own birth date. He had grown taller than I expected, with dark hair, and a snub nose he never grew out of.

The surgeon entered the hall and approached us. He was a fine-looking gentleman in his fifties, with a mustache and a calm air. Barker stood and walked toward him.

"The surgery went well, gentlemen," Treves explained, pulling on a heavy Chesterfield coat. "It was a typical thrust to the stomach. With care I believe he shall recover. Fortunately, these surgeries rarely go septic. However, they hurt like the dickens, and it will be a slow recovery. The wound is awash in bile and stomach acid, not a positive environment for recovery. However, he's young and healthy, and I feel no especial reason for concern."

We were suddenly thrust aside, and a girl not yet twenty approached the doctor. She had dark hair and eyes, which were full of anxiety.

"Is it Victor?" she asked. "Is he dead? Tell me he isn't dead! Promise me he won't die, Doctor!"

My word, I thought. *The boy has a sweetheart. Would wonders never cease?*

The doctor placated her as best he could as the Guv and I seated ourselves again. After a few minutes, Dr. Treves escaped. Then she rounded on us.

"Are you Mr. Barker?" she demanded.

"I am, miss."

"It's your fault he's here, nearly dying," she claimed. "Why'ncha leave him alone?"

"I merely asked him to see if there was mischief afoot in Whitechapel and Bethnal Green," the Guv replied. "Apparently, there was. I'm sorry, I don't know your name."

"Bella," she said. "Bella Czajka."

Ho ho, I thought. He had not chosen an English girl but had returned to his Polish roots. Before this enquiry, I hadn't spoken to him in months, having been too wrapped up in my own domestic bliss, but then it had been an eventful year in the Llewelyn household.

Cyrus Barker gestured to the barrier door, and the girl was off like a shot. The Guv is ever the gentleman with women. *Blast,* I told myself. She would go first, and who knew how long she would be there, with midnight fast approaching. It would be nice to have two full nights' sleep together, but that seemed a far-off dream.

The Guv leaned back in the hard wooden chair, rested his head upon the top edge, and was fast asleep within a minute. I longed for such an ability. There was nothing to do but sit and stare at the walls.

A half hour dragged by. Then Miss Czajka stepped out into the corridor again, gave us a look of contempt, and strode out of the building into the cold night, though she was inadequately dressed for the weather. Without a word, my partner stood and went through the door. I dragged myself after him.

We passed through two rooms, which had once been monk's cells. There were a few orderlies in the corridor, and one took us to Vic, who lay there looking decidedly pale and spindly. I understood the look, having seen it and even experienced it myself before. He was drugged with laudanum. Before we questioned him about his ordeal it was necessary to test his lucidity. I bent over him and examined his eyes. His pupils were small.

"Vic," I said. "Vic, can you hear me?"

"Baboon face," he said, if a bit groggily.

"Troglodyte. How are you feeling?"

"Like I've been stabbed."

I looked up at the Guv. "If he can insult me and complain, I suppose he can answer some simple questions," I pronounced.

Barker pulled a chair from against the wall and sat beside the bed.

"Victor, what happened?" the Guv asked.

"I was in Drury Lane, sir," he said. His voice had a dreamy quality to it. "In a public house, having a pint, just listening."

"Which public house?" Barker asked. Somewhere a nurse shushed him.

Victor stared at the ceiling in thought, as if grasping for words that were flapping about in his head. "The White Hart."

"Ah," the Guv replied. "The Grady Boys. What were they discussing?"

"Someone very powerful, sir. The fellow was trying to get the gangs to make peace. Word is . . . word is gang leaders were killed in Calcutta."

"What did you take that to mean?" Barker asked, like a headmaster quizzing one of his charges.

Soho Vic looked dazed, but it was obvious he was trying to answer him. "He wanted to . . . bring them together."

"Consolidate them?" Barker asked. "Would he be the leader?"

There was no answer. Vic's eyes were closed. We nodded and stood, but he spoke again.

"No one knows . . . who he is, or what he wants."

An orderly suddenly appeared at the foot of the bed.

"Stop browbeating the patient," he insisted. "He's been stabbed, stitched up, and filled full of opium. Leave him alone, and I'm not asking."

Barker looked as if he were ready to challenge him, then changed his mind.

"Of course," he replied. "Victor, I'm glad you survived the ordeal. Thomas and I will let you rest."

We stood and donned our hats. I looked down at Victor and saw the twelve-year-old I'd first met. He had begun to snore quietly. His mind was floating free, tethered to the damaged body below it. We passed through the door, then out into the street. The wind was chill, and I lifted the collar of my coat.

"Go home, lad," my partner ordered.

"Yes, sir," I responded.

I turned and left before the man changed his mind. Out in the street I waved for a cab. The hansom pulled up to the curb and I jumped aboard, giving my address as I sat back in the leather seat. There was a blanket there for the use of his customers and I draped it over me.

"Sir?" I heard a voice overhead, waking me from a light doze. "Sir, we're here."

I opened my eyes and found we were in Camomile Street. I paid the man, giving him a generous tip, and staggered to the door. When I opened it, I heard Rachel crying. I sighed. Surely teething didn't go on forever.

Inside, Mrs. Skaleski came to the upstairs landing and looked over the banister. For once she did not seem inclined to pass the baby to me. I called to her in greeting, over the crying. Then I struggled out of my coat and hung it along with my bowler on the hall stand.

I found Rebecca when I reached the bedroom. She was sound asleep, but roused as I unbuttoned my vest.

"Hello, darling!" she murmured, sitting up and propping herself against the pillows. "How's Victor doing?"

"He underwent surgery around midnight and managed

to survive somehow," I told her. "He's drugged. The Guv wants to have him moved to London Hospital in the next couple of days so he can get the best care."

"So, he'll be all right, then?" she asked.

"He will," I said with more confidence than I felt. "There was something interesting, however. A young woman came in and pushed Barker around, demanding to see Vic first."

My wife's eyes grew large. "That is interesting. What was she like?"

"She was very young, but she certainly knew her own mind. Barker let her have her way. It was a quite a sight."

She straightened the coverlet and looked at me. "There's something I want to talk to you about. I'd like to do something with Sarah."

"Sarah Fletcher?"

She cocked her head. "Do we know any other Sarah?"

"Thank goodness, no."

"She asked me to attend a meeting with her."

"What sort of meeting?" I asked distractedly, buttoning on my pajama sleeping suit.

"Oh, you know, just a woman's meeting."

I folded my trousers and hung them over a chair. "What sort of meeting? I can't exactly see Sarah in a knitting circle."

"It's a suffragists meeting," she replied.

I'd lifted the covers and had one leg in the bed. "A suffragist meeting! Why would you attend such a thing?"

"To hear what the speakers have to say, obviously."

"I don't know if that's the kind of meeting you should attend."

Her eyes narrowed. "Why not?"

"Well, I mean, you're a mother now."

She gave me a look then. It wasn't angry, but it was withering. "Being a father hasn't kept you from being out at all hours of the night. Besides, we have a nanny if you recall."

"I do recall, yes, but I worry about your safety."

"Sarah trains with Mr. Barker, you know."

"Still." I frowned. "Are you a suffragist?"

"Who wouldn't want women to have the vote?"

I had to concede the matter. "You may come and go as you choose, but Sarah Fletcher is another matter. I suspect she looks for trouble."

"You don't like her," she said. It wasn't a tiff, as such, but the wrong word might create one.

"Rather, she doesn't like me," I assured her.

"There seem to be many people you don't get along with," she remarked, one side of her mouth rising.

"I'm fair-minded," I replied. "However, I can't help how other people react."

"Oh?" she asked. "Like Mac?"

"He's just a prig," I said dismissively. "And he wanted my position before I was hired. He's never forgiven me for it. I can't fault his tailor, though. Also, he was in the same class as you at the Jews' Free School. I can't help but be a little jealous."

"And Victor," she continued. "I've heard you call him the most awful names."

"It's a game we play, although he is the most exasperating of fellows," I explained. "He was a terror as a youth, with his own gang of child thieves."

"What of Inspector Poole?" she asked, poking my chest.

"Ah. He's fine enough, I suppose, but I've lost count of the times he tossed me in jail. I tend to take that sort of thing personally."

"And now poor Sarah is the victim of your loathing."

"I don't loathe her," I argued, the picture of wounded

pride. "I merely find her bloodthirsty. I'm concerned that she might take you into a dangerous neighborhood. I swear she was a pirate queen in another life."

"You are merely jealous that she is so adept in your antagonistics class."

"Very well," I said. "I'll admit that defense comes to her naturally."

"Then there is the Chinaman," she said. "What is his name?"

"Ho, and he's a demon. He despises me. He wants Barker to give me to him for a week, to teach me how to work."

Rebecca raised a brow. "You could do with a lesson or two. Why don't you volunteer? That would impress him and Mr. Barker as well, or perhaps even shock them."

I mimicked writing something in the air.

"I'm adding you to my list," I said.

"The only disagreeable one here is you," she insisted. "You can't get along with anyone."

I tried to be angry, but I finally broke out laughing.

"Very well," I said. "I concede that it might . . . might, mind you, be my fault, but I still maintain that Sarah is a bad influence and will only get you into trouble. She'll take you to a suffrage meeting and I'll have to come and bail you out of jail in the middle of the night."

"It's better than a dull garden party." She looked at me curiously. "Do you find the suffragist cause objectionable?"

I shrugged. "Well, I certainly believe the women at the shelter have legitimate reasons to find a place of safety. As for the wealthy ones, I suspect they are out for a lark, or to prove a point if they are serious."

One of her brows raised at the corner. It was the dangerous one.

"The 'wealthy ones' never have a bit of trouble, then? Their fathers marry them always to perfect men who always meet their needs and never causes any concern."

It was the eyebrow that did it. The time to retreat from the field in disorder was now. I raised my hands in surrender.

"Very well, I admit you're right. You should be a barrister yourself. Go out with Sarah or whomever you like. Have a party with all my mortal enemies. I'll give you a more complete list tomorrow."

She broke out laughing.

"Poor dear," she said. "Oh, listen! Rachel has stopped crying. Let's get some sleep. You must be exhausted."

"At least someone has noticed."

"Mr. Barker has been ordering you about all night, hasn't he?" she asked. "I'll add him to your list."

"Thank you," I said.

"I don't believe it's a list of everyone you dislike," my wife pronounced. "More likely it's a list of everyone you know."

CHAPTER 23

The following morning, Cyrus Barker and I arrived in the office at eight o'clock sharp. Jenkins had the newspapers spread out across our desks, but the Guv didn't open one. Instead, he turned to me.

"I'm feeling inclined to go to the House of Lords and see if we can speak to Hugh Danvers," he said.

"Speak to him about what?" I asked.

"I'd like to know what he knew about May Evans's plans to marry Dunbarton," he replied, putting on his coat again.

I followed suit. "Shall we walk?"

He nodded. Twenty minutes later, we stepped into the Palace of Westminster, under the stern eye of the principal doorkeeper who sat on his perch by the entrance to the building. We passed along the corridors until we reached the chambers of the House of Lords. They had their own ceremonial doorkeepers there who, I understand, are more stringent than the ones on the Commons side, because so many lords are public figures. The doorkeepers were a dapper bunch, in swallow-tailed coats, white ties, and silver badges of office. Going into the chamber was out of the question, but we were able to write a message on a green card to be delivered to His Lordship. It was our best option. We sat on a bench and waited.

I glanced at one of the doorkeepers and he at me. These men had been around for hundreds of years, guarding the lords and speakers, and even the Queen herself. They are police officers, an army unto themselves, although a small one. The House of Lords had two dozen of them, the Commons closer to three.

Waiting was dull, but it was warm inside, so I was contented enough. The bench was hard as marble, but I was accustomed to that. The door to the chamber opened and who should appear but G. C. Havelock, who immediately buttonholed the most senior doorkeeper and pointed to us both. The next I knew we were surrounded by several men in formal dress.

"Good afternoon, gentlemen," Cyrus Barker said, civil and restrained.

"Come with us, please," the doorkeeper ordered.

I bit my lip and waited. Matters could get out of hand very quickly. My mind occupied itself going over several scenarios, most ending with us in the cell at Scotland Yard we had escaped from earlier that week.

"Certainly," my partner replied, being polite. He hadn't punched anyone yet. I considered keeping a list of policing agencies in London and which ones we had unfortunate dealings with.

I'd put the doorkeepers on the list.

As it happened it went well as far as confrontations go. We were walked firmly but politely to the front doors. One man even opened them for us.

"Was that Mr. Havelock?" Barker asked.

"Yes, it was," he replied.

I looked at him curiously. "Why was he here?"

"Why shouldn't he be here?" the doorkeeper asked, as if I were a dunce. "He is Lord Danvers's secretary."

"Thank you, sir," Barker replied. "Good day!"

That was the end of the matter. There were no blows, no kicks, or struggles. One would think the doorkeepers and we were the best of friends. In front of Parliament, I raised my hat, then we made our way north again. I wondered if my partner was disappointed.

"Private secretary," Barker rumbled from deep within his broad chest. "The rascal."

"What's he doing running a construction site in the East End?" I asked.

"I would imagine he's keeping his eye on his master's interests."

Cyrus Barker and I decided to have tea at the Shades public house down the street, a few buildings south of our offices. We ordered a pot of Darjeeling and settled in.

"Who is this Mr. Havelock?" Barker asked. "And why did he just prevent us from seeing Lord Danvers?"

I paused a moment while the tea was placed before us.

"He didn't look like a private secretary who belongs in the House of Lords," I replied after the barman had gone.

"It's illogical for His Lordship to throw out the two men he hired for an enquiry. I wonder if our message reached him at all."

"You suspect Havelock is working on his own behalf and is taking advantage of Danvers?" I asked.

"He wouldn't be the first secretary to take advantage."

"True," I replied.

"However," the Guv continued. "It is more likely he was fulfilling his normal duties to his employer."

I frowned. "Why then would Lord Danvers have us removed from the chamber?"

"I don't know," Barker answered in reply. "Why did Lady Danvers send us away from her mansion?"

We drank our tea and considered the matter.

"I have a theory," I said.

"Elaborate," the Guv replied, as if I were a barrister and he the judge.

"Hugh Danvers is in the House of Lords for hours each day working on behalf of his constituency, making deals and compromises. Meanwhile, Havelock is free to go about his duties, whatever they are, and to go to Whitechapel for whatever reason. I'm convinced his men have been causing most of the trouble in the East End, from the scuffle in the alleyway to taking Dutch from the mission." I nodded at the Guv. "Havelock said they were workers who were in the country illegally. You said yourself they might be mercenaries. If so, Lord Danvers could not be involved in the matter. More likely it was that fellow Havelock, whoever he is."

"What matters are Havelock's antecedents," the Guv pronounced. "He could be an anarchist for all we know. Danvers may have no idea what his secretary is doing while he is in Parliament."

I was still trying to gather more ammunition against the man when we opened the door of our offices ten minutes later and were confronted by Jeremy Jenkins.

"Sir!" he cried, seizing my shoulder. "Your stable is afire!"

I said not a word to Barker, but turned and ran to the curb, waving my arms for a cab. There seemed to be none in the area, and I hopped frantically up and down when one reluctantly pulled to a stop and set the brake. The man must have thought me a nutter, but he couldn't fault my money.

"The Minories!" I shouted. "As fast as you can!"

The brake was released, and there was the crack of a whip overhead. The horse's hooves dug into the cobbles, and we shot off like a cannonball. This fellow was going to earn his fare.

"What's happened, sir, if I may ask?" he called through the trap above my head.

"A stable is on fire," I replied. "My horse is there. I've got to save her! You understand."

"'Course I do. I'd be lost without my little Dolly here. Sit back and I'll get you there in a trice."

I held to the strap beside the window, and I needed to, because he took the first corner, then the second, and he barely missed the third, but not for want of trying. At one point the left wheel lost contact with the road, and I thought we would topple, but the cab righted itself again and plunged forward.

"There it is!" I cried, seeing smoke up ahead.

The hansom cab skittered around the corner. Thick, oily smoke billowed from the open doorway of the stable. Could I hear any horses from within, or was it my imagination? I stuffed notes into the driver's hand without knowing what denomination I was giving him and ran headlong into the stable. It was like hell itself in there. The heat of the flames hit me like a wall, and I retreated into the street. I started to go in again, but two men pulled me back.

"It's gone, sir," one of them said in my ear. I staggered back and fell over a curb. Then I sat there in utter shock and misery, holding my head and watching the old building burn. In a few moments I heard the familiar bell of a fire vehicle clanging in the distance, but I knew it was too late.

Out of nowhere, something wet ran along my face. I opened my eyes and glared into another, much larger eye than mine. Juno nickered and licked me again. I thought I had trained her not to do that, but I didn't care at that moment. I hugged her as I would my own child.

"I wouldn't let her get hurt, sir," the stable man said behind me with a lopsided grin. "I knowed she means so much to you."

"You've just earned the reward I offered for her," I called over the chaos, the yelling, and the inferno in front of us. "What is your name?"

"Horace, sir. Horace Squibly."

"What's to become of the stable, Horace?" I asked.

"It's a goner, sir!" he replied, a logical answer.

"What are you going to do?"

"It's not my stable, sir," he answered. "The owner may try to rebuild."

"Here is the twenty-five pounds reward money," I said, pulling the Guv's wallet from my pocket.

"Bless you, sir," he said, and suddenly burst out crying, the tears running down his unshaven face. There was soot on it as well, and a reddish burn on his cheek.

"Are you hurt?" I asked.

"Nah, sir, but I loved this work, and it's all I have. I've got a bum leg and am not much good for other work. This money will help until I can find another position."

"Is there any place I can board Juno nearby?"

"There's another stable in Chamber Street."

"I'll take her there, then."

I led Juno through the streets until I found the place Mr. Squibly had recommended. She was skittish from the effects of the fire and the ensuing chaos. She was inclined to rear, and her back legs were shivering. I stroked her neck and tried to soothe her. Of course, she didn't understand the words, but I believe she found comfort in the sound of my voice.

The owner of the Chamber Street stables allowed me to rent a stall for a month. It looked no better or worse than the last one, and I would be able to decide if it was satisfactory then. The man filled the trough in her stall with water and put down fresh hay under my watchful eye. The conditions were good, but the price was steep. However, the main concern was that she was safely out of harm's way.

Once Juno was settled into her new stall, I returned to our offices. The Guv was waiting for me when I came through our chamber door.

"How is Juno?" he asked. I could hear the concern in his voice.

"She's well," I replied. "But the stable burnt to the ground. I've moved her to a different one nearby."

I threw myself into my office chair and looked at my partner.

"You know, sir, I don't mind people taking a shot at me occasionally or trying to beat me. I know it's part of our occupation. I've even been known to shoot someone, as Rebecca is always telling me, and you've trained me extensively to defend myself."

"Aye," Barker muttered.

"But when someone comes after me and mine, that's another matter. I'm a husband now, and a father. I own property. Before you hired me, I didn't own a brush to clean my teeth. Sometimes I wish we didn't even live in London."

"Are you resigning?" asked the Guv, his face impassive.

"No, I'm just complaining."

"You do it so well."

"Ha," I replied. "But I mean what I say. Juno nearly died a terrible death two hours ago, and all because I took her out for a stroll to the Mile End Mission."

"Ours is a dangerous profession," he countered, sitting down in his green leather chair.

"Yes, but a constable may get beaten or shot once in his career. We're being attacked constantly!"

Barker nodded. "That's what makes us different from the detectives in Craig's Court, lad. Many are retired officers, no longer able to do what we do. Others can get by in a scrape but aren't trained in warfare."

"Warfare?" I asked. "Is that what we do? Are we soldiers?"

"Not always, but often, yes," he answered. "If you were an officer, your horse would be in danger, would it not?"

I took it in for a moment. "When did I volunteer?"

"It was May of 1884, as I recall. And it really isn't war. I've been involved in war before. They come at you from all sides, and they always try to kill you. Did it occur to you, lad, that I need you? I'd already be dead if you didn't literally guard my back."

"Really?" I asked. It sounded absurd.

"We do the work—I do the work—because it needs to be done, and very few are willing to do it. I won't apologize for it."

"However, most soldiers are young and I'm over thirty now," I reasoned. "You're however old you are and have been severely injured dozens of times. What will happen when you are gone?"

"You'll be in charge, Thomas, and you'll hire a man of your own. The agency must go on."

I sighed. "The agency must go on."

Afterward, Barker sent me to Scotland Yard to the records room to see if G. C. Havelock had a criminal record. I was hopeful, but after digging through files for the next two hours with a sergeant, I discovered that alas, he did not. I left that evening dispirited. The stable was in ruins, Juno was in the care of a man I had never met before, and Havelock might have been nothing more than the private secretary he purported to be. I needed a balm in the form of my comfortable slippers, my caring wife, and my adorable, teething daughter. I might even pat the unnamed dog. I really hoped to return her to her rightful owners soon.

CHAPTER 24

I returned home that evening to a cold reception. Charges of neglect, the occasional unsympathetic ear, or a pair of shoes out where someone can trip on them, I can frequently confess to. But then, most men do that. But something was different. Had I forgotten an anniversary? No, none that I could recall. Had I casually said something stupid, or which could have been misconstrued? It was possible, but if so, I had no idea what it was. I was mystified. Rebecca is not the sort to get upset over nothing.

It began when I entered the house. Lily was rough with my coat and silent when I said good evening. She seemed out of temper, but I couldn't speak to her about her behavior, it being more Rebecca's bailiwick.

"Where is Mrs. Llewelyn?" I asked.

"Upstairs, sir," she stated, and went off in a huff, as if I had been short with her, when it was quite the reverse. I put my hat on the hook and my stick in the stand. I was left alone in the hall to work out what was happening. I had no idea what it could be, but I felt as if the entire house harbored ill feelings against me.

I found my wife draped across the bed with a sick headache. She was buried under a pillow as if to say she couldn't look at anyone. I was baffled and becoming increasingly upset.

"Rebecca," I said. "What is it? Are you ill?"

There was no response from the pillow, which I took to mean I should know very well what it was, and I was a fool if I didn't.

"Tell me, dear," I pleaded. "Have I done something to upset you?"

Nothing happened. There was no reply, not so much as a shrug.

"Look, whatever this is, I'm sure we can talk it through," I insisted. "I'm sure it's nothing."

"Nothing?" she cried, ripping the pillow from her face. Her eyes were an angry red. It wasn't merely bad. Whatever I had done must have been monumental. I tried to think of something, anything. Rebecca does not keep me on tenterhooks with no reason. Had I simply been caught up in work? Had she heard I had been arrested the day before and broken out of jail? Some wives would want to know such things. I had planned to tell her, but it slipped my mind. That must be it. It was the only logical explanation.

"Look," I said, trying to sound sensible. "The Scotland Yard business . . . Barker was in a contrary mood that day. Yes, I know, I shouldn't have given him the penknife, but it all worked out in the end. No foul, as they say at Lords."

In response she buried her face in the pillow again. I made

the mistake of patting her shoulder. She shrugged off my hand.

"Rebecca, I'm truly sorry. Please tell me what I've said or done. I'm a dunderhead, I know, and I don't deserve you, but would you at least give me a hint?"

She threw the pillow and sat up. We were suddenly face-to-face. I slipped back on the counterpane and the next I knew I was on the floor. She sat high above me on the bed with fire in her eyes. She reminded me of the judge who had sentenced me to eight months.

"I give up!" I cried. "What in hell is wrong?"

"Don't use that language in front of me, Thomas Llewelyn!" she snapped. "And you know perfectly well what you have done!"

"I don't!" I said, as if I were three, and wouldn't confess to anything.

"How could you do this to me?" she continued. "And with her, of all women!"

"Her?" I shouted. "What 'her'? What are you talking about?"

She threw herself back on the bed and ripped a drawer open from the table by the bed. Then she flung the evidence of my guilt at my head, where it fluttered down like a butterfly.

"I hope you have a good explanation for that!" she cried.

I looked down and saw that it was a photograph. In fact, it was the photograph of Miss May Evans that Lord Danvers had given Cyrus Barker. I had been the last to examine it, so it must have found its way into my pocket, like many of the clues and detritus of our cases. I am a walking filing cabinet. The Guv likes to keep his own pockets free, save for his throwing coins. Everything else came into my possession.

"Where did you get this?" I asked.

"From your suitcoat pocket, obviously! Lily found it there when she was brushing your coat. How could you, Thomas? You have no idea how embarrassing this is. You may stay the night, since you have no club, like a decent husband would, but you may spend the night in your study!"

"Rebecca, this is the woman our client is searching for," I explained. "He gave us the photograph so that we could track her. Her name is May Evans."

"You're lying!" she replied. "This is a photograph of Maud Kemple, only the most horrid temptress in London. Have you any idea how many marriages she has destroyed? I never imagined ours would be one of them."

I controlled myself. This was some kind of mistake, but now I knew what we were fighting over.

"Dear," I said. "I don't know anyone named Maud Kemple. Lord Hugh Danvers gave us this photograph, and told us it was Miss May Evans, his sister-in-law. She's the American heiress for whom we have been searching. Perhaps he had this photograph in his pocket as well and gave us the wrong one. Or perhaps he was caught with it in his pocket and was trying to get rid of it. His wife was in the room. That could be more likely. He's a good-looking fellow, rich, and important. Which one of us do you suppose this harpy here would be likely to give her personal photograph to?"

She gave no response, but I hoped she would start wavering in a minute. Her face still looked like thunder. Now I had to convince my wife of the truth.

A flush appeared on each of Rebecca's cheeks. "You really don't know who she is?"

"I have no idea," I said. "She's no beauty, obviously. Look at that upturned nose."

"You're lying," she said solemnly. "She is the season's beauty."

I sat in a chair and folded my hands. "Rebecca, I'm no good at lying to you. You know when I steal a chocolate out of the sweets dish. You probably know when I pass by that I'm thinking of taking one."

She pushed herself up on her hands and sniffed.

"I must look a fright," she said, and left for the powder room.

That was the only apology I should expect, I told myself. If I were fortunate enough, we were going to put this whole matter behind us. I could live with that and forgive her immediately. I tried to put myself in her shoes. I'd be just as enraged as she would, possibly more, but it was merely a misunderstanding.

I went downstairs and gave her time to get herself in order. My first thought after I retreated to my study was to call Cyrus Barker. My second was to wonder whether my wife had told her mother. If so, the news would reach the newspapers in Borneo, Burma, and Kathmandu in hours. She would arrive in the morning to help pack the trunk. My third and final thought was whether Lily had been told. She served my porridge every morning, after all. There's no telling what sort of potion she could pour into it.

"Sir," I said, after the Guv had come to the telephone. "I've inadvertently learned something regarding the photograph Lord Danvers gave us. It isn't May Evans at all. My wife recognized it as an infamous demimondaine named Maud Kemple. Have you heard of her?"

"Kemple," he rumbled. "I seem to recall she was involved in divorce proceedings over at least two aristocrats. Quite a busy little woman. I'm pleased you learned her identity. Good work."

"It wasn't me, sir," I replied. "Mrs. Llewelyn recognized her for me."

"Oh?" he remarked, his voice heavy with innuendo. "Has there been a difficulty?"

"Nothing that cannot be sorted, I hope. Shall we confront His Lordship?"

"One of the most powerful men in London?" Barker asked. "No, let me consider our next step. It's possible he could assume we're trying to blackmail him. I'll see you in the morning."

"Yes, sir."

"Tell Mrs. Llewelyn she has been instrumental in solving a case. She can share the credit with Inspector Dew."

"I shall," I said, returning the receiver to its cradle. "Providing she is speaking to me."

I went upstairs and found my wife. Rebecca and I discussed the matter over the next hour and concluded that it was a mere disagreement, and our marriage was as strong as ever. We had both made baseless accusations and jumped to conclusions. Fortunately, she had not seen fit to make a telephone call to her mother, so there would be no lasting damage. However, my oatmeal the next morning was surprisingly lumpy and a trifle cold. Lily did not meet my eye for half a week. She hasn't my wife's forgiving nature.

Soon, I was in Barker's basement in my trousers and singlet, punching the heavy bag. The Guv held two fifty-pound dumbbells and was lifting them alternately. Since they amounted to most of my weight, I had never tried them. Casually, my partner asked after my wife.

I said she seemed in bright spirits that morning. I told him that our conversation the night before sounded like a Jane Austen novel, and having said that I had to tell the Guv who the lady was. Since she was neither an ancient stoic or a contemporary of John Calvin, I had to explain Miss Austen's history and why her literature had merit. Fortunately, I was able to do so, and promised to bring a copy of *Pride and Prejudice* with me the next day, violating his personal rule that all literature published after 1750 was not edifying to the soul, and fiction in general being suspect, save for *The Pilgrim's Progress.*

We arrived in our chambers at our usual time, sat in our usual chairs, and consumed our usual newspapers. Lord Danvers was mentioned in several of them. He was proposing a bill to lower the excise tax from goods arriving from China, thereby cultivating a stronger relationship with the Manchu government. I didn't know what our current relationship with China was regarding goods, but it sounded positive, and that was important as far as the Celestial City was concerned. Really, we only know what the newspapers tell us, without asking who influences them. We assume everything written is for our edification, but we might just as well make our decisions with a dartboard. I stated that opinion to my partner, but he considers me a pessimist as far as politics are concerned.

"What shall we do this morning?" I asked when I had digested *The Times, The Post,* and *The Chronicle.*

"I think we should have a conversation with His Lordship's secretary, Mr. G. C. Havelock. I did not appreciate being escorted from Parliament. If there is information available regarding this enquiry, I suggest we frighten it out of him."

"Should we go to his offices in the East End, or track him down in our own little street, Whitehall?" I asked.

"Let us try Osborn Street," Barker said. "It is always difficult to get beyond the Cerberus guarding the House of Lords."

When we reached Osborn Street, Barker and I triangulated which back door was most likely to be Havelock's and

I waited with a pistol at the ready. My partner was to play goatherd and push him into my waiting arms. For once, everything came off as planned. The fellow nearly ran head-first onto the business end of my Webley.

"Hello, Havelock," I said. "Remember me?"

"Mr. Llewelyn!"

Havelock was still a dandy, with every hair in place, but his eyes started from his face. I'd wager he'd never come face-to-face with a pistol before.

Barker's plate-sized hand seized the back of his collar and dragged him inside. By the time I entered he had thrown the unfortunate secretary into his chair. Havelock was in a panic and attempted a second escape. I was forced to drag him back to the chair again.

"There's no need for that!" he said.

"Mr. Havelock," Barker said, full of goodwill. "I wonder if you would do me the favor of coming to the local constabulary with us for questioning?"

"I think not," the secretary answered, frowning in return.

"I'm afraid I must insist," the Guv said. "Will you come willingly, or shall you cut up rough?"

"I have nine men nearby who will do that for me," Havelock countered.

"Perhaps," my partner conceded, "but Mr. Llewelyn has twelve bullets in his pistols, and I have a pair of Colts of my own."

"You do not frighten me, sir," Danvers's man said, though by the timbre of his voice, we suspected we did.

"Tell me, Mr. Llewelyn," my partner said, turning to me. "What would be a proper place to shoot Mr. Havelock if we cannot convince him to come along quietly?"

"Between the eyes, I should think," I replied.

"You wouldn't!" Havelock protested. "I saved your horse!"

"You stole my horse," I corrected. "Then you burned my barn. Are you coming along, or shall I make you an example for your men?"

"Wait!" he cried. "I'll talk! I'll tell you everything!"

"I told you he was a clever fellow, did I not, Thomas?" the Guv rumbled.

"You did, sir, and as usual, you pegged him right," I replied. "Where shall we take him for questioning? Dew is nearby, but Scotland Yard might be better."

"Nay, Thomas," Cyrus Barker answered. "I don't want this rascal so close to the Houses of Parliament where he could escape to his master. 'H' Division it is. And I like Dew well enough. He deserves the next arrest."

"Arrest?" Havelock asked, heaving in desperation. "Arrest for what? I've done nothing wrong!"

Barker sighed. "That's what we're going to discuss at 'H' Division."

Barker went to stand in front of a large map of the East End on the wall.

"Sir," he said. "Before we leave, why did you have us thrown out of the Palace of Westminster yesterday?"

"It was a misunderstanding, sir," he replied. "Mine entirely. It wasn't until His Lordship returned from his session and I told him of your wish to see him that I realized I was in error. It was my fault, Mr. Barker. I apologize for any embarrassment it may have caused you."

"Lord Danvers did not inform you that he had hired us?" the Guv continued.

"No, sir," Havelock said, shaking his head. "I'm merely his secretary and am not privy to his personal matters. I understand he is hunting for Her Ladyship's sister, but I've never met the woman."

The Guv paced with his chin sunk upon his breast. "Tell us more about H and D Associates."

"It's a business Lord Danvers and I run together," Havelock said. "We provide flats for workers in the City. His Lordship has often admired the architecture in the area and wanted to see it restored. He then realized they could be offered to professional men for a price comparable to ones in the city. He bought the land for next to nothing. We incorporated, and he made me the head of the company, while he was the backer. The first street, George Yard, sold out immediately, so we plunged the money into purchasing properties in Osborn Street. We are now negotiating for another street nearby."

"Very clever," Barker admitted.

"Mere supply and demand," Havelock said. "We wouldn't have had this opportunity if His Lordship wasn't interested in East End architecture. You're correct; he is a clever fellow, and many of his projects do well financially. He has the Midas touch, as they say."

Barker nodded at Havelock.

"If you recall, sir," he remarked, "none of King Midas's family or associates profited from his ability. They were sacrificed to his constant need to acquire. Do you understand?"

"Yes," the young man replied.

My partner bent over him with an air of menace.

"Yes, Mr. Barker. This is all my fault. His Lordship has had no hand in the matter!"

The Guv turned and circled around the desk. He sat down, facing Havelock.

"Now, tell me about your workers. Where are they from?"

"Gdansk, sir. They are Polish."

"I know where Gdansk is. How did you acquire your crew?"

Havelock shrugged his shoulders. He was so thin and dapper, they appeared birdlike. "We hired them on the docks. They were sailors."

Cyrus Barker and I glanced at each other. It was either the truth or a plausible lie. On the one hand, we thought them mercenaries, on the other, hiring a group of brawling sailors made sense.

"They've been seen about the city doing some rough work and fighting with local gangs," I told him.

"Have they?" he asked. "I had no idea. They don't know our laws. I knew they were heavy drinkers, but I had no idea they were doing anything illegal."

"Come," the Guv said. "We must get this gentleman to 'H' Division so he can give a statement to Scotland Yard."

We ushered Havelock into Osborn Street, where I hailed a cab. Havelock climbed aboard, but my partner held me back for a moment.

"Did you notice the map on the wall inside his office?" Barker said in a low voice.

"I saw it," I replied. "It depicts the districts in the East End."

Barker nodded. "I thought so as well until I took a closer look. There are cryptic notes in pencil you can't see from three feet away."

"Cryptic in what way, sir?" I asked.

"I don't think it's a map of districts at all. More likely it's a map of the gangs of London and their territories."

CHAPTER 25

H" Division is in Commercial Road, which happens to be in Spitalfields, where this case began. It is a small constabulary in the most crime-ridden area of London. We had walked these streets during the Whitechapel enquiry. Barker refuses to call them the Ripper Murders since he suspects that the letter sent to the authorities with that infamous name was concocted by the gentlemen of the press.

"We wish to speak to Detective Constable Dew, please," Barker stated to the desk sergeant after we entered.

"Works the early morning shift, don't he?" the sergeant answered, as if only an idiot wouldn't know this.

"I see," Barker replied. "May we speak to another inspector, then? I am Cyrus Barker."

The sergeant lifted his head and studied us for a second. Then he nodded toward a bench along the wall.

"Sit," he said. "I'll let someone know."

It had been some time since we had been forced to wait, even in Scotland Yard. Finally, a slovenly and irritable man came to stand over us. I looked up at him. It was Inspector Lang, whom we had exiled here.

"Welcome to Spitalfields, Barker," he crowed. "What brings you here?"

The Guv stood. "We'd like this gentleman to be put in a cell pending arrest. He has been supervising a group of men who are involved in a number of crimes in the area."

"Oh, really?" Lang replied, turning to Havelock. "Who's your boss, Mr. Dandy? We don't generally get such well-dressed gents in this part of the city."

Havelock reached into a pocket and retrieved a visiting card. "I work for Lord Danvers, leader of the Tory Party."

Lang examined the card as if it could speak for itself, which in a way it could.

"Very impressive," he replied. "Very well, you gentlemen come with me to an interrogation room."

Lang led us through a succession of halls. I noticed him glance and nod at a constable or two along the way, which gave me an unsettled feeling. We came to a door and were led through it. Havelock was seated in the interrogation chair and Lang put down a pair of darbies for the secretary's wrists.

"Well, Mr. Havelock," he said. "That is the name on the card, innit? What have you to say for yourself?"

"I don't know what these ruffians are about," Havelock said. "They burst into my office in Osborn Street. The one with the new construction. I'm sure you've seen it."

"I have indeed. Put out your hands, Mr. Havelock, there's a good fellow."

Reluctantly, the secretary raised his hands to be cuffed. Then Lang dived across the table and landed atop Barker. I heard the studs inside the darbies ratchet up as Barker gave a roar. The door flew open, and then constables poured into the room.

"You may go, Mr. Havelock," Lang said. Lord Danvers's secretary needed no second invitation. He evaporated like a morning dew.

"As for you, my boyos," spat Lang. "Thought you could get away with escaping Scotland Yard because you know the boss, did you? Trying to make me look stupid and getting me transferred to this refuse heap."

"It's where you belong," the Guv stated.

"Shut it!" Lang bellowed. "You've damaged my reputation. I was in 'A' Division, where things happen. I could get promoted! Now here I am, back in the alleyways again."

"That's your fault, not ours," I protested.

Lang smacked me across the head. Years of practice had perfected his art. Barker yelled, and suddenly everyone leapt onto him. There were groans from my partner's attackers, as several of his kicks and elbows hit home. A couple of the men jumped on me as well. Barker had taught me how to harden the muscles in my stomach so that a punch would not hurt, but there were too many blows for that. I received two or three taps across the top of my head with truncheons, and when I fell to the floor, they began kicking anywhere they could reach. Pain bloomed everywhere at once and I tasted the metallic tang of blood in my mouth. Goodness knows what they were doing to the Guv. He wouldn't go down easily.

We were all too close together. One couldn't pull back an arm to throw a punch, or raise a foot to kick, whereas the constables seemed perfectly at home with this close fighting. They had practice. Who knows how many had been attacked this way before, and how many would come after. People were beaten into confessions, beaten into denials, beaten into recanting testimony. Enough of this treatment and witnesses would say practically anything.

It was highly illegal, and they knew it. Their uniforms concealed the fact that they were little better than the criminals they faced every day. Perhaps they had convinced themselves that this was the only way to deal with crime in the worst part of London. I don't condone it, but I could understand it. What concerned me, beyond the fact that I was being beaten like a drum, was that if it happened to me, someone not guilty of anything, how many others had received this kind of punishment to produce a confession?

"Right, lads," Lang said at last, breathing heavily. "Put 'em in the carts."

I was lifted roughly, and might have passed out, for the next I knew I was being rolled across old cobblestones in a barrow, the kind the Met uses to transport the injured and the dead. Every jolt made me flinch, every missing stone jarred the cart.

I tried to see through a swelling eye. Cyrus Barker was being rolled nearby, his limbs hanging slack around the sides of the cart. He had to be unconscious, or he'd still be fighting. Absurdly, someone had placed his pristine bowler hat neatly on his chest, as a kind of housecleaning. We rolled over a broken stone, and I hissed in pain.

"Oh, did that hurt, Mr. Private Enquiry Agent?" asked the constable wheeling the barrow. "Try this 'un!" Then he slapped the side of the cart. The movement felt like an electric jolt to my system.

We traveled for who only knew how long. My addled brain

could no longer conceive of time. A minute, an hour, they seemed rather the same in the scheme of things.

"Here we are, lads," I heard Lang remark with a degree of satisfaction. I smelled it then, a mixture of offal, fish heads, and salt. We were near the river. The barrows were rolled along the dock, jarring with every warped plank, and suddenly Barker and I were unceremoniously upended into the water. It was frigid cold, but in a way it helped. My hot, angry wounds were at least temporarily quenched. Then the cold got its hooks into my skin, and I couldn't stand it.

Barker and I were picked up by the current and carried slowly east. The water was foul, little better than a sewer. The Thames is one of the most pestilent rivers in Europe, and we were steeping in it like a biscuit in a cup of Earl Grey. How deep was the water, I wondered? I reached down a foot and my toe could not touch the bottom.

"Sir!" I called.

There was a groan from somewhere nearby.

"Mr. Barker, can you hear me?"

There was a sudden grunt. I assumed it was the only answer I was going to get. Something rose high above me, then. We were floating under Tower Bridge, which seemed a thousand feet tall over our heads.

I floated along, freezing until I could no longer feel my limbs. Was this it? Would we die here, frozen in the river, to be found in the morning? Or would the tide turn and bring us floating back to where we had begun? Neither was a savory end to our career. The Barker and Llewelyn Agency brought to this.

I'd finally seen it: Cyrus Barker bested. It took ten years and a half dozen men to do it, with us trapped in a small room, but I had seen something I hadn't thought possible.

I had believed the man impervious, implacable, impossible to best. I had relied on him completely. Any scrape he could get us out of, but you know, he's just a man. An unusual one, of course, but just a man. He could be bested, and I had just witnessed it.

What now, I wondered? Would we be found floating here like the beginning of Dickens's *Our Mutual Friend,* when Flora and her father are out looking for corpses in the Thames to rob? It wasn't the money I was concerned about, though there was almost a hundred pounds in my wallet, something the constables hadn't considered. Whoever wanted could have the money, but not my wedding band. No, I would fight tooth and nail for that. Kill, if need be. I intended to be buried in that ring. I only hoped it wasn't soon.

Abruptly, I was seized by the collar and dragged to the river's edge. Then, I was hauled up onto the bank, where I lay gasping like a flounder.

"Are you alive, lad?" Barker asked.

"Just, sir!" I answered.

He came into view leaning over me.

"Don't just lie about like that. We've got things to do, matters to settle!"

I'd been there a grand total of twenty seconds. The Guv took my arm and pulled me to my feet. Pain came with it, but then pain is part of life, and sometimes all of it.

"Keep up, Thomas!" my partner called. "We have nae got all day!"

His Scottish accent had grown stronger, as it did when he was angry. I could hear him snorting like a bull.

"Where are we, sir?" I asked.

"Whitechapel, near the curve south," he replied. "The Strand should not be far."

"We can't walk down the Strand like this!" I cried.

"We're turning back east into Whitechapel," he said. "No one cares how we look there."

"Have you got a destination, or are we going to walk about London like this until we dry?" I asked.

"I know where I'm going."

I could see it there, hear it, sense it in the air. Rage. Vengeance. Wrath. It sounded in the back of my partner's throat like bile, like the disgusting effluvia we had been forced to swallow in that Styx-like river, which I hated with all my heart and soul.

We continued in silence after that, foul water dripping from our clothing onto the pavement. My shoes were sodden. At least one of them was. The other was gone. My hose were particularly frigid. We stepped through an alley into a street full of warehouses and anonymous industrial businesses. The few pedestrians we passed did not seem especially surprised to find two adult men soaked to the bone plodding down a street. It was growing exceedingly difficult to walk, so I threw the lone shoe into a dustbin, and my hose with them.

Abruptly, Cyrus Barker stepped into a doorway, and unlocked a door. I recognized it now. It was a bolt-hole of sorts, where Barker kept a change of clothes, a sink, and a cot. I'd only been there once before. I stepped inside and found a few improvements. There was a bath, a room containing old clothing, a makeshift kitchen, and even a telephone set.

"Freshen up and change," he ordered. "I've taken the liberty of purchasing some clothing in your size from Petticoat Lane."

"Thank you, sir."

I did as he requested, and quickly, too, although the suit I chose was more likely meant for the dustbin.

"Call your wife," he said. "Have a presentable suit laid out for you. Meet back here in half an hour."

"Yes, sir," I repeated, suspecting they were the only two words he wanted to hear. I called our home, gave Rebecca the briefest of requests, and rung off. Barker watched me throughout the conversation not three feet away.

"I'm off, then," I said.

"Half an hour," he insisted. "Hold a moment."

He reached forward and tugged on my nose. It was excruciating, and I cried out in surprise.

"It was out of alignment," he stated. "As I said, half an hour. Go."

I escaped. My new shoes, new to me anyway, were overlarge, but would do for a cab journey.

Once I was in the hansom I sat back and felt low. I'd been beaten and thrown in a river full of raw sewage. Everything hurt. Each movement brought forth a new type of pain.

When I entered our house both Rebecca and our maid stepped back at my appearance. They had been warned, however, and a second bath was waiting with proper soap and bath salts.

"You've been fighting again, haven't you?" my wife called through the door.

"Of course not," I replied. "What a thought! I was beaten to a pulp by the Whitechapel police and thrown in the Thames."

"I see," she said. "And why were you beaten by the police?"

"As it turned out, they are corrupt and we had brought them the wrong man, if you know what I mean."

I heard Rebecca sigh. "I don't, but I'll take your word for it. Why must you meet Mr. Barker again so soon?"

"I didn't dare ask," I replied. "I've never seen him like this. Of course, I've seen him angry before, but this, he's like a volcano about to spew."

I dried and dressed quickly. Then I kissed Rebecca and told her I had no idea when I would return. In answer, she gave me a pain au chocolat, my favorite. No one ever had so good a wife. Who knew when I'd be able to eat a proper dinner.

In the street, I offered the cabman double the fare. When I reached the anonymous street where the Guv kept his flat, I gave the cabman money to wait, jumped from the vehicle, and ran inside, arriving without a minute to spare.

Barker was just finishing a telephone call as I entered. He was impeccably dressed, and what he had worn that morning was in the fireplace, shoes included. The room smelled of sandalwood soap.

The Guv looked a trifle less angry than before. He even smiled, although I anticipated that it would be at someone else's expense.

"Well, sir," I said, appearing more game than I felt. "What shall we do now?"

"The same thing we just did, all over again. But I'm changing the rules."

I knew better than to ask what he meant. It would only spoil the surprise.

CHAPTER 26

I don't know why I wore a plain and respectable suit, while Barker looked resplendent. The Guv adjusted his tiepin in a mirror and seemed in good spirits for a man who had just been physically and figuratively beaten. I needed a few days to lie abed before even approaching his enthusiasm.

Out in the street, we clambered aboard the hansom, the Guv gave the address in Osborn Street, and we were off.

"You're not serious," I said.

"When have I not been serious, Thomas?"

"We're actually going back to the H and D offices?"

"I said so, didn't I?" he replied. "What in my character would make you believe I would not finish what I've started?"

I wanted to tell the man he was mad. It was right there on the tip of my tongue ready to spill out with all its consequences, but I swallowed it back. This was not the time nor the place.

"Are you armed, lad?" he asked.

"Two pistols, sir," I replied. "I'm not about to be caught out this time."

We rode through the mean streets of Whitechapel. It was raining lightly, and the brick and stone buildings looked darker and drearier than they had before, if such a thing were possible. Horse dung pooled on the sides of the roads and drained into the sewers.

"Look at it," my partner said. "God gave us Paradise and we prefer to sit here in the muck."

He brooded for the rest of the short journey. He does that from time to time. He'll sit by the fire in his room and not move for two days altogether.

Barker had regained his optimism by the time we reached Havelock's offices. He jumped down and I followed more slowly, still rather sore. The office, however, was crowded. There were three men talking to Barker's quarry when we entered. One was the man I had fallen on in the alleyway. He gave us a murderous look and I pulled both pistols.

Havelock was indignant. "Damn you, you can't—"

Barker punched him once in the face. He didn't put his shoulder into it; it wasn't required. I watched as Havelock sagged onto the floor and the room went silent. My partner came around the desk, threw the fellow over his shoulder as if he weighed no more than a sack of rice, and pulled his own pistol, a Colt, ironically called a "peacemaker." Americans can be unintentionally ironic sometimes. Then he left as casually as if he'd just stepped into a tobacconist for some Arcadia mixture. I followed, walking backward, pistols aimed at the duo we had left gnashing their teeth.

We left afoot, Barker still carrying the fastidious criminal over his shoulder. A small crowd gathered as we passed. Did they think he'd been drinking? I'm sure it was commonplace here, people trying to forget their blasted existence.

"Sir, you don't really intend to walk into 'H' Division again, do you?" I asked. "It will be suicide! I don't care to be beaten and thrown into the river again."

"You should have thought of that sooner, Thomas." he said, stoically.

We approached the Spitalfields constabulary. I wasn't content with the way we had left the building and preferred not to visit it again so soon. However, there was one difference between this time and the last: we were armed. Normally carrying a weapon would be a comfort in our line of work, but here, walking into a division of the London Metropolitan Police Force, they were a hindrance. One doesn't walk into such a building armed. They take exception to it.

"Sir?" the sergeant at the desk asked with a raised brow.

"I've got a package here for Inspector Lang," the Guv said. "He left it the last time we were here. I'm Cyrus Barker, and this is my partner, Thomas Llewelyn. We'll wait here if you will let him know."

He crossed to a bench and lay Havelock down beside him like a coat. The poor fellow was fully off in dreamland, although I didn't feel sorry for him. It was his fault that we were thrown into the ghastly Thames.

Looking down the hall, I saw a constable hare it down to the inspector's office and a verbal explosion followed. A minute later Lang burst into the hall and came toward us like the express to Edinburgh. His face was purple with anger.

"Barker, I thought we'd seen the last of you," he snapped. "Back for more, are you? Seize him, men. And I see you've brought your partner with you. Excellent. So, Barker, would you like to come into the interrogation room again, or would you prefer to step outside?"

"I'm not certain," the Guv replied. "What do you think, James?"

The door to the constabulary opened and Commissioner Munro of Scotland Yard walked inside and removed his gloves.

"What's going on, Cyrus?" he asked, but I knew better. Barker must have called him on the telephone in his bolt-hole while I was gone.

"Nothing of much import," the Guv replied. "I brought this man in under suspicion of criminal activity, but I expect he and the inspector are already acquainted."

"I find that difficult to believe," Munro answered. "I thought the gentlemen at this constabulary were exemplary officers. I understand there was an altercation here an hour or so ago. Is that so, Mr. Llewelyn?"

"Yes, sir," I said, surprised to be called out without warning.

"Could you point out the men involved?"

"Yes, sir," I replied. "That one, the two there, the one in the corner. That fellow with the short beard. Are there any more, sir?"

"Aye, the big one there," Cyrus Barker replied. "He's a kidney puncher. I hate kidney punchers."

Munro nodded sagely.

"Someone toss Mr. Lang in a cell," he ordered. "I cannot abide the sight of him. I'd hang the man if I could, for bringing the name of this division and the whole of the Met into disrepute.

"As for the rest of you, this will go on your record, pending your next evaluation. You have been a disgrace to this city and to our noble profession. Where is Detective Constable Dew?"

"He works the night shift, sir," the sergeant said behind him.

"No longer. I'm making him an inspector, temporarily in charge of this station. I suspect he alone is above the taint which has infected these halls."

Munro passed along the hall, examining the men who stood about, not certain of what to do.

He reached Lang's office and stepped inside.

"Look at this," he said. "Have you ever seen such a slovenly office? You can count the rings on that corner where pint glasses have been set! The man must have been drunk here every day!

"It's what comes of having public houses near stations," Barker said.

I could count six or seven pubs between our offices and Scotland Yard, but it thought it politic not to mention it.

"Calm yourself, James," Barker said. "You know what your doctor said."

Munro sat behind Lang's desk, like a man deciding whether to purchase it.

"Mr. Llewelyn, would you be so good as to see if there is a bucket of water in this wretched hovel?"

"Yes, sir!" I said, leaving the small office. On the one hand I'd like to have heard what was being said, but on the other it felt good not to sit so close to the fire, so to speak. I asked the sergeant at the desk, and soon returned with a full bucket. Havelock now occupied the seat I had taken, but he was welcome to it. Munro dashed the contents of the bucket in his face. The young man coughed and sputtered, then looked about him. The last thing he recalled was speaking with his Polish workers. Now he was among strangers. Sober-looking strangers, at that.

"Sir," Munro said, "I am the superintendent of the Metropolitan Police. You are under arrest for fraud. I have reason to believe H and D Associates is the headquarters of a number of illegal activities. Do you have anything to say to this allegation?"

"I wish to speak to my solicitor," the young man mumbled. He was soaked to the bone and shivering. I felt no sympathy, however. It wasn't river water.

"You may, certainly," Munro stated amiably. I'd never seen him so agreeable. "What is your name again, boy?"

"Havelock, sir."

"There may be more than one of you responsible for this situation. However, someone must receive a slap on the wrist, so we'll pin the crimes on your pocket. Of course, I am not a judge, but I don't see why five years in Princetown would be unreasonable."

"Five years?" Havelock gasped, as if seeing an eternity of punishment ahead of him.

"That's if you find a sympathetic judge," Barker said, putting in his oar.

"Of course," the commissioner continued. "Let us say you pay your debt to society by the time you are forty. You'll still have plenty of years to live. Of course, you'll have to find steady work after prison, which can be difficult at that age. You'll have to learn to be economical, but I'm sure you'll acquire the skills as you go along."

Munro was looking for a knife to pry open this particular oyster. Perhaps he had found it.

"Is that the only way?" Havelock asked, beginning to look desperate.

"You could cooperate with the Yard and tell us if anyone is colluding with you. If you are aiding Her Majesty's Government, you cannot be punished."

"It's really your only choice," I added. "That is, if you wish to avoid prison."

The commissioner turned and looked at me as if he hadn't known I was in the room. However, I had something to contribute to the conversation.

"I did eight months in Oxford Prison once," I told the secretary. "It was hell. The food, the beatings, picking oakum until your fingers bled. The treadmill. I can't believe I lived through it. Then I was ruined after."

"Ruined?" Havelock asked. "Ruined in what way?"

"Who would hire you after prison?" I asked. "What woman would marry you? Who would wish to be your friend? Then there are the memories that haunt you afterward, that steal your sleep. Mate, believe me, it breaks you for any kind of normal life."

There was a long pause in the room. I found myself holding my breath. *Come on, Havelock, take my advice,* I thought.

"Very well, sir," he said at last. "I can give you the names of all the men who have been doing these crimes, as well as provide evidence. Most of our paperwork is in a safe in the office. Records, receipts of payments, that sort of thing. I keep meticulous paperwork."

"Take him to 'A' Division," Munro said to a pair of constables who had come with him. "I'll need a stenographer for his confession."

G. C. Havelock gripped the edge of the desk. "Is there another place we could go? I can see the building from the steps of the Houses of Parliament."

The commissioner nodded. "True. There should be a closed Maria nearby. I'll have an officer transport you to a southern division across the river in Surrey. You cannot be seen inside the vehicle. You should be safe there."

"Thank you, sir."

Havelock was soon placed inside the closed van and taken south to safety. Two constables were sent to seize the offices of H & D. The door suddenly burst open, and Detective Constable Dew stepped in, having arrived early for his shift. I wondered if someone had warned him about Munro.

"What in the world?" he asked.

"Good afternoon, Inspector," I said. "They say a new broom sweeps clean."

He gave me a puzzled look.

"You've earned your inspector's badge due to your excellent work and because you've stood above your colleagues," Munro said. "I have here a note from last year that you complained about several issues. All the complaints have turned out to be true. Wait for me in the hall. You have a promotion coming."

After Dew had stepped out, the commissioner turned to me.

"Mr. Llewelyn, your partner and I have Templar business to discuss. It may take some time. I suggest you go home to your wife. You have been ill-used today, much of which is my fault, I'm afraid. You look like you need some rest."

I looked at Barker and he nodded.

"Yes, sir."

I wasn't about to argue with him, and I certainly couldn't stay when secret society business was being discussed. I had promised my sainted mother that I would not mix in such questionable circles. Therefore, I found a cab and did my best to put some distance between myself and Spitalfields. Perhaps I was nervous, but I didn't feel safe exposed in the open carriage, knowing the Polish workers were still nearby. I kept a pistol in my hand all the way home, just to make myself feel safer.

"Darling!" Rebecca said, coming into the hall from the study. She kissed my cheek and I winced.

"Oh dear, I think you may have broken your nose again. It has the same look as last time. Your eyes will puff up overnight and you'll look like a ferret. Or a burglar." She gave a mischievous grin.

"You should be in the music halls," I said, grimacing in pain.

I'd attempted to remove my coat unaided. There was no telling what I had been thinking.

"You get into bed, and I will bring you some liniment," she said. "Go!"

She waved a cushion at me as if I were an insect that had wandered in an open window.

I climbed the stairs to change. Of course, everything began to ache again. Even the act of undressing made the pain increase.

"Rebecca?" I called.

She returned with a brown glass jar and unscrewed the lid. "This is from Mr. Barker."

"It smells of camphor and tea," I complained. "Probably snake spleen as well if they have spleens. I think Barker's precious Dr. Wong is some kind of sorcerer."

"He told me you'd say that, almost word for word. Now let me apply this or no dessert tonight!"

"What kind of dessert is it?" I asked.

"Gooseberry fool. If you're good, I'll let you have a second helping."

Suddenly, the telephone jangled down in the hall. I thought of not answering it but bounded down the stairs before the final ring. The Guv was already there.

"Sir?"

"He's smarter than we realized, Thomas," Barker growled. "The H and D building was on fire when we arrived. Every shred of evidence gone. And that's not the worst of it."

"Havelock?"

"The Maria never arrived. I suspect he'll be found in the river tomorrow morning. Possibly the two constables, as well."

"Should I return to the office, sir?" I asked.

Suddenly, the thought of that liniment, snake spleens and all, sounded tempting.

"No, Thomas," he replied. "There's nothing more we can do tonight. We'll let Scotland Yard do their work. I'm sure the Black Maria will be found. Did Mrs. Llewelyn use the liniment I gave her?"

"Of course she did," I replied.

"You've got a good woman there, Thomas," he replied.

"Don't I know it!"

CHAPTER 27

The following morning, there was a dull thrumming in our offices for which I could not account. Then I saw that it was the pads of Cyrus Barker's fingertips drumming on the glass sheet that covered his desk. They moved one at a time, like a pianist playing a sonata. He was trying to reconcile the events that had occurred over the last week, to see if they made sense. There was the very real chance that all the events we were dealing with were unconnected to our enquiry. That was my opinion, but then, he had not asked for it.

"Lad, type a letter for me," he said. "The good paper. I desire an interview with Mrs. Maud Kemple."

"Yes, sir," I said, trying to keep the excitement out of my voice.

He was actually doing something besides brooding. And

the good paper! I rarely had the chance to use it. It was a stiff vellum of pale cream, with the agency's name and address embossed upon it, and his name in smaller letters. I had some with my own name, but I surmised he was only being kind when he ordered it. As beautiful as it was, I'd never used it and saw no likelihood that I ever would.

I lifted my old Hammond typewriter and placed it on my desk, where it fit exactly. I crossed to his, opened a drawer, and removed a single sheet of the vellum. Then I carefully placed it in the typewriting machine and adjusted it.

It is preferable in such a situation to write the letter in longhand, but the Guv's handwriting looks as if he has some form of nervous condition. The last time we faced a similar situation we considered me writing the note for him, but we settled on this compromise.

We knew what Mrs. Kemple was. She was an adventuress. I didn't know the particulars of her life, but I could probably imagine them with some accuracy. She was separated from her husband, who had settled a certain amount upon her for long-term living expenses. She had been seen with various nobles, some married, some not, and even had an acquaintance with the Prince of Wales. There had been at least two court trials and divorces because of her, and according to Rebecca, several scandals. She had frightened most of the important women in good society at one time or another. They could not refuse her, however, because she was witty and gay, and everyone was intrigued; no party was complete that season without her. In other words, she was a societal thorn in the flesh, and the sooner some minor member of royalty from across the Channel took her away, the better. All of Belgravia would breathe a sigh of relief.

"Ready, sir," I said.

"To Mrs. Maud Kemple," he said, settling back in his

chair and looking up at the ceiling. Dull light from the window was reflected in his brass-framed black spectacles. "You have her address?"

"It's in the Kelly's Directory, sir."

"Excellent," he replied. "Let's begin. 'Dear Mrs. Kemple, Please forgive the impertinence of a perfect stranger's request to see you on such short notice. I am a private enquiry agent, and your name was mentioned in relation to an enquiry we are investigating, and I hoped you might be available to answer a question or two. The matter is of some delicacy, but I assure you this is in no way a threat to you. Lady Philippa Ashleigh of Seaford, Sussex, will vouch for my character and discretion, and I shall bring my partner, Mr. Thomas Llewelyn, along with me. I am, your humble servant, Cyrus Barker.'

"Is that satisfactory, Mr. Llewelyn?"

"A bit antique, sir," I replied. "But I think it proper in this situation."

"Do you suppose she is aware of Lady Ashleigh?"

"A woman who trades in her social circle would most certainly know of her," I replied. "I imagine she is aware of everyone of consequence, and Philippa is important."

Lady Ashleigh had been Barker's partner in life since before I met him. She and Rebecca had become friends, as well. The matter had become complicated. The Guv does not like complications in his world, and yet they keep coming, unbidden.

As for me, the last thing I wanted was to speak with Maud Kemple. A mere photograph of the woman had sparked an argument in my house. I had no desire to meet her. I even considered asking Barker to allow me to miss this interview, before I realized he had asked me because he too needed a witness, a chaperone, and a recorder. Perhaps all at once.

None of the common weapons or defenses will work on a woman.

For the briefest second, I considered not telling my wife. Then I realized I couldn't help but tell her, and if I didn't, she would probably learn about it anyway, or intuit it on her own. I could not call her and warn her. There was no option but to see it through and then confess, putting myself at the mercy of the court. I'm by no means a great prize, but a certain kind of woman enjoys sharpening her claws on me. Barker hired a commissionaire to deliver the letter and brought back an answer shortly. She would see us at three o'clock.

Mrs. Kemple's address was in Holland Park. The cabman took us right to the front door, where we were passed to the butler, who ushered us to an informal sitting room with a roaring fire and rococo furnishings. Our hostess was awaiting us, draped across an overstuffed chaise longue like a painting I'd once seen of Sarah Bernhardt.

She was not extremely beautiful, but she had a way of captivating one without being obvious about it. She didn't play the coquette because she didn't need to. Most women, seeing visitors, would jump to their feet, but Maud Kemple was not most women.

"Gentlemen, good afternoon," she said. "Mr. Barker, what a pleasure to meet you. I've heard so much about you, yet absolutely nothing of value. London society knows not what to make of you. It's as if their opinions don't matter a jot to you or your work."

Barker took the hand offered to him and bowed over it.

"Madam," he said, "they don't."

"And Mr. Llewelyn," she said, turning to me, "you are far too handsome and innocent-looking to be an enquiry agent, but I've heard about you, as well. I've had my spies collecting information since your message arrived. I must say, you put me all aflutter."

She was perhaps forty, with blond hair that to my untrained eye looked dyed. There was too much yellow about it. Her eyes were green, and her nose aquiline and aristocratic, but I suspected that, like most women of her kind, she did not come from a good family. What she had acquired in order to survive in this hateful world was due to her own wiles and initiative, and even hate. I suspected this meeting had been a rare miscalculation on Cyrus Barker's part. We had stepped into a cage with a viper unawares and our chances of emerging unscathed were small.

"Mr. Barker," she said, drawing the back of her hand along her chin seductively. "How is it that so rough and, dare I say, uncouth a fellow as you has captured the heart of so magnificent a creature as Philippa Ashleigh?"

Was that an insult or a compliment, I wondered? In either case it was a flirtation.

"I have wondered the same thing myself, madam," he replied.

"And how is it that so domestic a woman as my dear Philippa should capture so rare a beast as you?" she continued. "I've only met your like once before: it was the explorer, Sir Richard Francis Burton. You bear many of the same scars as he and have a similar aspect. One could drop you into a jungle anywhere on the globe and you would either emerge unscathed or become king of a native tribe."

"You flatter me, madam."

It was the words my partner used that conveyed his personal opinion. The kind but resourceful Miss Orme was "ma'am," a sign of respect. This woman was "madam."

"This is too delicious. I can stand it no longer," she

exclaimed. "What is it that has brought you to my door? Who is in your sights? There are so many choices."

I looked up from my notebook and decided to speak. I reached into my pocket for the carte de visite.

"A gentleman came to our offices recently, madam," I said. "He was looking for his missing sister-in-law, but either accidentally or intentionally gave us this photograph."

"I see," she said, glancing at the card before returning it. "There are hundreds of these floating about London. I am popular among a certain set. Some men want to control me, others want to possess me, if only a pasteboard version."

"Are you in the habit of giving out such favors?" the Guv asked. "Mr. Llewelyn tells me that they are available in stationery stores and newsstands for purchase."

She sat up languidly like a cat from a nap. "I do from time to time, but only to those I want to impress. Now you must tell me who has been carrying my card about and showing it to people. This is an old photograph, and I have had another portrait taken since then, although this one is still available to the public."

The two stared at each other, a battle of wills. I might as well have not been in the room. Would he answer her question, or put her off, and protect our client's identity?

"It was given to us by Sir Hugh Danvers," he revealed.

"No!" she cried, then laughed and clapped her hands. "He kept the card all this time? How precious! I slipped it to him at Lady Bramley's anniversary party three or four years ago. I assumed he had refused my offer but carrying it about so long means he must be still considering my invitation."

"Madam, you could do better than this life," Barker said. "I will not sermonize, but surely there is a man out there for you who is unattached."

"I find one from time to time," she admitted. "But they are inevitably impoverished. When I have tucked away enough in a private bank account to last the rest of my life, I shall marry a university professor and retire to Cambridge or Oxford. There I shall be a model professor's wife, and no one will ever hear of me again."

Suddenly she gasped and I stopped writing in my notebook. Then she wagged a finger at the Guv.

"You are good, Mr. Barker. I don't believe I have ever revealed my personal plan to anyone before. I believe you shamed me into it."

"Tell me," my partner asked, ignoring the remark. "Have you tucked away enough?"

She sighed and her face and shoulders fell. "Never. It always leaks away. There is a permanent hole in my proverbial pocket. I have developed an appreciation for pretty things, you see."

"Then find your professor and share your savings with him," he suggested. "They are paid for their work."

"Yes, but not enough," she confessed.

Barker cleared his throat. "We have strayed from our earlier conversation."

"Ah, yes!" she replied, her expression changing. "Sir Hugh Danvers. I assumed he was taken."

"He is taken, Mrs. Kemple," he stated firmly. "As you know, he is a married man."

"Yes, yes," she replied. "That rich American. Now there's a fellow who knows how to make wise decisions. His bank account is always full."

The door opened and a servant entered with a cart containing a full tea set. I assumed she drank wine or absinthe in the afternoons. Tea was poured and sugared and garnished with lemon, and everyone was momentarily civilized, even the roughest and most uncouth of us. We spoke for a while on polite subjects. Then Barker returned to the subject we came to discuss, and not a moment too soon. Tea with lemon is an abomination, and the sugar was not cubed. Philippa would be scandalized.

"That was your only association with Lord Danvers, then?" Barker asked. "You made an offer, and he refused it?"

Our hostess frowned and waved a finger to emphasize her point. "He did not actually refuse, and you recall he still carried my card. I consider that a small triumph at least."

"He returned to his wife."

"Yes, an heiress worth millions of dollars," she purred. "Such a difficult choice to make, sir! I feel sorry for him. He returned to his wife, and his mistress."

The Guv's dark brows slid behind his spectacles in a frown. "He had a mistress, Mrs. Kemple? Who was she? Perhaps I am speaking to the wrong woman."

"There is always a first time," Maud Kemple answered. "I don't know her name. He told a rival of mine, but she refused to reveal the woman's identity to me, just to tweak my nose. Aren't we horrid? Hugh marries a nice girl, and the rest of us circle about like sharks because of his new money. It's how we think, you see. Surely, he could not refuse me something so trivial as a diamond bracelet. Alas, it went to another woman. What bad luck!"

I wondered whether he was going to lecture her on her behavior, or on the existence or nonexistence of luck as a concept. It was a toss-up.

"Did your rival know the mistress's name, and was she certain, or was she just 'tweaking your nose'?"

"Oh, she knew," Maud Kemple replied. "I have no doubt of that."

"Would you be willing to reveal the woman's name?"

"I could, but it won't be of much use to you. She has given up the life, married, and started to work as an actress. You know, *Macbeth* and *She Stoops to Conquer.*"

Cyrus Barker had no idea what she was suggesting, but I knew just whom she was speaking about. Rebecca and I saw the second play together.

"Would she speak to us on the matter?" the Guv asked.

"No, I'm afraid she found a husband and moved to California to raise horses and make wine. But you seem a canny fellow, Mr. Barker. I suspect you know of whom we speak."

"No, madam."

I looked up from my notebook. "I do."

Barker stood and bowed and gave all the pleasantries a man can give to such a woman without finding himself in jeopardy. I nodded to her and left, having asked Maud Kemple only the one question, aware I would be answering questions myself from Rebecca that evening.

"I know who her friend was," I said when we were back on the street. "It was Lillie Langtry. But who was Lord Danvers's mistress?"

Barker gave me a superior look, the master explaining to the lowly, dull-witted student.

"That should be obvious," he said. "It was his sister-in-law, May Evans."

CHAPTER 28

I tried to digest the information that the Guv had given me, but having difficulty doing so. Cyrus Barker stood at a corner, looking about like a tourist, but I knew he was deciding where to go next. Without a word, he began walking and I followed behind. At the first opportunity, he plunged into the Underground and a few minutes later, we were rattling along in the bowels of London.

"Which was she, this May Evans?" I demanded, over the din of the car. "Was she having a dalliance with her own brother-in-law, or trying to escape with Lord Dunbarton?"

"Possibly both, Thomas," he replied. "With millions of pounds at stake, and one naïve girl standing in his way, Danvers understood he must secure either her cooperation or her silence, whether it was consensual or not."

"Are you saying he assaulted her?" I asked, appalled.

"That is a complicated question," he admitted. "She might have been confused and fancied herself in love with him. He may have convinced her that he was in love with her, as well, and they must escape together. You see why I avoid such enquiries, lad? The waters grow murky almost immediately. There is even the possibility that she seduced Lord Danvers herself and is not the innocent we believe her to be. If that is the case, she is most definitely not at the bottom of the Tiber."

"I find it hard to believe she seduced her brother-in-law," I argued, as the train sped down the dark tunnel. "It's too far-fetched."

"Is it?" he asked. "Lady Jane had everything: a title, a handsome husband, a mansion. Miss May was living at the mercy of her sister. She was supposed to be attracting a husband of her own. Perhaps she found one under her very roof."

"Wait!" I said, putting out my hand. "Are you saying the trousseau might have been meant for her and Danvers?"

"It is possible."

"Why would she attempt to go off with Lord Dunbarton, then?" I asked.

"Subterfuge, perhaps," the Guv stated.

I shook my head. "I'm getting a headache. Are you saying it was May's plan to seduce her brother-in-law, or his plan to seduce her?"

"It's possible they were in love with each other but did not want to tell Her Ladyship," he rumbled. "It is even possible Lady Jane killed her sister to save her marriage. Do you see? We are left trying to decide who loved whom, and how much. It is absurd, and imponderable. Perhaps even they did not know their own motives."

I glanced about and realized that an old lady on the bench behind us was trying to eavesdrop. In our profession, we often had interesting conversations.

"Where is she, then?" I persisted, lowering my voice. "Has she really drowned herself in Rome? Or is she there, angry that her lover did not follow after her? Did Lady Danvers find out their plans before he left, and convince His Lordship to stay? And if so, did she do it out of love, or did she fear a scandal? So many possibilities!"

"You have put it most succinctly," the Guv stated.

"Can we eliminate any of them?" I asked.

"We can, Thomas, but only by theorizing."

"Very well," I replied. "Lord Dunbarton confirmed that the two of them intended to run off together. If he were a part of this, one would have assumed he'd have tried to harm Danvers, not May. If Danvers planned to marry his sister-in-law, they would never be able to return to any civilized country, since bigamy is illegal. But if he had decided to go that far, why not simply ask his wife for a divorce, to marry her sister? It would destroy his career, of course, and cause an immense scandal, but some are willing to go through it, I suppose. One cannot help whom one loves."

"Of course one can," my partner said. "But let us remove romance from this equation. Danvers does not appear the sort of fellow who falls in love at the drop of a hat. If he seduced his sister-in-law, it was for a good reason. Getting hold of a second dowry seems a more likely inducement."

"It isn't a matter of passion, then," I remarked. "It's down to pounds and shillings."

"Most likely," he agreed.

"Then where is the woman?"

"Have you not worked that out?" he asked, one brow rising above his dark spectacles. "Dutch is May Evans. Now we have proven the photograph was Maud Kemple, it is the logical conclusion."

"No," I exclaimed. "I won't believe it."

"There's one motivation we haven't considered."

"Which is?" I demanded.

"Spite," Cyrus Barker replied. "Lord Danvers is punishing May for attempting to run off with Dunbarton. I suspect if you were to ask Lady Danvers, she will recall that her sister can make birdcalls."

"Surely not," I answered, shaking my head. "The idea is absurd."

"Let us test the theory, then. Where did Scotland Yard say they took her?"

I thought for a moment, then pulled out my notebook and thumbed through it.

"They didn't say," I informed him.

"Blast!" my partner growled. "The lass has slipped off again! She could be anywhere."

"If your theory is correct," I began. "Dunbarton has been pining for her, convinced she's either in Rome or has killed herself, while she could have crawled along in front of his charity this very morning."

The Guv nodded. "Dunbarton has kept her trousseau as a shrine, in the hope that she will return someday. It is certainly evidence that he cares for her."

"I wonder how he will feel when he finds her in her present condition," I remarked. "I cannot see the two of them standing at the altar together."

"This will be a test of his character, then," he stated.

"I think the fact that he opened a charity for wayward men is a sign of that," I said, aware that character is very important to Cyrus Barker. "Unless you suspect he has ulterior motives, as well."

"He seemed genuine enough," my partner answered. "And there is a need for such an institution. Many wealthy families send their troubled sons off to other countries as remittance men. There is no one to show them the path back to a life of self-respect and honor. If there is anyone in this case whom I suspect of having proper motives it is he. It would have been so much easier for Lord Dunbarton to return to his errant ways."

"May Evans will refuse to see him," I remarked. "She's ashamed of her condition, and she's already proven she's very proud."

We reached Mile End, the last place we had seen Dutch, hoping against hope she would still be there. When the train stopped, we alighted from the Underground and walked quickly toward the mission. We went straight to the office and found Miss Orme, Miss Lawrence, and Brigadier Booth talking over a matter.

"Gentlemen," Booth said as we entered the room. "How may we help you today?"

"We are looking for Dutch, sir," the Guv replied. "In fact, we are very much hoping that she has made her way back to you."

"Miss Dutch?" Miss Lawrence replied. "No, sir, I'm afraid we haven't seen her in a few days."

"We need to locate her as quickly as possible," the Guv continued. "Do you have any idea where she might be?"

"She could be anywhere in the East End," Miss Orme said. "I doubt very much that she would be able to make her way to any other part of London."

"Could you pass the word along that we are trying to find her?" Cyrus Barker asked.

"Of course," said Miss Orme. "But it may be difficult if she doesn't wish to be found."

"It's worth a try," he replied. "Thank you for your cooperation."

"What now, sir?" I asked as we left the mission. "Scouring the district again, I presume?"

"I'm afraid we have no choice, lad."

My partner and I walked the streets of Whitechapel for an hour with no success. We had gone to all of the places we had previously seen her, but May Evans was nowhere to be found. Barker decided we should return to our chambers and plan our next move. We made our way by omnibus to Liverpool Street station, and then by Underground to Charing Cross. Finally, we were in Craig's Court again.

"Welcome back, sirs," Jeremy Jenkins said as we entered, lifting his salver. "A message arrived while you were gone."

Barker lifted the soiled scrap of paper, which was torn from the margin of an old newspaper. He read it once and then handed it to me.

"'I give up,'" I read. "'It's too hard. Fetter Lane.'"

I looked up at the Guv in astonishment.

"Look at the handwriting," he said. "It was written by a cultured hand."

"So, it is May Evans," I replied.

"She wouldn't surrender unless she was in desperate straits," my partner remarked. "Come, Thomas."

Fetter Lane was but a ten-minute ride by hansom cab. We found her in an alley, leaning against a brick wall and wrapped in a blanket. Barker lifted her as easily as if she weighed no more than a child, and I retrieved her teapot from where it lay on the ground. She said nary a word. We took her to the mission, where the nurse and Miss Orme took charge. They took her to the infirmary and found her a change of clothing before arranging for a meal for the half-starved young woman.

"I'm sending for a doctor," Barker told Miss Orme when we reached the office again. "That limb must be seen at to once."

CHAPTER 29

Early the next morning, Cyrus Barker and I stood on the platform in Camberley again. I saw little reason for returning, expecting the same refusal at the door to Danvers's estate. Still, it was a beautiful morning, with a brilliant sun after another night's frost. Every tree, building, and bush wore a crisp mantle of white. Barker seemed inclined to sit in his own thoughts, so I left him to it.

The town was still waking when we arrived, though there were few people on the platform. It was Saturday, and the shops both here and in London would not open for a few more hours. My partner wore a long, black coat with a burgundy scarf and leather gloves. I wished I'd brought a sturdier coat.

"Why are we here again, sir?" I asked, trying not to make

it sound like a complaint. "It won't do any good. We won't get past the gargoyle at the front door."

"I spoke to Lady Ashleigh late last night and asked her impression of Jane Danvers. They only met once, but she said the young woman seemed spirited and vivacious. Did Her Ladyship strike you as being spirited and vivacious when she came into our chambers?"

"No," I admitted. "She certainly did not. She looked sickly and pale, even subdued."

"Aye," Barker said, nodding. "Philippa could not account for it. She mentioned that in the past, Lady Danvers enjoyed going out in society to balls, concerts, and events, but she hasn't been out all year. When a young woman with millions of pounds starts to become sickly, I begin to worry."

"What are you suggesting?" I asked.

"I'm suggesting I'd like to speak to her myself," he replied.

I shook my head. "We were not permitted to see her the last time we were here."

"We won't be stopped this time."

I soon realized the Guv wasn't walking toward Danvers's estate, he was heading somewhere else. He asked directions, and we made our way to the town constabulary. It, too, was nearly deserted. We were fortunate that morning that the district inspector of police for much of Surrey was in residence, yawning over his morning tea. He was perhaps sixty, with a white mustache and a competent air. Barker gave him his card, which the man read over while sitting behind the desk.

"I'm Superintendent Whitfield," he said, gesturing for us to take a seat. "What brings you to Camberley, Mr. Barker?"

"A mystery I'm trying to solve," my partner answered, removing his hat. "A domestic one, as it happens. A week ago, Lord and Lady Danvers arrived at our offices in Whitehall, asking us to look into the disappearance of Her Ladyship's sister, Miss May Evans. Are you familiar with the matter?"

"I am," the superintendent replied. "I investigated the case myself."

"Excellent," the Guv said. "Has the matter been concluded?"

"It has, insomuch as the family is convinced that she ran away to Rome," the superintendent replied. "They think that she was going to meet a lover, perhaps, although the most likely candidate remained in London."

Barker nodded. "Alan Dunbarton? We questioned him regarding the matter."

"Is there any new information about the case?" Whitfield asked.

"There may be," my partner said. "I need to speak to Her Ladyship about her sister."

"May Evans was last seen on the platform by the stationmaster," Whitfield replied, leaning back in his chair. "The staff notices when young and pretty heiresses are in the area. It's a way for the porters to earn a bob or two. What precisely brings you here today?"

Barker leaned forward in his seat. "Mr. Llewelyn and I visited Danvers's estate earlier this week to speak to Lady Jane about the case. We knocked on the front door and were met by a butler, large, muscular, and with a thick beard. Do you recall what the butler looked like during your investigation?"

"Nothing like that," the superintendent replied, tapping a pencil on his blotter. "He was a middling-looking fellow, growing bald. A stiff breeze could knock him over. This one must be new. What happened?"

"We introduced ourselves, and the man closed the door in our faces without a word."

The inspector gave a short laugh. "Yes, nobles are known for that."

"Aye, but I came with pertinent information about the case, and specific questions for Her Ladyship," Barker stated. "She had come to London specifically to hire me. That is, her husband hired me on her behalf. Have you seen her lately?"

The superintendent shook his head. "No, but I've heard she was unwell. Some say consumption, others scarlet fever. What exactly do you want from her, Mr. Barker?"

I liked this fellow. He was assertive yet relaxed and seemed to know what he was about. He represented in my mind the best example of a career sheriff in England. Barker came to the quick of it without fuss.

"To be truthful, sir, I believe we've found May Evans living in London as a beggar," my partner stated. "She is in a bad way. We need Her Ladyship to make an identification of the woman as soon as possible. However, Mr. Llewelyn and I have been barred from the house without explanation. I hoped you might help me gain access to Lady Danvers, so I could ask a question or two, and provide her with the information I have uncovered so far. She is paying for our services and deserves a report. If the enquiry is done, we have other cases awaiting us in London. If this beggar woman is not her sister, she's not to be found. It's possible she has done away with herself as His Lordship fears."

"The thought had occurred to me," Whitfield admitted. "The general opinion of her was that the young lady was a bit fragile. His Lordship had to keep an eye on her. Would you like me to come with you and help you speak to Lady Jane personally?"

"Aye, and to get past that Cerberus of theirs."

"Before I do, I'll require some proof of what you say. I'm

not going to vouch for you to the landed gentry with no more than your say-so."

Barker nodded and reached into the breast pocket of his coat. He placed an envelope on the desk and pushed it his way. Whitfield's eyes narrowed. Was it some kind of bribe? He opened the envelope and took out a letter. It was written on heavy paper, and even the sound of it being unfolded had the weight of authority in it. The superintendent read, nodding as he did so.

"Well," he said. "If the commissioner of Scotland Yard agrees with you, there's no reason for me to question it. It appears that your royal warrant is genuine, although I never heard of a detective receiving one."

"It is rare, sir," Barker admitted.

"Did you go to Rome?" Whitfield asked, handing back the letter.

"There was nothing there except her luggage."

It wasn't an actual answer to the question. The Guv is good at that. He does not like to give a bald-faced lie, but he'll let someone draw their own erroneous conclusions.

We took our leave of the constabulary and followed Superintendent Whitfield up the road.

"This is a beautiful town," Barker said, for the man's benefit. "Far enough from London, but not too far."

"Yes, it's a beautiful country hereabout," Whitfield replied, nodding. "There's the estate up ahead. I hope we can clear this matter up without any conflict."

"Indeed, sir," Cyrus Barker answered.

When we reached Danvers's estate, the Guv seized the knocker on one of the double doors and pounded it twice. There was an awkward silence as we waited. I found myself wanting to fiddle with my tie or reach for my revolver. Finally, one of the doors was opened by the same rude man as before.

"Sir?" he asked, acid dripping from the word.

"We wish to speak to Lady Danvers," Barker informed him.

The butler frowned. "As I told you the last time, she is not receiving visitors."

"I'm not a visitor," the Guv rumbled in his gruff voice. "I am working for her. She hired me to find her sister."

"First I've heard of it," he said. He was an ugly brute with bad skin, a broad nose, and little piggy eyes. "Off with you, or I'll call the constabulary or worse! And take your rascally friends with you."

"I am the superintendent of police, my good man," Whitfield stated, stepping forward. "Choose your words carefully."

"I don't care if you're the Queen of Sheba," the butler replied, shrugging. "This is private property."

Whitfield drew his foot up and caught the man in the lower abdomen. The fellow fell in the doorway, moaning in pain.

We entered a wide hall and searched through drawing rooms, lounges, and libraries. Not a soul was to be found. It was as if the house had been closed for the season.

"Let us look upstairs," the Guv said.

It was in the eighth room that I found Lady Danvers. The door was not locked. I supposed security had grown lax when no one came to the door anymore. The Guv and Whitfield were at my heels, but before we could speak, a nurse came into the room, holding a medicine bottle. Barker reached out, snatching it from her fingers. Then he unstopped it, holding it to his nose.

"Just as I suspected," he cried. "Arsenic!"

The woman cried out in terror and ran out of the room. We could hear her clambering down the stairs.

"She won't go far," Whitfield remarked, glancing at the bottle in Barker's hands. "By the way, you do know arsenic has no smell."

"I know that, and you know that, sir, but she did not," my partner replied. "I'll wager she suspected the tonic she has been giving Her Ladyship was poisoned, but she convinced herself it wasn't until I said the word."

"Poor Lady Danvers," I said, looking at the figure in the bed before us. Her skin was pale and waxen, her cheeks hollow. Even a week earlier, she had seemed more robust and healthier.

Just then, the door burst open, and the butler stumbled inside, armed with a shotgun. Superintendent Whitfield did not hesitate. He pulled a regulation police pistol from his pocket and shot the man in the chest. A red bloom appeared on the white expanse of his shirtfront, and the fellow clutched at it, falling to the carpet. He coughed once and rolled over onto his side. Slowly, he exhaled and went still. The Guv bent over the body, but it was clear that it was too late.

"Is there a doctor nearby?" Barker asked.

"I can find one," Whitfield stated. "Let me look for a telephone set."

I went down the stairs with the superintendent and helped him find a telephone set. When I returned to Her Ladyship's room, Cyrus Barker was grasping Jane Danvers's wrist for a pulse. It woke her, something the gunshot had not done.

"Who are you?" she murmured.

"It is Mr. Barker, ma'am."

She looked confused for a moment, having only met us once before. Then it came to her.

"Did you find May?" she asked faintly.

"I think I have, Lady Danvers," he replied. "But like you she is ill and must recover. You will be reunited with her soon."

"Thank you, Mr. Barker," she said, barely able to keep her eyes open. "I'm so terribly tired."

"You've been drugged, Your Ladyship, but we'll put you to rights. Rest, now."

We heard Whitfield on the stairs, and he returned to Lady Danvers's room.

"A doctor is on his way," he stated. "How is Her Ladyship?"

"We need to remove her from this house as soon as possible," Barker replied. "Her husband has endangered her life."

The superintendent gave him a skeptical look. "Gentlemen, I'm not sure whether His Lordship can be kept in the dark about his own wife's whereabouts."

"He's the one who imprisoned her here," I remarked. "He's responsible for the condition she's in now."

"We plan to take her to the Mile End Mission in London where her sister is receiving care," the Guv stated. "Lady Danvers is the only person who can vouch for her identity."

"My word, what a day," Whitfield replied, looking at the body on the floor. "To be truthful, I wasn't sure this old service revolver would still shoot. I thought it might blow up in my face. I've never shot anyone in the performance of my duties, let alone killed someone."

"Let us move the body into the next room," the Guv said. "Then we need to find out if anyone else is lurking about the premises."

There was a cook downstairs, preparing lunch for her mistress, apparently unaware of what had happened, or even that Lady Danvers had been in danger. She was startled when we came into the kitchen.

"Forgive the interruption, ma'am," Barker said. "We are private enquiry agents employed by Lady Danvers, and this is Police Superintendent Whitfield. How long have the new members of staff been employed by His Lordship?"

The woman was stout and phlegmatic, a typical English

cook in an apron. She had been making a cottage pie and paused to think about her answer.

"Less than a month ago, sir," she replied, frowning. "That fellow is a beast. Always snapping at me and stealing food from the kitchen. Not like our usual butler, Chalmers. One day he said something innocent to His Lordship and he sacked him on the spot. Two days later this oaf arrives on the stoop, him and Nurse Peabody."

"What's she like?" Whitfield asked.

"Keeps herself to herself, which is always a good policy."

"Ma'am, I don't mean to alarm you, but events have just occurred of a deadly nature," Barker said. "Perhaps you should sit down."

She took hold of a stool and sat, staring at us.

"The butler tried to stop us from seeing Lady Danvers," the superintendent said. "I'm afraid he's been shot."

The woman gasped.

"I heard a shot," she said. "But I thought it came from outside. I assumed it was a hunter."

"Go home," Superintendent Whitfield told her. "There isn't anyone to cook for today. These gentlemen are taking Lady Danvers to London for her safety."

"Now what shall we do?" the Guv asked after the woman had gathered her things and left the house. "Her Ladyship is unable to walk."

"I saw a bath chair in one of the rooms, sir," I said. "Perhaps we can get Lady Danvers to the station in it."

"Good lad," the Guv replied. "Let's do it."

Three quarters of an hour later, we carefully loaded a half-conscious patient into a first-class compartment bound for London with the help of two porters. Whitfield put out a hand to the Guv, and then to me.

"I wish I could accompany you, Mr. Barker," he said. "But I've got a body to deal with. Not to mention that when you reach the river, my jurisdiction is at an end."

"Alas, sir, it is," my partner replied. "However, my home is open to you. Perhaps you can come to dinner soon. We can discuss enquiries if you like, and you can see my garden."

"I will, sir."

As the train slowly steamed out of Camberley station, I glanced at Lady Danvers, who was in a fitful sleep.

"Imagine," I murmured. "Five million American dollars. Danvers could do anything he wanted with money like that."

"Ten million," Barker countered. "You're forgetting May Evans's share."

"Good heavens," I replied. "He could buy the prime ministership!"

Cyrus Barker took a lungful of air. "There is no limit on what a man might do if the motivation is strong enough. Can you manage here?"

"Of course, sir."

"Then I'm off to the smoking car," he replied. "I need to think."

CHAPTER 30

Lady Danvers awoke when we were halfway to London. She lifted her head and looked at the ceiling and around the compartment before her gaze finally lit upon me.

"Where are we?" she asked, trying to sit up. "You're Mr. Llewelyn, aren't you?"

"That's right, Lady Danvers," I replied. "We left Camberley and are now headed to London."

She trembled in her seat. "Where is that dreadful nurse?"

"She has fled and shall harm you no longer."

"And that monster who guards the door?" she asked.

"Shot dead, I'm afraid," I admitted.

Her Ladyship stared out the window at the passing countryside, and I wondered if she had heard me. I was certain she had been drugged as well as poisoned.

"Good," she said finally.

"When was the last time you spoke to your husband?" I asked.

"I don't know," she replied. "Days, perhaps. I've lost count."

"Your Ladyship," I said, standing. "Let me call for Mr. Barker. He'll want to speak to you."

I stepped out and waved to a guard, giving him Cyrus Barker's name. Then I closed the door to our compartment and sat down across from Jane Danvers again. The Guv joined us momentarily. She was sitting up and looking more lucid as the minutes went by.

"Where are you taking me when we get to London?" she asked, a frightened look in her eye. "Tell me you're not working for Hugh."

"Lady Danvers, I work for you, and no one else," Cyrus Barker assured her. "As to where we are going, there is a shelter for women in the East End of London. I am taking you there, where no one will think of looking for you. Your sister is already there, under their care."

"May!" she cried. "You found her!"

"She has been through an ordeal, as you have," my partner explained. "You'll find her much changed."

The woman leaned forward. "Is she all right? I promised my father I'd look after her. I haven't done very well, have I?"

"She's under a doctor's care," Barker assured her. "I made certain Miss Evans is getting proper medical treatment to help her recover."

"Hugh has done us both great harm," she replied.

"Your Ladyship, can you tell me the circumstances as you recall them, please?" Barker asked, crossing his arms over his broad chest.

"I worked out his plans," she said, grasping the arms of the chair fiercely. "May had created a will, leaving her money to me. If both of us were to die, he would inherit a fortune.

I began to realize he is a wicked man, but I had no idea of the depths to which he would go. Father loved his title and Hugh's plans for our future, but they were just honeyed words, and I fell for them just as he did. I was a fool!"

"Ye weren't to know the truth, ma'am," my partner replied. "He concealed his intentions well."

"They were going to kill me, you know," Lady Jane stated. "Hugh even had a doctor willing to forge a death certificate, a respectable surgeon. He can buy practically anyone and anything. And with my money! I'm going to divorce him and get back every penny he has stolen from us."

She sat silently for a moment. The only sound to be heard was the lullaby of the wheels running rhythmically along the rails.

"You know, don't you, Mr. Barker?" she murmured. "That he turned his attentions to my sister?"

"Aye, we'd worked that out."

"He called her Dutch."

"Short for Duchess," the Guv replied.

"It was his pet name for her," she continued. "He told her he no longer loved me, that she had captured his heart. But she refused to betray me, so he decided to punish her."

"Why didn't you tell us when you met us?" Barker asked.

"I only found out the truth when I was confined to my room," she replied. "He couldn't resist the opportunity to gloat while I was still alive."

"Lady Jane, has your husband confessed any of his other plans to you?"

She nodded vigorously. "He said that he shall take control of all London. That's it. All London. I don't know what he meant."

"He's made a good start, as a matter of fact," the Guv replied. "He's being considered as the head of Scotland Yard, and there's a chance of him even becoming prime minister. The man has been very busy. We're going to stop him, Lady Danvers."

"You know, sir, I very much suspect that you will. Pull him down, Mr. Barker. Tear down the noble edifice that is my husband. It is rotten at the core."

After we reached London, we took a hansom cab to the mission. When we arrived, we found it locked as tight as a fortress. The usual two women in the familiar matron uniforms of brown and white stood behind the gate. The Guv and I looked at each other.

"I am Cyrus Barker," he said to the woman in charge. "I am here with Lady Jane Danvers. Her sister is Miss May Evans, who is in the infirmary. We need to speak to her at once."

She nodded and unlocked the gate. The two of them helped Her Ladyship inside. The Guv and I followed as the gate swung closed behind us. We were led to the infirmary where May Evans lay in a crisp white bed, the only patient in the room. Jane Danvers ran to her sister and took her in her arms as Barker and I waited by the door. After a few minutes of whispered conversation, Lady Jane took a seat next to her sister and invited us to join them.

Dutch had undergone a transformation since we had seen her last. Her blond hair was now curling about her head and her rough skin was healing. However, her expression was grave.

"They are taking my leg tomorrow, Mr. Barker," she stated quietly. "There is no hope for it, I'm afraid. Hugh and his men threw me down a long set of steps in Whitechapel, leaving me a cripple, because I dared try to escape from him."

Lady Jane began to cry.

"We were mere trophies to him, Mr. Barker," Her Ladyship said, her arms around her sister. "He tried to seduce her and I was so unsuspecting, she left rather than tell me about it."

"I was ashamed, Mr. Barker," May Evans said. "I hoped if I was gone, he would repent of his actions."

"We would have identified you sooner if His Lordship had not given us a photograph of another woman entirely," my partner stated. "We would still be uninformed if Mr. Llewelyn's wife had not recognized the young woman's image. It appears she is a society beauty with a questionable reputation."

"Another conquest of my husband's, I presume," Lady Jane stated.

Barker turned to May Evans. "How long were you aware of what sort of man he was?"

"I had no idea of Hugh's intentions for some time," she replied. "It was only by chance I saw his reflection in a mirror one day, revealing his hidden feelings. I faced him the next morning in the drawing room, expecting an apology. Instead, he attacked me there in broad daylight. I had no idea a man could be so brutal."

"How did you escape?" I asked.

"I stayed in my room until the bruises healed. Our butler, Chalmers, sent a message for me to Alan Dunbarton. Then early one morning I slipped out and went to the train station to meet him in London. We had planned to run away together. Hugh overtook me along with some of his men."

"You see, Mr. Barker," Her Ladyship remarked. "We'd been raised out in the West where men might be brutal, but not devious. May was afraid to tell me something was wrong, but even if she had I would not have believed her. In fact, I'd have thought the worst of her. So, she did the only sensible thing, deciding to escape."

"What of Alan Dunbarton now?" I asked. "We could let him know where to find you."

"No!" May cried, shaking her head furiously. "He's forgotten about me. In any case, he would find me repellent."

"But Mr. Dunbarton went after you," I said. "He scoured Rome for you. He even found your trunk, which I suspect Lord Danvers sent along to cover your trail."

"How do you know?" she exclaimed, her eyes widening. "Did you speak to him?"

"We did, ma'am," I replied. "His office is not far from here. He's even aware of this mission. We can bring him to you if you wish."

"Heavens, no!" she cried. "I am hideous, and I'm going to lose a limb tomorrow. I never want to see him again."

"As you wish," Barker said, bowing. "You ladies have a great deal to talk about. Mr. Llewelyn and I will leave you to have some time to yourselves."

The Guv and I made our way to the mission's office. There Barker removed his bowler hat and bowed as the two women rose from their seats to shake our hands.

"Miss Orme, Miss Lawrence," the Guv said. "We have brought Lady Jane Danvers to see her sister, May Evans."

"Come inside, gentlemen," Eliza Orme murmured. "I need a word with you, please."

"Of course," Barker replied.

"We are expecting an attack on the mission tonight," Raina Lawrence said, handing us a scribbled note on a piece of soiled paper. It read: *Ben says they comin tonite six. Nan.*

Barker examined the note. "This woman, Nan, I presume has stayed at the shelter before? She was told that a group of men are coming tonight to attack the mission?"

"That's how we have interpreted it," Miss Orme stated. "Nan Hardy comes here when her husband has beaten her after a drinking bout. It's happened four or five times. They always reconcile. She isn't strong enough to leave him, and she has no family to help her. She has sent notes, however, with information about other victims. Ben Hardy is a member of a local gang. He hasn't worked out that when he brags about his work, she informs us, and we tell the local police if necessary. He believes she is illiterate, and that he is merely unlucky."

My partner frowned. "Do you believe the attack is due to Miss Evans being brought back here again?"

"We don't know," she replied. "And neither do we know if we will be facing one man or several. Not long ago, we had a group of them holding placards and protesting the unlawful detainment of their wives. But I still don't understand. Why was May Evans taken before? And what reason would anyone have for pursuing her and her sister now?"

The Guv cleared his throat. "Miss Orme, we were hired by Lady Danvers to find May Evans. Their lives are under threat by her husband. Our duty is to keep them safe, and by extension, secure the safety of everyone here at the mission."

"What should we do?" she asked.

"I am an old soldier," he replied. "I fought in the Taiping Rebellion. I know military tactics, and I happen to be armed."

"No guns, Mr. Barker," she protested. "I insist. This needs to be as bloodless as possible."

Sympathy was what they wanted. Sympathy and donations. Legitimacy, too, if it wasn't asking too much. The women who ran the mission had a different agenda from the Barker and Llewelyn Agency. We were fighting to defend Lady Jane and her sister. Miss Orme and Miss Lawrence were standing for those who couldn't stand up for themselves and in the process were proving their right to be in the community.

"In that case, may I avail myself of your telephone set?" the Guv asked.

She nodded and both women stood. "Certainly. We will give you some privacy."

"Is Sarah Fletcher here?"

"She's in the gymnasium," Miss Lawrence replied.

The Guv turned to me. "Would you have a word with her, Mr. Llewelyn?"

"Of course," I said, leaving him to his telephone call.

Approaching the door of the oldest structure in the compound, I tried to decide whether to walk in or knock on the door. It would probably be wiser to knock, I decided. It was answered after a moment by Miss Fletcher herself. She gave me the slightly annoyed look she always gave me when we met.

"Mr. Llewelyn," she said coldly.

"Miss Fletcher."

"How may I help you?"

"Mr. Barker sent me," I said. There were two dozen women standing about in groups. "What, pray, are you doing?"

"I am guarding these women," she said, taking me aside. "This is the most fortified building in the compound. As soon as Miss Orme received a note, she had us come here for everyone's safety. Is Mr. Barker with you?"

I nodded. "He is, and we've seen the note Miss Orme received."

"Do you have any idea who is coming to attack us, or how many of them there will be?" she asked.

"We are convinced that Lord Danvers is sending the men

himself," I explained. "I've seen a dozen or so of his gang members, but I suspect there may be more."

"What about Scotland Yard?" she asked.

"Mr. Barker is calling for support."

"I hope they arrive soon," Sarah Fletcher said.

"As do I. However, I do not believe these women could be in better hands."

It was a compliment I hadn't realized I would make. She looked at me warily, but I meant it. She was fearless. There wasn't a woman in London I thought more capable of defending them.

"Thank you," she said, giving me a slight smile, although I knew we would still have more work to do to mend the rift between us. I thought it was worth the effort.

I returned to the office to see the Guv, but he was still on the telephone set. I would have thought his time would be better spent putting up barricades. Barker hung the receiver, and I stepped forward.

"Who have you been calling?" I asked.

He grunted. "Anyone who will listen. It is a difficult sell. There aren't many willing to come to the East End in the middle of the night."

I leaned forward. "What about Ho's crew, the Blue Dragon Triad?"

"This is not their fight, and they don't involve themselves in domestic problems."

"Blast," I muttered. "Then who's coming?"

"Possibly no one," he answered. "There may be a few who will arrive belatedly, but I won't know until the time comes."

"This could be a bloodbath," I said. It was the sort of situation we had hoped to avoid, a confrontation in Brother Andrew's peaceful compound.

I stepped outside and studied the property. It had natural defenses. The walls were twelve feet tall or more and made of planed logs. The gates were made of sturdy iron. However, the chains on the gates were flimsy and needed to be replaced. I wondered if the Guv had called for the police, but it was possible that even they did not believe that women should leave their husbands.

"I'm going to speak to Miss Fletcher," the Guv said.

He stood and left the building while I went to the front gate, where Bridget and Bertha were standing sentinel.

"Any sign of trouble?" I asked.

"We haven't seen anyone," she replied. "It's strangely quiet."

It was growing dark quickly and people in London were going home to their tea. As six o'clock approached, I felt a sense of unease. Barker came up beside me to wait.

"I think I hear something!" Bertha whispered a few minutes later.

We went up to the gate, craning our necks. There was a phalanx of men carrying torches heading in our direction.

"Blast," I muttered.

"'Tis a ruse, Thomas," the Guv said in my ear. "When they get closer, I believe you'll find that many of them are carrying two torches. Also, some are merely following to watch the excitement, and have no intention of getting involved in an altercation."

We watched as they came closer, and there he was, Lord Hugh Danvers himself leading the procession, his torch raised high. It was the last thing we expected. One could feel the tension in the air.

"This is staged, sir," I murmured. "Staged for effect, like a play."

"Casting him as the protagonist, and us as the villains," Barker rumbled. "If he wants a fight, I'll give him one."

The men in the street rushed to the gate and began calling for blood.

"Mr. Barker," Lord Danvers called, "stand back. We are taking charge of this mission."

"No," the Guv thundered, standing firm. "We are protecting these women from you and your criminal mob."

"Release them, I say! I know my wife and sister-in-law are inside. You have no business locking them up here!" Lord Hugh Danvers took the iron bars in his fists and gave them a mighty shake. "Open this gate!"

Cyrus Barker shook his head. "I'll fight you to the last man."

Danvers's face grew livid. Suddenly, the door of the gymnasium flew open, and the women came rushing out. I turned to the Guv in shock as Danvers's men converged on the gate and began shaking the bars.

"Here we go," I muttered.

CHAPTER 31

B arker, you swine!" Danvers exclaimed through the gate. "I demand that you bring out my wife and sister-in-law immediately before I call the police!"

I wondered how he knew we had brought Lady Jane to the mission, but the fellow seemed to have spies everywhere.

"Let us be clear," Cyrus Barker rumbled. "Would this be the woman whom you imprisoned in your own house, or the woman that you asked me to find, that you tried to send me to Italy for, when you had her under your very nose in the East End the whole time?"

"That is my business, not yours," Danvers said curtly. "It was a mistake to hire you. Release them and we won't trouble you any further, you have my word. Otherwise, we'll come through this gate and take them ourselves."

"You have no business here," my partner spat. "You and your men need to leave at once."

"Don't push me, Barker, or you'll regret it!" His Lordship thundered.

Barker shook his head. "You seduced a woman worth millions of pounds despite the fact that you had already married her wealthy sister. If anyone is a swine, Danvers, it is you. That is more money than the whole of the Mile End will see in their lifetimes. Wasn't your wife's dowry enough for you? Did you have to spoil another young woman's life?"

"We're going in!" Danvers yelled, signaling to his men. "Don't try to stop us!"

One of the foreign laborers came forward with a saw. The Guv and I retreated a few paces. The chain gave away so easily I could not believe it had held during any previous assault. The gate was flung open with a loud squeal of protest, and the gang rushed in. I counted at least sixteen men, possibly twenty. I knew they were battle-hardened soldiers, recruited to control the criminals in the East End.

"What's this?" Danvers demanded, once he and his men were inside the compound. "Women? We are facing a handful of incompetent females?"

Behind us, the inhabitants of the missions stood, daring the men to come forward. Then they parted and two women stepped toward us slowly, Lady Danvers and Miss Orme, their faces illuminated by the men's torches. Danvers looked taken aback.

"Jane!" he cried. "Come with me at once. You're not well. You should be at home in bed!"

"To drink the poison you've been giving me?" she replied. "Thank you, no. I have something to give you."

Miss Orme placed an envelope in Lord Danvers's hand. Impatiently, he tore it open.

"What is this?" he asked.

"It is a petition of divorcement, Your Lordship," she stated. "You are now cut off from your wife's fortune. And here is a second legal document from your sister-in-law, denying you access to any of her funds as well."

"Hugh," a voice came from the darkness behind me, and a bath chair was pushed forward, with May Evans sitting in it. "You have some nerve showing up here."

Behind him the gates slowly closed. I saw Bridget on one side and Bertha on the other. The latter was carrying a much heavier chain. They wrapped it around the gate again and locked it.

"Is this intended as some sort of joke?" Danvers asked. Suddenly, he seized his wife's wrist and pulled her into his grasp. He took a pistol from his pocket and lifted it to her temple. "Open that gate, or I will kill her."

As if in answer, something flew out of the darkness and struck the man beside him, a stone from a catapult Miss Fletcher held in her hand. The man clasped a hand to his head and slumped to the ground, bleeding but not unconscious.

Suddenly, everything broke into pandemonium. Lights flashed in our eyes, smoke drifted across the mission, and there were explosions behind the front gate. I tensed, but then I realized it was photographers from the London newspapers recording the sight of the Tory leader holding a pistol to his wife's head. Reporters strained against the gate, taking down every word.

"It would be in your best interests to put down your weapon and stop threatening your wife," Cyrus Barker said. "I believe you have put her through quite enough."

Danvers clutched Lady Jane tighter. Although she was

weak, she managed to reach up and scratch his cheek. He stepped back, making a strangled sound in his throat, which the men with him interpreted as a call to attack. They sprung forward like dogs of war. The women scattered, running toward the back of the buildings. I could not blame them. Magnesium smoke filled the air, clogging my throat as I surged forward, nearly blinded by the flashes.

One of Danvers's men tried to punch me, but I batted his fist away and smacked him in the jaw with my elbow. When he stepped back, clutching his face, I swept one leg out from under him.

Barker bellowed and caught a man up, using him as a battering ram, and then tossed him into the communal well near the front gate. His cries echoed as he fell. Before I could react, someone punched me in the chin. After ten years in class with Barker, fighting back had become second nature. When a man seized me, I jammed a heel into his chest.

Taking a second to glance around, I saw a photographer on the other side of the gate take a photograph holding the camera by its storklike legs. I pushed my way through the crowd and looked about. Suddenly, I noticed strangers advancing behind us, pitching into the battle. Where had they come from? The mission gate had been sealed.

"Who are you?" I demanded of one who came near me.

"C.I.D.," he replied. "Plainclothes Division."

"Poole's men?" I asked.

"Yes, he's around here somewhere," he answered as he fended off a blow.

"How did you get in?" I asked, putting one of Danvers's men in a headlock. "The gate is chained."

"There's a back entrance," he replied.

We clashed with some of Danvers's men, and I lost sight of him. I spied Poole, however, engaged with an opponent.

I seized the man he was fighting by the arms, and Poole punched him several times in the stomach until he fell.

"Ta, Thomas," he called out. "Where's Lord Danvers?"

"He was holding his wife, the last I saw him."

I looked through the crowd until I spied Lord Hugh Danvers being put in darbies by Detective Constable Dew, who had arrived on the scene. Munro had put him in charge of the Whitechapel division, and this was the perfect opportunity for its resurrection. Dew looked embarrassed by the need for the press, with the latter straining to get the best photographs. They hadn't had such a thrilling story in years.

The remaining men of Danvers's crew were still being batted about. By now they wished they'd never come to England. I ran to the rear of the mission, hoping to find Lady Jane and her sister. Instead, I ran into Sarah Fletcher, who had been punched in the eye.

"Are you all right?" I asked.

"Never better," she replied. "I have fought for the Cause!"

"You held your own," I told her. "Barker will be proud."

Sarah grinned.

"You should get something on that eye," I told her. "I think things are all but over now."

The gate had been opened and I found Barker lifting an injured man into the back of an ambulance bound for the London Hospital. Terence Poole left for Scotland Yard with his creel full, and we were in the stage the Yard calls "mopping up." There was bound to be a criminal or two still lurking in the bushes.

"Oy!" called one of the reporters, walking toward the Guv. "You're Cyrus Barker, aren't you?"

"Aye," my partner answered, "but the trouble is over now. You are free to go."

"Wait!" he cried. "What was Lord Hugh Danvers's interest in coming here tonight?"

"We have no comment," I replied.

"Come on, a fellow's got to earn a living."

We turned and went inside the mission. We could not remark upon what this would do to the House of Lords and possible upcoming elections. We were just average blokes, workingmen, who by chance read all the newspapers front to back every day, who just happened to know a number of important people, and get ourselves into a scrape now and then because, frankly, no one else would bother. That was fine with us. We like what we do. I hadn't always, but now I wouldn't trade it for anything.

CHAPTER 32

When I awoke the next morning, I was slow to get out of bed, stiff and sore from the fight the night before.

"Does it hurt for long?" Rebecca asked, throwing open the curtains.

"Only for a few hours," I replied. "I've had much worse. Do you think Lily has prepared breakfast yet?"

"I believe so," she answered. Just then, the baby cried, and we looked at each other. "I'll go. You can check on breakfast."

I went downstairs. Lily is a fine young woman, and a competent maid, but under no circumstances would one call her a cook. There was a plate of fresh buns on the table. I dared lift one. It was as heavy as a stone and burnt along one edge. Goodness knew what was in it. Suet pudding, perhaps. I pocketed one, then poured myself a cup of coffee and returned upstairs.

"It's indigestible," I complained.

"You say that every morning," Rebecca said, balancing Rachel on her hip.

"I mean it every morning."

She smiled. "Why don't you go see what Etienne is serving?"

"I think I will."

I shaved and dressed and found a cab within half an hour. It was just six. I gave the cabman the address in Newington, then sat back in the hansom and closed my eyes. A quarter hour later I opened the door at No. 3 Lion Street and removed my bowler. Suddenly I was surrounded by the most marvelous aroma. My stomach constricted to the size of a peach pit, and I went into the dining room. There were eggs and bacon, sausages, white and black puddings, beans, mushrooms, fried tomatoes, and toast, an English breakfast with all the trimmings.

Etienne Dummolard, Barker's chef, handed me a cup of steaming coffee as I entered the kitchen.

"What's the occasion?" I asked.

"*Mon capitaine* thought everyone deserved a proper breakfast after last night," he replied, a French cigarette jammed between his teeth.

Etienne had been a galley cook aboard Barker's ship the *Osprey* during their exploits in China. They had come to England together with Ho. He'd gone on to open one of the best restaurants in London, Le Toison d'Or, but he still began most mornings in Barker's kitchen.

"I want you to see this," I said, handing him the offending bun.

He examined it as if with a magnifying glass.

"You pay this woman to make this?" he asked. "Are you mad?"

I sat, just as the Guv entered.

"Ah, lad," he said. "Exercise is canceled for today. I thought a small banquet was in order. I hope you haven't eaten already?"

I heard the thump of the bun striking the bottom of the kitchen scrap bin.

"No, sir. Thank you."

"How are you feeling?" he asked, as we filled our plates.

"Well enough, sir," I replied. "I cannot wait to see the newspapers this morning."

"The enquiry is not over completely," the Guv said. "Terry called me not an hour ago and said Lord Danvers has posted bail. He's due to be released shortly."

"Blast," I said around a mouthful of bacon. "I thought he'd spend more than one night in a cell. There's no chance he'll do a bunk, is there?"

"There would be if the Yard wasn't watching him closely," my partner answered. "Let us say they are not kindly disposed toward His Lordship."

I cut a sausage neatly with my fork, the steam rising as I did so. "Excellent. What will happen to him?"

"I have no idea," the Guv replied. "I'm as anxious to read the morning editions as you. I considered smuggling in a copy of *The Times,* but you know it would crush Jeremy's spirit."

After the meal, we struggled to our feet. I felt something swish between my boots. It was Harm, spinning in circles about the house, hoping for a bit of sausage or bacon. I slipped him a few bites. Afterward, he would spend the rest of the day on his back, sleeping off the feast.

Before we hailed a cab, Mac handed me a small hamper.

"Something for Jeremy," he said.

When we arrived in Craig's Court, I placed the hamper on Jenkins's desk. Our clerk lifted the lid and inhaled the nirvana that is Etienne's cooking.

Then a second feast began, the feast of information. The office was awash in newspapers and journals, and these were merely the early editions. The images on the front pages were the largest I had ever seen, and those that used engravings must have had their artists up all night making etchings. Each had their own sensational image: Danvers holding a pistol to his wife's head; Lady Danvers and Miss Orme handing the divorce request to His Lordship; the brawl at the mission. The topper, however, was Hugh Danvers in darbies, being led off by the fledgling Inspector Dew.

"What a sensation!" Jenkins cried. "It's a mosaic; each newspaper has information the other does not!"

Barker nodded. "There is enough here to fill part of a bound journal, and it's still early days yet."

Detective Chief Inspector Poole wandered into our office at that moment and snatched a sausage from Jenkins's hamper. After downing it in two bites, he helped himself to a cigar from the box on Barker's desk. He bit the end of the cigar, spat it into the waste can, and lit the cigar with a flourish. Then he reclined in the visitor's chair, looking content.

"I never much cared for Hugh Danvers's politics," he said, settling his boot over his knee. "It was a pleasure to see him clapped in irons. There's nothing worse than a politician who believes his fortune gives him the right to do as he pleases."

"Agreed," Barker rumbled.

"He's gone to his club," Poole stated. "I have officers there to keep an eye on him. We don't want him to leave for the Continent and have the one night he spent in a cell be all the punishment he receives."

"He was far too close to taking the reins of the country in one form or another," Barker remarked.

"He was nearly my boss," Poole replied.

"What brings you here, Terence?" the Guv asked. "Besides to eat my sausages and smoke my Dunhills?"

"To get out of the Yard for a moment," the C.I.D. man admitted. "But also, to tell you that the Old Man is leaving for India this afternoon and wants to see you before he leaves. His train departs at two thirty-five."

"Thank you," the Guv replied. "We shall be there to see him off."

"I wish he wasn't going," Poole remarked. "But the Yard is regulated so that one man cannot remain in power for too long. I know you and Munro did not get along during the Whitechapel Murders, but you seem to have patched things up since then."

Barker glanced my way. Not being a member of the Templars, Poole didn't know the two had been sharing the duties as co-leaders, although he would never hear it from us. We keep many secrets at the Barker and Llewelyn Agency.

"Who were the men who were arrested last night?" I asked, guiding the conversation to a safer topic.

"They were a group of immigrants without proper papers," Poole answered, tapping his cigar against the ashtray. "I assume they worked for Danvers, but their story is that they were just walking down the street and happened to wander in. In a pig's eye! They'll be deported."

Just then, a messenger boy ran into our offices with a note for Barker. I flipped him a sixpence for his trouble, and he dashed out again. Jenkins brought the scrap of paper into the office on the silver salver. He does enjoy his little ceremonies. Poole puffed on his cigar and watched the smoke encircling his head.

"You're barmy, all of you," he commented, as Barker read the note.

"May Evans is having her limb removed this morning," the Guv said somberly, folding the note. "I think we should be there, Thomas. We'll see Munro before he leaves this afternoon. Thank you for the information, Terence. We should be going. Stay and finish your cigar."

"No, I'll take it with me," our friend replied. "Most of the cigars in Scotland Yard smell like burnt rope."

CHAPTER 33

When we stepped into the London Hospital a half hour later, we found a red-faced and distraught Alan Dunbarton pacing the halls, nervous as a cat. When we arrived, he rushed up to us and seized Barker by the lapels, an exercise I would not recommend to anyone.

"You should have told me, sir!" he cried. "Merciful heavens, she was only a few streets away from my office. Why did you not tell me?"

"It was Miss Evans's decision whether or not to inform you," Barker replied. "Have they begun the surgery?"

"A short while ago," Dunbarton said. "Still, it feels like hours. Come, her sister is here!"

He led us to a waiting room where Lady Jane was seated in the middle of a row of chairs. She looked stronger than she had the night before, but still as pale as death.

"Good morning, Your Ladyship," Barker said, always remembering the social graces. "How is your sister this morning?"

"She began running a fever last night," Lady Jane replied. "The doctor suspects it is blood poisoning. There was no help for the limb. In fact, she's in a grave condition, but we won't give up praying and hoping. This is a vigil. Some of the women from the mission are in the chapel with Brigadier Booth."

"Booth is here?" I asked.

"Yes," she answered. "He came immediately."

We were a motley group, clustered in the small room: a Salvation Army general, a reformed rake, two private enquiry agents, an American heiress, and a female barrister, for Miss Orme had arrived, leaving Reina Lawrence to direct the repairs at the mission. We were soon joined by Sarah Fletcher and Rebecca, who brought flowers. We did not have much of a chance to chat, however. We filled much of the lobby, as we waited for news.

The brigadier apologized for the events of the night before, as if they were his doing. I was in the last seat at the end of the row, listening to the three or four conversations that were occurring around me when Barker came and sat next to me.

"Have you heard anything new about Vic?" I asked.

"He's still at the priory," the Guv answered. "He's due to be released within a week."

"We should visit him again."

Just then, a doctor came into the waiting hall to see us, and everyone stood to hear the news.

"I am Doctor Treves," the man said. "The surgery went as well as can be expected. She'll require a long convalescence, including time to grow accustomed to a wooden limb. We anticipate that one day she will be able to walk without a cane. At the moment, she is heavily sedated, of course."

"When can she be moved?" Lady Danvers asked. "I've taken some rooms at the Savoy for us, and will arrange for a private physician to look after her."

"She shouldn't be moved for at least two weeks, I'm afraid," Treves replied. "You can give me the name of her doctor and we shall discuss the arrangements."

"Can she receive visitors?" Dunbarton asked, breathlessly.

"Not today," said the doctor, shaking his head. "Perhaps not even tomorrow, I'm afraid."

"That's all right," the aristocrat answered. "I'll wait as long as necessary."

Barker dug into his pocket and retrieved his turnip watch, before glancing at me. It was time to be off. Like a shark, he must constantly move. Across the room, Rebecca was speaking animatedly with Miss Orme. I waved at her and then followed Barker out of the hospital.

At two fifteen, we arrived at St. Pancras station and waited on the platform for James Munro to arrive. When he reached the train, he joined us, and the conversation turned immediately to Hugh Danvers.

"The man had practically everything," I said. "He was good-looking, titled, well educated. He held a high position, and married a beautiful heiress, but still, it wasn't enough. There was something he couldn't have, so of course he wanted it."

"You've put it in a nutshell, Mr. Llewelyn," Munro said.

"Thank you, Commissioner."

"Commissioner no longer as of twenty minutes ago."

"Who holds the position now?" the Guv asked.

"I have nothing more to do with it," Munro replied. "The sword of Damocles hangs over other heads, not mine. My successor hasn't been decided yet, but I am free. Tomorrow

I'll be on the express to Istanbul, and none of this will even matter."

Barker nodded. "India will be quite the change for you."

"I'm sorry to leave everything up in the air so that you must catch it, but the leadership of the Templars is still undecided. There will be a meeting next week to vote on the outcome. Your time would be best spent there tonight."

"I've been sent down in disgrace, if you recall," the Guv replied.

"I have un-disgraced you," Munro said. "Power has its privileges. I'm not saying you may assume the leadership position again, but at least you can steer the nomination toward someone you can trust."

"Thank you, James," my partner said, shaking Munro's hand. "I shall. Like you, I am exhilarated by the freedom."

Munro shook my hand as well, then climbed aboard the express to Dover. We watched it steam out of the station. When we stepped out into Euston Road again, we looked up in wonder. The first snowfall of the season had begun. We watched it from the station canopy all the way to Whitehall. London is uncommonly beautiful in the snow.

Returning to his desk, Cyrus Barker lowered himself into the recesses of his green leather wingback chair and turned his attention to the latest editions of the newspapers. Some attempted to support Lord Danvers, in particular, those associated with his political party, while others painted him as the worst of blackguards. It was a scandal, and there is nothing a Londoner enjoys more than a good scandal, if one is not caught up in it.

"I see Mrs. Kemple may be involved in another divorce," I noted.

Barker shrugged his broad shoulders. The case was over,

and we had read the relevant information. Jenkins would paste articles into his scrapbooks. The entire matter ceased to be of interest to him.

"Hugh Danvers is still ensconced at the Junior Carlton Club," I remarked.

"I seem to recall there was a suicide there six months ago," he rumbled. "Lord Cummings was implicated in an embezzlement scheme and was disgraced."

The Guv and I looked at each other.

"Why do I have the feeling this may all end badly?" I asked.

CHAPTER 34

We were at the mercy of Mr. Bell's telephone service, and I was growing weary of it. We were men of derring-do. Enquiry work by telephone wire offended me. If this were a sign of things to come, Barker would sit about all day, sending and receiving telephone calls until he grew sleek and fat in that large chair of his. He wouldn't leave our chambers except to eat long lunches, get a haircut and shave, and hang about Astley's, deciding on a new meerschaum pipe.

My partner hung the telephone receiver on the hook and put the stalk down on his desk. He frowned and crossed his arms before settling back in his chair.

"What has happened now?" I asked.

"Lord Danvers is still sequestered in a private room in the

Junior Carlton Club. Terry is there now awaiting developments."

I spun my chair and looked at the Guv. "What do you think will happen, sir?"

"Most men in his situation write a confession. After all, this would be the time for reflection and to explain one's actions."

An hour later we were still waiting for word.

"This is maddening," I said. "I've run out of things to do."

"Read the newspaper Jeremy brought you or go to a bookstall."

Normally I'd take him up on such an offer, it being given so sparingly, but I was too agitated. I would pace, but I don't have my partner's gravitas.

"Should we be at the Junior Carlton ourselves?" I asked.

"I am not a member of the Junior Carlton Club, and I will not crowd that noble institution, nor would I circle about like a vulture. Reporters and the police are aware of where Danvers is, and want to be in at the kill, if that is not a distasteful analogy."

"It is, but I see your point."

"We don't know what will happen," he said firmly. "We must sit and wait."

"It's easy for you," I replied. "I have a hard wooden chair on casters."

Barker tented his fingers on his desk. "Perhaps when this matter is finished you will purchase a new chair for yourself."

"Perhaps I shall."

The dratted telephone jangled. Barker cradled it in his hand a split second later.

"Terry?" he barked into the receiver. I could hear Poole's disembodied voice on the other end of the line. "You cannot be serious! Blast! Do you know where he went?"

He slammed the receiver so hard he broke the hook. I jumped to my feet just before he did.

"The man's escaped," he growled. "He bribed one of the waiters to change clothes with him and slipped out below-stairs."

He seized his coat and ran out the door, so I did the same.

"Where do you think he went?" I asked, trying to get my arm in a sleeve.

"To Camberley, though I'm not certain how he'll get there, especially in this weather."

"Back to Victoria station, then?"

"And not a second to spare!"

We found a hansom cab which took us to the station, where we bought our tickets. We took seats in the return suburban run. In the compartment I saw the latest edition of *The Illustrated Police News*. It had a corking engraving made from a photograph of Danvers brandishing a pistol.

The express ate up the miles to Camberley, although it was not fast enough for us. I was impatient. It was growing dark by the time we reached the old town. We alighted from the train and ran from the small station toward the Danvers estate. However, slush was getting into the cuffs of my trousers, and traction was difficult.

From the gate we couldn't see any lights from the house, but then it should be empty with the owners in London and the staff having fled. It was a gamble to come all this way. Danvers could be anywhere. Barker outpaced me, but we soon reached the house. There were footprints in the snow in front of the entrance. We looked in windows, jiggled all the doorknobs, but could not get in. Even the skeleton key did not work. Barker stood in the back garden, arms akimbo, staring up at the windows in frustration.

"We tried, sir," I said. There was nothing else to say.

Then I became aware of a thrumming sound coming from the stable, like a growling bear. Barker and I ran toward it, and just as we arrived the doors burst open, knocking us both back. Something with goggling eyes as bright as the moon flew past. We stood and looked at the apparition.

"A horseless carriage!" Barker exclaimed.

"That, sir, is a Racine Victoria Motorette!" I cried. "I never thought I'd see one in person!"

"Stop!" the Guv bellowed at the retreating motorcar.

Hugh Danvers glanced back at us through his goggles but kept going. The Motorette wasn't moving very quickly, but the advertisements in the newspapers said that it could run for an hour without stopping. There were railway lamps at the back of the contraption, and we chased after them as they receded in the distance.

"Stop, sir, at once!" Barker cried again.

Danvers ignored the Guv's shouts.

"Nothing for it, lad," Cyrus Barker said, pulling out his pistol. It spat bullets ahead of us, and a second later I pulled out mine, as well. This thing, this sleek new creature birthed in faraway Wisconsin, ran on petrol and pneumatic tires.

"The wheels, sir!" I yelled. "Aim for the wheels!"

We fired our pistols until they were empty. I stomped in frustration. Then the Guv produced a second revolver. Though the vehicle was barely visible in the darkness, Barker pointed his Colt at the spindly tires and pulled the trigger.

The automobile drove off the road and descended a hill, heading straight for an enormous oak. We watched in shock as it increased in speed, and without stopping, ran into the tree. A fireball ignited everything. We stood for several minutes, watching it burn in the velvet blackness.

"There's nothing we can do here, lad," Barker finally said.

We made our way toward the village, through the trees,

until we found a lively pub. We went inside and ordered a pint to steady our nerves. Then we stepped out the door with our drinks and watched the distant blaze with the rest of the patrons, one of whom was Superintendent Whitfield. We explained the circumstances and the man shook his head.

"I'm surprised he came back here," Whitfield remarked.

"We were trying to stop him," the Guv stated. "We wanted to return him to the authorities in London to face the consequences of his actions."

"It appears that he has," the superintendent replied. "He knew very well you were pursuing him, and he refused to stop. But how do we know that the tire didn't blow out on its own while he was driving?"

We solemnly shook hands and caught the final express to London, which arrived around eight thirty in the evening. There's a feeling of great lethargy after events like this, I have experienced. I nodded wordlessly to Barker, and we each found a hansom cab. I was feeling stunned. In Camomile Street, I struggled from the cab.

Inside, Rachel was in Rebecca's lap, examining her tiny stockinged feet.

"Thomas, you're home!" my wife exclaimed.

"Thank goodness," I said. "It's been a very long day."

She stood and came over to kiss me on the cheek.

"We have a new pie in the larder," she stated. "Mac brought it when he came by this morning. It's apple chess."

"Apple chess," I repeated, exhaustion taking over. They were merely words, which had no meaning to me.

She put the baby in my arms. It amazes me that a baby can feel so heavy at times, and light as a feather at others. My daughter was making sounds, little noises that one day would be words. At the sound, the dog came up and nuzzled against her side. I reached out a hand and patted her.

It occurred to me then what a misery I had been. Here I was in a beautiful home, far nicer than I had ever imagined. I had a wonderful wife, and even now I wake up and ask myself what I've done to deserve her. After years of wanting a child, here was a miracle in my very arms. I had no right to complain when others had so little.

I'd struggled after I left prison, before I was hired by Cyrus Barker. If things had been different, I could have ended my days like the members of the Dawn Gang. Instead, I was blessed beyond measure. Just then, the dog looked up at me and wagged her wiry tail. She was as glad to be there as I.

"She's a love, isn't she, Thomas?" my wife murmured. "And she loves Rachel."

"What will we call her?" I asked. "Just bear in mind that if you name her, we must keep her. Let's consider the matter."

"Come, Thomas," Rebecca said. "I'll pour some milk and cut a slice of that pie for you."

CHAPTER 35

I'd never been inside the Savoy before. Posh doesn't begin to describe it. It stands between the Strand and the Thames, where John of Gaunt had built a palace in thirteen-something-or-other. More recently, Richard D'Oyly Carte, the famous impresario, purchased the land to build a theater for the Messieurs Gilbert and Sullivan, and then decided to build a luxury hotel instead. Of course, it wasn't just a luxury hotel. It was *the* luxury hotel.

We had been summoned to see Lady Jane Danvers and her sister, May Evans. One could not imagine how Miss Evans must have felt to be in such a place. She had been starving in the East End for half a year, crawling through the muck, and now she was recovering from surgery in a place that made Buckingham Palace look tatty.

We were shown to the rooms by a porter who looked as if

he suspected we would nick the silver. Perhaps he was right. A souvenir would not have gone amiss, just to prove I'd been there. As for Cyrus Barker, one place is like another. He'd have been just as happy in the muck if an enquiry were involved.

A maid met us at the door, and we were shown into an opulent suite. Lady Danvers was there, dressed in black. Her face was filled out nicely and there was color to it. She smiled when we entered and shook our hands.

"Mr. Barker, Mr. Llewelyn, you've been most forbearing," she said. "The two of you must have begun to feel we'd skipped off without paying you."

Barker chuckled, something he almost never does. Lady Jane crossed to a bureau, took out a bankbook, and wrote a cheque then and there. No one had ever discussed an amount. She ripped the check from the book and folded it, handing it to me. I put it in my pocket unread. That was that, as far as I was concerned. Once a payment is received, the enquiry is closed.

We were shown into a second room as luxurious as the first. May Evans was sitting in a chair by the window. I could not believe the change that had come over her in so short a time. We knew that she had been fitted with a prosthetic limb, but one would never know it by looking at her. Any sign of Dutch, the crawler, had been eradicated.

"Miss Evans," Barker said, approaching her to take her hand. "You are looking well."

"Thank you, sir," she replied. She gestured to the cane in her hand. "I'm beginning to take a few steps now."

The Guv smiled. "That's excellent news, Miss Evans."

Her manner still betrayed the suffering she had undergone for many months, both physical and emotional. Danvers had proved the vilest of men, and I could not believe how agreeable he had appeared to us all. One suspects that a man's sins will be evident on his countenance like Oscar Wilde's Dorian Gray, but sometimes they aren't. It's as simple as that.

"Mr. Barker," May Evans said. "I owe you many apologies for the things I said to you. I believed you to be an adversary who could endanger my sister's life. Hugh warned me he had no compunction about killing Jane if you got too close, if in any way I took you into my confidence or revealed my identity. He was afraid of you because of your reputation."

My partner nodded. "I'll admit he fooled me for a time. Not because he was so clever, but because he used Her Ladyship as a distraction, presenting himself as so preoccupied he couldn't be concerned with your disappearance. I should have known better. There were so many elements to his plan, I did not suspect he could possibly succeed, but he very nearly did."

"You are too modest, sir," Miss Evans said. It was still novel to hear her speak like an American. "You were very close, a bloodhound sniffing at my heels."

"How did this all begin?" Cyrus Barker asked.

She would not look her sister in the eye, and only glanced the Guv's way now and then.

"Hugh ingratiated himself with me almost from the very first," she replied at last. "I assumed it was due to his courting my sister. He wanted me to think well of him and we became fast friends."

"I was rather jealous, I confess," Lady Jane said. "I thought it possible that, had my husband met May first, he might have courted her instead."

"I thought he was just being friendly," May stated. "And I had no idea of his plans for some time. I was a fool. He played upon my vanity. I should have realized that, but I wasn't used to the guile of such men."

"What happened after you realized his intentions?" my partner prompted.

"He tried to seduce me, Mr. Barker," she replied. "I'm sorry, Jane. I must speak plainly. One night he went to pass me in the hall, and the next I knew I was in his arms. He was telling me how much he loved me, that marrying my sister was a mistake. I didn't know how I felt about him precisely, but I kept silent while he pursued me, though Jane was often in the next room. Too soon I began to fancy myself in love with him. Then I met Alan Dunbarton at a ball, and he was very sweet. A bit of a rascal, but also naïve in his own way. Looking back now, I see his life was also in danger from that very first night."

The Guv cleared his throat. "When did you and Lord Dunbarton decide to go to Italy?"

"I soon realized that I never wanted Hugh and that I wanted to marry Alan," she said. "Hugh found out about it and tried to paint him in the worst light, telling me that he was a libertine from a degenerate family that was after my fortune. All the things, in fact, that Hugh was himself."

Here Miss Evans stopped, and dared look at her sister. Her cheeks colored. Jane gave her a wan smile, and a nod of encouragement.

"And then?" Barker asked, with a certain delicacy.

May leaned forward, recalling the incidents that damaged her so. "The next day I went into Camberley to speak to a friend."

"Henrietta Styles," I spoke up. It was my sole addition to the conversation. I was scrawling notes in Pitman's shorthand.

"Yes!" Miss Evans said, turning to me as if I had done a magic trick.

"Continue," Barker said.

"I was with her when a boy came into her shop with a message for me. It was from Alan, asking me to meet him in a nearby tearoom. I slipped out the back door of Henrietta's shop and went there immediately. I was shown to the kitchen where Alan revealed that he had been trying to see me for days, but that Hugh had hired men to beat him. He proposed in that kitchen, and I accepted. It wasn't the most romantic of spots, but we had little time."

I could tell Miss Evans was reliving the events in her mind, unburdening herself to the point that she was nearly gasping. For a moment I thought she might cry, but she rallied. She was made of sterner stuff. Suffering had molded her.

"We agreed to meet in London the next morning and travel on to Italy to be married. Then Henrietta put together my trousseau."

"But you were being watched," Barker stated.

"I was!" she answered. "Hugh appeared on the platform with several men, who carried me to the train by force. I called out for the stationmaster, but he was unaccountably absent."

"Imagine that," I muttered.

"They took me to London, where they put me into a cab bound for the East End. Hugh had been almost silent during the entire ride, but after dragging me from the cab to the river he began to shout at me. He knew about my secret engagement and would do anything to stop my escape."

"Horrible man!" Lady Danvers said between gritted teeth.

"He wanted me to sign a document giving over my dowry to him."

Cyrus Barker nodded. "Which you refused to do."

"Yes," she answered. "Then he said that if I didn't sign my money over to him, or if told anyone about this, he'd have Jane murdered."

"But again, you refused," the Guv said.

"I did," she said, nodding.

"And he threw you down the stairs."

"Yes," she replied, looking down at her limbs.

"Oh, May," her sister said, "how much you have suffered because of me."

"He left me there to consider my choices, and had someone follow me, to make sure I wouldn't tell anyone. He refused to take me to a doctor. That was six months ago. I was moved from one area to another, if it seemed like someone was going to help me. I was starving, and fell ill, but received no help whatsoever."

"Tragic," Barker murmured.

"Life is brutal on the street, gentlemen," she said. "I was dressed in rags, filthy from the grime of the street, and left alone to starve. Desperate for food after several days, I recalled something from my childhood. Jane and I had a bachelor uncle when we were young who taught me how to make birdcalls. I began making them on street corners and earned just enough to feed myself. I met an old woman then, who taught me how to survive on the streets in the East End. She helped me purchase my kettle."

"You became a crawler, miss," the Guv said. "And all because you would not sign over your fortune to him."

"Yes, Mr. Barker," she said. "I swore to myself I would never do that."

Barker turned to Lady Danvers. "Meanwhile, ma'am, you tried to convince your husband to find your beloved sister."

Her Ladyship nodded. "She hadn't left a note and didn't send a telegram. I waited day after day. I pushed Hugh for months to hire someone to go after her. He said he had hired men to look into the matter."

"And then, Lady Jane, you began to feel ill and weak."

"I did, sir," she answered. "I thought it was a slight fever.

I never suspected I was being deliberately poisoned. It's hard to imagine anyone could be that cruel."

"Did you ever suspect he knew where your sister was?" I asked.

She looked down, then extracted a handkerchief from her pocket. My partner looked apprehensive, but she only patted her nose with it.

"No, sir, but he was apathetic when I begged him to hire a detective to find May, saying his man would find her. Finally, he relented, and we visited Scotland Yard. An inspector named Lang promised to look but after a few months, found nothing. I begged Hugh again, and so he took us to your door."

"Indeed."

"He did not strike me as a bad husband, that is, until the end," she said. "He did not beat me. He was civil, even kind at times. My only regret was in marrying him before I learned how ambitious he was. How could he poison his own wife? He swore he loved me. He followed me about like a puppy when we were courting. And by the end, he was dosing me with poison and torturing my sister! What sort of man does that?"

"A disturbed one," Barker replied.

Her Ladyship sighed. "I will never forget what he did to you, May. He grew up an aristocrat from an impoverished line. You know what they are like; we've met our share at parties since we arrived. The wealthier families give them short shrift. It warped him, I think."

Miss Evans shook her head. "No, Jane. If you had seen the glee with which he seized my arm and threw me down those dockside steps. He could have told one of his men to do it, but no, he wanted to do it himself. He enjoyed the triumph, Mr. Barker, and the exaltation caused by destroying my life. I hope his soul languishes at the lowest level of perdition."

Barker nodded absently. I could tell he wanted his pipe. He was cogitating.

"Mr. Barker, you will attend our wedding when it happens next year," May Evans stated. "And you, Mr. Llewelyn, scribbling away in the corner. Bring your wife, as well."

"I will, Miss Evans," I promised. "We shall look forward to it."

A few minutes later, we stepped out into the street and hailed a cab. Then we bowled away toward our offices.

"What a wonderful creature is man, Mr. Llewelyn," Barker said. "Yet the evils he can create are nearly endless."

"Yes, sir," I replied. "But it certainly keeps us employed."

The Guv sat back in the recesses of the cab, looking satisfied with himself.

"Mr. K'ing has returned from Canton, I hear," he said. "And the various gangs have found new leaders. Terry Poole says the East End has become singularly uninteresting."

"As a homeowner, that's how I prefer it," I replied.

"Aye, and the Calcutta hole has been filled with granite from Devon and Cornwall, mixed with good Portland cement. It shall be a normal-looking street by the summer."

"What about Mr. Soft?" I asked.

"He was buried in a pauper's grave," the Guv replied. "None of his relatives would claim him. Such are the wages of sin."

"I wonder what will become of H and D Associates?"

Barker shrugged. "I doubt Her Ladyship will have anything more to do with the East End. The properties will be sold, probably at significant profit."

"Is Booth still at the mission?"

"Miss Evans and Lord Dunbarton have purchased the property. The Salvation Army has given it up, which I suspect is as they prefer. Miss Orme and Miss Lawrence may stay on if they wish, and local women are still free to seek shelter there. The work for the men at Dunbarton's charity, Second Start, will continue as well. I understand William T. Stead has been asked to be the director."

"What will become of Brother Andrew's boxing ring?" I asked.

The Guv looked out at the traffic and bustle of the season. Christmas was a week away and shops were festooned with pine boughs and full of customers.

"I believe I'll purchase all the equipment, if only to remember him by."

I nodded in approval.

"I'm glad you thought of it before it was carted away," I said.

There was a sudden flare in his corner of the hansom as he took a match to his pipe. Smoke filled the cab.

"And how are things with the Templars, sir?"

We came to a stop in front of Craig's Court and alighted from the cab.

"It is no longer in my hands, I'm happy to say, lad. It was becoming more trouble than it was worth. Let it be someone else's problem for a while."

We stepped inside and hung our hats on the stand. Within a minute he was settling between the leather wings of his chair. I suddenly realized I had never looked at the check from Lady Danvers. I took it from my pocket and read it. Then I gave a long, satisfied whistle.

"Thomas!" Cyrus Barker chided.

"To think that you nearly offered to take the case for free," I replied.

ABOUT THE AUTHOR

Justin Greiman

Will Thomas is the winner of the Shamus Award for best novel and the Oklahoma Book Award for his critically acclaimed Cyrus Barker and Thomas Llewelyn series, including *Some Danger Involved, Heart of the Nile,* and most recently, *Death and Glory.*